CALAMITY TOWN

Books by Ellery Queen in HarperPerennial:

CALAMITY TOWN

THERE WAS AN OLD WOMAN

THE ORIGIN OF EVIL

FACE TO FACE

CALAMITY TOWN

ELLERY QUEEN

HarperPerennial

A Division of HarperCollins*Publishers*

Printed by arrangement with the Ellery Queen (Manfred B. Lee and Frederic Dannay) Trusts and Scott Meredith Literary Agency, Inc.

First HarperPerennial edition published 1992.

Library of Congress Cataloging-in-Publication Data

Queen, Ellery
  Calamity Town / Ellery Queen
    p. cm.
  ISBN 0-06-097437-0 (pbk.)
  I. Title.
PS3533.U4C3 1992
813'.52—dc20   91-50531

---

92 93 94 95 96 RRD 10 9 8 7 6 5 4 3 2 1

Part One

1

Mr Queen Discovers America

Ellery Queen stood knee-deep in luggage on the Wrightsville station platform and thought: 'This makes me an admiral. Admiral Columbus.' The station was a squatty affair of black-red brick. On a rusty hand truck under the eaves two small boys in torn blue overalls swung their dirty legs and chewed gum in unison, staring at him without expression. The gravel about the station was peppered with horse droppings. Cramped two-story frame houses and little stoop-shouldered shops with a cracker-barrel look huddled to one side of the tracks—the city side, for up a steep street paved with square cobbles Mr Queen could see taller structures beyond and the fat behind of a retreating bus. To the other side of the station there were merely a garage, an ex-trolley labeled PHIL'S DINER, and a smithy with a neon sign. The rest was verdure and delight.

'Country looks good, by jake,' murmurs Mr Queen enthusiastically. 'Green and yellow. Straw colors. And sky of blue, and clouds of white'—bluer blue and whiter white than he recalled ever having seen before. City—country; and here they met, where Wrightsville station flings the twentieth century into the astonished face of the land.

'Yes, sir, my boy. You've found it. *Porter!*'

The Hollis Hotel, Upham House, and the Kelton among them could not offer the stranger at their desks one pitiful room. It seemed boom times had hit Wrightsville two jumps ahead of Mr Queen. The last room at the Hollis was filched from under his nose by a portly man with 'defense industry' written all over him. Undiscouraged, Mr Queen checked his bags at the Hollis, ate a leisurely lunch in the Coffee Shoppe, and read a copy of the *Wrightsville Record*—Frank Lloyd, Publisher and Editor. He memorized as many of the names mentioned in the *Record* as seemed to have local prominence, bought two packs of Pall Malls and a Wrightsville street map from Mark Doodle's son Grover at the lobby cigar stand, then struck out across the red-cobbled Square under the hot sun.

At the horse trough in the center of the Square, Mr Queen paused to admire Founder Wright. Founder Wright had once been a bronze, but he now looked mossy, and the stone trough on which he stood had obviously been unused for years. There were crusty bird droppings on the Founder's Yankee nose. Words on a plaque said that Jezreel Wright had founded Wrightsville when it was an abandoned Indian site, in the Year of Our Lord 1701, had tilled the land, started a farm, and prospered. The chaste windows of the Wrightsville National Bank, *John F. Wright, Pres.*, smiled at Mr Queen from across the Square, and Mr Queen smiled back: O Pioneers!

Then he circumnavigated the Square (which was round); peered into Sol Gowdy's Men's Shop, the Bon Ton Department Store, Dunc MacLean—Fine Liquors, and William Ketcham—Insurance; examined the three gilded balls above the shop of J. P. Simpson, the jardinieres of green and red liquid in the window of the High Village Pharmacy, *Myron Garback, Prop.*, and turned to survey the thoroughfares which radiated like spokes from the

4

hub of the Square. One spoke was a broad avenue: the red-brick Town Hall, the Carnegie Library, a glimpse of park, tall praying trees, and beyond, a cluster of white new WPA-looking buildings. Another spoke was a street lined with stores and full of women in house dresses and men in work clothes. Consulting his street map, Mr Queen ascertained that this avenue of commerce was Lower Main; so he made for it. Here he found the *Record* office; he peered in and saw the big press being shined up by old Phinny Baker after the morning's run. He sauntered up Lower Main, poking his nose into the crowded five-and-dime, past the new Post Office building, past the Bijou Theater, past J. C. Pettigrew's real estate office; and he went into Al Brown's Ice Cream Parlor and had a New York College Ice and listened to the chatter of tanned boys and red-cheeked girls of high-school age. He heard Saturday night 'dates' being arranged right and left—for Danceland, in the Grove, which he gathered was at Wrightsville Junction three miles down the line, admission one dollar per person, 'and for pete's sake Marge keep your mother away from the parking lot, will you? I don't wanna get caught like two weeks ago and have you start bawling!'

Mr Queen strolled about the town, approving and breathing deeply of wet leaves and honeysuckle. He liked the stuffed eagle in the Carnegie Library vestibule; he even liked Miss Aikin, the elderly Chief Librarian, who gave him a very sharp look, as if to say: 'Don't you try to sneak a book out of *here!*' He liked the twisting narrow streets of Low Village, and he went into Sidney Gotch's General Store and purchased a package of Old Mariner Chewing Tobacco just as an excuse to smell the coffee and rubber boots and vinegar, the cheeses and kerosene. He liked the Wrightsville Machine Shop, which had just reopened, and the old cottonmill factory, diagonally across from the Low Village World War Memorial. Sidney Gotch told him about the cotton mill. It had been a cotton mill, then an empty building, then a shoeshop, then an empty building again; he could see for himself the splintery holes in the windows where the Low Village boys threw rocks in summer and snowballs in winter on their way to that vine-covered building up Lower Dade Street there—St John's Parochial School. But now 'specials' prowled around the mill with long fat holsters strapped to their thighs and eyes in their heads that would not smile; the boys, said Sidney Gotch, just yelled 'Yahhhh!' and took it out on Mueller's Feed Store three doors up the block, near the corner of Whistling Avenue. And the woollen mill had taken on extra help—army orders. 'Boom times, brother! No wonder you couldn't get a room. I've got an uncle from St. Paul and a cousin from Pittsburgh doublin' up with me and Betsy right now!' In fact, Mr Queen liked everything. He glanced up at the big clock on the Town Hall steeple. Two-thirty. No room, eh? Walking rapidly, he made his way back to Lower Main and neither paused nor pried until he reached the shop marked J. C. PETTIGREW, REAL ESTATE.

2

Calamity House

His number twelves up on his desk, J.C. was napping when Mr Queen came in. He had just come from the weekly Chamber of Commerce lunch at Upham House, and he was full of Ma Upham's fried chicken. Mr Queen woke him up. 'My name,' said Mr Queen, 'is Smith, I've just landed in Wrightsville, and I'm looking for a small furnished house to rent on a month-to-month basis.'

'Glad to know you, Mr Smith,' said J.C., struggling into his gabardine 'office' jacket. 'My, it's warm! Furnished house, hey? I can see you're a stranger. No furnished houses in Wrightsville, Mr Smith.'

'Then perhaps a furnished apartment—'

'Same thing.' J.C. yawned. 'Excuse me! Certainly is hotting up, isn't it?'

'It certainly is,' said Ellery.

Mr Pettigrew leaned back in his swivel chair and picked a strand of chicken out of his teeth with an ivory pick, after which he examined it intently. 'Housing's a problem. Yes, sir. People pouring into town like grain in a hopper. To work in the

Machine Shop especially. Wait a minute!' Mr Queen waited. 'Course!' J.C. flicked the shred of chicken off his pick delicately. 'Mr Smith, you superstitious?'

Mr Queen looked alarmed. 'I can't say I am.'

'In that case,' said J.C. brightening; then he stopped. 'What business you in? Not that it makes any difference, but—'

Ellery hesitated. 'I'm a writer.'

The real estate man gaped. 'You write *stories*?'

'That's it, Mr Pettigrew. Books and such.'

'Well, well,' beamed J.C. 'I'm real honored to meet you, Mr Smith. Smith…Now that's funny,' said J.C. 'I'm a reading man myself, but I just don't seem to recollect an author named—what did you say your first name was, Mr Smith?'

'I didn't say, but it's Ellery. Ellery Smith.'

'Ellery Smith,' said J.C., concentrating.

Mr Queen smiled. 'I write under a pen name.'

'Ah! Name of…?' But when Mr Pettigrew saw that Mr 'Smith' simply kept smiling, he rubbed his jaw and said: 'Course you'd give references?'

'Would three months' rent in advance give me a good character in Wrightsville, Mr Pettigrew?'

'Well, I should smile!' grinned J.C. 'You come with me, Mr Smith. I've got exactly the house you're looking for.'

'What did you mean by asking me if I'm superstitious?' asked Ellery as they climbed into J.C.'s pea-green coupé and drove off. 'Is the house haunted?'

'Uh…no,' said J.C. 'Though there *is* a sort of a queer yarn connected with that house—might give you an idea for one of your books now, hey?' Mr 'Smith' agreed; it might. 'This house, it's next door to John F.'s own place on the Hill. John F. Wright, that is. He's president of the Wrightsville National. Oldest family in town. Well, sir, three years ago one of John F.'s three daughters— the middle one, Nora—Nora got herself engaged to this Jim Haight. Jim was head cashier at John F.'s bank. Wasn't a local boy—he'd come to Wrightsville from New York a couple of years before that with fine recommendations. Started out as an assistant teller, and he was making good. Steady boy, Jim; stayed away from the bad element, went to the library a lot, didn't have much fun, I s'pose—a movie at Louie Cahan's Bijou, or standing around Band Concert Nights with the rest of the boys, watching the girls parade up and down eating popcorn, and joshing 'em. Worked hard—plenty of up-and-go, Jim had, and independent? Say, I never saw a lad stand on his two feet like Jim did. We all liked him a heap.' Mr Pettigrew sighed, and Ellery wondered why such a glowing subject should depress him.

'I take it Miss Nora Wright liked him more than anyone,' said Ellery, to grease the wheels of the story.

'That's a fact,' muttered J.C. 'Wild about the boy. Nora'd been the quiet kind before Jim came along—has to wear specs, and I guess it made her think she wasn't attractive to boys, 'cause she used to sit in the house while Lola and Patty went out with fellows—reading or sewing or helping her ma with organization work. Well, sir, Jim changed all that. Jim wasn't the kind to be stopped by a pair of eye-glasses. Nora's a pretty girl, and Jim started to rush her, and she changed...my, she changed!' J.C. frowned. 'S'pose I'm blabbing too much. Anyway, you get the idea. When Jim and Nora got engaged, the town said it was a fine match, especially after what had happened to John's oldest daughter, Lola.'

Ellery said quickly: 'And what was that, Mr Pettigrew?'

J.C. swung the coupé into a broad country road. They were well away from town now, and Ellery feasted his eyes on the succulent greens of the countryside.

'Did I say something about Lola?' asked the real estate man feebly. 'Why...Lola, she'd run away from home. Eloped with an actor from a visiting stock company. After a while she came back home to Wrightsville. Divorced.' J.C. set his lips stubbornly, and Mr Queen realized he wasn't going to hear any more about Miss Lola Wright. 'Well, anyway,' continued J.C., 'John and Hermione Wright decided to give Jim and their Nora a furnished house for a wedding present. John cut off part of his property near his own house and built. Right next door, 'cause Hermy wanted Nora as close by as possible, seeing she'd…lost one of her girls already.'

'Lola,' nodded Mr Queen. 'Divorced, you said? Came back home afterwards. Then Lola Wright doesn't live with her father and mother any more?'

'No,' said J.C. shortly. 'So John built Jim and Nora a sweet little six-roomer next door. Hermione was putting in rugs and furniture and drapes and linen and silver—the works—when all of a sudden it happened.'

'What happened?' asked Mr Queen.

'To tell the truth, Mr Smith, nobody knows,' said the real estate man sheepishly. 'Nobody 'cepting Nora Wright and Jim Haight. It was the day before the wedding and everything looked fine as corn silk, when Jim Haight ups and leaves town! Fact. Ran away. That was three years ago, and he's not been back since.' They were on a winding, rising road. Ellery saw wide old houses on voluptuous lawns, and elms and maples and cypress and weeping willows taller than the houses. Mr Pettigrew scowled at the Hill road. 'The next morning John F. found a note of resignation on his desk at the bank, but not a word as to why Jim'd skipped town. And Nora wouldn't say a blessed word. Just shut herself up in her bedroom and wouldn't come out for her father or mother or sister Patricia or even old Ludie, the hired girl who's practically brought the three Wright girls up. Nora just kept bawling in her room. My daughter Carmel and Patty Wright are thick as molasses, and Pat told Carmel the whole thing. Pat did a heap of crying herself that day. I guess they all did.'

'And the house?' murmured Mr Queen.

J.C. drove his car to the side of the road and shut off the motor. 'Wedding was called off. We all thought Jim'd turn up, thinking it was just a lovers' spat; but he didn't. Whatever broke those two up must have been awful important!' The real estate man shook his head. 'Well, there was the new house, all ready to be lived in, and no one to live in it. Terrible blow to Hermione. Hermy let out that Nora'd jilted Jim. But people did keep jawing about it, and after a while...' Mr Pettigrew paused.

'Yes?' prompted Ellery.

'After a while people began saying Nora'd gone...crazy and that that little six-roomer was jinxed.'

'Jinxed!'

J.C. smiled a sickly smile. 'Funny how some folks are, isn't it? Thinking the house had anything to do with Jim and Nora's breaking up! And of course ain't nothing wrong with Nora. I mean, she's not crazy. Crazy!' J.C. snorted. 'That wasn't the whole of it. When it looked like Jim wasn't coming back, John F. decided to sell that house he'd built for his daughter. Pretty soon along came a buyer—relative of Judge Martin's wife Clarice, man named Hunter of the Boston branch of the family. I was handling the deal.'

J.C. lowered his voice. 'Mr Smith, I give you my word I'd taken this Mr Hunter over to the house for a last inspection before signing the papers, and we were looking around the living room and Mr Hunter was saying, "I don't like the sofa just there," when he gets kind of a scared look all of a sudden and grabs his heart and falls down right in front of me! Died on the spot! I didn't sleep for a week.' He swabbed his forehead. 'Doc Willoughby said it was heart failure. But that's not what the town said. The town said it was the house. First Jim ran away, then a buyer dropped dead. And to make it worse, some smart-aleck of a cub reporter on Frank Lloyd's *Record* wrote up Hunter's death and he called the house "Calamity House" in his yarn. Frank fired him. Frank's friendly with the Wrights.'

'Of all the nonsense!' chuckled Mr Queen.

'Just the same, nobody'd buy,' muttered J.C. 'John offered to rent. Nobody'd rent. Too unlucky, people said. Still want to rent, Mr Smith?'

'Yes, indeed,' said Mr Queen cheerfully. So J.C. started his car again. 'Family seems ill-fated,' observed Ellery. 'One daughter

11

running off and another's life blasted by a love affair. Is the youngest daughter normal?'

'Patricia?' J.C. beamed. 'Prettiest, smartest filly in town next to my Carmel! Pat's going steady with Carter Bradford. Cart's our new County Prosecutor…Here we are!'

The real estate man steered his coupé into the driveway of a Colonial-style house sunk into the hillside far off the road. It was the largest house, and the trees on its lawns were the tallest trees, that Ellery had seen on the Hill. There was a small white frame house close by the large one, its windows shuttered.

Mr Queen kept looking at the blind and empty little house he intended to rent all the way up to the wide Wright porch. Then J.C. rang the bell and old Ludie in one of her famous starched aprons opened the front door and asked them what in tarnation.

3

'Famed Author to Live in Wrightsville'

'I'll tell Mr John you're callin',' sniffed Ludie, and she stalked out, her apron standing to each side of her like a Dutch cap.

'Guess Ludie knows we're here to rent Calamity House,' grinned Mr Pettigrew.

'Why should that make her look at me as if I were a Nazi *Gauleiter?*' asked Mr Queen.

'I expect Ludie doesn't think it proper for folks like the John F. Wrights to be renting out houses. Sometimes I don't know who's got more pride in the family name, Ludie or Hermy!'

Mr Queen took inventory. Lived in. There were a few aged mahogany pieces of distinction, and a beautiful fireplace of Italian marble. And at least two of the oil paintings had merit. J.C. noticed his interest. 'Hermione picked out all the pictures herself. Knows a lot about art, Hermy does—Here she is now. And John.'

Ellery rose. He had expected to meet a robust, severe-faced female; instead, he saw Hermy. Hermy always fooled strangers

13

that way; she's so tiny and motherly and sweet-looking. John Fowler Wright was a delicate little man with a brown country-club face. Ellery liked him at sight. He was carrying a stamp album with practised care. 'John, this is Mr Ellery Smith. He's looking to rent a furnished house,' said J.C. nervously. 'Mr Wright, Mrs Wright, Mr Smith. A-hrmm!'

John F. said in his reedy voice that he was mighty proud to meet Mr Smith, and Hermy held out her hand at arm's length with a sweet 'How do you do, Mr Smith,' but Mr 'Smith' saw the iced gleam in Hermy's pretty blue eyes and decided that in this instance, too, the female was deadlier than the male. So he was most gallant with her. Hermy unbent a little at that and poked her slender lady's fingers in her sleek gray hair, the way she always did when she was pleased, or fussed, or both.

'Of course,' said J.C. respectfully, 'I thought right off of that beautiful little six-roomer you built next door, John—'

'I don't at all like the idea,' said Hermione in her coolest voice, 'of renting, John. I can't imagine, Mr Pettigrew—'

'Maybe if you knew who Mr Smith *is*,' said J.C. quickly.

Hermy looked startled. John F. hitched forward in his wing chair near the fireplace. 'Well?' demanded Hermy. 'Who is he?'

'Mr Smith,' said J.C., throwing it away, 'is Ellery Smith, the famous author.'

'Famous *author!*' gasped Hermy. 'But I'm so bowled *over!* Here on the coffee table, Ludie!' Ludie clanked down a tray bearing a musical pitcher filled with ice and grape-juice-and-lemonade punch, and four handsome crystal goblets. 'I'm *sure* you'll like our house, Mr Smith,' Hermy went on swiftly. 'It's a little dream house. I decorated it with my own hands. Do you ever lecture? Our Women's Club—'

'Good golfing hereabouts, too,' said John F. 'How long would you want to rent for, Mr Smith?'

'I'm sure Mr Smith is going to like Wrightsville so well he'll stay on and *on*,' interrupted Hermy. 'Do have some of Ludie's punch, Mr Smith—'

'Thing is,' said John F., frowning, 'the way Wrightsville's shooting up, I'll probably be able to sell pretty soon—'

'That's easy, John!' said J.C. 'We can write in the lease that in case a buyer comes along Mr Smith is to vacate pending reasonable notice—'

'Business, business!' said Hermy gaily. 'What Mr Smith wants is to *see* the house. Mr Pettigrew, you stay here and keep John and his poky old stamps company. Mr Smith?' Hermy held on to Ellery's arm all the way from the big house to the little house, as if she were afraid he'd fly away if she let go. 'Of course, the furniture's protected by dust covers now, but it's really lovely. Early American bird's-eye maple, and brand-new. Just look, Mr Smith. Isn't it *darling?*'

Hermy dragged Ellery upstairs and downstairs, from cellar to peaked attic, exhibited the chintzy master bedroom, extolled the beauties of the living room with its maple pieces and art-filled niches and hooked rug and half-empty bookshelves…'Yes, yes,' said Ellery feebly. 'Very nice, Mrs Wright.'

'Of course, I'll see you get a housekeeper,' said Hermy happily. 'Oh, dear! Where will you do your Work? We could fix over the second bedroom upstairs into a study. You *must* have a study for your Work, Mr Smith.' Mr 'Smith' said he was sure he'd manage handsomely. 'Then you do like our little house? I'm so glad!' Hermione lowered her voice. 'You're in Wrightsville incognito, of course?'

'Such an impressive word, Mrs Wright…'

'Then except for a few of our *closest* friends I'll make sure nobody knows who you are,' beamed Hermy. 'What kind of Work are you planning, Mr Smith?'

'A novel,' said Ellery faintly. 'A novel of a particular sort, laid in a typical small city, Mrs Wright.'

'Then you're here to get Colour! How *apt!* You chose our own dear Wrightsville! You must meet my daughter Patricia immediately, Mr Smith. She's the cleverest child. I'm sure Pat would be a great help to you in getting to know Wrightsville…'

Two hours later Mr Ellery Queen was signing the name 'Ellery Smith' to a lease whereunder he agreed to rent Number 460 Hill Drive, furnished, for a period of six months beginning August 6, 1940, three months' rental paid in advance, one month's vacating notice to be given by lessor in event of a sale, at the rental of $75 per month.

'The truth is, Mr Smith,' confided J.C. as they left the Wright house, 'I kind of held my breath in there for a minute.'

'When was that?'

'When you took that pen of John F.'s and signed the lease.'

'You held your breath?' Ellery frowned. 'Why?'

J.C. guffawed. 'I remembered the case of poor old Hunter and how he dropped dead in that very house. Calamity House! That's a hot one! Here you are, still fit as a fiddle!'

And he got into his coupé still overcome by mirth, bound for town to pick up Ellery's luggage at the Hollis Hotel...and leaving Ellery in the Wright driveway feeling irritated.

When Ellery returned to his new residence, there was a tingle in his spine. There *was* something about the house, now that he was out of Mrs Wright's clutches, something—well, *blank*, unfinished, like Outer Space. Ellery almost said to himself the word 'inhuman,' but when he got to that point he took himself in hand, sternly. Calamity House! As sensible as calling Wrightsville Calamity Town! He removed his coat, rolled up his shirt sleeves, and sailed into things.

'Mr Smith,' cried a horrified voice, 'what are you *doing*?' Ellery guiltily dropped a dust cover as Hermione Wright rushed in, her cheeks flushed and her gray hair no longer sleek. 'Don't you dare touch a thing! Alberta, come in. Mr Smith won't bite you.' A bashful Amazon shuffled in. 'Mr Smith, this is Alberta Manaskas. I'm sure you'll find her most satisfactory. Alberta, don't stand there. Start the upstairs!' Alberta fled. Ellery murmured his gratitude and sank into a chintz-cloaked chair as Mrs Wright attacked the room about him with terrifying energy.

'We'll have this in apple-pie order in a jiffy! By the way, I trust you don't mind. On my trip into town to fetch Alberta, I *happened* to drop into the *Record* office—whoo! this dust!—and had a confidential chat with Frank Lloyd. The editor and publisher, you know.' Ellery's heart scuttled itself.

'By the way, I also took the liberty of giving Logan's a grocery and meat order for you. Although of course you'll dine with *us* tonight. Oh, dear, did I forget...? Electricity...gas...water...no, I attended to everything. Oh, the telephone! I'll do that first thing tomorrow. Well, as I was saying, I knew that no matter *how* hard we tried, sooner or later everyone would know you're in Wrightsville, Mr Smith, and of course as a newspaper man Frank would *have* to do a story on you, so I thought I'd better ask Frank as a personal favour not to mention in his write-up that you're the famous author—Patty baby! Carter! Oh, my darlings, I have *such* a surprise for you!' Mr Queen rose, fumbling for his jacket. His only coherent thought was that she had eyes the colour of brook water bubbling in the sun.

'So you're the famous author,' said Patricia Wright, looking at him with her head cocked. 'When Pop told Carter and me just now what Mother had snagged, I thought I'd meet a baggy-pantsed poet with a hangdog look, melancholy eyes, and a pot. I'm *pleased*.' Mr Queen tried to look suave, and mumbled something.

'Isn't it wonderful, dearest?' cried Hermy. 'You must forgive me, Mr Smith. I know you think I'm terribly provincial. But I really *am* overwhelmed. Pat dear—introduce Carter.'

'Carter! Darling, I'm so sorry. Mr Smith, Mr Bradford.' Shaking hands with a tall young man, intelligent-looking but worried, Ellery wondered if he were worried about how to hold on to Miss Patricia Wright. He felt an instant sympathy.

'I suppose,' said Carter Bradford politely, 'We must all seem provincial to you, Mr Smith. Fiction or nonfiction?'

'Fiction,' said Ellery. So it was war.

'I'm *pleased*,' said Pat again, looking Ellery over. Carter frowned; Mr Queen beamed. 'I'll do this room, Muth...You won't be hurting *my* feelings, Mr Smith, if after we've stopped interfering in your life you change things around again. But for now—'

As he watched Pat Wright setting his house in order under Carter Bradford's suspicious eye, Ellery thought: 'May the saints grant me calamities like this each blessed day. Carter my boy, I'm sorry, but I'm cultivating your Patty!'

His good humor was not dispelled even when J.C. Pettigrew hurried back from town with his luggage and flourished the last edition of the *Wrightsville Record*. Frank Lloyd, publisher and editor, had kept his word to Hermione Wright only technically. He had said nothing about Mr Smith in the body of the news item except that he was 'Mr Ellery Smith of New York.' But the headline on the story ran:—FAMED AUTHOR TO LIVE IN WRIGHTSVILLE!

4

The Three Sisters

Mr Ellery 'Smith' was a sensation with the *haut monde* on the Hill
and the local intelligentsia: Miss Aikin, the Librarian, who had
studied Greek; Mrs Holmes, who taught Comparative Lit at
Wrightsville High; and, of course, Emmeline DuPré, known to
the irreverent as the 'town crier,' who was nevertheless envied
by young and old for having the miraculous good fortune to be
his neighbor. Emmy DuPré's house was on Ellery's other side.
Automobile traffic suddenly increased on the Hill. Interest
became so hydra-headed that Ellery would have been unmoved
if the Wrightsville Omnibus Company had started running a
sightseeing bus to his door. Then there were invitations. To tea,
to dinner, to luncheon; and one—from Emmeline DuPré—asking
him to breakfast, 'so that we may discuss the Arts in the coolth
of a Soft Morning, before the Dew vanishes from the Sward.' Ben
Danzig, High Village Rental Library and Sundries, said he had
never had such a rush on Fine Stationery.

So Mr Queen began to look forward to escaping with Pat in
the mornings, when she would call for him dressed in slacks and
a pullover sweater and take him exploring through the County

in her little convertible. She knew everybody in Wrightsville and Slocum Township, and introduced him to people named variously O'Halleran, Zimbruski, Johnson, Dowling, Goldberger, Venuti, Jacquard, Wladislaus, and Broadbeck—journeymen machinists, toolers, assembly-line men, farmers, retailers, hired hands, white and black and brown, with children of unduplicated sizes and degrees of cleanliness. In a short time, through the curiously wide acquaintanceship of Miss Wright, Mr Queen's notebook was rich with funny lingos, dinner-pair details, Saturday-night brawls down on Route 16, square dances and hepcat contests, noon whistles whistling, lots of smoke and laughing and pushing, and the color of America, Wrightsville edition.

'I don't know what I'd do without you,' Ellery said one morning as they returned from Low Village. 'You seem so much more the country-club, church-social, Younger-Set type of female. How come, Pat?'

'I'm that, too,' grinned Pat. 'But I'm a Sociology Major, or I was—got my degree in June; and I guess I just can't help practising on the helpless population. If this war keeps up—'

'Milk Fund?' asked Ellery vaguely. 'That sort of thing?'

'Barbarian! Milk Funds are Muth's department. My dear man, sociology is concerned with more than calcium for growing bones. It's the science of civilization. Now take the Zimbruskis—'

'Spare me,' moaned Mr Queen, having met the Zimbruskis. 'By the way, what does Mr Bradford, your local Prosecutor, think of all this, Patty?'

'Of me and sociology?'

'Of me and you.'

'Oh.' Pat tossed her hair to the wind, looking pleased. 'Cart's jealous.'

'Hmmm. Look here, my little one—'

'Now don't start being noble,' said Pat. 'Trouble with Cart, he's taken me for granted too long. We've practically grown up together. Do him good to be jealous.'

'I don't know,' smiled Ellery, 'that I entirely relish the role of love-irritant.'

'Oh, please!' Pat was shocked. 'I *like* you. And this is more fun.' Suddenly, with one of her quick sidelong glances: 'You know what people are saying, incidentally—or don't you?'

'What now?'

'You told Mr Pettigrew that you're a famous writer—'

'Mr Pettigrew supplied the adjective "famous" all by himself.'

'You've also said you don't write under the name Ellery Smith, that you use a pseudonym...but you didn't tell anyone *which* pseudonym.'

'Lord, no!'

'So people are saying that maybe you aren't a famous author after all,' murmured Pat. 'Nice town, huh?'

'Which people?'

'People.'

'Do *you* think I'm a fraud?'

'Never mind what I think,' retorted Pat. 'But you should know there's been a run on the Authors' Photograph File at the Carnegie Library, and Miss Aikin reports you're simply not there.'

'Pish,' said Ellery. 'And a couple of tushes. I'm just not famous enough.'

'That's what I told her. Mother was furious at the very thought, but I said: "Muth, how do we *know*?" and do you know—poor Mother didn't sleep a wink all night?'

They laughed together. Then Ellery said: 'Which reminds me. Why haven't I met your sister Nora? Isn't she well?'

He was appalled by the way Pat stopped laughing at mention of her sister's name. 'Nora?' repeated Pat in a perfectly flat voice, a voice that told nothing at all. 'Why, Nora's all right. Let's call it a morning, Mr Smith.'

That night Hermione officially unveiled her new treasure. The list was *intime*. Just Judge and Clarice Martin, Doc

Willoughby, Carter Bradford, Tabitha Wright, John F.'s only living sister—Tabitha was the 'stiff-necked' Wright who had never quite 'accepted' Hermione Bluefield—and editor-publisher Frank Lloyd of the *Record*. Lloyd was talking politics with Carter Bradford; but both men merely pretended to be interested in each other. Carter was hurling poisonous looks at Pat and Ellery in the 'love seat' by the Italian fireplace; while Lloyd, a brown bear of a man, kept glancing restlessly at the staircase in the foyer.

'Frank had a crush on Nora before Jim...He's still crazy about her,' explained Pat. 'When Jim Haight came along and Nora fell for him, Frank took the whole thing pretty badly.' Ellery inspected the mountainous newspaper editor from across the room and inwardly agreed that Frank Lloyd would make a dangerous adversary. There was iron in those deep-sunk green eyes. 'And when Jim walked out on Nora, Frank said that—'

'Yes?'

'Never mind what Frank said,' Pat jumped up. 'I'm talking too much.' And she rustled towards Mr Bradford to break another little piece off his heart. Pat was wearing a blue taffeta dinner gown that swished faintly as she moved.

'Milo, this is *the* Ellery Smith,' said Hermy proudly, coming over with big, lumbering Doc Willoughby in tow.

'Don't know whether you're a good influence or not, Mr Smith,' chuckled Doc. 'I just came from another confinement at the Jacquards'. Those Canucks! Triplets this time. Only difference between me and Dr Dafoe is that no lady in Wright County's been considerate enough to bear more than four at one time. Like our town?'

'I've fallen in love with it, Dr Willoughby.'

'It's a good town. Hermy, where's my drink?'

'If you're broad-minded,' snorted Judge Martin, strolling up with Clarice hanging—heavily—on his arm. Judge Martin was a gaunt little man with sleepy eyes and a dry manner. He reminded Ellery of Arthur Train's Mr Tutt.

'Eli Martin!' cried Clarice. 'Mr Smith, you just ignore this husband of mine. He's miserable about having to wear his dinner jacket and he'll take it out on you because you're the cause. Hermy, everything's just *perfect*.'

'It's nothing at all,' murmured Hermione, pleased. 'Just a little intimate dinner, Clarice.'

'I don't like these doodads,' growled the Judge, fingering his bow tie. 'Well, Tabitha, and what are *you* sniffing about?'

'Comedian!' said John F.'s sister, glaring at the old jurist. 'I can't imagine what Mr Smith must be thinking of us, Eli!'

Judge Martin observed dryly that if Mr Smith thought less of him for being uncomfortable in doodads, then *he* thought less of Mr Smith. A crisis was averted by the appearance of Henry Clay Jackson announcing dinner. Henry Clay was the only trained butler in Wrightsville, and the ladies of the upper crust, by an enforced Communism, shared him and his rusty 'buttlin' suit.' It was an unwritten law among them that Henry Clay was to be employed on ultra-special occasions only.

'Dinnuh,' announced Henry Clay Jackson, 'is heaby suhved!'

Nora Wright appeared suddenly between the roast lamb-wreathed-in-mint-jelly-flowers and the pineapple mousse. For an instant the room was singing-still. Then Hermione quavered: 'Why, *Nora* darling,' and John F. said gladly: 'Nora baby,' through a mouthful of salted nuts, and Clarice Martin gasped: 'Nora, how *nice*!' and the spell was broken.

Ellery was the first man on his feet. Frank Lloyd was the last; the thick neck under his shaggy hair was the color of brick. Pat saved the day. 'I must say this is a fine time to come down to dinner, Nora!' she said briskly. 'Why, we've finished Ludie's best lamb. Mr Smith, Nora.'

Nora offered him her hand. It felt as fragile and cold as a piece of porcelain. 'Mother's told me all about you,' said Nora in a voice that sounded unused.

'And you're disappointed. Naturally,' smiled Ellery. He held out a chair.

'Oh, no! Hello, Judge, Mrs Martin. Aunt Tabitha...Doctor... Carter ...'

Frank Lloyd said, 'Hullo, Nora,' in gruff tones; he took the chair from Ellery's hands neither rudely nor politely; he simply took it and held it back for Nora. She turned pink and sat down. Just then Henry Clay marched in with the magnificent mousse, molded in the shape of a book, and everybody began to talk.

Nora Wright sat with her hands folded, palms up, as if exhausted; her colorless lips were twisted into a smile. Apparently she had dressed with great care, for her candy-striped dinner gown was fresh and perfectly draped, her nails impeccable, and her coiffure without a single stray wine-brown hair. Ellery glimpsed a sudden, rather appalling, vision of this slight bespectacled girl in her bedroom upstairs, fussing with her nails, fussing with her hair, fussing with her attractive gown...fussing, fussing, so that everything might be just so...fussing so long and so needlessly that she had been an hour late to dinner.

And now that she had achieved perfection, now that she had made the supreme effort of coming downstairs, she seemed emptied, as if the effort had been too much and not entirely worthwhile. She listened to Ellery's casual talk with a fixed smile, white face slightly lowered, not touching her mousse or demitasse, murmuring a monosyllable occasionally...but not as if she were bored, only as if she were weary beyond sensation.

And then, as suddenly as she had come in, she said: 'Excuse me, please,' and rose. All conversation stopped again. Frank Lloyd jumped up and drew her chair back. He devoured her with a huge and clumsy hunger; she smiled at him, and at the others, and floated out...her step quickening as she approached the archway from the dining room to the foyer. Then she disappeared; and everyone began to talk at once and ask for more coffee.

24

Mr Queen was mentally sifting the evening's grist as he strolled
back to his house in the warm darkness. The leaves of the big
elms were talking; there was an oversize cameo moon; and his
nose was filled with the scents of Hermione Wright's flowers.
But when he saw the small roadster parked by the curb before
his house, dark and empty, the sweetness fled. It was simply
night; and something was about to happen. A gun-metal cloud
slipped across the moon, and Mr Queen made his way along the
edge of his lawn on the muffling grass toward the little house. A
point of fire took shape on his porch. It was swaying back and
forth about waist-high to a standing man.

'Mr Smith, I presume?' A woman's contralto. Slightly fuzzed
with husk. It had a mocking quality.

'Hullo!' he called, mounting the porch steps. 'Mind if I turn
on the porch light? It's so beastly dark—'

'Please do. I'm as curious to see you as you are to see me.'

Ellery touched the light switch. She was curled up in a corner
of the slide-swing blinking at him from behind the streaming
veil of her cigarette. The dove suède of her slacks was tight over
her thighs; a cashmere sweater molded her breasts boldly. Ellery
gathered a full-armed impression of earthiness, overripe, and
growing bitter. She laughed, a little nervously he thought, and
flipped her cigarette over the porch rail into the darkness.

'You may turn off the light now, Mr Smith. I'm a fright, and
besides I shouldn't want to embarrass my family by making
them aware I'm in their immediate neighborhood.'

Ellery obediently switched off the porch light. 'Then you're
Lola Wright.' The one who had eloped, and come back divorced.
The daughter the Wrights never mentioned.

'As if you didn't know!' Lola Wright laughed again, and it
turned into a hiccup. 'Excuse *me*. Seventh hiccup of a seventh
Scotch. I'm famous too, you know. The *drinking* Wright girl.'

Ellery chuckled. 'I've heard the vile slanders.'

'I was all prepared to hate your guts, from the kow-towing
that's been going on, but you're all right. Shake!' The swing

creaked, and steps shuffled to the tune of an unsteady laugh, and then the moist heat of her hand warmed his neck as she groped. He gripped her arms to save her from falling.

'Here,' he said, 'You should have stopped at number six.'

She placed her palms against his starched shirt and pushed strongly. 'Whoa, Geronimo! The man'll think li'l Lola's stinko.' He heard her totter back to the swing, and its creak. 'Well, Mr Famous Author Smith, and what do you think of us all? Pygmies and giants, sweet and sour, snaggled-toothed and slick-magazine ads—good material for a book, eh?'

'Elegant.'

'You've come to the right place.' Lola Wright lit another cigarette: the flame trembled. 'Wrightsville! Gossipy, malicious, intolerant...the great American slob. More dirty linen to the square inch of backyard than New York or Marseilles.'

'Oh, I don't know,' argued Mr Queen. 'I've spent a lot of loose time prowling, and it seems a pretty nice place to me.'

'Nice!' She laughed. 'Don't get me started. I was born here. It's wormy and damp—a breeding place of nastiness.'

'Then why,' murmured Mr Queen, 'did you come back to it?'

The red tip of her cigarette waxed three times in rapid succession. 'None of your business. Like my family?'

'Immensely. You resemble your sister Patricia. Same physical glow, too.'

'Only Patty's young, and my light's going out.' Lola Wright mused for a moment. 'I suppose you'd have to be polite to an old bag named Wright. Look, Brother Smith. I don't know why you came to Wrightsville, but if you're going to be palsy with my kind, you'll hear a lot about little Lola eventually, and...well...I don't give a damn what Wrightsville thinks of me, but an alien...that's different. Good grief! I still have vanity!'

'I haven't heard anything about you from your family.'

'No?' He heard her laugh again. 'I feel like baring my bosom tonight. You'll hear I drink. True. I learned it from—I learned it. You'll hear I'm seen in all the awful places in town, and what's worse, *alone*. Imagine! I'm supposed to be "fast." The truth is

I do what I damned please, and all these vultures of women on the Hill, they've been tearing at me with their claws!'

She stopped. 'How about a drink?' asked Ellery.

'Not now. I don't blame my mother. She's narrow, like the rest of them; her social position is her whole life. But if I'd play according to her rules, she'd still take me back—she's got spunk, I'll give her that. Well, I won't play. It's my life, and to hell with rules! Understand?' She laughed once more. 'Say you understand. Go on. Say it.'

'I understand,' Ellery said.

She was quiet. Then she said: 'I'm boring you. Goodnight.'

'I want to see you again.'

'No. Goodbye.'

Her shoes scraped the invisible porch floor. Ellery turned on the light again. She put up her arm to hide her eyes.

'Well, then, I'll see you home, Miss Wright.'

'Thanks no. I'm—' She stopped.

Patricia Wright's gay voice called from the darkness below: 'Ellery? May I come up and have a goodnight cigarette with you? Carter's gone home and I saw your porch light—' Pat stopped, too. The two sisters stared at each other.

'Hello, Lola!' cried Pat. She vaulted up the steps and kissed Lola vigorously. 'Why didn't you tell me you were coming?'

Mr Queen put the light out again very quickly. But he had time to see how Lola clung—briefly—to her taller, younger sister.

'Lay off, Snuffles,' he heard Lola say in a muffled voice. 'You're mussing my hair-do.'

'And that's a fact,' said Pat cheerfully. 'You know, Ellery, this sister of mine is the most attractive girl ever to come out of Wrightsville. And she insists on hiding her light under frumpy old slacks!'

'You're a darling, Pats,' said Lola, 'but don't try so hard. It's no dice, and you know it.'

Pat said miserably: 'Lo dear...why don't you come back?'

'I think,' remarked Mr Queen, 'I'll walk down to that hydrangea bush and see how it's making out.'

'Don't,' said Lola. 'I'm going now. I really am.'

'Lola!' Pat's voice was damp.

'You see, Mr Smith? Snuffles. She was always snuffling as a brat. Pat, now stop it. This is old hat for us two.'

'I'm all right.' Pat blew her nose in the darkness. 'I'll drive home with you.'

'No, Patsy. Night, Mr Smith.'

'Goodnight.'

'And I've changed my mind. Come over and have a drink with me any time you like. Night, Snuffy!' And Lola was gone.

When the last rattle of Lola's 1932 coupé died, Pat said in a murmur: 'Lo lives in a two-room hole down in Low Village, near the Machine Shop. She wouldn't take alimony from her husband, who was a rat till the day he died, and she won't accept money from Pop. Those clothes she wears—six years old. Part of her trousseau. She supports herself by giving piano lessons to Low Village hopefuls at fifty cents a throw.'

'Pat, why does she stay in Wrightsville? What brought her back after her divorce?'

'Don't salmon or elephants or something come back to their birthplace...to die? Sometimes I think it's almost as if Lola's...hiding.' Pat's silk taffeta rustled suddenly. 'You make me talk and talk. Good night, Ellery.'

'Night, Pat.'

Mr Queen stared into the dark for a long time. Yes, it was taking shape. He'd been lucky. The makings were here, rich and bloody. But the crime—the crime. Where was it? *Or had it already occurred?*

Ellery went to bed in Calamity House with a sense of events past, present, and future.

On the afternoon of Sunday, August twenty-fifth, nearly three weeks from the day of Ellery's arrival in Wrightsville, he was smoking a postprandial cigarette on his porch and enjoying the improbable sunset when Ed Hotchkiss's taxicab charged up the

Hill and squealed to a stop before the Wright house next door. A hatless young man jumped out of the cab. Mr Queen felt a sudden agitation and rose for a better view.

The young man shouted something to Ed Hotchkiss, bounded up the steps, and jabbed at the Wright doorbell. Old Ludie opened the door. Ellery saw her fat arm rise as if to ward off a blow. Then Ludie scuttled back out of sight, and the young man dashed after her. The door banged. Five minutes later it was yanked open; the young man rushed out, stumbled into the waiting cab, and yelled to be driven away.

Ellery sat down slowly. It might be. He would soon know. Pat would come flying across the lawn...There she was...'Ellery! You'll never guess!'

'Jim Haight's come back,' said Ellery.

Pat stared. 'You're wonderful. Imagine—after three years! After the way Jim ran out on Nora! I can't believe it yet. He looks so much *older*...He had to see Nora, he yelled. Where was she? Why didn't she come down? Yes, he knew what Muth and Pop thought of him, but that could wait—where was Nora? And all the time he kept shaking his fist in poor Pop's face and hopping up and down on one foot like a maniac!'

'What happened then?'

'I ran upstairs to tell Nora. She went deathly pale and plopped down on her bed. She said: "*Jim?*" and started to bawl. Said she'd rather be dead, and why hadn't he stayed away, and she wouldn't see him if he came crawling to her on his hands and knees—the usual feminine tripe. Poor Nora!'

Pat was in tears herself.

'I knew it was no good arguing with her—Nora's awfully stubborn when she wants to be. So I told Jim, and he got even more excited and wanted to run upstairs, and Pop got mad and waved his best mashie at the foot of the stairs, like Horatius at the bridge, and ordered Jim out of the house, and—well, Jim would have had to knock Pop down to get by him, so he ran out of the house screaming that he'd see Nora if he had to throw

29

bombs to get in. And all of this time I was trying to revive Muth, who conveniently fainted as a sort of strategic diversion...I've got to get back!' Pat ran off. Then she stopped and turned around. 'Why in heaven's name,' she asked slowly, 'do I come running to you with the most intimate details of my family's affairs, Mr Ellery Smith?'

'Maybe,' smiled Ellery, 'because I have a kind face.'

'Don't be foul. Do you suppose I'm f—' Pat bit her lip, a faint blush staining her tan. Then she loped away.

Mr Queen lit another cigarette with fingers not quite steady. Despite the heat, he felt chilled suddenly. He threw the unsmoked butt into the grass and went into the house to haul out his typewriter.

5

Lover Come Back

Gabby Warrum, the one-toothed agent at the railroad station, saw Jim Haight get off the train. Gabby told Emmeline DuPré. By the time Ed Hotchkiss dropped Jim off at Upham House, where Ma for old times' sake managed to wangle a bed for him, Emmy DuPré had phoned nearly everyone in town who wasn't picnicking in Pine Grove or swimming in Slocum Lake.

Opinion, as Mr Queen ascertained by prowling around town Monday and keeping his steel-trap ears open, was divided. J. C. Pettigrew, Donald Mackenzie, and the rest of the Rotary bunch, who were half Country Club and half tradespeople, generally opined that Jim Haight ought to be run out on a rail. The ladies were stoutly against this: Jim was a nice young man; whatever'd happened between him and Nora Wright three years ago wasn't *his* fault, you can bet your last year's bonnet!

Frank Lloyd disappeared. Phinny Baker said his boss had gone off on a hunting trip up in the Mahoganies. Emmeline DuPré sniffed. 'It's funny Frank Lloyd should go hunting *the very next morning* after James Haight gets back to Wrightsville. Ran away, of course. That big windbag!' Emmy was disappointed that Frank hadn't taken one of his deer rifles and gone stalking through the streets of Wrightsville for Jim, like Owen Wister's Virginian (starring, however, Gary Cooper).

Old Soak Anderson, the town problem, discovered by Mr Queen Monday noon lying on the stone pedestal of the Low Village World War Memorial, rubbed his salt-and-pepper stubble and declaimed: '"O most lame and impotent conclusion!"'

'Are you feeling well this morning, Mr Anderson?' asked Ellery, concerned.

'Never better, sir. But my point is one with the Proverb, the twenty-sixth, I believe, which states: "Whoso diggeth a pit shall fall therein." I refer, of course, to the reappearance in this accursed community of Jim Haight. Sow the wind, sir; sow the wind!'

The yeast in all this ferment acted strangely. Having returned to Wrightsville, Jim Haight shut himself up in his room at Upham House; he even had his meals served there, according to Ma Upham. Whereas Nora Wright, the prisoner, began to show herself! Not in public, of course. But on Monday afternoon she watched Pat and Ellery play three sets of tennis on the grass court behind the Wright house, lying in a deck chair in the sun, her eyes protected by dark glasses hooked over her spectacles; and she kept smiling faintly. On Monday evening she strolled over with Pat and a hostile Carter Bradford 'to see how you're coming along with your book, Mr Smith.' Ellery had Alberta Manaskas serve tea and oatmeal cookies; he treated Nora quite as if she were in the habit of dropping in. And then on Tuesday night...

Tuesday night was bridge night at the Wrights.' Carter Bradford usually came to dinner, and Carter and Pat paired against Hermione and John F. Hermy thought it might be 'nice' to have Mr Smith in on Tuesday, August twenty-seventh to make a fifth; and Ellery accepted with alacrity.

'I'd much rather watch tonight,' said Pat. 'Carter dear—you and Pop against Ellery and Mother. I'll heckle.'

'Come on, come on, we're losing time,' said John F. 'Stakes, Smith? It's your option.'

'Makes no difference to me,' said Ellery. 'Suppose I toss the honour over to Bradford.'

'In that case,' said Hermy quickly, 'let's play for a tenth. Carter, *why* don't they pay Prosecutors more?' Then she brightened. 'When you're Governor...'

'Penny a point,' said Carter; his lean face was crimson.

'But Cart, I didn't mean—' wailed Hermione.

'If Cart wants to play for a cent, by all means *play* for a cent,' said Pat firmly. 'I'm sure he'll win!'

'Hello,' said Nora. She had not come down to dinner—Hermy had said something about a 'headache.' Now Nora was smiling at them from the foyer. She came in with a basket of knitting and sat down in the big chair under a piano lamp. 'I'm really winning the war for Britain,' she smiled, 'all by myself. This is my tenth sweater!'

Mr and Mrs Wright exchanged startled glances, and Pat absently began to ruffle Ellery's hair. 'Play cards,' said Carter in a smothered voice.

The game began under what seemed to Ellery promising circumstances, considering the warm vital hand in his hair and Carter's outthrust lower lip. And, in fact, after two rubbers Cart slammed his cards down on the table.

'Why, Cart!' gasped Pat.

'Carter Bradford,' said Hermy, 'I never *heard*—'

'What on earth?' said John F., staring at him.

'If you'd stop *jumping around*, Pat,' cried Carter, 'I'd be able to concentrate on this ding-busted game!'

'Jumping *around*?' said Pat indignantly. 'Cart Bradford, I've been sitting here on the arm of Ellery's chair all evening not saying a word!'

'If you want to play with his beautiful hair,' roared Cart, 'why don't you take him outside under the moon?'

Pat turned the machine-gun of her eyes on him. Then she said contritely to Ellery: 'I'm sure you'll forgive Cart's bad manners. He's really had a decent bringing-up, but associating with hardened criminals so much—'

Nora yelped. Jim Haight stood in the archway. His Palm Beach suit hung tired and defeated; his shirt was dark with perspiration. He looked like a man who has been running at top speed in a blazing heat without purpose or plan—just running. And Nora's face was a cloud-torn sky.

'Nora.' The pink in Nora's cheeks spread and deepened until her face seemed a mirror to flames. Nobody moved. Nobody said a word.

Nora sprang toward him. For an instant Ellery thought she meant to attack him in a spasm of fury. But then Ellery saw that Nora was not angry; she was in a panic. It was the fright of a woman who had long since surrendered hope of life to live in a suspension of life, a kind of breathing death; it was the fear of joyous rebirth.

Nora darted by Jim and skimmed up the stairs. Jim Haight looked exultant. Then he ran after her. And silence. Living Statues, thought Ellery. He ran his finger between his neck and his collar; it came away dripping. John F. and Hermy Wright were saying secretive things to each other with their eyes, as a man and woman learn to do who have lived together for thirty years. Pat kept glaring at the empty foyer, her chest rising and falling visibly; and Carter kept glaring at Pat, as if the thing that was happening between Jim and Nora had somehow become confused in his mind with what was happening between him and Pat.

Later...later there were overhead sounds: the opening of a bedroom door, a slither of feet, steps on stairs. Nora and Jim appeared in the foyer. 'We're going to be married,' said Nora. It was as if she were a cold lamp and Jim had touched the button. She glowed from within and gave off a sort of heat.

'Right off,' said Jim. He had a deep defiant voice; it was harsher than he meant, rasped by emery strain. 'Right off!' Jim said. 'Understand?' He was scarlet from the roots of his sandy hair to the chicken skin below his formidable Adam's apple. But he kept blinking at John F. and Hermy with a dogged, nervous bellicosity.

'Oh, Nora!' cried Pat, and she pounced and kissed Nora's mouth and began to cry and laugh. Hermy was smiling the stiff smile of a corpse. John F. mumbled, 'I'll be dinged,' and heaved out of his chair and went to his daughter and took her hand, and he took Jim's hand, just standing there helplessly. Carter said: 'It's high time, you two lunatics!' and slipped his arm about Pat's waist. Nora did not cry. She kept looking at her mother. And then Hermy's petrification broke into little pieces and she ran to Nora, pushing Pat and John F. and Carter aside. She kissed Nora and kissed Jim and said something in a hysterical tone that made no sense but seemed the right thing to say just the same.

Mr Queen slipped out, feeling a little lonely.

6

'Wright–Haight Nuptials Today'

Hermy planned the wedding like a general in his field tent surrounded by maps of the terrain and figures representing the accurate strength of the enemy's forces. While Nora and Pat were in New York shopping for Nora's trousseau, Hermione held technical discussions with old Mr Thomas, sexton of the First Methodist Church; horticultural conferences with Andy Birobatyan, the one-eyed Armenian florist in High Village; historic conversations with the Reverend Dr Doolittle *in re* rehearsals and choir-boy arrangements; talks with Mrs Jones the caterer, with Mr Graycee of the travel agency, and with John F. at the bank on intrafamiliar banking business.

But these were Quartermaster's chores. The General Staff conversations were with the ladies of Wrightsville. 'It's just like a movie, dear!' Hermy gushed over the telephone. 'It was nothing more than a lover's quarrel to begin with—Oh, yes, darling, *I* know what people are saying!' said Hermy coldly. 'But my Nora doesn't have to grab anybody. I don't suppose you recall last year how that handsome young Social Registrite from Bar Harbor...Of course not! Why should we have a *quiet* wedding? My dear, they'll be married in church and...*Naturally* as a bride...Yes, to South America for six weeks...Oh, John is taking Jim back into the bank...Oh, no, dear, an *officer's* position...Of course, darling! Do you think I'd marry my Nora off and not have *you* at the wedding?'

On Saturday, August thirty-first, one week after Jim's return to Wrightsville, Jim and Nora were married by Dr Doolittle in the First Methodist Church. John F. gave the bride away, and Carter Bradford was Jim's best man. After the ceremony, there was a lawn reception on the Wright grounds. Twenty Negro waiters in mess jackets served; the rum punch was prepared from the recipe John F. had brought back with him from Bermuda in 1928. Emmeline DuPré, full-blown in an organdie creation and crowned with a real rosebud tiara, skittered from group to group remarking how 'well' Hermione Wright had carried off a 'delicate' situation, and didn't Jim look interesting with those purple welts under his eyes? Do you suppose he's been drinking these three years? How romantic! Clarice Martin said rather loudly that *some* people were born troublemakers.

During the lawn reception Jim and Nora escaped by the service door. Ed Hotchkiss drove the bride and groom over to Slocum Township in time to catch the express. Jim and Nora were to stay overnight in New York and sail on Tuesday for Rio. Mr Queen, who was prowling, spied the fleeing couple as they hurried into Ed's cab. Wet diamonds in her eyes, Nora clung to her husband's hand. Jim looked solemn and proud; he handed his wife into the cab gingerly, as if she might bruise under less careful manipulation.

Mr Queen also saw Frank Lloyd. Lloyd, returning from his 'hunting trip' the day before the wedding, had sent a note to Hermy 'regretting' that he couldn't attend the ceremony or

37

reception as he had to go upstate that very evening to attend a newspaper publishers' convention in the Capital. Gladys Hemmingworth, his Society reporter, would cover the wedding for the *Record*. 'Please extend to Nora my very best wishes for her happiness. Yours, F. Lloyd.'

But F. Lloyd, who should have been two hundred miles away, was skulking behind a weeping willow near the grass court behind the Wright house. Mr Queen experienced trepidation. What had Patty once said? 'Frank took the whole thing pretty badly.' And Frank Lloyd was a dangerous man...Ellery, behind a maple, actually picked up a rock as Jim and Nora ran out of the kitchen to get into the cab. But the weeping willow wept quietly, and as soon as the taxi disappeared F. Lloyd left his hiding place and stamped off into the woods behind the house.

Pat Wright trudged up onto Ellery's porch the Tuesday night after the wedding and said with artificial cheeriness: 'Well, Jim and Nora are somewhere on the Atlantic.'

'Holding hands under the moon.'

Pat sighed. Ellery sat down beside her on the swing. They rocked together, shoulders touching. 'What happened to your bridge game tonight?' Ellery finally asked.

'Oh, Mother called it off. She's exhausted—been in bed practically since Sunday. And poor old Pop's pottering around with his stamp albums, looking lost. I didn't realize—quite—what it means to lose a daughter.'

'I noticed your sister Lola—'

'Lola wouldn't come. Mother drove down to Low Village to ask her. Let's not talk about...Lola.'

'Then whom shall we talk about?'

Patty mumbled: 'You.'

'Me?' Ellery was astonished. Then he chuckled. 'The answer is yes.'

'*What?*' cried Pat. 'Ellery, you're ribbing me!'

'Not at all. Your dad has a problem. Nora's just married. This house, under lease to me, was originally designed for her. He's thinking—'

'Oh, El, you're such a darling! Pop hasn't known what to do, the coward! So he asked me to talk to you. Jim and Nora do want to live in their...well, I mean who'd have thought it would turn out this way? As soon as they get back from their honeymoon. But it's not fair to you—'

'All's fair,' said Ellery. 'I'll vacate at once.'

'Oh, no!' said Pat. 'You've a six-month lease, you're writing your novel, we've really no right, Pop feels just awful—'

'Nonsense,' smiled Ellery. 'That hair of yours drives me quite mad. It isn't human. I mean it's like raw silk with lightning bugs in it.'

Pat grew very still. And then she wiggled into the corner of the swing and pulled her skirt down over her knees.

'Yes?' said Pat in a queer voice.

Mr Queen fumbled for a match. 'That's all. It's just—extraordinary.'

'I see. My hair isn't human, it's just extraordinary,' Pat mocked him. 'Well, in that case I must dash. Cart's waiting.'

Mr Queen abruptly rose. 'Mustn't offend Carter! Will Saturday be time enough? I imagine your mother will want to renovate the house, and I'll be leaving Wrightsville, considering the housing shortage—'

'How stupid of me,' said Pat. 'I almost forgot the most important thing.' She got off the swing and stretched lazily. 'Pop and Mother are inviting you to be our house guest for as long as you like. Goodniiiiiight!'

And she was gone, leaving Mr Queen on the porch of Calamity House in a remarkably better humor.

7

Hallowe'en: The Mask

Jim and Nora returned from their honeymoon cruise in the middle of October, just when the slopes of Bald Mountain looked as if they had been set on fire and everywhere you went in town you breathed the cider smoke of leaves burning. The State Fair was roaring full blast in Slocum: Jess Watkins's black-and-white milker, *Fanny IX*, took first prize in the Fancy Milch class, making Wrightsville proud. Kids were sporting red-rubber hands from going without gloves, the stars were frostbitten, and the nights had a twang to them. Out in the country you could see the pumpkins squatting in mysterious rows, like little orange men from Mars. Town Clerk Amos Bluefield, a distant cousin of Hermione's, obligingly died of thrombosis on October eleventh, so there was even the usual 'important' fall funeral. Nora and Jim stepped off the train the color of Hawaiians. Jim grinned at his father-in-law. 'What! Such a small reception committee?'

'Town's thinking about other things these days, Jim,' said John F. 'Draft registration tomorrow.'

'Holy smoke!' said Jim. 'Nora, I clean forgot!'

'Oh, lordy,' breathed Nora. 'Now I've got something else to

worry about!' And she clung to Jim's arm all the way up the hill.

'The town's just agog,' declared Hermy. 'Nora baby, you look *wonderful!*'

Nora did. 'I've put on ten pounds,' she laughed.

'How's married life?' demanded Carter Bradford.

'Why not get married and find out for yourself, Cart?' asked Nora. 'Pat dear, you're ravishing!'

'What chance has a man got,' growled Carter, 'with that smooth-talking hack writer in the house—'

'Unfair competition,' grinned Jim.

'In the *house*,' exclaimed Nora. 'Mother, you never wrote me!'

'It was the least we could do, Nora,' said Hermy, 'seeing how sweet he was about giving up his lease.'

'Nice fella,' said John F. 'Bring back any stamps?'

But Pat said impatiently: 'Nora, shake off these men and let's you and I go somewhere and…talk.'

'Wait till you see what Jim and I brought—' Nora's eyes grew big as the family limousine stopped in the Wright driveway. 'Jim, *look!*'

'Surprise!' The little house by the big one glistened in the October sunshine. It had been repainted: the fresh white of the clapboard walls, the turkey-red of the shutters and 'trim,' the Christmas green of the newly landscaped grounds made it look like a delectable gift package.

'It certainly looks fine,' said Jim. Nora smiled at him and squeezed his hand.

'And just wait, children,' beamed Hermy, 'till you see the *inside.*'

'Absolutely spick and utterly span,' said Pat. 'Ready to receive the lovebirds. Nora, you're blubbing!'

'It's so beautiful,' wept Nora, hugging her father and mother. And she dragged her husband off to explore the interior of the house that had lain empty, except for Mr Queen's short tenure, for three frightened years.

* * *

41

Mr Queen had packed an overnight bag the day before the newlyweds' return and had taken the noon train. It was a delicate disappearance, under the circumstances, and Pat said it showed he had 'a fine character.' Whatever his reason, Mr Queen returned on October seventeenth, the day after national registration, to find bustle and laughter in the little house next door, and no sign whatever that it had recently been known as Calamity House. 'We do want to thank you for giving up the house, Mr Smith,' said Nora. There was a housewifely smudge on her pert nose.

'That hundred-watt look is my reward.'

'Flatterer!' retorted Nora, and tugged at her starchy little apron. 'I look a sight—'

'For ailing eyes. Where's the happy bridegroom?'

'Jim's down at the railroad station picking his things up. Before he came back from his apartment in New York he'd packed his books and clothes and things and shipped them to Wrightsville care of General Delivery, and they've been held in the baggage room ever since. Here he is! Jim, did you get everything?'

Jim waved from Ed Hotchkiss's cab, which was heaped with suitcases and nailed boxes and a wardrobe trunk. Ed and Jim carried them into the house. Ellery remarked how fit Jim looked, and Jim with a friendly handclasp thanked him for 'being so decent about moving out,' and Nora wanted Mr 'Smith' to stay for lunch. But Mr 'Smith' laughed and said he'd take advantage of that invitation when Nora and Jim weren't so busy getting settled; and he left as Nora said: 'Such a mess of boxes, Jimmy!' and Jim grunted: 'You never know how many books you've got till you start packing 'em. Ed, lug these boxes down the cellar meanwhile, huh?'

The last thing Ellery saw was Jim and Nora in each other's arms. Mr Queen grinned. If the bride's house hid a calamity within its walls, the calamity was hidden superlatively well.

*   *   *

42

Ellery attacked his novel with energy. Except for mealtimes he remained within the sanctuary of his quarters on the top floor, the whole of which Hermy had placed at his disposal. Hermy and Pat and Ludie could hear his portable clacking away until immoral hours. He saw little of Jim and Nora, although at dinner he kept his ears alert for dissonances in the family talk. But Jim and Nora seemed happy. At the bank Jim had found waiting for him a private office with a new oak desk and a bronze plaque saying MR HAIGHT V.-PRES. Old customers dropped in to wish him luck and ask about Nora, not without a certain vulturous hope.

The little house was popular, too. The ladies of the Hill called and called, and Nora gave them tea and smiles. Sharp eyes probed corners, looking for dust and despair; but they were disappointed, and Nora giggled over their frustrated curiosity. Hermy was very proud of her married daughter.

So Mr Queen decided he had been an imaginative fool and that Calamity House was buried beyond resurrection. He began to make plans to invent a crime in his novel, since life was so uncooperative. And, because he liked all the characters, he was very glad.

The twenty-ninth of October came and went, and with it the published figures of the Federal draft lottery in Washington. Jim and Carter Bradford drew high order-numbers; Mr Queen was observed to drop in at the Hollis Hotel early on the morning of the thirtieth for a New York newspaper, upon reading which he was seen by Mark Doodle's son Grover to shrug and toss the paper away.

The thirty-first was mad. People on the Hill answered mysterious doorbells all day. Menacing signs in colored chalk appeared on pavements. As evening came on, costumed gnomes began to flit about town, their faces painted and their arms flapping. Big sisters complained bitterly about the disappearance of various compacts and lipsticks, and many a gnome went to bed with a tingling bottom. It was all gay and nostalgic, and Mr

Queen strolled about the neighborhood before dinner wishing he were young again, so that he, too, might enjoy the wicked pleasures of Hallowe'en. On his way back to the Wright house, he noticed that the Haight place next door was lit up; and on impulse he went up the walk and rang his ex-doorbell.

But it was Pat, not Nora, who answered the door. 'Thought you'd run out on me,' said Pat. 'We *never* see you any more.' Ellery fed his eyes for a moment. 'Now what?' demanded Pat, blushing. 'If you aren't the wackiest man! *Nora?* It's the famous author.'

'Come in!' called Nora from the living room. He found her struggling with an armful of books, trying to pick up more from disorderly stacks on the floor.

'Here, let me help you,' said Ellery.

'Oh, dear, no,' said Nora. 'You just watch us.' And Nora plodded up the stairs.

'Nora's turning the second bedroom upstairs into a study for Jim,' explained Pat.

Pat was stacking books from the floor in her arms and Ellery was idly examining titles on the half-filled bookshelves when Nora came downstairs for more books. 'Where's Jim, Nora?' asked Ellery.

'At the bank,' said Nora, stooping. 'An awfully important director's meeting.' And just then a book slid off the top of the fresh pile in her arms, and another, and another, while Nora crouched there horrified at the cascade. Half the books were on the floor again.

Pat said: 'Oh, look, Nor! Letters!'

'Letters? Where? Of all—They are!' One of the volumes which had fallen from Nora's arms was over-sized and fat, bound in tan cloth. From among the leaves some envelopes had tumbled. Nora picked them up curiously. They were not sealed.

'Oh, three poky old envelopes,' said Pat. 'Let's get going with these books or we'll never be through, Nora.'

But Nora frowned. 'There's something inside each one, Pat.

44

These are Jim's books. I wonder if…' She removed a single sheet of folded notepaper from one of the envelopes and spread it smooth, reading slowly to herself.

'Nora,' said Mr Queen. 'What's the matter?'

Nora said faintly: 'I don't understand—' and returned the sheet to its envelope. She took a similar sheet from the second envelope, read it, returned it to its envelope, the third, read it…And as she thrust it back into the third envelope, her cheeks were the color of wet sand. Pat and Ellery glanced at each other, puzzled.

'*Boo!*'

Nora whirled, shrieking. In the doorway crouched a man wearing a papier-mâché mask; his fingers were curled before his fantastic face, opening and closing hungrily. Nora's eyes turned up until they were all whites. And then she crumpled, still clutching the three envelopes.

'Nora!' Jim ripped off the ludicrous Hallowe'en mask. 'Nora, I didn't mean—'

'Jim, you fool,' panted Pat, flinging herself to her knees by Nora's still body. 'That's a smart joke! Nora dear—Nora!'

'Look out, Pat,' said Jim hoarsely; he seized Nora's limp figure, scooped her up, half-ran up the stairs with her.

'It's only a faint,' said Ellery, as Pat dashed into the kitchen. 'She'll be all right, Patty!' Pat came stumbling back with a glass of water, which slopped over with each step. 'Here, wench.' Ellery took it from her and sped up the stairs with the glass, Pat treading on his heels.

They found Nora on her bed, in hysterics, while Jim chafed her hands and groaned self-abasements. 'Excuse me,' said Ellery. He shouldered Jim aside and put the glass to Nora's blue lips. She tried to push his hand away. He slapped her, and she cried out; but she drank the water, choking. Then she sank back on the pillow, covering her face with her palms. 'Go away,' she sobbed.

'Nora, you all right now?' asked Pat anxiously.

'Yes. Please. Leave me alone. Please!'

'Go on, now,' said Jim. 'Leave us alone.'

Nora let her hands fall. Her face was swollen and puffed. 'You, too, Jim.'

Jim gaped at her. Pat steered him out. Ellery shut the bedroom door, frowning, and they went downstairs. Jim made for the liquor cabinet, poured himself a stiff Scotch, and tossed it down with one desperate motion. 'You know how nervous Nora is,' said Pat disapprovingly. 'If you hadn't had too much to drink tonight—'

Jim was angry, sullen. 'Who's tight? Don't you go telling Nora I've been drinking! Understand?'

'Yes, Jim,' said Pat quietly. They waited. Pat kept going to the foot of the stairs and looking up. Jim shuffled around. Ellery whistled a noiseless tune. Suddenly Nora appeared.

'Nora! Feeling better?' cried Pat.

'Worlds.' Nora came downstairs smiling. 'Please forgive me, Mr Smith. It was just being scared all of a sudden.'

Jim seized her in his arms. 'Oh, Nora—'

'Forget it, dear,' laughed Nora.

There was no sign of the three envelopes.

8

Hallowe'en:
The Scarlet Letters

When Jim and Nora came up on the porch after dinner, Nora was quite gay.

'Pat told me about that silly mask, Jim Haight,' said Hermy. 'Nora dearest, you're sure you're all right?'

'Of course, Mother. All this fuss over a scare!'

John F. was studying his son-in-law in a puzzled, secretive way. Jim seemed a little sheepish; he grinned vaguely.

'Where's Carter, Pat?' demanded Hermy. 'Wasn't he supposed to go with us to Town Hall tonight?'

'I've a headache, Muth. I phoned Cart to say I was going to bed. Night!' Pat went quickly into the house.

'Come along, Smith,' said John F. 'There's a good speaker—one of those war correspondents.'

'Thanks, Mr Wright, but I've some work on my novel. Have a nice time!'

When Jim's new car rolled off down the Hill, Mr Ellery Queen stepped off the Wright porch and, by the light of the pumpkin moon, noiselessly crossed the lawn. He circled Nora's house once, inspecting the windows. All dark. Then Alberta had already left—Thursday night was her night off. Ellery opened the kitchen door with a skeleton key, locked it behind him and, using his flashlight sparingly, made his way through the hall to the living room. He climbed the stairs making no sound. At the landing, he paused, frowning. There was a luminous line under Nora's bedroom door! He listened intently. Inside, drawers were being pulled open and pushed shut. A thief? Another Hallowe'en prank? Gripping the flashlight like a club, Ellery kicked the door open. Miss Patricia Wright screamed as she sprang from her stooped position over the lowest drawer of Nora's vanity. 'Hello,' said Mr Queen affably.

'Worm!' gasped Pat. 'I thought I'd *die*.' Then she blushed under his amused glance. 'At least *I* have an excuse! I'm her sister. But you...you're just a plain snoop, *Mr Ellery Queen!*'

Ellery's jaw waggled. 'You little demon,' he said admiringly. 'You've known me all along.'

'Of course,' retorted Pat. 'I heard you lecture once on *The Place of the Detective Story in Contemporary Civilization*. Very pompous it was, too.'

'Wellesley?'

'Sarah Lawrence. I thought at the time you were very handsome. *Sic transit gloria*. Don't look so concerned. I shan't give your precious incognito away.' Mr Queen kissed her. 'Mmm,' said Pat. 'Not bad. But inopportune...No, please, Ellery. Some other time. Ellery, those letters—you're the only one I can confide in. Muth and Pop would worry themselves sick—'

'And Carter Bradford?' suggested Mr Queen dryly.

'Cart,' said Miss Wright, flushing, 'is...well, I just wouldn't want Cart to know anything's wrong. If it is,' she added quickly. 'I'm not sure anything is.'

Ellery said: 'Yes, you are. Delicious lipstick.'

'Wipe it off. Yes,' said Pat damply, 'I am...Why didn't Nora say what was in those letters?' she burst out. 'Why did she come back to the living room tonight without them? *Why did she chase us all out of her bedroom?* Ellery, I'm...scared.'

Ellery squeezed her cold hands. 'Let's look for them.'

He found them in one of Nora's hatboxes. The hatbox lay on the shelf of Nora's closet, and the three envelopes had been tucked between the tissue paper and the floor of the box beneath a little flowered hat with a saucy mauve veil.

'Very clumsy technique,' mourned Mr Queen.

'Poor Nor,' said Pat. Her lips were pale. 'Let me see!' Ellery handed her the three letters. In the upper right-hand corner of each envelope, where a stamp should have been, appeared a date written in red crayon. Pat frowned. Ellery took the envelopes from her and arranged them in chronological order, according to the crayoned dates. The dates were 11/28, 12/25, and 1/1. 'And all three,' mused Pat, 'are addressed to "Miss Rosemary Haight." She's Jim's only sister. We've never met her. But it's queer there's no street or city address...'

'Not necessarily,' said Ellery, his brows together. 'The queerness lies in the use of the crayon.'

'Oh, Jim's always used a thin red crayon instead of a pencil—it's a habit of his.'

'Then his sister's name on these envelopes is in Jim's handwriting?'

'Yes. I'd recognize this scrawl of Jim's anywhere. For pete's sake, Ellery, what's *in* them?'

Ellery removed the contents of the first envelope, crumpled a bit from Nora's clutch when she had fainted. The note was in Jim's handwriting, too, Pat said, and written in the same red crayon:—

Nov. 28

DEAR SIS: I know it's been a long time, but you can imagine I've been rushed. Haven't time to drop you more than a line, because my wife got sick today. Doesn't seem like much, but I don't know. If you ask me, the doctor doesn't

know what it is, either. Let's hope it's nothing. Of course,
I'll keep you posted. Write me soon.

Love, JIM

'I can't understand it,' said Pat slowly. 'Nora's never felt better. Muth and I were just remarking about it the other day.
Ellery—'

'Has Nora seen Dr Willoughby recently?'
'No. Unless...But I'm sure she hasn't.'
'I see,' said Ellery in a voice that told nothing.
'Besides, that date—November twenty-eighth. That's a month
away, Ellery! How could Jim know...?' Pat stopped. Then she
said hoarsely: 'Open the second one!'
The second note was shorter than the first, but it was written
in the same red crayon in the same scrawl.

December 25th
SIS: I don't want to worry you. But I've got to tell you.
It's much worse. My wife is terribly ill. We're doing every-
thing we can.

In haste, JIM

'In haste, Jim,' repeated Pat. 'In haste—and dated December
twenty-fifth!' Ellery's eyes were clouded over now, hiding. 'But
how could Jim know Nora's illness is worse when Nora isn't
even sick?' cried Pat. 'And two months in advance!'

'I think,' said Mr Queen, 'We'd better read the third note.'
And he took the sheet of paper from the last envelope.
'Ellery, what...?'
He handed it to her and began to walk up and down Nora's
bedroom, smoking a cigarette with short, nervous puffs.
Pat read the note wide-eyed. Like the others, it was in Jim's
hand, a red-crayon scrawl. It said:—

50

DEAREST SIS: She's dead. She passed away today.

My wife, gone. As if she'd never been. Her last moments were—I can't write any more. Come to me if you can.

JIM

Ellery said: 'Not now, honey child,' and threw his arm about Pat's waist.

'What does it mean?' she sobbed.

'Stop blubbering.' Pat turned away, hiding her face.

Ellery replaced the messages in their envelopes and returned the envelopes to their hiding place exactly as he had found them. He set the hatbox back on the shelf of the closet, closed the vanity drawer in which Pat had been rummaging, straightened Nora's hand mirror. Another look around, and he led Pat from the room, switching off the ceiling light by the door. 'Find the door open?' he asked Pat.

'Closed,' she replied in a strangled voice.

He closed it. 'Wait. Where's that fat tan book—the one the envelopes fell out of this evening?'

'In Jim's study.' Pat seemed to have difficulty pronouncing her brother-in law's name.

They found the book on one of the newly installed shelves in the bedroom Nora had converted into a study for her husband. Ellery had switched on the mica-shaded desk lamp, and it threw long shadows on the walls. Pat clung to his arm, throwing glances over her shoulder. 'Pretty fresh condition,' said Ellery in a mutter, plucking the book from the shelf. 'Cloth hasn't even begun to fade, and the edges of the pages are clean.'

'What is it?' whispered Pat.

'Edgcomb's *Toxicology*.'

'Toxicology!' Pat stared at it in horror.

Ellery sharply scrutinized the binding. Then he let the book fall open in his hands. It broke obediently to a dog-eared page— the only dog-eared page he could find. The book's spine showed

51

a deep crack which ran parallel with the place in the book where it had broken open to reveal the dog-eared page. The three envelopes, then, had been lying between these two pages, thought Ellery. He began to read—to himself.

'What,' said Pat feverishly, 'What would Jim Haight be doing with a book on toxicology?'

Ellery looked at her. 'These two facing pages deal with various arsenious compounds—formulae, morbific effects, detection in organs and tissues, antidotes, fatal dosages, treatment of diseases arising from arsenious poisoning—'

'Poisoning!'

Ellery laid the book down within the brightest focus of the lamp. His finger pointed to the words in bold type: *Arsenious Oxid* (As_2O_3). His finger moved down to a paragraph which described arsenious oxid as 'white, tasteless, poisonous,' and gave the fatal dosage. This paragraph had been underlined in light red crayon.

In a quite clear voice that emerged from between dry, unwilling lips, Pat said: *'Jim is planning to murder Nora.'*

Part Two

9

Burnt Offering

'Jim is planning to murder Nora.'

Ellery set the book upon the shelf. With his back to Pat, he said: 'Nonsense.'

'You saw the letters yourself! You read them!'

Mr Queen sighed. They went downstairs in the dark, his arm about her waist. Outside, there was the old moon, and a stencil of cold stars. Pat shivered against him, and his clasp tightened. They drifted across the silver lawn and came to rest beneath the tallest elm. 'Look at the sky,' said Ellery, 'and tell me that again.'

'Don't feed me philosophy! Or poetry. This is the good old USA in the Year of Our Madness nineteen-forty. Jim is insane. He must be!' She began to cry.

'The human mind—' began Mr Queen; and he stopped. He had been about to say that the human mind was a curious and wonderful instrument. But it occurred to him in time that this was a two-way phrase, a Delphic hedge. The fact was...it looked bad. Very bad.

'Nora's in danger,' sobbed Pat. 'Ellery, what am I going to do?'

'Time may spade up some bones of truth, Patty.'

'But I can't take this alone! Nora—you saw how Nora took it. Ellery, she was scared green. And then…just as if nothing had happened. She's decided already, don't you see? *She's decided not to believe it.* If you waved those letters under her nose, Nora wouldn't admit anything now! Her mind opened for just a second; now it's shut down tight, and she'd lie to God.'

'Yes,' said Ellery, and his arms comforted her.

'He was so much in love with her! You saw it all happen. You saw the look on his face that night when they came downstairs to say they were going to be married. Jim was *happy*. When they got back from their honeymoon he seemed even happier.' Pat whispered: 'Maybe he *has* gone mad. Maybe that's been the whole thing all along. A dangerous maniac!' Ellery said nothing. 'How can I tell Mother? Or my father? It would kill them, and it wouldn't do any good. And yet—I've got to!'

A car throbbed up the Hill in the darkness.

'You're letting your emotions get in the way of your thinking, Pat,' said Ellery. 'A situation like this calls for observation and caution. And a disciplined tongue.'

'I don't understand…'

'One false accusation, and you might wreck the lives not only of Jim and Nora, but of your father and mother too.'

'Yes…And Nora waited so long—'

'I said there's time. There is. We'll watch, and we'll see, and meanwhile it will be a secret between us…Did I say "we"?' Ellery sounded rueful. 'It seems I've declared myself in.'

Pat gasped. 'You wouldn't back out *now*? I took it for granted. I mean, I've counted on you from that first awful moment. Ellery, you've *got* to help Nora! You're trained to this sort of thing. Please don't go away!' Pat shook him.

'I just said "we," didn't I?' said Ellery, almost irritably. There was something wrong. A sound had gone wrong somewhere. A sound that had stopped. A car? Had that been a car before? It hadn't passed…'Cry it out now, but when it's over it's over, do you understand?' And now he shook her.

'Yes,' wept Pat. 'I'm a snuffling fool. I'm sorry.'

'You're not a fool, but you must be a heroine. No word, no look, no *attitude*. As far as the rest of Wrightsville is concerned, those letters don't exist. Jim is your brother-in-law, and you like him, and you're happy about him and Nora.' She nodded against his shoulder. 'We mustn't tell your father or mother or Frank Lloyd or—'

Pat raised her head. 'Or whom?'

'No,' said Ellery with a frown. 'I can't make *that* decision for you, too.'

'You mean Cart,' said Pat steadily.

'I mean the Prosecutor of Wright County.'

Pat was silent. Ellery was silent. The moon was lower now, its bosom ruffled with slate flounces of cloud. 'I couldn't tell Carter,' murmured Pat. 'It never even occurred to me. I can't tell you why. Maybe it's because he's connected with the police. Maybe it's because he's not in the family—'

'I'm not in the family, either,' said Mr Queen.

'You're different!'

Despite himself, Mr Queen experienced a chill of pleasure. But his voice was impersonal. 'At any rate, you've got to be my eyes and ears, Pat. Stay with Nora as much as possible without arousing her suspicions. Watch Jim without seeming to. Report everything that happens. And whenever possible you must work me into your family gatherings. Is all that clear?'

Pat actually smiled up at him. 'I *was* being silly. Now it doesn't seem half so bad, with you under this tree, and the moonlight touching that flat plane of your right cheek...you're very handsome, you know, Ellery—'

'Then why in hell,' growled a male voice from the darkness, 'don't you kiss him?'

'Cart!' Pat snuggled against the black chest of the elm.

They could hear Bradford breathing somewhere near—breathing short deep ones. Too absurd, thought Mr Queen. A man of logic should evade such encirclements by chance. But at

57

least it cleared up the minor irritation of the sound-that-had-stopped. It had been Carter Bradford's car.

'Well, he *is* handsome,' said Pat's voice from the tree trunk. Ellery grinned to himself.

'You lied to me,' cried Carter. He materialized: no hat, and his chestnut hair angry. 'Don't hide in a bush, Pat!'

'I'm not hiding,' said Pat peevishly, 'and it isn't a bush, it's a tree.' She came out of the darkness, too; and they faced each other with punctilio. Mr Queen watched with silent enjoyment.

'You told me over the phone that you had a headache!'

'Yes.'

'You said you were going to bed!'

'I am.'

'Don't quibble!'

'Why not? You raise such unimportant points, Mr Bradford.'

Carter's arms flapped under the unfriendly stars. 'You lied to get rid of me. You didn't want me around. You had a date with this scribbler! Don't deny it!'

'I do deny it.' Pat's voice softened. 'I did lie to you, Cart, but I didn't have a date with Ellery.'

'That,' remarked Mr Queen from his observation post, 'happens to be the truth.'

'Stick your two cents out, Smith!' shouted Carter. 'I'm trying to keep my temper or I'd drape you over the lawn!'

Mr 'Smith' grinned and held his peace.

'All right, so I'm jealous,' muttered Cart. 'But you don't have to be a sneak, Pat! If you don't want me, say so.'

'This has nothing to do with my wanting you or not wanting you,' said Pat in a timid-turtle voice.

'Well, do you or don't you?'

Pat's eyes fell. 'You've no right to ask me that—here—now.' Her eyes flashed up. 'You wouldn't want a sneak, anyway, would you?'

'All right! Have it your way!'

'Cart...!'

58

His voice came back in a bellow of defiance. 'I'm through!'

Pat ran off toward the big white house.

Thought Mr Queen as he watched her slim figure race across the lawn: In a way it's better...much better. You don't know what you're in for. And Mr Carter Bradford, when you meet him next, may very well be an enemy.

When Ellery returned from his pre-breakfast walk the next morning, he found Nora and her mother whispering on the Wright porch. 'Good morning!' he said cheerfully. 'Enjoy the lecture last night?'

'It was very interesting.' Nora looked distressed, and Hermione preoccupied, so Ellery began to go into the house.

'Mr Smith,' said Hermy. 'Oh, dear, I don't know how to say it! Nora dear—'

'Ellery, what happened here last night?' asked Nora.

'Happened?' Ellery looked blank.

'I mean with Pat and Carter. You were home—'

'Is anything wrong with Pat?' asked Ellery quickly.

'Of course there is. She won't come down to breakfast. She won't answer any questions. And when Pat sulks—'

'It's Carter's fault,' Hermy burst out. 'I *thought* there was something queer about her "headache" last night! Please, Mr Smith, if you know anything about it—if something happened after we went to Town Hall last night which her mother ought to know—'

'Has Pat broken off with Cart?' asked Nora anxiously. 'No, you don't have to answer, Ellery. I can see it in your face. Mother, you'll simply have to give Patty a talking-to. She can't keep doing this sort of thing to Cart.'

Ellery walked Nora back to the little house. As soon as they were out of earshot of Mrs Wright, Nora said: 'Of course you had something to do with it.'

'I?' asked Mr Queen.

'Well...don't you agree Pat's in love with Carter? I'm sure you could help by not making Carter jealous—'

'Mr Bradford,' said Mr Queen, 'would be jealous of a postage stamp Patty licked.'

'I know. He's so hotheaded, too! Oh, dear.' Nora sighed. 'I'm making a mess of it. Will you forgive me? And come in to breakfast?'

'Yes to both questions.' And as he helped Nora up the porch steps, he wondered just how guilty he really was.

Jim was full of political talk, and Nora...Nora was wonderful. No other word for it, thought Ellery. Watching and listening, he could detect no least tinkle of falsity. They seemed so much like two young people luxuriating in the blessedness of early marriage that it was a temptation to dismiss the incidents of the previous evening as fantasy.

Pat arrived, with Alberta and eggs, in a rush. 'Nora! How nice,' she said, as if nothing at all had happened. 'Can you spare a starving gal an egg or two? Morning, Jim! Ellery! Not that Ludie didn't have breakfast for me. She *did*. But I just felt that nosy impulse to look in on the lovebirds...'

'Alberta, another setting,' said Nora, and she smiled at Pat. 'You *do* talk in the morning! Ellery, sit down. The honeymoon being over, *my* husband doesn't rise for my family any more.'

Jim stared. 'Who—Patso?' He grinned. 'Say, you *are* grown-up! Let me look. Yep. A real glamour girl. Smith, I envy you. If I were a bachelor—'

Ellery saw the swift cloud darken Nora's face. She pressed more coffee on her husband. Pat kept chattering. She wasn't a very good actress—couldn't look Jim in the eye. Heroic, though. Remembering instructions in the midst of her own troubles...But Nora was superb. Yes, Pat had been right. Nora had decided not to *think* about the letters or their horrible implication. And she was using the minor crisis of Pat and Cart to help her not to think.

'I'll fix your eggs myself, darling,' said Nora to Pat. 'Alberta's a jewel, but how could she know you like four-minute coddling, to the second? Excuse me.' Nora left the dining room to join Alberta in the kitchen.

'That Nora,' chuckled Jim. 'She's a real hen. Say! What time is it? I'll be late at the bank. Patty, you been crying? You're talking sort of funny, too. Nora!' he shouted. 'Didn't the mail come yet?'

'Not yet!' Nora called from the kitchen.

'Who, me?' said Pat feebly. 'Don't—don't be a goop, Jim.'

'*All* right, *all* right,' said Jim, laughing. 'So it's none of my damn business. Ah! There's Bailey now. 'Scuse!' Jim hurried out to the foyer to answer the postman's ring. They heard him open the front door; they heard old Mr Bailey's cracked 'Mornin', Mr Haight,' Jim's joshing response, the little slam of the door, and Jim's slow returning footsteps, as if he were shuffling through the mail as he came back. Then he walked into the field of their vision and stopped, and they saw him staring at one of the several envelopes the postman had just delivered. His face was liverish. And then he vaulted upstairs. They heard his feet pound on the carpeting and a moment later a door bang.

Pat was gaping at the spot Jim had just vacated. 'Eat your cereal,' said Ellery.

Pat flushed and bent quickly over her plate. Ellery got up and walked without noise to the foot of the staircase. After a moment he returned to the breakfast table. 'He's in his study, I think. Heard him *lock the door*…No! Not now. Here's Nora.'

Pat choked over her Crackle-Crunch. 'Where's Jim?' asked Nora as she set the eggs before her sister.

'Upstairs,' said Ellery, reaching for the toast.

'Jim?'

'Yes, Nora.' Jim reappeared on the stairs; he was still pale, but rigidly controlled. He had his coat on, and carried several unopened letters of assorted sizes.

'Jim! Is anything wrong?'

'Wrong?' Jim laughed. 'I never saw such a suspicious woman! What the devil should be wrong?'

'I don't know. But you look so pale—'

Jim kissed her. 'You ought to've been a nurse! Well, got to be going. Oh, by the way. Here's the mail. The usual junk. Bye, Patty! Smith! See you soon.' Jim raced out.

After breakfast, Ellery said something about 'strolling in the woods' behind the house and excused himself. A half hour later Pat joined him. She came hurrying through the underbrush with a Javanese scarf tied around her head, looking back over her shoulder as if someone were chasing her. 'I thought I'd never get away from Nora,' Pat panted. She dropped to a stump. 'Whoo!'

Ellery blew smoke thoughtfully. 'Pat, we've got to read that letter Jim just received.'

'Ellery...where's this all going to end?'

'It stirred Jim up tremendously. Can't be coincidence. Somehow this morning's letter ties in with the rest of this puzzle. Can you lure Nora out of the house?'

'She's going to High Village this morning with Alberta to do some shopping. There's the station wagon! I'd recognize that putt-putt in Detroit.'

Mr Queen ground out his cigarette carefully. 'All right, then,' he said.

Pat kicked a twig. Her hands were trembling. Then she sprang off the stump. 'I feel like a skunk,' she moaned. 'But what else can we do?'

'I doubt if we'll find anything,' said Ellery as Pat let him into Nora's house with her duplicate key. 'Jim locked the door when he ran upstairs. He didn't want to be caught doing...whatever it was he did.'

'You think he destroyed the letter?'

'Afraid so. But we'll have a look, anyway.'

In Jim's study, Pat set her back against the door. She looked ill. Ellery sniffed. And went directly to the fireplace. It was clean except for a small mound of ash. 'He burned it!' said Pat.

'But not thoroughly enough.'

'Ellery, you've found something!'

'A scrap that wasn't consumed by the fire.'

Pat flew across the room. Ellery was examining a scrap of charred paper very carefully. 'Part of the envelope?'

'The flap. Return address. But the address has been burned off. Only thing left is the sender's name.'

Pat read: '"Rosemary Haight." Jim's sister.' Her eyes widened. 'Jim's sister Rosemary! Ellery, the one he wrote those three letters to about Nora!'

'It's possible that—' Ellery did not finish.

'You were going to say it's possible there was a first letter we didn't find, because he'd already sent it! And that this is the remains of his sister's answer.'

'Yes.' Ellery tucked the burnt scrap away in his wallet. 'But on second thought I'm not so sure. Why should his sister's reply bother him so much, if that's what it is? No, Patty, this is something different, something new.'

'But what?'

'That,' said Mr Queen, 'is what we've got to find out.' He took her arm, looking about. 'Let's get out of here.'

That night they were all sitting on the Wright porch watching the wind blow the leaves across the lawn. John F. and Jim were debating the presidential campaign with some heat, while Hermy anxiously appeased and Nora and Pat listened like mice. Ellery sat by himself in a corner, smoking.

'John, you know I don't like these political arguments!' said Hermy. 'Goodness, you men get so hot under the collar—'

John F. grunted. 'Jim, there's dictatorship coming in this country, you mark my words—'

Jim grinned. 'And you'll eat 'em...*All* right, Mother!' Then he said casually: 'Oh, by the way, darling, I got a letter from my sister Rosemary this morning. Forgot to tell you.'

'Yes?' Nora's tone was bright. 'How nice. What does she write, dear?'

Pat drifted toward Ellery and in the darkness sat down at his

63

feet. He put his hand on her neck; it was clammy. 'The usual stuff. She does say she'd like to meet you—all of you.'

'Well, I should think so!' said Hermy. 'I'm very anxious to meet your sister, Jim. Is she coming out for a visit?'

'Well…I *was* thinking of asking her, but—'

'Now, Jim,' said Nora. 'You know I've asked you dozens of times to invite Rosemary to Wrightsville.'

'Then it's all right with you, Nor?' asked Jim quickly.

'All right!' Nora laughed. 'What's the matter with you? Give me her address and I'll drop her a note tonight.'

'Don't bother, darling. I'll write her myself.'

When they were alone, a half hour later, Pat said to Ellery: 'Nora was scared.'

'Yes. It's a poser.' Ellery circled his knees with his arms. 'Of course, the letter that stirred Jim up this morning was the same letter he just said he got from his sister.'

'Ellery, Jim's holding something back.'

'No question about it.'

'If his sister Rosemary just wrote about wanting to come out for a visit, or anything as trivial as that…*why did Jim burn her letter?*'

Mr Queen kept the silence for a long time. Finally he mumbled: 'Go to bed, Patty. I want to think.'

On November the eighth, four days after Franklin Delano Roosevelt had been elected to the Presidency of the United States for a third term, Jim Haight's sister came to Wrightsville.

10

Jim and the Fleshpot

'Miss Rosemary Haight,' wrote Gladys Hemmingworth in the Society column of the *Wrightsville Record*, 'was strikingly accoutered in a *naturel* French suède travelling suit with sleeveless jerkin to match, a dashing jacket of platinum-fox fur topped with the jauntiest fox-trimmed archery hat of forest green, and green suède wedgies and bag...'

Mr Ellery Queen happened to be taking a walk that morning...to the Wrightsville station. So he saw Rosemary Haight get off the train at the head of a safari bearing luggage and pose for a moment, in the sun, like a movie actress. He saw her trip over to Jim and kiss him, and turn to Nora with animation and embrace her, presenting a spruce cheek; and Mr Queen also saw the two women laugh and chatter as Jim and the safari picked up the visitor's impedimenta and made for Jim's car. And Mr Queen's weather eye clouded over.

That night, at Nora's, he had an opportunity to test his first barometric impression. And he decided that Rosemary Haight was no bucolic maiden on an exciting journey; that she was pure metropolis, insolent and bored and trying to conceal both. Also, she was menacingly attractive. Hermy, Pat, and Nora disliked her instantly; Ellery could tell that from the extreme politeness with which they treated her. As for John F., he was charmed, spryly gallant. Hermy reproached him in the silent language of the eye. And Ellery spent a troubled night trying to put Miss Rosemary Haight together in the larger puzzle, and not succeeding.

Jim was busy at the bank these days and, rather with relief, Ellery thought, left the problem of entertaining his sister to Nora. Dutifully Nora drove Rosemary about the countryside, showing her the 'sights.' It was a little difficult for Nora to sustain the charming-hostess illusion, Pat confided in Ellery, since Rosemary had a supercilious attitude towards everything and wondered 'how in heaven's name you can be *happy* in such a dull place, Mrs. H!'

Then there was the gauntlet of the town's ladies to run...teas for the guest, very correct with hats on in the house and white gloves, an ambitious mah-jongg party, a wiener roast on the lawn one moonlit night, a church social...The ladies were cold. Emmeline DuPré said Rosemary Haight had a streak of 'commerce' whatever that was, Clarice Martin thought her clothes too 'you know,' and Mrs Mackenzie at the Country Club said she was a born bitch and look at those silly men drooling at her! The Wright women found themselves constrained to defend her, which was hard, considering that secretly they agreed to the truth of all the charges.

'I wish she'd leave,' said Pat to Ellery a few days after Rosemary's arrival. 'Isn't that a horrid thing to say? But I do. And now she's sent for her trunks!'

'But I thought she didn't like it here.'

'That's what I can't understand, either. Nora says it was supposed to be a "flying" visit, but Rosemary acts as if she means to dig in for the winter. And Nora can't very well discourage her.'

'What's Jim say?'

'Nothing to Nora but—' Pat lowered her voice and looked around—'apparently he's said something to Rosemary, because I happened in just this morning and there was Nora trapped in the serving pantry while Jim and Rosemary, who evidently thought Nora was upstairs, were having an argument in the dining room. That woman has a temper!'

'What was the argument about?' asked Ellery eagerly.

'I came in at the tail end and didn't hear anything important, but Nora says it was...well, frightening. Nora wouldn't tell me what she'd heard, but she was terribly upset—she looked the same way as when she read those three letters that tumbled out of the toxicology book.'

Ellery muttered: 'I wish I'd heard that argument. Why can't I put my finger on *something*? Pat, you're a rotten assistant detective!'

'Yes, sir,' said Pat miserably.

Rosemary Haight's trunk arrived on the fourteenth. Steve Polaris, who ran the local express agency, delivered the trunk himself—an overgrown affair that looked as if it might be packed with imported evening gowns. Steve lugged it up Nora's walk on his broad back and Mr Queen, who was watching from the Wright porch, saw him carry it into Nora's house and come out a few minutes later accompanied by Rosemary, who was wearing a candid red, white, and blue negligee. She looked like an enlistment poster. Ellery saw Rosemary sign Steve Polaris's receipt book and go back into the house. Steve slouched down the walk grinning—Steve had the most wolfish eye, Pat said, in all of Low Village.

'Pat,' said Ellery urgently, 'do you know this truckman well?'

'Steve? That's the only way you *can* know Steve.'

Steve tossed his receipt book on the driver's seat of his truck and began to climb in. 'Then distract him. Kiss him, vamp him, do a striptease—anything, but get him out of sight of that truck for two minutes!'

Pat instantly called: 'Oh, Ste-e-e-eve!' and tripped down the

67

porch steps. Ellery followed in a saunter. No one was in sight anywhere on the Hill.

Pat was slipping her arm through Steve's and giving him one of her quick little-girl smiles, saying something about her piano, and there wasn't a man she knew strong enough to move it from where it was to where she wanted it, and of course when she saw Steve...Steve went with Pat into the Wright house, visibly swollen. Ellery was at the truck in two bounds. He snatched the receipt book from the front seat. Then he took a piece of charred paper from his wallet and began riffling the pages of the book...When Pat reappeared with Steve, Mr Queen was at Hermione's zinnia bed surveying the dead and dying blossoms with the sadness of a poet. Steve gave him a scornful look and passed on.

'Now you'll have to move the piano back,' said Pat. 'I *am* sorry—I could have thought of something not quite so bulky...Bye, Steve!' The truck rolled off with a flirt of its exhaust.

'I was wrong,' mumbled Ellery.

'About what?'

'About Rosemary.'

'Stop being cryptic! And why did you send me to lure Steve away from his truck? The two are connected, Mr Queen!'

'I had a flash from on high. It said to me: "This woman Rosemary doesn't seem cut from the same cloth as Jim Haight. They don't seem like brother and sister at all—"'

'Ellery!'

'Oh, it was possible. But my flash was wrong. She *is* his sister.'

'And you proved that through Steve Polaris's truck? Wonderful man!'

'Through his receipt book, in which this woman had just signed her name. I *have* the real Rosemary Haight's signature, you'll recall, my dear Watson.'

'On that charred flap of envelope we found in Jim's study— the remains of his sister's letter that he'd burned!'

'Precisely, my dear Watson. And the signature "Rosemary

Haight" on the flap of the letter and the signature "Rosemary Haight" in Steve's receipt book are the work of the same hand.'

'Leaving us,' remarked Pat dryly, 'exactly where we were.'

'No,' said Mr Queen with a faint smile. 'Before we only *believed* this woman was Jim's sister. Now we *know* it. Even your primitive mind can detect the distinction, my dear Watson?'

The longer Rosemary Haight stayed at Nora's, the more inexplicable the woman became. Jim was busier and busier at the bank; sometimes he did not even come home to dinner. Yet Rosemary did not seem to mind her brother's neglect half so much as her sister-in-law's attentions. The female Haight tongue was forked; more than once its venom reduced Nora to tears...shed, it was reported to Mr Queen by his favourite spy, in her own room, alone. Towards Pat and Hermione, Rosemary was less obvious. She rattled on about her 'travels'—Panama, Rio, Honolulu, Bali, Banff, surf riding and skiing and mountain climbing and 'exciting' men—much talk about exciting men—until the ladies of the Wright family began to look harried and grim, and retaliated.

And yet Rosemary stayed on.

Why? Mr Queen was pondering this poser as he sat one morning in the window seat of his workroom. Rosemary Haight had just come out of her brother's house, a cigarette at a disgusted angle to her red lips, clad in jodhpurs and red Russian boots and a Lana Turner sweater. She stood on the porch for a moment, slapping a crop against her boots with impatience, at odds with Wrightsville. Then she strode off into the woods behind the Wright grounds.

Later, Pat took Ellery driving; and Ellery told her about seeing the Haight woman enter the woods in a riding habit.

Pat turned into the broad concrete of Route 16, driving slowly. 'Bored,' she said. 'Bored blue. She got Jake Bushmill the blacksmith to dig her up a saddle horse from somewhere—yesterday was her first day out, and Carmel Pettigrew saw her tearing along the dirt road toward Twin Hill like—I quote—one of the

Valkyries. Carmel—silly dope!—thinks Rosemary's just too-too.'

'And you?' queried Mr Queen.

'That panther laziness of hers is an act—underneath, she's the restless type, and hard as teak. A cheap wench. Or don't you think?' Pat glanced at him sidewise.

'She's terribly attractive,' said Ellery evasively.

'So's a man-eating orchid,' retorted Pat; and she drove in silence for eight-tenths of a mile. Then she said: 'What do you make of the whole thing, Ellery—Jim's conduct, Rosemary, the three letters, the visit, Rosemary's staying on when she hates it...?'

'Nothing,' said Ellery. But he added: 'Yet.'

'Ellery—look!' They were approaching a gaudy bump on the landscape, a one-story white stucco building on whose walls oversized red lady-devils danced and from whose roof brittle cut-out flames of wood shattered the sky. The tubing of the unlit neon sign spelled out VIC CARLATTI'S *Hot Spot*. The parking lot to the side was empty except for one small car.

'Look at what?' demanded Ellery, puzzled. 'I don't see anything except no customers, since the sun is shining and Carlatti's patrons don't creep out of their walls until nightfall.'

'Judging from that car on the plot,' said Pat, a little pale, 'there's *one* customer.'

Ellery frowned. 'It does look like the same car.'

'It is.' Pat drove up to the entrance, and they jumped out.

'It might be business, Pat,' said Ellery, not with conviction.

Pat glanced at him scornfully and opened the front door. There was no one in the chrome-and-scarlet leather interior but a bartender and a man mopping the postage-stamp dance floor. Both employees looked at them curiously. 'I don't see him,' whispered Pat.

'He may be in one of those booths...No.'

'The back room...'

'Let's sit down.'

They sat down at the nearest table and the bartender came over, yawning. 'What'll it be, folks?'

'Cuba Libre,' said Pat, nervously looking around.

'Scotch.'

'Uh-huh.' The bartender strolled back to his bar.

'Wait here,' said Ellery. He got up and made for the rear, like a man looking for something.

'It's over that way,' said the man with the mop, pointing to a door marked HE. But Ellery pushed against a partly open red-and-gold door with a heavy brass lock. It swung noiselessly.

The room beyond was a gambling room. In a chair at the empty roulette table sprawled Jim Haight, his head on one arm of the table. A burly man with a cold cigar stub in his teeth stood half turned away from Ellery at a telephone on the far wall. 'Yeah. I said Mrs Haight, stoopid.' The man had luxuriant black brows which almost met and a gray flabby face. 'Tell her Vic Carlatti.'

'Stoopid' would be Alberta. Ellery stood still against the red-and-gold door. 'Mrs Haight? This is Mr Carlatti of the *Hot Spot*,' said the proprietor in a genial bass. 'Yeah...No, I ain't making no mistake, Mrs Haight. It's about Mr Haight...Now wait a minute. He's settin' in my back room right now, cockeyed...I mean drunk...Now don't get bothered, Mrs Haight. Your old man's okay. Just had a couple of shots too many and passed out. What'll I do with the body?'

'Just a moment,' said Ellery pleasantly.

Carlatti slewed his big head around. He looked Ellery up and down. 'Hold on a second, Mrs Haight...Yeah? What can I do for you?'

'You can let me talk to Mrs Haight,' said Ellery, crossing over and taking the phone from the man's furry hands. 'Nora? This is Ellery Smith.'

'Ellery!' Nora was frantic. 'What's the matter with Jim? How is he? How did you happen to—'

71

'Don't get excited, Nora. Pat and I were driving past Carlatti's place and we noticed Jim's car parked outside. We're in here now and Jim's all right. Just had a little too much to drink.'

'I'll drive right down—the station wagon—'

'You'll do nothing of the kind. Pat and I will have him home in half an hour. Don't worry, do you hear?'

'Thank you,' whispered Nora, and hung up.

Ellery turned from the telephone to find Pat bending over Jim, shaking him. 'Jim. Jim!'

'It's no use, girl friend,' growled Carlatti. 'He's carrying a real load.'

'You ought to be ashamed of yourself, getting him tight!'

'Now don't get tough, babe. He came in here under his own steam. I got a licence to sell liquor. He wants to buy, he can buy. Get him outa here.'

'How did you know who he was? How did you know whom to call?' Pat was fizzing with indignation.

'He's been here before, and besides I frisked him. And don't gimme that fishy eye. Come on, pig. Blow!'

Pat gasped. 'Excuse me,' said Ellery. He walked past Carlatti as if the big man were not there, and then suddenly he turned and stepped hard on Carlatti's bulldog toe. The man bellowed with pain and reached swiftly for his back pocket. Ellery set the heel of his right hand against Carlatti's chin and pushed. Carlatti's head snapped back; and as he staggered Ellery punched him in the belly with the other hand. Carlatti groaned and sank to the floor, clutching his middle with both hands and staring up, surprised. 'Miss Pig to you,' said Ellery. He yanked Jim out of his chair and got him in a fireman's grip. Pat picked up Jim's crushed hat and ran to hold the door open.

Ellery took the wheel going back. In the open car, with the wind striking his face and Pat shaking him, Jim began to revive. He goggled glassily at them.

'Jim, whatever made you do a silly thing like this?'

'Huh?' gurgled Jim, closing his eyes again.

'In mid-afternoon, when you should be at the bank!'

Jim sank lower in the seat, muttering. 'Stupefied,' said Ellery. There was a deep cleft between his brows. His rear-vision mirror told him a car was overtaking them rapidly—Carter Bradford's car. Pat noticed, and turned. And turned back, very quickly. Ellery slowed down to let Bradford pass. But Bradford did not pass. He slowed down alongside and honked his horn. A lean gray Yankee with a red face and jellyfish eyes sat beside him. Obediently, Ellery pulled up at the side of the road; and Bradford stopped his car, too.

Pat said: 'Why, *hello*, Cart,' in a surprised voice. 'And Mr Dakin! Ellery, this is Chief Dakin of the Wrightsville police. Mr Ellery Smith.'

Chief Dakin said: 'How do, Mr Smith,' in a polite voice, and Ellery nodded.

'Anything wrong?' asked Carter Bradford, a little awkwardly. 'I noticed Jim here was—'

'Well, that's extremely efficient, Cart,' said Pat warmly. 'Practically Scotland Yardish, or at the very least F.B.I. Isn't it, Ellery? The Public Prosecutor and the Chief of Police—'

"There's nothing wrong, Bradford,' said Ellery.

'Nothing that a bicarbonate of soda and a good night's sleep won't fix,' said Chief Dakin dryly. 'Carlatti's?'

'Something like that,' said Ellery. 'Now if you don't mind, gentlemen, Mr Haight needs his bed—badly.'

'Anything I can do, Pat...' Cart was flushed. 'Matter of fact, I was thinking of calling you up—'

'You were thinking of calling me up.'

'I mean—'

Jim stirred between Pat and Ellery, mumbling. Pat said severely: 'Jim. How do you feel?' He opened his eyes again. They were still glassy, but something behind the glaze made Pat look at Ellery with a swift fear. 'Say, he's in a bad way, at that,' said Dakin.

'Relax, now, Jim,' soothed Ellery. 'Go to sleep.'

73

Jim looked from Pat to Ellery to the men in the other car, but he did not recognize any of them. The mumble became intelligible: 'Wife my wife damn her oh damn wife…'

'Jim!' cried Pat. 'Ellery, get him home!'

Ellery released his hand brake quickly. But Jim was not to be repressed. He pulled himself up and his cheeks, pale from sickness, grew scarlet. 'Rid of her!' he shouted. 'Wait'n' see! I'll get rid of the bas'ard! I'll kill 'a bas'ard!'

Chief Dakin blinked, and Carter Bradford looked immensely surprised and opened his mouth to say something. But Pat pulled Jim down savagely and Ellery shot the convertible forward, leaving Bradford's car behind. Jim began to sob, and in the middle of a sob he suddenly fell asleep again. Pat shrank as far from him as she could. 'Did you hear what he *said*, Ellery? Did you?'

'He's crazy blind.' Ellery stepped hard on the gas pedal.

'It's true, then,' moaned Pat. 'The letters—Rosemary…Ellery, I tell you Rosemary and Jim have been putting on an act! They're in cahoots to—to—And Cart and Chief Dakin heard him!'

'Pat.' Ellery kept his eyes on the road. 'I haven't wanted to ask you this before, but…Has Nora any considerable sum of money, or property, in her own right?'

Pat moistened her lips very slowly. 'Oh…no. It couldn't be…that.'

'Then she has.'

'Yes,' Pat whispered. 'By my grandfather's will. Pop's father. Nora automatically inherited a lot of money when she married, held in trust for her if and when. Grandfather Wright died soon after Lola eloped with that actor—he'd cut Lola off because of that, and divided his estate between Nora and me. I get half when I marry, too—'

'How much did Nora get?' asked Ellery. He glanced at Jim. But Jim was stertorously asleep.

'I don't know. But Pop once told me it's more than Nora and I could ever spend. Oh Lord—Nora!'

'If you start to cry,' said Ellery grimly. 'I'll dump you overboard. Is this inheritance to you and Nora a secret?'

'Try to keep a secret in Wrightsville,' said Pat. 'Nora's money ...' She began to laugh. 'It's like a bad movie. Ellery—what are we going to *do*?' She laughed and laughed.

Ellery turned Pat's car into the Hill drive. 'Put Jim to bed,' he muttered.

11

Thanksgiving:
The First Warning

The next morning Mr Queen was knocking at Nora's door before eight. Nora's eyes were swollen. 'Thanks for—yesterday. Putting Jim to bed while I was being so silly—'

'Rubbish,' said Ellery cheerfully. 'There hasn't been a bride since Eve who didn't think the world was going under when hubby staggered home under his first load. Where's the erring husband?'

'Upstairs shaving.' Nora's hand trembled as she fussed with the gleaming toaster on the breakfast table.

'May I go up? I shouldn't want to embarrass your sister-in-law by prowling around the bedroom floor at this hour—'

'Oh, Rosemary doesn't get up till ten,' said Nora. 'These wonderful November mornings! Please do—and tell Jim what you think of him!'

Ellery laughed and went upstairs. He knocked on the master-bedroom door, which was half-open, and Jim called from the

76

bathroom: 'Nora? Gosh, darling, I knew you'd be my sweet baby and forgive—' His voice blurred when he spied Ellery. Jim's face was half shaved; the shaved half was pasty, and his eyes puffed. 'Morning, Smith. Come in.' ·

'I just dropped by for a minute to ask you how you were feeling, Jim.' Ellery draped himself against the bathroom jamb.

Jim turned, surprised. 'How did *you* know?'

'How did *I* know! Don't tell me you don't remember. Why, Pat and I brought you home.'

'Gosh,' groaned Jim, 'I wondered about that. Nora won't talk to me. Can't say I blame her. Say, I'm awfully grateful, Smith. Where'd you find me?'

'Carlatti's place on Route 16. The *Hot Spot.*'

'That dive?' Jim shook his head. 'No wonder Nora's sore.' He grinned sheepishly. 'Was I sick during the night! Nora fixed me up, but she wouldn't say a word to me. What a dumb stunt!'

'You did some pretty dumb talking on the ride home, too, Jim.'

'Talking? What did I say?'

'Oh…something about "getting rid of" some bastard or other,' said Ellery lightly.

Jim blinked. He turned back to the mirror again. 'Out of my head, I guess. Or else I was thinking of Hitler.' Ellery nodded, his eyes fixed on the razor. It was shaking. 'I don't remember a damn thing,' said Jim. 'Not a damn thing.'

'I'd lay off the booze if I were you, Jim,' said Ellery amiably. 'Not that it's any of my business, but…well, if you keep saying things like that, people might misunderstand.'

'Yeah,' said Jim, fingering his shaved cheek. 'I guess they would at that. Ow, my head! Never again.'

'Tell that to Nora,' laughed Ellery. 'Well, morning, Jim.'

'Morning. And thanks again.'

Ellery left, smiling. But the smile vanished on the landing. It seemed to him that the door to the guest room was open a handsbreadth wider than when he had gone in to talk to Jim.

Mr Queen found it harder and harder to work on his novel. For one thing, there was the weather. The countryside was splashy with reds and oranges and yellowing greens; the days were frost-touched now as well as the nights, hinting at early snows; nights came on swiftly, with a crackle. It was a temptation to roam back-country roads and crunch the crisp dry corpses of the leaves underfoot. Especially after sunset, when the sky dropped its curtains, lights sparkled in isolated farmhouses, and an occasional whinny or howl came from some black barn. Wilcy Gallimard came into town with five truckloads of turkeys and got rid of them in no time. 'Yes, sir,' said Mr Queen to himself. 'Thanksgiving's in the air—everywhere except at 460 Hill Drive.'

Then there was Pat, whose recent habit of peering over her own shoulder had become chronic. She clung to Ellery so openly that Hermione Wright began to make secret plans in her head and even John F., who never noticed anything but flaws in mortgages and rare postage stamps, looked thoughtful...It made work very difficult.

But most of all it was watching Jim and Nora without seeming to that occupied Ellery's time. Things were growing worse in the Haight household. For Jim and Nora no longer 'got along.' There were quarrels so bitter that their impassioned voices flew through the November air all the way across the driveway to the Wright house through closed windows. Sometimes it was about Rosemary; sometimes it was about Jim's drinking; sometimes it was about money. Jim and Nora continued to put up a brave show before Nora's family, but everyone knew what was going on.

'Jim's got a new one,' reported Pat to Ellery one evening. 'He's gambling!'

'Is he?' said Mr Queen.

'Nora was talking to him about it this morning.' Pat was so distressed she could not sit still. 'And he admitted it—*shouted* it at her. And in the next breath asked her for money. Nora pleaded with him to tell her what was wrong, but the more Nora pleads the angrier and harder Jim gets. Ellery, I think he's touched. I really do!'

'That's not the answer,' said Ellery stubbornly. 'There's a pattern here. His conduct doesn't *fit*, Patty. If only he'd talk. But he won't. Ed Hotchkiss brought him home in the cab last night. I was waiting on the porch—Nora'd gone to bed. Jim was pretty well illuminated. But when I began to pump him—' Ellery shrugged. 'He swung at me...*Pat.*'

Pat jerked. 'What?'

'He's pawning jewelry.'

'Pawning jewelry! Whose?'

'I followed him at lunch today, when he left the bank. He ducked into Simpson's, on the Square, and pawned what looked to me like a cameo brooch set with rubies.'

'That's Nora's! Aunt Tabitha gave it to her as a high-school graduation present!'

Ellery took her hands. 'Jim has no money of his own, has he?'

'None except what he earns.' Pat's lips tightened. 'My father spoke to him the other day. About his work. Jim's neglecting it. You know Pop. Gentle as a lamb. It must have embarrassed him dreadfully. But Jim snapped at him, and poor Pop just blinked and walked away. And have you noticed how my mother's been looking?'

'Dazed.'

'Muth won't admit anything's wrong—even to me. Nobody will, nobody. And Nora's worse than any of them! And the town—Emmy DuPré's busier than Goebbels! They're all whispering...I hate them! I hate the town, I hate Jim...'

Ellery had to put his arms around her.

Nora planned Thanksgiving with a sort of desperation—a woman trying to hold on to her world as it growled and heaved about her. There were two of Wilcy Gallimard's fanciest toms, and chestnuts to be grated in absurd quantities, and cranberries from Bald Mountain to be mashed, and turnips and pumpkins and goodies galore...all requiring preparation, fuss, work, with and without Alberta Manaskas's help...all requiring *concentration*. And while her house filled with savory odors, Nora would brook no assistance from anyone but Alberta—not Pat, not Hermione, not even old Ludie, who went about muttering for days about 'these snippy young know-it-all brides.'

Hermy dabbed at her eyes. 'It's the first Thanksgiving since we were married, John, that I haven't made the family dinner. Nora baby—your table's so beautiful!'

'Maybe this time,' chuckled John F., 'I won't have indigestion. Bring on that turkey and stuffing!'

But Nora shooed them all into the living room—things weren't quite ready. Jim, a little drawn, but sober, wanted to stay and help. Nora smiled pallidly at him and sent him after the others.

Mr Queen strolled out to the Haight porch, so he was the first to greet Lola Wright as she came up the walk.

'Hello,' said Lola. 'You bum.'

'Hello yourself.'

Lola was wearing the same pair of slacks, the same tight-fitting sweater, the same ribbon in her hair. And from her wry mouth came the same fumes of Scotch. 'Don't look at me that way, stranger! I'm invited. Fact. Nora. Family reunion an' stuff. Kiss and make up. I'm broad-minded. But you're a bum just the same. How come no see little Lola?'

'Novel.'

'Your eye,' laughed Lola, steadying herself against his arm. 'No writer works more than a few hours a day, if that. It's my Snuffy. You're making love to Pat. 'Sall right. You could do worse. She's even got a brain on that swell chassis.'

'I could do worse, but I'm not doing anything, Lola.'

'Ah, noble, too. Well, give 'em hell, brother. Excuse me. I've got to go jab my family's sensibilities.' And Lola walked, carefully, into her sister's house. Mr Queen waited on the porch a decent interval, and then followed. He came upon a scene of purest gaiety. It took keen eyes to detect the emotional confusion behind Hermy's sweet smile, and the quivering of John F.'s hand as he accepted a Martini from Jim. Pat forced one on Ellery; so Ellery proposed a toast to 'a wonderful family,' at which they all drank grimly.

Then Nora, all flushed from the kitchen, hustled them into the dining room; and they dutifully exclaimed over the magazine-illustration table...Rosemary Haight holding on to John F.'s arm.

It happened just as Jim was dishing out second helpings of turkey. Nora was passing her mother's plate when she gasped, and the full platter fell into her lap. The plate—Nora's precious Spode—crashed on the floor. Jim gripped the arms of his chair. Nora was on her feet, palms pressed against the cloth, her mouth writhing in a horrid spasm.

'Nora!'

Ellery reached Nora in one leap. She pushed at him feebly, licking her lips, white as the new cloth. Then with a cry she ran, snatching herself from Ellery's grip with surprising strength. They heard her stumble upstairs, the click of a door.

'She's sick. Nora's sick!'

'Nora—where are you?'

'Call Doc Willoughby, somebody!'

Ellery and Jim reached the upper floor together, Jim looking around like a wild man. But Ellery was already pounding on the bathroom door. 'Nora!' Jim shouted. 'Open the door! What's the matter with you?'

Then Pat got there, and the others. 'Dr Willoughby will be right over,' said Lola. 'Where is she? Get out of here, you men!'

'Has she gone crazy?' gasped Rosemary.

'Break the door down!' commanded Pat. 'Ellery, break it down! Jim—Pop—help him!'

'Out of the way, Jim,' said Ellery. 'You're a bloody nuisance!'

But at the first impact, Nora screamed. 'If anyone comes in here I'll—I'll...*Don't come in!*'

Hermy was making mewing sounds, like a sick cat, and John F. kept saying: 'Now Hermy. Now Hermy. Now Hermy.'

At the third assault the door gave. Ellery catapulted into the bathroom, and pounced. Nora was leaning over the basin, trembling, weak, greenish, swallowing huge spoonfuls of milk of magnesia. She turned a queerly triumphant look on him as she slumped, fainting, into his arms.

But later, when she came to in her bed, there was a scene. 'I feel like a—like an animal in a zoo! Please, Mother—get everybody out of here!' They all left except Mrs Wright and Jim. Ellery heard Nora from the upper-hall landing. Her tone was stridulous; the words piled on one another. 'No, no, no! I *won't* have him! I don't *want* to see him!'

'But dearest,' wailed Hermy, 'Dr Willoughby—surely the doctor who brought you into the world—'

'If that old—old goat comes near me,' screamed Nora, 'I'll do something desperate! I'll commit suicide! I'll jump out the window!'

'Nora,' groaned Jim.

'Get out of here! Mother, you too!'

Pat and Lola went to the bedroom door and called their mother urgently. 'Mother, she's hysterical. Let her alone—she'll calm down.' Hermy crept out, followed by Jim, who was red about the eyes and seemed bewildered.

They heard Nora gagging inside. And crying.

When Dr Willoughby arrived, breathless, John F. said it was a mistake, and sent him away.

Ellery softly closed his door. But he knew before he turned on the light that someone was in the room. He pressed the switch and said: 'Pat?'

Pat lay on his bed in a cramped curl. There was a damp spot on the pillow, near her face. 'I've been waiting up for you.' Pat blinked in the light. 'What time is it?'

'Past midnight.' Ellery switched the light off and sat down beside her. 'How is Nora?'

'She says she's fine. I guess she'll be all right.' Pat was silent for a moment. 'Where did *you* disappear to?'

'Ed Hotchkiss drove me over to Connhaven.'

'Connhaven! That's seventy-five miles.' Pat sat up abruptly. 'Ellery, what did you do?'

'I took the contents of Nora's plate over to a research laboratory. Connhaven has a good one, I discovered. And...' He paused. 'As you say, it's seventy-five miles—from Wrightsville.'

'Did you—did they—?'

'They found nothing.'

'Then maybe—'

Ellery got off the bed and began to walk up and down in the dark room. 'Maybe anything. The cocktails. The soup. The hors d'oeuvres. It was a long shot; I knew it wouldn't work out. Wherever she got it, though, it was in her food or drink. Arsenic. All the symptoms. Lucky she remembered to swallow milk of magnesia—it's an emergency antidote for arsenic poisoning.'

'And today is...Thanksgiving Day,' said Pat stiffly. 'Jim's letter to Rosemary—dated November twenty-eighth...today. "My wife is sick." *My wife is sick*, Ellery!'

'Whoa, Patty. You've been doing fine...It could be a coincidence.'

'You think so?'

'It may have been a sudden attack of indigestion. Nora's in a dither. She's read the letters, she's seen that passage about arsenic in the toxicology book—it may all be psychological.'

'Yes...'

'Our imaginations may be running away with us. At any rate, there's time. If a pattern exists, this is just the beginning.'

'Yes...'

'Pat, I promise you: *Nora won't die*.'

'Oh, Ellery.' She came to him in the darkness and buried her face in his coat. 'I'm so glad you're here...'

'Get out of my bedroom,' said Mr Queen tenderly, 'before your pa comes at me with a shotgun.'

12

Christmas:
The Second Warning

The first snows fell. Breaths steamed in the valleys. Hermy was busy planning her Christmas baskets for the Poor Farm. Up in the hills skis were flashing and boys watched restlessly for the ponds to freeze. But Nora...Nora and Jim were enigmas. Nora recovered from her Thanksgiving Day 'indisposition,' a little paler, a little thinner, a little more nervous, but self-possessed. But occasionally she seemed frightened, and she would not talk. To anyone. Her mother tried. 'Nora, what's wrong? You can tell me—'

'Nothing. What's the matter with everybody?'

'But Jim's drinking, dear. It's all over town,' groaned Hermy. 'It's getting to be a—a national disgrace! And you and Jim *are* quarreling—that *is* a fact...'

Nora set her small mouth. 'Mother, you'll simply have to let me run my own life.'

'Your father's worried—'

'I'm sorry, Mother. It's my life.'

'Is it Rosemary who's causing all these arguments? She's always taking Jim off and whispering to him. How long is she going to stay with you? Nora darling, I'm your mother. You can confide in your mother—' But Nora ran away, crying.

Pat was ageing visibly. 'Ellery, the three letters…they're still in Nora's hatbox in her closet. I looked last night. I couldn't help it.'

'I know,' sighed Ellery.

'You've been keeping tabs, too?'

'Yes. Patty, she's been rereading them. They show signs of being handled—'

'But why won't Nor face the truth?' cried Pat. 'She knows that November twenty-eighth marked the first attack—that first letter told her so! Yet she won't have the doctor, she won't take any steps to defend herself, she refuses help…I can't understand her!'

'Maybe,' said Ellery carefully, 'Nora's afraid to face the scandal.' Pat's eyes opened wide. 'You told me how she retreated from the world when Jim left her on their scheduled wedding day several years ago. There's a deep streak of small-town pride in your sister Nora, Pat. She can't abide being talked about. If this ever came out—'

'That's it,' said Pat in a wondering voice. 'I was stupid not to have seen it before. She's ignoring it, like a child. Close your eyes and you won't see the bogeyman. You're right, Ellery. *It's the town she's afraid of!*'

The Monday evening before Christmas Mr Queen was sitting on a stump just beyond the edge of the woods, watching 460 Hill Drive. There was no moon; but it was a still night and sounds carried crisply and far. Jim and Nora were at it again. Mr Queen chafed his cold hands. It was about money. Nora was shrill. Where was he spending his money? What had happened to her cameo brooch? 'Jim, you've got to tell me. This can't go on. It can't!'

Jim's voice was a mutter at first, but then it began to rise, like lava. 'Don't put me through a third degree!'

Mr Queen listened intently for something new, a clue to conduct. He heard nothing he had not already learned. Two young people screaming at each other on a winter's night, while he sat like a fool in the cold and eavesdropped. He rose from the stump and, skirting the fringe of woods, made for the Wright house and warmth. But then he stopped. The front door of Calamity House—how much apter the phrase seemed these days!—had slammed. Ellery sprinted through the snow, keeping in the shadows of the big house. Jim Haight was plowing down the walk unevenly. He jumped into his car. Ellery ran to the Wright garage. He had an arrangement with Pat Wright: she always left the keys of her convertible in the ignition lock for his use in an emergency. Jim's car sloshed down the Hill at a dangerous pace, and Ellery followed. He did not turn on Pat's headlights; he could see well enough by the lights of Jim's car. Route 16...Vic Carlatti's...

It was almost ten o'clock when Jim staggered out of the *Hot Spot* and got into his car again. By the weave and lurch of the car Ellery knew Jim was very drunk. Was he going home? No. The turn-off to town. Going into town! Where?

Jim skidded to a stop before a poor wooden tenement in the heart of Low Village. He reeled into the dark hallway. A 25-watt bulb burned drearily in the hall; by its light Ellery saw Jim creep up the stairs, knock at a door with a split, paint-blistered panel. 'Jim!' Lola Wright's exclamation. The door closed.

Ellery slipped up the stairs, feeling each step for its creaky spot before putting his full weight on it. At the landing he did not hesitate; he went swiftly to Lola's door and pressed his ear to the thin panel. 'But you got to,' he heard Jim cry. 'Lola, don' turn me down. 'M a desp'r't man. 'M desp'r't...'

'But I've told you, Jim, I haven't any money,' said Lola's cool voice. 'Here, sit down. You're filthy drunk.'

'So I'm drunk.' Jim laughed.

'What are you desperate about?' Lola was cooing now. 'There—isn't that more comfortable? Come on, Jim, tell little Lola all about it...' Haight began to weep. His weeping became muffled, and Ellery knew that his face was pressed to Lola's breast. Lola's maternal murmur was indistinct. But then she gasped, as if in pain, and Ellery almost crashed through the door. 'Jim! You pushed me!'

'All 'a same! Goo-goo. Tell Lola. Oh, yeah? Take your han's off me! I'm not tellin' you anything!'

'Jim, you'd better go home now.'

'Gonna gimme dough or you gonna not gimme dough?'

'But Jim, I told you...'

'Nobody'll gimme dough! Get in trouble, his own wife won' shell out. Know what I oughta do? Know what? I oughta—'

'What, Jim?'

'Nothin'. Nothin'...' His voice trailed. There was a long interval. Apparently Jim had dropped off. Curious, Ellery waited. And then he heard Lola's faint cry and Jim's awakening snort. 'I said take your han's off me!'

'Jim, I wasn't—you fell asleep—'

'You were s-searchin' me! What you lookin' for? *Huh?*'

'Jim. Don't...do that. You're hurting me.' Lola's voice was beautifully controlled.

'I'll hurt you plen'y! I'll show you—'

Mr Queen opened the door. Lola and Jim were dancing on a worn patch of carpet in the middle of a poor, neat room. His arms were around her and he was trying drunkenly to bend her backward. She had the heel of her hand under his chin. His head was far back, his eyes glaring. 'The United States Marines,' sighed Mr Queen, and he plucked Jim from Lola and sat him down on a sagging sofa. Jim covered his face with his hands. 'Any damage, Lola?'

'No,' panted Lola. 'You *are* a one! How much did you hear?' She straightened her blouse, fussed with her hair, turned a bit away. She took a bottle of gin from the table and, as if it didn't matter, put it in a cupboard.

'Just a scuffling,' said Ellery mildly. 'I was coming up to pay you that long-overdue visit. What's the matter with Jim?'

'Plastered.' Lola gave him her full face now. Composed. 'Poor Nora! I can't imagine why he came *here*. Do you suppose the idiot's fallen in love with me?'

'You ought to be able to answer that yourself,' grinned Ellery. 'Well, Mr Haight, I think you'd best say nighty-night to your attractive sister-in-law and let your old pal take you home.'

Jim sat there rocking. And then he stopped rocking and his head flopped. He was asleep doubled up, like a big rag doll with sandy hair. 'Lola,' said Ellery quickly. 'What do you know about this business?'

'What business?' Her eyes met his, but they told nothing.

After a moment Ellery smiled. 'No hits, no runs, one error. Some day I'll fight my way out of this unmerciful fog! Night.'

He slung Jim across his shoulders; Lola held the door open. 'Two cars?'

'His and mine—or rather Pat's.'

'I'll drive Jim's back in the morning. Just leave it parked out-side,' said Lola. 'And Mr Smith—'

'Miss Wright?'

'Call again.'

'Perhaps.'

'Only next time,' Lola smiled, 'knock.'

With unexpected firmness, John F. took command for the fam-ily. 'No fuss, Hermy,' he said, waggling his thin forefinger at her. 'This Christmas somebody else does the work.'

'John Fowler Wright, what on earth—?'

'We're all going up to the mountains for Christmas dinner. We'll spend the night at the Lodge, and roast chestnuts around Bill York's fire, and we'll have *fun*.'

'John, that's a *silly* idea! Nora took my Thanksgiving away from me, now you want my Christmas. I won't hear of it.'

But after looking into her husband's eyes, Hermy decided his command was not a whim, and she stopped arguing.

So Ed Hotchkiss was hired to drive the Christmas gifts up to

Bill York's Lodge on top of Bald Mountain, with a note to Bill from John F. concerning dinner, and lodgings, and 'special preparations'—old John was mighty mysterious about the whole thing, chortling like a boy.

They were to drive up to Bald Mountain in two cars directly after dinner Christmas Eve. Everything was ready—the snow chains were on the rear tires, old Ludie had already left, released for the holiday, and they were stamping about outside the Wright house waiting for Jim and Nora to join them...when the door of Nora's house opened and out came Rosemary Haight, alone. 'Where are Jim and Nora, for goodness' sake?' called Hermy. 'We'll never get to the Lodge!'

Rosemary shrugged. 'Nora's not going.'

'What!'

'She says she doesn't feel well.'

They found Nora in bed, still weak and greenish, and Jim prowling aimlessly about the room. 'Nora baby!' cried Hermy.

'Sick again?' exclaimed John F.

'It's nothing,' said Nora; but it was an effort for her to talk. 'Just my stomach. You all go on ahead to the Lodge.'

'We'll do no such thing,' said Pat indignantly. 'Jim, haven't you called Dr Willoughby?'

'She won't let me.' Jim said it in a lifeless voice.

'Won't *let* you! What are you—a man or a worm—? What's she got to say about it? I'm going downstairs this minute—'

'Pat,' faltered Nora. Pat stopped. 'Don't.'

'Now Nora—'

Nora opened her eyes. They burned. 'I won't have it,' said Nora through her teeth. 'I'm saying this for the last time. I won't have interference. Do you understand? I'm all right. I'm—all—right.' Nora bit her lip, then with an effort continued: 'Now please. Go on. If I feel better in the morning, Jim and I will join you at the Lodge—'

'Nora,' said John F., clearing his throat, 'it's time you and I had an old-fashioned father-and-daughter talk...'

'*Let me alone!*' Nora screamed.

They did so.

On Christmas Day Ellery and Pat drove up to Bald Mountain, retrieved the gifts from Bill York at the Lodge, and drove back to Wrightsville with them. They were distributed in a distinctly unhallowed atmosphere.

Hermy spent the day in her room. Pat fixed a Christmas 'dinner' of left-over lamb and a jar of mint jelly, but Hermy would not come down, and John F. swallowed two mouthfuls and dropped his fork, saying he wasn't hungry. So Pat and Ellery ate alone. Later, they walked over to see Nora. They found Nora asleep, Jim out, and Rosemary Haight curled up in the living room with a copy of *Look* and a box of chocolates. She shrugged at Pat's question about Jim. Had another fight with Nora and ran out. Nora was fine...weak, but getting along all right. What does one do for excitement in this one-horse town? Wrightsville! Christmas! And, petulantly, Rosemary went back to her magazine.

Pat ran upstairs to satisfy herself about Nora. When she came back she winked urgently, and Ellery took her outside again. 'I tried to talk to her—she wasn't asleep at all. I...almost told her I knew about those letters! Ellery, Nora's got me frightened. She threw something at me!' Ellery shook his head. 'She won't talk. She got hysterical again. And she's sick as a cat! I tell you,' Pat whispered, 'the schedule's working out. Ellery, *she was poisoned again yesterday!*'

'You're getting to be as bad as Nora,' said Ellery. 'Go up and take a nap, Pat. Can't a woman be sick occasionally?'

'I'm going back to Nora. I'm *not* going to leave her alone!'

When Pat had run back, Ellery took a long walk down the Hill, feeling unhappy. The day before, while the others had been upstairs with Nora, he had quietly gone to the dining room. The table had not yet been cleared of the dinner dishes. He had sam-

90

pled the remains of Nora's corned-beef hash. It had been a minute sample, but the effects were not long in making themselves known. He felt extreme stomachic pain, and nausea. Very quickly, then, he had swallowed some of the contents of a bottle he had taken to carrying about with him—ferric hydroxid, with magnesia, the official arsenic antidote. No possible doubt. Someone had mixed an arsenic compound into Nora's corned-beef hash. And only Nora's. He had tasted the hash on the other two plates. The pattern was working out. First Thanksgiving, then Christmas. So death was scheduled for New Year's Day.

Ellery recalled his promise to Pat: to save her sister's life.

He plodded through the drifts. His mind was swirly with thoughts that seemed to take recognizable shapes, but did not.

13

New Year's: The Last Supper

Nora spent four days after Christmas Eve in bed. But on the twenty-ninth of December she appeared fresh, gay...too gay, and announced that she was through being sick, like some old lady; that she'd spoiled the family's Christmas, but she was going to make up for it, so everybody was invited to a New Year's Eve party! Even Jim brightened at that and clumsily kissed her. Pat, witnessing the embrace, choked up and turned away. But Nora kissed Jim back, and for the first time in weeks they looked at each other in the old, secret way of lovers.

Hermy and John F. were overjoyed by this sudden return of Nora's spirits. 'A dandy idea, Nora!' said Hermy. 'Now you plan the whole thing yourself. I shan't lift a *finger*. Unless, of course, you'd like me to...'

'No, indeed!' smiled Nora. 'It's my party, and I'm going to boss it. Oh, darling,' and Nora threw her arms about Pat, 'you've been such an angel this week, and I was so mean to you...throwing things! Can you ever forgive me?'

'You mug,' said Pat grimly, 'I'd forgive you anything if you'd only keep acting this way!'

'It's a good mood for Nora to be in,' Ellery said to Pat when she told him. 'Who's Nora inviting?'

'The family, and the Judge Martins, and Doc Willoughby, and Nora's even going to ask Frank Lloyd!'

'Hmm. Get her to invite Carter Bradford, too.'

Pat blanched. 'Cart?'

'Now, now. Bury the hatchet. It's a new year—'

'But why Cart? The pig didn't even send me a Christmas card!'

'I want Bradford here New Year's Eve. And you've got to get him here if it takes crawling to do it.'

Pat looked him in the eye. 'If you insist—'

'I insist.'

'He'll be here.'

Cart told Pat over the phone that he would 'try' to come—nice of her to ask him—quite a surprise, in fact—but of course he had numerous other 'invitations'—he wouldn't want to disappoint Carmel Pettigrew—but—well—he'd 'manage' to drop in. Yes—yes, count on it. I'll drop in...

'Oh, Cart,' said Pat, despite herself, 'why can't people be friends?' But Cart had already hung up.

Editor-Publisher Frank Lloyd came early. He showed up in a vast and sulky unconviviality, greeting people in monosyllables or not at all, and at the first opportunity made for the 'bar,' which was a makeshift affair off the kitchen, in Nora's pantry.

One would have said Mr Queen's interest in matters culinary that evening was unnatural. He haunted the kitchen, watching Alberta, watching Nora, watching the stove and the ice box and who came in and went out and what they did in the vicinity of anything edible or potable. And he did it all with such a self-effacement and eagerness that when Alberta left for her own New Year's Eve party at the home of some Lithuanian friends in Low Village, Nora exclaimed: 'My goodness, Ellery, you *are* a homebody, aren't you? Here, stuff some olives.' And so Mr

93

Queen stuffed some olives, while Jim was busy in the adjacent pantry fixing drinks. From where Mr Queen stuffed the olives he had a perfect view of his host.

Nora served a sumptuous buffet supper, preceded by canapés and pigs-in-blankets and stuffed celery-stalks and relishes and cocktails; and before long Judge Eli Martin was saying to Aunt Tabitha, who glared about her disapprovingly: 'Come, come, Tabby, take a drink and oil that soul of yours. It creaks to high heaven. Here—a Manhattan—good for you!'

But John F.'s sister snarled: 'Reprobate!' and read Clarice Martin a lecture on the dangers of old fools drinking. Clarice, who was drifting about like the Lady of the Lake, misty-eyed, said of course Tabitha was *perfectly* right, and went on sipping her cocktail.

Lola was not there. Nora had invited her, but Lola had said over the phone: 'Sorry, sis. I have my own celebration planned. Happy New Year!'

Rosemary Haight held court in a corner, getting the men to fetch and carry for her—not out of interest in them, surely, for she seemed bored, but more as if she felt it necessary to keep in practice...until Pat, watching good old Doc Willoughby trotting off to replenish Rosemary's glass, said: 'Why can't men see through a woman like that?'

'Maybe,' said Mr Queen dryly, 'because they're stopped by the too, too, solid flesh.' And he strolled off to the kitchen again—in Jim's wake, Patty's troubled eyes noticed. For the dozenth time.

Gala evenings in the 'nice' homes of Wrightsville were not noted for their hilarity; but Rosemary Haight, the outlander, exercised an irresistible influence for the worst. She became quite merry on numerous Manhattans, to the pointed disgust of Aunt Tabitha. Her spirits infected the men especially, so that talk became loud and laughter a little unsteady, and twice Jim had to visit the pantry to concoct new delights with rye and vermouth, and Pat had to open another bottle of maraschino cherries. And both times, Mr Queen appeared smiling at Jim's elbow, offering to help.

There was no sign of Carter Bradford. Pat kept listening for the doorbell. Someone turned on the radio, and Nora said to Jim: 'We haven't danced since our honeymoon, darling. Come on!' Jim looked unbelieving; then a grin spread over his face and, seizing her, he danced her madly off. Ellery went into the kitchen abruptly to mix himself a drink—his first of the evening.

It was fifteen minutes to midnight when Rosemary waved a dramatic arm and commanded: 'Jim! 'Nother drink!'

Jim said pleasantly: 'Don't you think you've had enough, Rosemary?' Surprisingly, Jim had drunk very little himself.

Rosemary scowled. 'Get me one, killjoy!' Jim shrugged and made for the kitchen, followed by the Judge's admonition to 'mix up a mess of 'em, boy!' and Clarice Martin's giggle.

There was a door from the hall to the kitchen, and an archway from the kitchen to the butler's pantry; there was a dining-room door to the butler's pantry, too. Mr Ellery Queen stopped at the hall door to light a cigarette. It was half-open; he could see into the kitchen, and into the butler's pantry. Jim moved about the pantry, whistling softly as he got busy with the rye and vermouth. He had just finished filling a fresh batch of glasses with Manhattans and was reaching for the bottle of maraschino cherries when someone knocked on the back door of the kitchen. Ellery became tense; but he resisted the temptation to take his eyes off Jim's hands.

Jim left the cocktails and went to the door 'Lola! I thought Nora said—'

'Jim.' Lola sounded in a hurry. 'I had to see you—'

'Me?' Jim seemed puzzled. 'But Lo—'

Lola pitched her voice low; Ellery was unable to make out the words. Jim's body blocked Lola out; whatever was happening, it took only a few moments, for suddenly Lola was gone and Jim had closed the back door, crossing the kitchen a little abstractedly to return to the pantry. He plopped a cherry into each glass.

95

Ellery said: 'More fixin's, Jim?' as Jim came through to the hall carrying the tray of full glasses carefully. Jim grinned, and they went into the living room together to be greeted by jubilant shouts.

'It's almost midnight,' said Jim cheerfully. 'Here's a drink for everyone to toast the New Year in.' And he went about the room with the tray, everyone taking a glass.

'Come on, Nora,' said Jim. 'One won't hurt you, and New Year's Eve doesn't come every night!'

'But Jim, do you really think—'

'Take this one.' He handed her one of the glasses.

'I don't know, Jim—' began Nora doubtfully. Then she took it from him, laughing.

'Now you be careful, Nora,' warned Hermy. 'You know you haven't been well. Ooh! I'm *dizzy.*'

'Souse,' said John F. gallantly, kissing Hermy's hand. She slapped him playfully.

'Oh, one sip won't hurt me, Mother,' protested Nora.

'Hold it!' yelled Judge Martin. 'Here's the ol' New Year rolling in right now. Yip-ee!' And the old jurist's shout was drowned in a flood of horns and bells and noise makers coming out of the radio.

'To the New Year!' roared John F., and they all drank, even Aunt Tabitha, Nora dutifully taking a sip and making a face, at which Jim howled with laughter and kissed her.

That was the signal for everybody to kiss everybody else, and Mr Queen, struggling to keep everything in view, found himself seized from behind by a pair of warm arms. 'Happy New Year,' whispered Pat; and she turned him around and kissed him on the lips. For an instant the room, dim with candlelight, swam; then Mr Queen grinned and stooped for another; but Pat was snatched from his arms by Doc Willoughby, who growled: 'How about me?' and Ellery found himself foolishly pecking the air.

'More!' shrieked Rosemary. ''*Nother drink!* Let's all get stinking—what the hell!' And she waved her empty glass coyly at

Judge Martin. The Judge gave her a queer glance and put his arm around Clarice. Frank Lloyd drank two cocktails quickly. Jim said he had to go down to the cellar for another bottle of rye—he was all 'out' upstairs here.

'Where's my drink?' insisted Rosemary. 'What kinda joint is this? New Year's an' no drinks!' She was angry. 'Who's got a drink?' Nora was passing her, on her way to the radio. 'Hey! Nora! *You* got a drink…!'

'But Rosemary, I've drunk from it—'

'I wanna drink!'

Nora made a face and gave her unfinished cocktail to Rosemary, who tossed it down like a veteran and staggered over to the sofa, where she collapsed with a silly laugh. A moment later she was fast asleep.

'She *snores*,' said Frank Lloyd gravely. 'The beaushous lady snores,' and he and John F. covered Rosemary with newspapers, all but her face; and then John F. recited 'Horatius at the Bridge' with no audience whatever, until Tabitha, who was a little flushed herself, called him another old fool; whereupon John F. seized his sister and waltzed her strenuously about the room to the uncoöperative strains of a rumba. Everybody agreed that everybody was a little tight, and wasn't the new year *wonderful?* All but Mr Ellery Queen, who was again lingering at the hall door to the kitchen watching Jim Haight make cocktails.

At thirty-five minutes past midnight there was one strange cry from the living room and then an even stranger silence. Jim was coming out of the kitchen with a tray and Ellery said to him: 'That's a banshee, at least. What are they up to now?' And the two men hurried to the living room. Dr Willoughby was stooped over Rosemary Haight, who was still lying on the sofa half covered with newspapers. There was a tiny, sharp prickle in Mr Queen's heart.

Doc Willoughby straightened up. He was ashen. 'John.' The old doctor wet his lips with his tongue.

John F. said stupidly: 'Milo, for jiminy sake. The girl's passed out. She's been…sick, like other drunks. You don't have to act and look as if—'

Dr Willoughby said: 'She's dead, John.' Pat, who had been the banshee, sank into a chair as if all the strength had suddenly gone out of her. And for the space of several heartbeats the memory of the sound of the word 'dead' in Dr Willoughby's cracked bass darted about the room, in and out of corners and through still minds, and it made no sense.

'Dead?' said Ellery hoarsely. 'A…heart attack, Doctor?'

'I think,' said the doctor stiffly, 'arsenic.'

Nora screamed and fell over in a faint, striking her head on the floor with a thud. As Carter Bradford came briskly in. Saying: 'Tried to get here earlier—where's Pat?—Happy New Year, everybody…*What the devil!*'

'Did you give it to her?' asked Ellery Queen, outside the door of Nora's bedroom. He looked a little shrunken; and his nose was pinched and pointy, like a thorn.

'No doubt about it,' croaked Dr Willoughby. 'Yes, Smith. I gave it to her…Nora was poisoned, too.' He blinked at Ellery. 'How did you happen to have ferric hydroxid on you? It's the accepted antidote for arsenic poisoning.'

Ellery said curtly: 'I'm a magician. Haven't you heard?' and went downstairs. The face was covered with newspapers now. Frank Lloyd was looking down at the papers. Carter Bradford and Judge Martin were conferring in hoarse low tones. Jim Haight sat in a chair shaking his head in an annoyed way, as if he wanted to clear it but could not. The others were upstairs with Nora. 'How is she?' said Jim. 'Nora?'

'Sick.' Ellery paused just inside the living room. Bradford and the Judge stopped talking. Frank Lloyd, however, continued to read the newspapers covering the body. 'But luckily,' said Ellery, 'Nora took only a sip or two of that last cocktail. She's pretty sick, but Dr Willoughby thinks she'll pull through all right.' He sat down in the chair nearest the foyer and lit a cigarette.

'Then it was the cocktail?' said Carter Bradford in an unbelieving voice. 'But of course. Both women drank of the same glass—both were poisoned by the same poison.' His voice rose. 'But that cocktail was Nora's! *It was meant for Nora!*'

Frank Lloyd said, still without turning: 'Carter, stop making speeches. You irk the hell out of me.'

'Don't be hasty, Carter,' said Judge Martin in a very old voice.

But Carter said stridently: 'That poisoned cocktail was meant to kill Nora. And *who mixed it? Who brought it in?*'

'Cock Robin,' said the newspaper publisher. 'Go 'way, Sherlock Holmes.'

'I did,' said Jim. 'I did, I guess.' He looked around at them. 'That's a queer one, isn't it?'

'Queer one!' Young Bradford's face was livid. He went over and yanked Jim out of the chair by his collar. 'You damn murderer! You tried to poison your own wife and by pure accident got your sister instead!'

Jim gaped at him. 'Carter,' said Judge Martin feebly.

Carter let go, and Jim fell back, still gaping. 'What can I do?' asked the Wright County Prosecutor in a strangled voice. He went to the phone in the foyer, stumbling past Mr Queen's frozen knees, and asked for Chief Dakin at Police Headquarters.

Part Three

Chapter 14

Hangover

The Hill was still celebrating when Chief Dakin hopped out of his rattletrap to run up the wet flags of the Haight walk under the stars of 1941. Emmeline DuPré's house was dark, and old Amos Bluefield's—the Bluefield house bore the marks of mourning in the black smudges of its window shades. But all the others—the Livingstons', the F. Henry Minikins', the Dr Emil Poffenbergers', the Granjons', and the rest—were alive with lights and the faint cries of merriment.

Chief Dakin nodded: it was just as well. Nobody would notice that anything was wrong. Dakin was a thin, flapping countryman with light dead eyes bisected by a Yankee nose. He looked like an old terrapin until you saw that his mouth was the mouth of a poet. Nobody ever noticed that in Wrightsville except Patricia Wright and, possibly, Mrs Dakin, to whom the Chief combined the best features of Abraham Lincoln and God. Dakin's passionate baritone led Mr Bishop's choir at the First Congregational Church on West Livesey Street in High Village each Sunday. Being a temperance man, and having his woman, the Chief would chuckle, what was there left in life but song? And, in fact,

Dakin was interrupted by Prosecutor Bradford's telephone call in the midst of an 'at-home' New Year's Eve carol fest.

'Poison,' said Dakin soberly to Carter Bradford over the body of Rosemary Haight. 'Now I wonder if folks don't overdo this New Year celebrating. What kind of poison, Doc?'

Dr Willoughby said: 'Arsenic. Some compound. I can't tell you which.'

'Rat-killer, hey?' Then the Chief said slowly, 'I figure this kind of puts our Prosecutor in a spot—hey, Cart?'

'Awkward as hell! These people are my friends.' Bradford was shaking. 'Dakin—take charge, for God's sake.'

'Sure, Cart,' said Chief Dakin, blinking his light eyes at Frank Lloyd. 'Hi, Mr Lloyd.'

'Hi yourself,' said Lloyd. 'Now can I go peddle my papers?'

'Frank, I told you—' began Carter peevishly.

'If you'll be so kind as not to,' said Dakin to the newspaper publisher with an apologetic smile. 'Thank you. Now how come this sister of Jim Haight's swallowed rat-killer?'

Carter Bradford and Dr Willoughby told him. Mr Queen, seated in his corner like a spectator at a play, watched and listened and pondered how much like a certain New York policeman Chief Dakin of Wrightsville seemed. That ingrown air of authority...Dakin listened to the agitated voices of his townsfellows respectfully; only his light eyes moved—they moved over Mr 'Smith's' person three times, and Mr 'Smith' sat very still. And noted that, after the first quick glance on entering the room, Chief Dakin quite ignored Haight, who was a lump on a chair.

'I see,' said Dakin, nodding. 'Yes, sir,' said Dakin. 'Hmm,' and he shambled off with his loose gait to the kitchen.

'I can't believe it,' groaned Jim Haight suddenly. 'It's an accident. How do I know how the stuff got into it? Maybe some kid. A window. A joke. Why, this is *murder*.'

No one answered him. Jim cracked his knuckles and stared owlishly at the filled-out newspapers on the sofa.

Red-faced Patrolman Brady came in from outdoors, a little

out of breath and trying not to look embarrassed. 'Got the call,' he said to no one in particular. 'Gosh.' He tugged at his uniform and trod softly into the kitchen after his chief.

When the two officers reappeared, Brady was armed with numerous bottles, glasses, and odds and ends from the kitchen 'bar.' He disappeared; after a few moments he came back, empty-armed. In silence Dakin indicated the various empty and half-empty cocktail glasses in the living room. Brady gathered them one by one, using his patrolman's cap as a container, picking them up in his scarlet fingers delicately, at the rim, and storing them in the hat as if they had been fresh-laid pigeon eggs. The Chief nodded and Brady tiptoed out. 'For fingerprints,' said Chief Dakin to the fireplace. 'You never can tell. And a chemical analysis, too.'

'What!' exclaimed Mr Queen involuntarily.

The Dakin glance X-rayed Mr Queen's person for the fourth time: 'How do, Mr Smith,' said Chief Dakin, smiling. 'Seems like we're forever meeting in jams. Well, twice, anyway.'

'I beg pardon?' said Mr 'Smith,' looking blank.

'That day on Route 16,' sighed the Chief. 'I was driving with Cart here. The day Jim Haight was so liquored up?' Jim rose; he sat down. Dakin did not look at him. 'You're a writer, Mr Smith, ain't you?'

'Yes.'

'Heard tell all over town. You said "What"?'

Ellery smiled. 'Sorry. Wrightsville—fingerprints…It was stupid of me.'

'And chem lab work? Oh, sure,' said Dakin. 'This ain't New York or Chicago, but the new County Courthouse building, she's got what you might call unexpected corners.'

'I'm interested in unexpected corners, Chief'

'Mighty proud to know a real live writer,' said Dakin. 'Course, we got Frank Lloyd here, but he's more what you'd call a hick Horace Greeley.' Lloyd laughed and looked around, as if for a drink. Then he stopped laughing and scowled. 'Know anything about this, Mr Smith?' asked Dakin, glancing at Lloyd's great back.

'A woman named Rosemary Haight died here tonight.' Ellery shrugged. 'The only *fact* I can supply. Not much help, I'm afraid, considering that the body's lying right here.'

'Poisoned, Doc Willoughby says,' said Dakin politely. 'That's another fact.'

'Oh, yes,' said Ellery with humility. And tried to become invisible as Dr Willoughby sent him a thick-browed question. Watch yourself. Doc Willoughby is remembering that little bottle of ferric hydroxid you whipped out when Nora Haight required an antidote against arsenic poisoning and even minutes were precious…Will the good doctor tell the good policeman the strange fact that a stranger to the house and the people and the case carried so strange a preparation as ferric hydroxid about with him when, strangely, one woman died and another was made seriously ill by the poison for which it was the official antidote? Dr Willoughby turned away. He suspects I know something involving the Wright family, thought Ellery. He's an old friend. He brought the three girls into the world…He's uneasy. Shall I make him still uneasier by confiding that I purchased the drug because I promised Patty Wright her sister Nora wouldn't die? Mr Queen sighed. It was getting complicated.

'The family,' said Chief Dakin. 'Where they at?'

'Upstairs,' said Bradford. 'Mrs Wright insists that Nora—Mrs Haight—be moved over to the Wright house.'

'This is no place for her, Dakin,' said Dr Willoughby. 'Nora's pretty sick. She'll need plenty of care.'

'It's all right with me,' said the Chief. 'If it's all right with the Prosecutor.'

Bradford nodded hastily and bit his lip. 'Don't you want to question them?'

'Well, now,' said the Chief slowly, 'I can't see the sense of making the Wrights feel worse'n they feel already. At least right now. So if you've got no objection, Cart, let's call it a night.'

Carter said stiffly: 'None at all.'

'Then we'll have a get-together right here in this room in the mornin',' said Dakin. 'You tell the Wrights, Cart. Sort of keep it unofficial.'

'Are you remaining here?'

'For a spell,' drawled Dakin. 'Got to call in somebody to haul this *corpus* out of here. Figure I'll phone old man Duncan's parlors.'

'No *morgue*?' asked Mr Queen, despite himself.

The Dakin eyes made another inspection. 'Well, no, Mr Smith...Okay for you, Mr Lloyd. Go easy on these folks in your paper, hey? This'll raise plenty of hallelujah as it is, I guess...No, sir, Mr Smith. Got to use a reg'lar undertaking parlor. You see,' and the Chief sighed, 'ain't never had a homicide in Wrightsville before, and I been Chief here for pretty near twenty years. Doc, would you be so kind? Coronor Salemson's up in Piny Woods on a New Year vacation.'

'I'll do the autopsy,' said Dr. Willoughby shortly. He went out without saying goodnight.

Mr Queen rose. Carter Bradford walked across the room, stopped, looked back. Jim Haight was still sitting in the chair. Bradford said in an angry voice: 'What are you sitting here for, Haight?'

Jim looked up slowly. 'What?'

'You can't sit here all night! Aren't you even going up to your wife?'

'They won't let me,' said Jim. He laughed, and took out a handkerchief to wipe his eyes. 'They won't let me.' He leaped from the chair and dashed upstairs. They heard the slam of a door—he had gone into his study.

'See you in the morning, gents,' said Chief Dakin, blinking at Ellery.

They left the Chief in the untidy living room, alone with Rosemary Haight's body. Mr Queen would like to have stayed, but there was something in Chief Dakin's eyes that discouraged company.

107

*　　*　　*

Ellery did not see Patricia Wright until they all gathered in the same untidy room at ten o'clock on the morning of New Year's Day...all except Nora, who was in her old bed in the other house, guarded by Ludie behind the closed vanes of the Venetian blinds. Dr Willoughby had already seen her this morning, and he forbade her leaving the room or even setting foot out of bed. 'You're a sick biddy, Nora,' he had said to her sternly. 'Ludie, remember.'

'She'll have to fight me,' said old Ludie.

'But where's Mother? Where's Jim?' moaned Nora, tossing on the bed.

'We've got to...go out for a few minutes, Nora,' said Pat. 'Jim's all right—'

'Something's happened to Jim, too!'

'Don't be a worry-wart,' said Pat crossly, fleeing.

Ellery waylaid her on Nora's porch. 'Before we go in,' he said quickly, 'I want to explain—'

'I don't blame you, Ellery.' Pat was almost as sick-looking as Nora. 'It might have been worse. It might have been...Nora. It almost was.' She shivered.

'I'm sorry about Rosemary,' said Ellery.

Pat looked at him blankly. Then she went inside. Ellery lingered on the porch. It was a gray day, like Rosemary Haight's face: a gray day and a cold day, a day for corpses...Someone was missing—Frank Lloyd. Emmy DuPré chittered by, stopped, studied Chief Dakin's car at the curb, frowned...walked on slowly, craning at the two houses. A car drove up. Frank Lloyd jumped out. Then Lola Wright. They ran up the walk together. 'Nora! Is she all right?' gasped Lola. Ellery nodded. Lola dashed inside.

'I picked Lola up,' said Lloyd. He was breathing heavily, too. 'She was walking up the Hill.'

'They're waiting for you, Lloyd.'

'I thought,' said the publisher, 'you might think it funny.'

There was a damp copy of the *Wrightsville Record* in his overcoat pocket.

'I think nothing funny on mornings like this. Did Lola know?' They walked into the house.

'No. She was just taking a walk, she said. Nobody knows yet.'

'They will,' said Ellery dryly, 'when your paper hits the streets.'

'You're a damn snoop,' growled Lloyd, 'but I like you. Take my advice and hop the first train out.'

'I like it here,' smiled Ellery. 'Why?'

'Because this is a dangerous town.'

'How so?'

'You'll see when the news gets around. Everybody who was at the party last night will be smeared.'

'There's always,' remarked Mr Queen, 'the cleansing property of a clear conscience.'

'That makes you apple pie.' Lloyd shook his heavy shoulders. 'I don't figure you.'

'Why bother? For that matter, you're not a simple sum in arithmetic yourself.'

'You'll hear plenty about me.'

'I already have.'

'I don't know,' said the newspaper publisher savagely, 'why I stand here in the foyer gassing with a nitwit!' He shook the floor striding into the living room.

'The poison,' said Dr Willoughby, 'is arsenic trioxid, or arsenious oxid, as you prefer. "White" arsenic.'

They were sitting in a rough circle, like unbelievers at a séance. Chief Dakin stood at the fireplace, tapping his false teeth with a rolled paper. 'Go ahead, Doc,' said Dakin. 'What else did you find? That part's right. We checked in our own lab during the night.'

'It's used in medicine mostly as an alternative or tonic,' said the doctor tonelessly. 'We never prescribe a bigger therapeutic dose than a tenth of a grain. There's no way of telling from the dregs of the cocktail, of course—at least with accuracy—but judging from the speed with which the poison acted, I'd estimate there were three or four grams in that glass.'

'Prescribe any of that stuff recently for…anyone you know, Doc?' muttered Carter Bradford.

'No.'

'We've established a bit more,' said Chief Dakin soberly, looking around. 'Most probably it was plain ordinary rat poison. And moreover, no trace of the poison was found anywheres except in that one cocktail which Mrs Haight and her sister-in-law drank—not in the mixing glass, nor the rye whisky, nor the vermouth, nor the bottle of cherries, nor any of the other glassware.'

Mr Queen surrendered. 'Whose fingerprints did you find on the poisoned cocktail glass, Chief Dakin?'

'Mrs Haight's. Rosemary Haight's. Jim Haight's. No others.' Ellery could see them translate silently. Nora's…Rosemary's…Jim's…no others. His own thoughts were admiring. Chief Dakin had not remained idle after they left him last night. He had taken the fingerprints of the corpse. He had found some object unmistakably Nora Haight's, probably in her bedroom, and had taken *her* fingerprints. Jim Haight had been in the house all night, but Ellery was willing to make a large bet that Jim had not been disturbed, either. There were plenty of *his* things in the house, too…Very pretty. Very considerate. It disturbed Mr Queen powerfully—the prettiness and considerateness of Chief Dakin's methods. He glanced over at Pat. She was watching Dakin as if the Chief had hypnotized her. 'And what did your autopsy show, Doc?' asked Dakin deferentially.

'Miss Haight died of arsenic trioxid poisoning.'

'Yes, sir. Now let's get this organized,' said Dakin. 'If you folks don't mind?'

'Go ahead, Dakin,' said John F. impatiently.

'Yes, Mr Wright. So we know the two ladies were poisoned by

110

that one cocktail. Now, who mixed it?' No one said anything. 'Well, I already know. It was you, Mr Haight. You mixed that cocktail.'

Jim Haight had not shaved. There were muddy ruts under his eyes. 'Did I?' There was a frog in his throat; he cleared it several times. 'If you say so—I mixed so many—'

'And who came in from the kitchen and handed out the tray of drinks?' asked Chief Dakin. 'Including the one that was poisoned? You did, Mr Haight. Am I wrong? Because that's my information,' he said apologetically.

'If you're trying to insinuate—' began Hermione in an imperious voice.

'All right, Mrs Wright,' said the Chief. 'Now maybe I'm wrong. But you mixed that cocktail, Mr Haight, you handed it out, so it looks like you're the only one could have dosed it up good with rat-killer. But it only looks that way. *Were* you the only one? Did you leave those cocktails you were making even for a few seconds any time up to the time you brought the tray into this room last night?'

'Look,' said Jim. 'Maybe I'm crazy. Maybe the things that happened last night knocked my brains for a loop. What is this? Am I suspected of having tried to poison my wife?'

As if this had been a fresh wind in a stale room, the air became breathable again. John F.'s hand dropped from his eyes, Hermy's color came back, and even Pat looked at Jim.

'This *is* nonsense, Chief Dakin!' said Hermy coldly.

'Did you, Mr Haight?' asked Dakin.

'Of course I brought that tray in here!' Jim got up and began to walk up and down before the Chief, like an orator. 'I'd just mixed the Manhattans—that last batch—and was going to put the maraschino cherries in, but then I had to leave the pantry for a few minutes. That's it!'

'Well, now,' said Dakin heartily. '*Now* we're getting places, Mr Haight. Could someone have slipped in from the living room and poisoned one of them cocktails without you knowing or seeing? While you were gone, I mean?'

The fresh wind died, and they were in choking miasma once more. *Could someone have slipped in from the living room—*

'I didn't poison that cocktail,' said Jim, 'so somebody *must* have slipped in.'

Dakin turned swiftly. 'Who left the living room while Mr Haight was mixing that last mess of drinks in the kitchen? This is very important, please. Think hard on it!' Ellery lit a cigarette. Someone must have noticed that he had been missing simultaneously with Jim. It was inevitable...But then they all began to chatter at once, and Ellery blew smoke in great clouds. 'We'll never get anywheres this way,' said the Chief. 'So much drinking and dancing going on, and the room dark on account of only candles being lit...Not,' added Dakin suddenly, 'that it makes much difference.'

'What do you mean?' asked Pat quickly.

'I mean that ain't the important point, Miss Wright.' And this time Dakin's voice was quite, quite chill. Its chill deepened the chill in the room. 'The important point is: Who had control of the *distribution* of the drinks? Answer me that! Because the one who handed that cocktail out—that's *got* to be the one who poisoned it!'

Bravo, bumpkin, thought Mr Queen. You're wasting your smartness on the desert air...You don't know what I know, but you've hit the essential point just the same. You ought to capitalize your talents...

'*You* handed 'em out, James Haight,' said Chief Dakin. 'No poisoner'd have dropped rat-killer in one of those drinks and left it to Almighty God to decide who'd pick up that poisoned one! No, sir. It don't make sense. *Your wife got that poisoned cocktail, and you was the one handed it to her. Wasn't you?*'

And now they were all breathing heavily like swimmers in a surf, and Jim's eyes were red liquid holes. 'Yes, I did hand it to her!' he yelled. 'Does that satisfy your damn snooping disposition?'

'A-plenty,' said the Chief mildly. 'Only thing is, Mr Haight, you didn't know one thing. You went out of the living room to make more drinks, or fetch another bottle, or something. You didn't know your sister Rosemary was going to yell for another drink, and you didn't know that your wife, who you figured would drink the whole glassful, would just take a couple of sips and then your sister would pull the glass out of her hand and guzzle the rest down. So instead of killing your wife, you killed your sister!'

Jim said hoarsely: 'Of course you can't believe I planned or did anything like that, Dakin.'

Dakin shrugged. 'Mr Haight, I only know what my good horse sense tells me. The facts say you, and only you, had the— what do they call it?—the opportunity. So maybe you won't have what they call motive—*I* dunno. Do you?'

It was a disarming question—man to man. Mr Queen was quite bathed in admiration. This was finesse exquisite.

Jim muttered: 'You want to know why I should try to murder my wife four months after our marriage. Go to hell.'

'That's no answer. Mr Wright, can you help us out? Do you know of any reason?'

John F. gripped the arms of his chair, glancing at Hermy. But there was no help there; only horror.

'My daughter Nora,' mumbled John F., 'inherited a hundred thousand dollars—her grandfather's legacy—when she married Jim. If Nora died...Jim would get it.'

Jim sat down, slowly, looking around, around. Chief Dakin beckoned to Prosecutor Bradford. They left the room. Five minutes later they returned, Carter paler than pale, staring straight before him, avoiding their eyes. 'Mr Haight,' said Chief Dakin gravely, 'I'll have to ask you not to try to leave Wrightsville.'

Bradford's work, thought Ellery. But not from compassion.

From duty. There was no legal case yet. Damning circumstances, yes; but no case. There would be a case, though. Glancing over the whole lean, shambling countryman that was Chief of Police Dakin, Mr Queen knew there would be a case and that, pending the proverbial miracle, James Haight was not long for the free streets of Wrightsville.

15

Nora Talks

At first all Wrightsville could talk about was the fact itself. The delicious fact. A body. A corpse. At the Wrights'. *At the Wrights'!* The snooty, stuck-up, we're-better-than-you-are First Family! *Poison!* Just *imagine.* Who'd have thought? And so soon after, too. Remember that wedding?

The woman. Who was she? Jim Haight's sister. Rosalie—Rose-Marie? No, Rosemary. Well, it doesn't make any difference. She's dead. I saw her once. Tricked up. You *felt* something about her. Not nice. My dear, I was telling my husband only the other day...

So it's murder. Rosemary Haight, that woman from heaven knows where, she got a mess of poison in a Manhattan cocktail, and it was really meant for Nora Haight. There it is right in Frank Lloyd's paper...Frank was *there.* Drinking. Wild party. Fell down dead. Foaming at the mouth. Shh, the children!...Cinch Frank Lloyd hasn't told the *whole* story...Of course not. After *all.* The *Record*'s a family newspaper!

Four-sixty Hill Drive. Calamity House. Don't you remember? That story in the *Record* years ago? First Jim Haight ran away from his own wedding, leaving Nora Wright looking silly—and the house all built and furnished and everything! Then that Mr Whozis from Where? Anyway, *he* dropped dead just as he was going to buy it from John F. Wright. And now—*murder* in it! Say, I wouldn't set foot in that jinxed house for all the money in John F.'s vaults!

Bess, did *you* hear? *They say*...For some days Wrightsville could talk about nothing but the fact.

Siege was laid, and Mr Ellery 'Smith' Queen found himself inadvertently a soldier of the defending force. People streamed up and down the Hill like trekking ants, pausing outside the Wright and Haight houses to pick up some luscious leaf-crumb and bear it triumphantly down into the town. Emmeline DuPré was never so popular. Right next door! Emmy, what do you *know*? Emmy told them. Emmy's porch became a hiring hall for the masses. If a face showed at a window of either house, there was a rush, and a gasp.

'What's happening to us?' moaned Hermione. 'No. I *won't* answer the phone!'

Lola said grimly: 'We're a Chamber of Horrors. Some Madame Tussaud'll start charging admission soon!' Since the morning of New Year's Day, Lola had not left. She shared Pat's room. At night she silently washed her underwear and stockings in Pat's bathroom. She would accept nothing from her family. Her meals she took with Jim in the 'unlucky' house. Lola was the only member of the family to show herself out of doors the first few days of January. On January second she said something to Emmy DuPré which turned Emmy pale and sent her scuttling back to her porch like an elderly crab in a panic. 'We're wax-works,' said Lola. 'Jack-the-Ripper multiplied by seven. Look at the damn body-snatchers!'

Alberta Manaskas had vanished in a Lithuanian dither, so Lola cooked Jim's meals. Jim said nothing. He went to the bank as usual. John F. said nothing. *He* went to the bank. In the bank father-in-law and son-in-law said nothing to each other. Hermy haunted her room, putting handkerchiefs to her little nose. Nora was in a tossing fever most of the time, wailing to see Jim, being horridly sick, keeping her pillow blue with tears. Carter Bradford shut himself up in his office at the County Courthouse. Large plain men came and went, and at certain times of the day he conferred in pointed secrecy with Chief of Police Dakin.

Through all this Mr Queen moved silently, keeping out of everyone's way. Frank Lloyd had been right. There was talk about 'that man Smith—who *is* he?' There were other remarks, more dangerous. He noted them all in his notebook, labeled: 'The Mysterious Stranger—a Suspect.' He was never far from Nora's room. On the third day after the crime, he caught Patty as she came out and beckoned her upstairs to his room. He latched the door. 'Pat, I've been thinking.'

'I hope it's done you good.' Pat was listless.

'When Dr Willoughby was here this morning, I heard him talk to Dakin on the phone. Your County Coroner, Salemson, has cut his vacation short and he's come back to town on the double. Tomorrow there will be an inquest.'

'Inquest!'

'It's the law, darling.'

'You mean we'll have to…leave the *house*?'

'Yes. And testify, I'm afraid.'

'Not Nora!'

'No, Willoughby refuses to let her leave her bed. I heard him say so to Dakin.'

'Ellery…what are they going to *do*?'

'Establish the facts for the record. Try to get at the truth.'

Pat said: 'The truth?' and looked terrified.

'Pat,' said Ellery gravely, 'you and I are at the crossroads in this labyrinth—'

'Meaning?' But she knew what he meant.

'This is no longer a potential crime. It's a crime that's happened. A woman has died—the fact that she died by accident makes no difference, since a murder was planned and a murder

117

was executed. So the law comes into it...' Ellery said grimly...'a most efficient law, I must say...and from now on it's snoop, sniff, and hunt until *all* the truth is known.'

'What you're trying to say, and are saying so badly,' said Pat steadily, 'is that we've got to go to the police with what *we* know...and *they* don't.'

'It's within our power to send Jim Haight to the electric chair.'

Patty sprang to her feet. Ellery pressed her hand. 'It can't be that clear! You're not convinced yourself! Even *I'm* not, and I'm her sister...'

'We're talking now about facts and conclusions from facts,' said Ellery irritably. 'Feelings don't enter into it—they certainly won't with Dakin, although they might with Bradford. Don't you realize you and I are in possession of four pieces of information not known to the police—four facts that convict Jim of having plotted and all but carried out the murder of Nora?'

'Four?' faltered Pat. 'As many as that?'

Ellery sat her down again. She looked up at him with her forehead all tight and wrinkled. 'Fact one: the three letters written by Jim and now at the bottom of Nora's hatbox next door—the three letters establishing his *anticipation of her death* at a time when she wasn't even ill! Clearly premeditation.' Pat moistened her lips. 'Fact two: Jim's desperate need for money. This fact, which *we* know because he's been pawning Nora's jewelry and demanding money of her, plus the fact *Dakin* knows—that on Nora's death Jim would come into a large inheritance—combined would fix a powerful motive.'

'Yes. Yes...'

'Fact three: the toxicology book belonging to Jim, with its underlined section in Jim's characteristic red crayon...a section dealing with arsenious trioxid, the very poison with which subsequently Nora's cocktail was spiked and from which Nora nearly died. And fourth,' Ellery shook his head, 'something I alone can establish, because I had Jim under observation every moment New Year's Eve: the fact that no one but Jim *could* have put poison into that fatal cocktail, *or did*. So I'm in a position to establish that Jim not only had the *best* opportunity to poison that drink, but the *only* opportunity.'

'And that doesn't even include his threat against Nora that afternoon when we brought him away from the *Hot Spot* blind drunk—when he said he was going to get rid of her. Dakin heard it, Cart heard it...'

'Or,' added Ellery gently, 'the two previous occasions on which Nora's been poisoned by arsenic—Thanksgiving and Christmas, coinciding with the dates of Jim's first two letters...Pretty conclusive, put together, Patty. How could anyone disbelieve, knowing all this, that Jim planned Nora's death?'

'Yet you don't believe it,' said Pat.

'I didn't say that,' said Ellery slowly. 'I said....' He shrugged. 'The point is: We've got to decide now. Do we talk at the inquest tomorrow, or don't we?'

Pat bit a fingernail. 'But suppose Jim is innocent? How can I— how can you—set up as judge and jury and condemn somebody to death? Somebody you *know*? Ellery, I couldn't.' Pat made faces, a distressed young woman. 'Besides,' she said eagerly, 'he won't try it again, Ellery! Not now. Not after he killed his sister by mistake. Not after the whole thing's out and the police—I mean, *if* he did...'

Ellery rubbed his hands together as if they itched, walking up and down before her, frowning, scowling. 'I'll tell you what we'll do,' he said at last. 'We'll put it up to Nora.' Pat stared. 'She's the victim, Jim's her husband. Yes, let Nora make the decision. What do you say?'

Pat sat still for a moment. Then she got up and went to the door. 'Mother's asleep, Pop's at the bank, Ludie's downstairs in the kitchen, Lola's next door...'

'So Nora's alone now.'

'And Ellery.' Ellery unlatched his door. 'Thanks for being such a swell clam—' He opened the door. 'Taking such a personal risk—being involved—' He gave her a little push towards the stairs.

Nora lay in a knot under the blue comforter, staring at the ceiling. Scared through and through, thought Ellery.

'Nora.' Pat went quickly to the bed, took Nora's thin hand between both her brown ones. 'Do you feel strong enough to talk?'

Nora's eyes flew from her sister to Ellery, and then darted into hiding like timid birds. 'What is it? What's the matter?' Her voice was tight with pain 'Is Jim—did they—?'

'Nothing's happened, Nora,' said Ellery.

'It's just that Ellery feels—I feel—it's time the three of us understood one another,' said Pat. Then she cried: 'Nora, please! Don't shut yourself up! Listen to us!' Nora braced herself and pushed against the bed until she was sitting up. Pat leaned over her and, for an instant, she looked like Hermy. She drew the edges of Nora's bed jacket together. Nora stared at them.

'Don't be frightened,' said Ellery. Pat propped the pillow against Nora's shoulders and sat down on the edge of the bed and took Nora's hand again. And then in a quiet voice Ellery told Nora what he and Pat had learned—from the beginning. Nora's eyes grew larger and larger.

'I tried to talk to you,' cried Pat, 'but you wouldn't listen! Nora, *why?*'

Nora whispered: 'Because it isn't true. Maybe at first I thought…But it's not. Not Jim. You don't know Jim. He's scared of people, so he acts cocky. But inside he's like a little boy. When you're alone with him. And he's weak. Much too weak to—to do what you think he did. Oh, please!' Nora began to cry in her hands. 'I love him,' she sobbed. 'I've always loved Jim! I'll never believe he'd want to kill me. Never. Never!'

'But the facts, Nora—' said Ellery wearily.

'Oh, the facts!' She took her hands away; her wet eyes were

blazing. 'What do I care about the facts? A woman *knows.* There's something so horribly wrong you can't make sense out of it. I don't know who tried to poison me three times, but I do know it wasn't Jim!'

'And the three letters, Nora? The letters in Jim's handwriting announcing your illness, your...death?'

'He didn't write them!'

'But Nora darling,' said Pat, 'Jim's handwriting—'

'Forged.' Nora was panting now. 'Haven't you ever heard of forgery? They were forged!'

'And the threat against you we heard him make, that day I told you about, when he was drunk?' asked Ellery.

'He wasn't responsible!'

No tears now. She was fighting. Ellery went over the whole damning case with her; she fought back. Not with counterfacts. With faith. With an adamant, frightening faith. And at the end Ellery was arguing with two women, and he had no ally. 'But you don't reason—' he exploded, throwing up his hands. Then he smiled. 'What do you want me to do? I'm softheaded, but I'll do it.'

'Don't say anything about these things to the police!'

'All right, I won't.'

Nora sank back, closing her eyes. Pat kissed her and then signalled to Ellery. But Ellery shook his head. 'I know you're pretty well pooped, Nora,' he said kindly, 'but as long as I'm becoming an accessory, I'm entitled to your full confidence.'

'Anything,' said Nora tiredly.

'Why did Jim run out on you that first time? Three years ago, just before you were to be married, when Jim left Wrightsville?'

Pat looked at her sister anxiously. 'That.' Nora was surprised. 'That wasn't anything. It couldn't have anything to do—'

'Nevertheless, I'd like to know.'

'You'd have to know Jim. When we met and fell in love and all, I didn't realize just how independent Jim was. I didn't see

121

anything wrong in—well, accepting help from Father until Jim got on his feet. We'd argue about it for hours. Jim kept saying he wanted me to live on his cashier's salary.'

'I remember those battles,' murmured Pat, 'but I didn't dream they were so—'

'I didn't take them seriously enough, either. When Mother told me Father was putting up the little house and furnishing it for us as a wedding gift, I thought I'd keep it a surprise for Jim. So I didn't tell him until the day before the wedding. He got furious.'

'I see.'

'He said he'd already rented a cottage on the other side of town for fifty dollars a month—it was all we'd be able to afford, he said, we'd just have to learn to live on what he earned.' Nora sighed. 'I suppose I lost my temper, too. We...had a fight. A bad one. And then Jim ran away. That's all.' She looked up. 'That's really all. I never told Father or Mother or anyone about it. Having Jim run out on me just because of a thing like that—'

'Jim never wrote to you?'

'Not once. And I...thought I'd die. The whole town was talking...Then Jim came back, and we both admitted what fools we'd been, and here we are.'

So from the very first it had been the house, thought Ellery. Queer! Wherever he turned in this case, the house was there. Calamity House...Ellery began to feel that the reporter who had invented the phrase was gifted with second sight. 'And these quarrels you and Jim have been having since your marriage?'

Nora winced. 'Money. He's been asking for money. And my cameo, and other things...But that's just temporary,' she said quickly. 'He's been gambling at that roadhouse on Route 16—I suppose every man goes through a phase like that—'

'Nora, what can you tell me about Rosemary Haight?'

'Not a thing. I know she's dead, and it sounds an awful thing to say, but...I didn't like her. At all.'

'Amen,' said Patty grimly.

122

'Can't say I was smitten myself,' murmured Ellery. 'But I mean—do you know anything about her that might tie her in with…well, the letters, Jim's conduct, the whole puzzle?'

Nora said tightly: 'Jim wouldn't talk about her. But I know what I felt. She was *no good*, Ellery. I don't see how she ever came to be Jim's sister.'

'Well, she was,' said Ellery briskly, 'and you're tired, Nora. Thanks. You'd have been wholly justified in telling me to mind my own business about all this.' Nora squeezed his hand, and he left as Pat went into the bathroom to wet a towel for her sister's head. Nothing. Utter nothing. And tomorrow the inquest!

16

The Aramean

Coroner Salemson was nervous about the whole thing. Any audience more numerous than three paralyzed his vocal cords; and it is a matter of public record that the only time the coroner opened his mouth at Town Meeting except for breathing purposes—he had asthma—was one year when J. C. Pettigrew reared up and demanded to know why the office of Coroner shouldn't be voted out of existence—Chic Salemson hadn't had a corpus to justify his salary in his nine years' tenure. And then all the Coroner could stammer was: 'But suppose!' And so now, at last, there was a corpus.

But a corpus meant an inquest, and that meant the Coroner had to sit up there in Judge Martin's court (borrowed from the County for the occasion) and preside; and that meant talk, and lots of it, before hundreds of glittering Wrightsville eyes—not to mention the eyes of Chief Dakin and Prosecutor Bradford and County Sheriff Gilfant and Lord knows who. To make matters worse, there was John F. Wright. To think of the exalted Name linked nastily with a murder weakened the Coroner's knees; John F. was his household god.

So as Coroner Salemson rapped feebly for order in the jammed courtroom he was a nervous, miserable, and desperate man. And all through the selection of the Coroner's Jury he became more nervous, and more miserable, and more desperate, until finally his nervousness and misery were swallowed by his desperation, and he saw what he must do to cut his ordeal short and save—if saving was possible—the honor of the Wright name.

To say that the old Coroner sabotaged the testimony deliberately would be unjust to the best horseshoe pitcher in Wright County. No, it was just that from the first the Coroner was convinced no one named Wright, or connected with anyone named Wright, could possibly have had the least pink or brownish stain on his conscience. So obviously it was either all a monstrous mistake, or the poor woman committed suicide or something, and strike this out, and that's just *supposing*...and the result was that, to the disgust of Dakin, the relief of the Wrights, the sad amusement of Mr Ellery Queen and—above all—the disappointment of Wrightsville, the confused Coroner's Jury brought in a harmless verdict of 'death at the hands of person or persons unknown' after several days of altercation, heat, and gavel breaking.

Chief Dakin and Prosecutor Bradford immediately retired to Bradford's office for another conference, the Wrights sped home thankfully, and Coroner Salemson fled to his twelve-room ancestral home in the Junction, where he locked himself in with trembling hands and got drunk on an old bottle of gooseberry wine left over from his orphaned niece Eppie's wedding to old man Simpson's son Zachariah in 1934.

Gently, gently, into one neat six-foot hole in the ground. What's her name? Rosalie? Rose-Marie? They say she was a glamour girl. The one they're burying—the one Jim Haight poisoned by mistake—his sister...Who says Jim Haight...? Why, it was right there in the *Record* only yesterday! Didn't you read it? Frank

Lloyd didn't *say* so, just like that; but you know if you read between the lines...Sure, Frank's sore. Sweet on Nora Wright, Frank was, and Jim Haight cut him out. Never did like Haight. Kind of cold proposition—couldn't look you in the eye, 'pears to me...So he was the one, huh? Why don't they arrest him? That's what I'd like to know!

Ashes to ashes...Think there's dirty work going on? Wouldn't be bowled over! Cart Bradford and that Patricia Wright started necking years ago. That's Haight's sister-in-law. Aaah, the rich always get away with murder. Nobody's getting away with murder in Wrightsville. Not if we have to take the law—

Gently, gently...Rosemary Haight was buried in East Twin Hill Cemetery, not (people were quick to remark) in West Twin Hill Cemetry, where the Wrights had interred their dead for two hundred-odd years. The transaction was negotiated by John Fowler Wright, acting for his son-in-law James Haight, and Peter Callendar, sales manager of the Twin Hill Eternity Estates, Inc., selling price sixty dollars. John F. handed Jim the deed to the grave in silence as they drove back from the funeral.

The next morning Mr Queen, rising early for purposes of his own, saw the words WIFE KILLER printed in red school chalk on the sidewalk before Calamity House. He erased them.

'Morning,' said Myron Garback of the High Village Pharmacy.

'Morning, Mr Garback,' said Mr Queen, frowning. 'I've got a problem. I've rented a house and there's a small greenhouse in the garden—found vegetables growing there, by George! In January!'

'Yes?' said Myron blankly.

'Well, now, I'm mighty fond of home-grown tomatoes and there's a fine tomato plant or two in my greenhouse, only the plant's overrun with some kind of round little bug—'

'Mmmm. Yellowish?'

'That's right. With black stripes on their wings. At least,' said Mr Queen helplessly, 'I think they're black.'

126

'Eating the leaves, are they?'

'That's just what the pests are doing, Mr Garback!'

Myron smiled indulgently. '*Doryphora decemlineata*. Pardon me. I like to show off my Latin. Sometimes known as the potato beetle, more commonly called a potato bug.'

'So that's all they are,' said Mr Queen with disappointment. 'Potato bugs! *Dory*—what?'

Myron waved his hand. 'It doesn't matter. I suppose you'll want something to discourage them, eh?'

'Permanently,' said Mr Queen with a murderous scowl.

Myron bustled off and returned with a small tin carton, which he began to wrap in the High Village Pharmacy's distinctive pink-striped wrapping paper. 'This'll do the trick!'

'What's in it that discourages them?' asked Mr Queen.

'Arsenic—arsenious oxid. About fifty per cent. Technically...' Myron paused. 'I mean, strictly speaking, it's copper aceto-arsenite in this preparation, but it's the arsenic that slaughters 'em.' He tied the package and Mr Queen handed him a five-dollar bill. Myron turned to the cash register. 'Want to be careful with that stuff, of course. It's poisonous.'

'I certainly hope so!' exclaimed Mr Queen.

'*And* five,' said Myron. 'Thank you. Call again.'

'Arsenic, arsenic,' said Mr Queen loquaciously. 'Say, isn't that the stuff I was reading about in the *Record*? I mean that murder case? Some woman swallowed it in a cocktail at a New Year's Eve party?'

'Yes,' said the pharmacist. He gave Ellery a sharp look and turned away, presenting his graying nape and heavy shoulders to his customer.

'Wonder where they got it,' said Mr Queen nosily, leaning on the counter again. 'You'd need a prescription, wouldn't you, from a doctor?'

'Not necessarily.' It seemed to Ellery that Pharmacist Garback's voice took on an edge. 'You didn't need one just now! There's arsenic in a lot of commercial preparations.' He fussed

127

with some cartons on the shaving-preparations shelf.

'But if a druggist did sell a person arsenic without a prescription—'

Myron Garback turned about hotly. 'They won't find anything wrong with *my* records! That's what I told Dakin, and the only way Mr Haight could have got it would have been when he bought—'

'Yes?' asked Ellery, breathing not at all.

Myron bit his lip. 'Excuse me, sir,' he said. 'I really mustn't talk about it.' Then he looked startled. 'Wait a minute!' he exclaimed. 'Aren't you the man who—?'

'No, indeed,' said Mr Queen hastily. 'Good morning!' And he hurried out. So it had been Garback's pharmacy. A something. A trail. And Dakin had picked it up. Quietly. They were working on Jim Haight—quietly.

Ellery struck out across the slippery cobbles of the Square towards the bus stop near the Hollis Hotel. An iced wind was whistling, and he put up his overcoat collar and half-turned to protect his face. As he turned, he noticed a car pull into a parking space on the other side of the Square. The tall figure of Jim Haight got out and strode quickly towards the Wrightsville National Bank. Five small boys with strapped books swinging over their shoulders spied Jim and began to troop after him. Ellery stopped, fascinated. They were evidently jeering Jim, because Jim stopped, turned, and said something to them with an angry gesture. The boys backed off, and Jim turned away.

Ellery shouted. One of the boys had picked up a stone. He threw it, hard. Jim went down on his face.

Ellery began to run across the Square. But others had seen the attack, and, by the time he reached the other side of the Square, Jim was surrounded by a crowd. The boys had vanished. 'Let me through, please!' Jim was dazed. His hat had fallen off. Blood oozed from a dark stain on his sandy hair.

'Poisoner!' said a fat woman. 'That's him—that's the poisoner!...' 'Wife killer!...' 'Why don't they arrest him?...' 'What kind

128

of law have we got in this town, anyway?...' 'He ought to be strung up!...' A small dark man kicked Jim's hat. A woman with doughy cheeks jumped at Jim, screaming.

'Stop that!' growled Ellery. He cuffed the small man aside, stepped between the woman and Jim, and said hastily: 'Out of this, Jim. Come on!'

'What hit me?' asked Jim. His eyes were glassy. 'My head—'

'*Lynch the dirty bastard!*'

'Who's the other one?'

'Get him, too!'

Ellery found himself, absurdly, fighting for his life with a group of blood-maddened savages who were dressed like ordinary people. As he struck back, he was thinking: This is what comes of meddling. Get out of this town. It's no good. Using his elbows, his feet, the heels of his hands, and occasionally a fist, he maneuvered the screeching crowd with him towards the bank building. 'Hit back, Jim!' he shouted. 'Defend yourself!'

But Jim's hands remained at his sides. One sleeve of his overcoat had disappeared. A rivulet of blood coursed down a cheek. He let himself be pushed, poked, punched, scratched, kicked. Then a one-woman Panzer division struck the crowd from the direction of the curb. Ellery grinned painfully over a swollen lip. Hatless, white-mittened, fighting mad. 'You cannibals! Let 'em alone!' Pat screamed.

'Ouch!'

'Serves you right, Hosy Malloy! And you—Mrs Landsman! Aren't you ashamed? And you drunken old witch, you—yes, I mean you, Julie Asturio! Stop it! *Stop it, I say.*'

'Attaboy, Patsy!' shouted a man from the edge of the crowd. 'Break it up, folks—come on, that's no way to carry on!'

Pat burst through to the struggling men. At the same moment Buzz Congress, the bank 'special,' ran out and hit the crowd with himself. Since Buzz weighed two hundred and fifteen pounds, it was a considerable blow; people squawked and scattered, and between them Ellery and Pat got Jim into the bank.

Old John F. ran by them and breasted the crowd, his gray hair whipping in the wind. 'Go home, you lunatics!' roared John F. 'Or I'll sail into you myself!'

Someone laughed, someone groaned, and then, with a sort of outgoing-tidal shame, the mob ebbed away. Ellery, helping Pat with Jim, saw through the glass doors, at the curb, the big silent figure of Frank Lloyd. There was a bitter twist to the newspaper publisher's mouth. When he saw Ellery watching him, he grinned without mirth, as if to say: 'Remember what I told you about this town?' and lumbered off across the Square.

Pat and Ellery drove Jim back to the little house on the Hill. They found Dr Willoughby waiting for them—John F. had phoned him from the bank. 'Some nasty scratches,' said Dr Willoughby, 'a few ugly bruises, and that's a deep scalp wound, but he'll be all right.'

'How about Mr Smith, Uncle Milo?' asked Pat anxiously. 'He looks like a fugitive from a meat grinder, too!'

'Now, now, I'm perfectly fine,' protested Ellery.

But Dr Willoughby fixed up Ellery, too.

When the doctor had gone, Ellery undressed Jim, and Pat helped get him into bed. He immediately turned over on his side, resting his bandaged head on a limp hand, and closed his eyes. They watched him for a moment and then tiptoed from the room. 'He didn't say a word,' moaned Pat. 'Not one word. All through the whole thing…He's like that man out of the Bible!'

'Job,' said Ellery soberly. 'The silent, suffering Aramean. Well, your Aramean had better stay away from town from now on!' After that day, Jim stopped going to the bank.

17

America Discovers Wrightsville

The activities of Mr Ellery Queen during the trying month between January and February were circumambient. For, no matter in how straight a line he started, he invariably finished by finding himself back in the same place...and, moreover, with the realization that Chief Dakin and Prosecutor Bradford had been there before him. Quietly, quietly. Ellery did not tell Pat what a web was being woven in those secret investigations of the law. There was no point in making her feel worse than she felt already.

Then there was the Press. Apparently one of Frank Lloyd's vitriolic editorials had splashed heavily enough to deposit a drop in Chicago; for early in January, and shortly after Rosemary Haight's funeral, a smartly dressed woman with a thirty-eight waistline, silver-sprayed hair, and tired eyes got off the afternoon express and had Ed Hotchkiss drive her directly to 460 Hill Drive. The next day the readers of two hundred and fifty-nine large newspapers in the United States learned that good old Roberta was in there once again battling for love.

The leading paragraph of *Roberta's Column*, by Roberta Roberts, said:—

Today in a small American city named Wrightsville there is being enacted a fantastic romantic tragedy, with a Man and a Woman the tragic protagonists and a whole community playing the role of villain.

That was enough for the others. Roberta had her nose in something yum-yummy. Editors began to call for back numbers of the *Wrightsville Record*. By the end of January a dozen first-line reporters had arrived in town to see what Bobby Roberts had dug up. Frank Lloyd was cooperative, and the first stories that trickled back over the wires put the name of Jim Haight on the front page of every newspaper in America.

The out-of-town newspaper men and women swarmed over the town, interviewing and writing and drinking straight bourbon at Vic Carlatti's *Hot Spot* and Gus Olesen's *Roadside Tavern* and making Dunc MacLean, next door to the Hollis Hotel, put in a hurry call to the liquor wholesaler. During the day they lolled about the County Courthouse spitting on Janitor Hernaberry's spotless lobby tiles, trailing Chief Dakin and Prosecutor Bradford for stories and photographs, and generally showing no decent respect for the opinions of mankind (although they wired same faithfully to their editors). Most of them stayed at the Hollis, commandeering cots when they could find no legitimate accommodations. Manager Brooks complained that they were turning his lobby into a 'slophouse.'

Later, during sessions of the trial, they spent their nights either on Route 16 or at the Bijou Theater on Lower Main, where they ganged up on young Louie Cahan, the manager, cracking Indian nuts all over the theatre and catcalling whenever the hero made love to the heroine. On Grab Bag Night one of the

132

reporters won a set of dishes (donated by A. A. Gilboon, House Furnishings, Long-Term Payments) and 'accidentally on purpose,' as everyone said indignantly, dropped all sixty pieces on the stage while the rest of them whistled, howled, and stamped their feet. Louie was good and sore, but what could he do?

Bitter speeches about 'those newspaper tramps' and 'self-constituted privileged characters' were delivered to good effect at a special meeting of the Country Club Board by Donald Mackenzie, President of the Wrightsville Personal Finance Corporation (PFC Solves Your Unpaid-Bills Problem!), and Dr Emil Poffenberger, Dental Surgeon, 132 Upham Block, High Village. Yet there was something infectious in their cynical high spirits, and Mr Ellery Queen was saddened to observe how Wrightsville gradually took on an air of County Fair. New and shiny stock began to appear in the shop windows; prices for food and lodging went up; farmers who had never before come into town on week nights began to parade the Square and Lower Main with their square-toed, staring families; and it became impossible to find parking space within a radius of six blocks of the Square. Chief Dakin had to swear in five new policemen to help direct traffic and keep the peace. The unwilling author of all this prosperity barricaded himself at 460 Hill Drive and refused to see anyone but the Wrights, Ellery, and later Roberta Roberts. To the remainder of the Press Jim was adamant. 'I'm still a taxpayer!' he cried to Dakin over the phone. 'I've got a right to some privacy! Put a cop at my door!'

'Yes, Mr Haight,' said Chief Dakin politely; and that afternoon Patrolman Dick Gobbin, who had been an invisible watcher in plain clothes for some time, on orders put on a uniform and became visible. And Jim went back to his cellaret.

'It's getting worse,' reported Pat to Ellery. 'He's drinking himself stupid. Even Lola can't do anything with him. Ellery, is it just that he's scared?'

'He's not scared at all. Goes deeper than funk, Patty. Hasn't he seen Nora yet?'

'He's ashamed to go near her. Nora's threatening to get out of bed and go over there herself, only Dr Willoughby said if she did he'd send her to the hospital. I slept with her last night. She cried all night.'

Ellery glumly surveyed his glass of Scotch, filched from John F.'s modest, little-used bar. 'Nora still thinks he's an innocent babe?'

'Of course. She wants him to fight back. She says if he'd only come over to see her she knows she could persuade him to stand up and defend himself from these attacks. Did you see what those damn reporters are writing about Jim *now*?'

'Yes,' sighed Ellery, emptying his glass.

'It's all Frank Lloyd's fault! That grump! Turning on his best friends! Pop's so furious he says he'll never speak to Frank again.'

'It's better to keep out of Lloyd's way,' said Ellery with a frown. 'He's a large animal, and he's thoroughly aroused. An angry beast with a hysterical typewriter. I'll tell your father myself.'

'Never mind. I don't think he wants to talk to...anybody,' said Pat in a low voice. Then she burst out: 'How can people be such vermin? Mom's friends—they don't call her any more, they're whispering the vilest things behind her back, she's being impeached by two of her organizations—even Clarice Martin's stopped calling!'

'The Judge's wife,' murmured Ellery. 'Which suggests another interesting problem...Never mind. Have you seen Carter Bradford lately?'

'No,' said Pat shortly.

'Patty. What do you know about this woman Roberta Roberts?'

'The only decent reporter in town!'

'Strange what different conclusions she draws from the same facts. Did you see this?' Ellery showed Pat a Chicago newspaper, flipped back to *Roberta's Column*. A paragraph had been ringed, and Pat read it quickly:—

> The longer I investigate this case, the surer I feel that James Haight is a misunderstood, hounded man, a martyr to what is at best a circumstantial case and the victim of Wrightsville's mobbism. Only the woman he is alleged by Wrightsville gossips to have tried to poison is standing by her husband four-square, with never a doubt or a backward look. More power to you, Nora Wright Haight! If faith and love still mean anything in this wretched world, your husband's name will be cleared and you will triumph over the pack.

'That's a *wonderful* tribute!' cried Pat.

'A little emotional, even for a famous *entrepreneuse* of love,' said Mr Queen dryly. 'I think I'll explore this female Cupid.'

But exploration only confirmed the evidence of his eyes. Roberta Roberts was heart and soul behind the struggle to get Jim a just hearing. One talk with Nora, and they became fighters in a common cause. 'If you could only get Jim to come up here for a talk,' said Nora urgently. 'Won't you try, Miss Roberts?'

'He'd listen to you,' Pat interposed. 'He said only this morning'—Pat neglected to mention his condition when he said it—'that you were the only friend he had in the world.'

'Jim's a queer love,' said Roberta thoughtfully. 'I've had two talks with him and I admit I haven't got anything but his confidence. Let me take another crack at the poor dope.'

But Jim refused to stir from the house.

'Why, Jim?' asked the newspaper woman patiently. Ellery was present, and Lola Wright—a more silent Lola these days.

'Lemme alone.' Jim had not shaved; under the stubble his skin was gray; and he had drunk a lot of whisky.

'You can't just lie around the house like a yellow dog and let these people spit on you, Jim! See Nora. She'll give you strength, Jim. She's ill—don't you know that? Don't you care?'

Jim turned a tortured face to the wall. 'Nora's in good hands. Her family's taking care of her. And I've done her enough harm already. Lemme alone!'

'But Nora believes in you, honey.'

'I'm not gonna see Nora till this is all over,' he muttered. 'Till I'm Jim Haight again in this town, not some lousy hyena.' And he raised himself and fumbled for his glass, and drank, and sank back, and not all of Roberta's urging and prodding could rouse him again.

When Roberta had gone, and Jim was asleep, Ellery said to Lola Wright: 'And what's *your* angle, my dear Sphinx?'

'No angle. Somebody has to take care of Jim. I feed him and put him to bed and see that he has a fresh bottle of pain-killer every once in a while.' Lola smiled.

'Unconventional,' said Mr Queen, smiling back. 'The two of you, alone, in this house.'

'That's me,' said Lola. 'Unconventional Lola.'

'You haven't expressed any opinion, Lola—'

'There's been too much expression of opinion,' she retorted. 'But if you want to know, I'm a professional underdog-lover. My heart bleeds for the Chinese and the Czechs and the Poles and the Jews and the Negroes—it's leaking practically all the time, and every time one of my underdogs is kicked, it leaks a little more. I see this poor slob suffering, and that's enough for me.'

'Apparently it's enough for Roberta Roberts, too,' mumbled Ellery.

'Miss Love-Conquers-All?' Lola shrugged. 'If you ask me, that dame's on Jim's side so she can get in where the other reporters can't!'

18

St Valentine's Day: Love Conquers Nothing

Considering that Nora was bedridden as a result of arsenic poisoning, that John F. was finding his cronies shying away from him and transferring their business to Hallam Luck's Public Trust Co., that Hermione was having the lady-finger put on her, Pat was sticking close to Nora's bedside, and even Lola had been jolted out of her isolation—considering all this, it was wonderful how the Wrights kept bravely pretending, even among themselves, that nothing out of the ordinary had happened. No one referred to Nora's condition except as an 'illness,' as if she were suffering from laryngitis or some mysterious but legal 'woman's complaint.' John F. talked business at his desk in his old dry way—if he attended far fewer board meetings it was because he was 'tied up'…obviously; and the fact that he quite disappeared from the weekly luncheons of the Chamber of Commerce at Ma Upham's was gravely excused on grounds of dyspepsia. As for Jim—he was not mentioned at all.

But Hermy, after the first emotional storms, did some calking and sail patching. No one was going to run *her* out of town. And grimly she began to employ her telephone again. When impeachment proceedings began at her Women's Club, Madame President astounded everyone by making a personal appearance, in her smartest winter suit, and acting as if nothing had happened whatsoever. She was impeached notwithstanding; but only after various abalone ears burned and the ladies grew scarlet under the lash of Hermy's scorn. And at home she took charge as of old. Ludie, who might have been expected to snarl back, instead went about with a relieved expression. And by the beginning of February things took on such an air of normality that Lola actually returned to her nun's flat in Low Village and, Nora being better, Pat assumed the task of cooking Jim's meals and straightening Nora's house.

On Thursday, February thirteenth, Dr Willoughby said that Nora could get out of bed. There was much joy in the household. Ludie baked a gargantuan lemon-meringue pie, Nora's favorite; John F. came home early from the bank with a double armful of American Beauty roses (and where he got them, in Wrightsville, in February, he refused to say!); Pat stretched as if she were cramped and then washed her hair and did her nails, murmuring things like: 'My God! How I've let myself go!' Hermy turned the radio on for the first time in weeks to hear the war news...It was like coming out of a restless sleep to find yourself safely awake. Nora wanted to see Jim instantly; but Hermione refused to let her out of the house—'The first day, dear! Are you insane?'—and so Nora phoned next door. After a while she hung up, helplessly; there was no answer. 'Maybe he's gone out for a walk or something,' said Pat.

'I'm sure that's what it is, Nora,' said Hermy, fussing over Nora's hair. Hermy did not say that Jim was in the house that very moment—she had just glimpsed his gray face pressed against the Venetian blinds of the master bedroom.

'I know!' said Nora, with a little excitement; and she telephoned Ben Danzig. 'Mr Danzig, send me the biggest, most expensive Valentine you've got. Right away!'

'Yes, ma'am,' said Ben; and in a half hour it was all over town that Nora Haight was all right again. Sending Valentines! *Is there another man, do you suppose?*

It was a gorgeous thing, quilted in pink satin and bordered with real lace, framing numerous fat Cupids and sweet with St Valentine sentiment—Ben Danzig's most exclusive number, 99A. Nora addressed the envelope herself, and licked the stamp and affixed it, and sent Ellery out to mail it. She was almost gay. Mr Queen, playing Hermes to Eros, dropped the Valentine in the box at the bottom of the Hill with the uncomfortable feeling of a man who watches a battered pugilist getting to his knees after the fourth knockdown.

In the mail Friday morning there was no Valentine for Nora. 'I'm going over there,' she said firmly. 'This is silly. Jim's sulking. He thinks the whole world's against him. I'm going—'

Ludie came in, very stiff and scared, and said: 'It's that Chief Dakin and Mr Bradford, Miss Hermy.'

'Dakin!' The color left Hermy's girlish cheeks. 'For...me, Ludie?'

'Says he wants to be seeing Miss Nora.'

Nora said: 'Me?' in a quivery voice.

John F. rose from the breakfast table. 'I'll handle this!' They went into the living room.

Mr Queen left his eggs and ran upstairs. Pat yawned 'Whoz-it?' when he rapped on her door.

'Come downstairs!'

'Whaffor?' He heard her yawn again. 'Come in, come in.' Ellery merely opened the door. Pat was bunched under the bed-clothes, looking rosy and mussed and young again.

'Dakin and Bradford. To see Nora. I think this is it.'

'Oh!' Panic. But only for a moment. 'Throw me my robe, like a darling. It's arctic in here.' Ellery handed it to her, turned to walk out. 'Wait for me in the hall, Ellery. I mean—I want to go down-stairs with you.'

Pat joined him in three minutes. She held onto his arm all the way downstairs. As they came in, Chief Dakin was saying: 'Course, Mrs Haight, you understand I've got to cover the whole ground. I'd told Doc Willoughby to let me know when you'd be up and about—'

'So kind of you,' said Nora. She was frightened almost out of her wits. You could see it. Her figure had a wooden stillness, and she looked from Dakin to Bradford and back again like a puppet being jerked by invisible hands.

'Hello,' said Pat grimly. 'Isn't it early for a social call, Mr Dakin?'

Dakin shrugged. Bradford regarded her with a furious misery. He seemed thinner, almost emaciated. 'Sit down and be quiet, baby,' said Hermione faintly.

'I don't know what you can expect Nora to tell you,' said John F. frigidly. 'Patricia, sit down!'

'Patricia?' said Pat. She sat down. 'Patricia' was a bad sign. John F. hadn't called her Patricia in such a formal voice since the last time he'd used his old-fashioned razor strop on her bottom, and that had been many many years ago. Pat contrived to grasp Nora's hand. She did not look at Bradford once; and after the first unhappy glance, Bradford did not look at her.

Dakin nodded pleasantly to Ellery. 'Glad to see you, Mr Smith. Now if we're all set—Cart, did you want to say some-thin'?'

'Yes!' exploded Cart. 'I wanted to say that I'm in an impossi-ble position. I wanted to say—' He made a helpless gesture and stared out of the window at the snow-covered lawn.

'Now, Mrs Haight,' said Dakin, blinking at Nora, 'would you mind telling us just what happened New Year's Eve as you saw it? I've got everybody else's story—'

'Mind? Why should I mind?' It came out froggy, and Nora cleared her throat. And began to talk shrilly and rapidly, making rapid little meaningless signs with her free hand. 'But I can't really tell you anything. I mean, all that I saw—'

'When your husband came around to you with the tray of cocktails, didn't he sort of pick out one special glass for you? I mean, didn't you want to take one glass and he fixed it so you took another?'

'How can I remember a thing like that?' asked Nora indignantly. 'And that's a—a nasty implication!'

'Mrs Haight.' The Chief's voice was suddenly chilly. 'Did your husband ever try to poison you before New Year's Eve?'

Nora snatched her hand from Pat's and jumped up. 'No!'

'Nora dear,' began Pat, 'you mustn't get excited—'

'You're sure, Mrs Haight?' insisted Dakin.

'Of course, I'm sure!'

'There's nothing you can tell us about the fights you and Mr Haight been having?'

'Fights!' Nora was livid now. 'I suppose it's that horrible DuPré creature—or—' The 'or' was so odd even Carter Bradford turned from the window. Nora had uttered the word with a sudden sickish emphasis and glared directly at Ellery. Dakin and Bradford glanced quickly at him, and Pat looked terrified. Mr and Mrs Wright were hopelessly lost.

'Or what, Mrs Haight?' asked Dakin.

'Nothing. Nothing! Why don't you let Jim alone?' Nora was crying hysterically now. 'All of you!'

Dr Willoughby came in with his big man's light step; Ludie's face, white and anxious, peered over his shoulder, then vanished. 'Nora,' he said with concern. 'Crying again? Dakin, I warned you—'

'Can't help it, Doc,' said the Chief with dignity. 'I got my job to do, and I'm doing it. Mrs Haight, if there's nothing you can tell us that helps your husband—'

'He didn't do it, I tell you!'

'Nora,' said Dr. Willoughby insistently.

'Then I'm afraid we got to do it, Mrs Haight.'

'Do what, for heaven's sake?'

'Arrest your husband.'

'Arrest—Jim?' Nora began to laugh, her hands in her hair. Dr Willoughby tried to take her hands in his, but she pushed him away. Behind the glasses her pupils were dilated. 'But you can't arrest Jim! He didn't do anything! You haven't a thing on him—!'

'We've got plenty on him,' said Chief Dakin.

'I'm sorry, Nora,' mumbled Carter Bradford. 'It's true.'

'Plenty on him,' whispered Nora. Then she screamed at Pat: 'I knew too many people knew about it! That's what comes of taking strangers into the house!'

'Nora!' gasped Pat. 'Darling...'

'Wait a moment, Nora,' began Ellery.

'Don't *you* talk to me!' Nora shrieked. 'You're against him because of those three letters! They wouldn't arrest Jim if you hadn't told them about the letters—!' Something in Ellery's gaze seemed to penetrate her hysteria, and Nora broke off with a gasp, swaying against Dr Willoughby, an enormous new fear leaping into her eyes. She looked quickly at Dakin, at Bradford, saw the astonishment, then the flash of exultation. And she backed up against the broad chest of the doctor and froze there, her hand to her mouth, sick with realization.

'What letters?' demanded Dakin.

'Nora, what letters?' cried Bradford.

'No! I didn't mean—'

Carter ran over to her and seized her hand. 'Nora! *What letters?*' he asked fiercely.

'No,' groaned Nora.

'You've got to tell me! If there are letters, you're concealing evidence—'

'Mr Smith! What do you know about this?' demanded Chief Dakin.

'Letters?' Ellery looked astonished, and shook his head.

Pat rose and pushed Bradford. He staggered back. 'You let

Nora alone,' said Pat in a passionate voice. 'You Judas!'

Her violence kindled an answering violence. 'You're not going to presume upon my friendship! Dakin, search this house, and the house next door!'

'Should have done it long ago, Cart,' said the Chief mildly. 'If you hadn't been so blamed set—' He disappeared.

'Carter,' said John F. in very low tones, 'you're never to come here again. Do you understand?'

Bradford looked as if he were going to cry. And Nora collapsed in Dr Willoughby's arms with a moan like a sick cat.

With Bradford's frigid permission Nora was taken upstairs to her bedroom by Dr Willoughby. Hermy and Pat hurried along with them, helpless and harried.

'Smith.' Bradford did not turn.

'Save your breath,' advised Mr Queen politely.

'I know it's no use, but I've got to warn you—if you're contributing to the suppression of evidence ...'

'Evidence?' echoed Mr Queen, as if he had never heard the word before.

'Those letters!'

'What *are* these letters you people are talking about?'

Cart spun around, his mouth working. 'You've been in my way ever since you came here,' he said hoarsely. 'You've wormed your way into this house, alienated Pat from me—'

'Here, here,' said Ellery kindly. 'Mind your verbs.'

Cart stopped, his hands two fists. Ellery went to the window. Chief Dakin was deep in conversation with little Dick Gobbin, the patrolman, on the Haight porch...The two policemen went into the house. Fifteen minutes later Messrs Queen and Bradford were still standing in the same positions. Pat came in with a noise. Her face shocked them. She went directly to Ellery. 'The most awful thing's happened.' And she burst into tears.

'Pat! For heaven's sake!'

'Nora—Nora is—' Pat's voice blurred and shook.

Dr Willoughby said from the doorway: 'Bradford?'

'What's happened?' asked Bradford tensely.

And then Chief Dakin came in, unknowing, and his face was like a mask. He was carrying Nora's hatbox and the fat tan book with the neat gilt title, Edgcomb's *Toxicology*. Dakin stopped. 'Happened?' he asked quickly. 'What's this?'

Dr Willoughby said 'Nora Haight is going to have a baby. In about five months.' And then there was no sound at all but Pat's exhausted sobs against Ellery's chest.

'No...' said Bradford in a wincing voice. 'That's...too much.' And with a queer gesture toward Chief of Police Dakin he stumbled out. They heard the front door slam.

'I won't be responsible for Mrs Haight's life,' said Dr Willoughby harshly, 'if she's put through any more scenes like the one just now. You can call in Wright County's whole medical fraternity to confirm what I just said. She's pregnant, in an extremely nervous condition, she has a naturally delicate constitution to begin with—'

'Look, Doc,' said Dakin, 'it ain't my fault if—'

'Oh, go to hell,' said Dr Willoughby. They heard him climbing furiously back up the stairs.

Dakin stood in the middle of the room, Nora's hatbox in one hand and Jim's book on poisons in the other. Then he sighed and said: 'But it *ain't* my fault. And now these three letters in Mrs Haight's hatbox, and this medical book with the arsenic part all marked up—'

'All right, Dakin,' said Ellery. His arms tightened about Pat.

'These three letters,' said Dakin doggedly. 'They practically make our case. And finding 'em in Mrs Haight's closet...Looks mighty odd to me. I don't get this—'

Pat cried: 'Doesn't that convince you? Would Nora have kept those letters if she thought Jim was trying to poison her? Are you all so stupid—'

'So you did know about the letters,' said the Chief, blinking. 'I see. And you're in on this, too, Mr Smith. Not that I blame you. I got a family, too, and it's good to be loyal to friends. I got nothing against Jim Haight, or you Wrights…But I got to find the facts. If Jim Haight's innocent he'll be acquitted never you worry…'

'Go away, please,' said Ellery.

Dakin shrugged and left the house, taking his evidence with him. He looked angry and bitter.

At eleven o'clock that morning, February fourteenth, the day of St Valentine, when all Wrightsville was giggling over comic cards and chewing candy out of heart-shaped boxes, Chief of Police Dakin returned to 460 Hill Drive with Patrolman Charles Brady, nodded to Patrolman Dick Gobbin, and Patrolman Dick Gobbin knocked on the front door. When there was no answer, they went in. They found Jim Haight snoring on the living-room sofa in a mess of cigarette butts, dirty glasses, and half-empty whisky bottles. Dakin shook Jim, not ungently, and finally Jim snorted. His eyes were all red and glassy. 'Hunh?'

'James Haight,' said Dakin, holding out a blue-backed paper, 'I hereby arrest you on the charge of the attempted murder of Nora Wright Haight and the murder of Rosemary Haight.'

Jim screwed up his eyes, as if he could not see well. Then he reddened all over his face. He shouted: 'No!'

'Better come without a fuss,' said Dakin; and he walked out with a quick, relieved step.

Charles Brady said later to the reporters at the Courthouse: 'Seemed like Haight just caved in. Never saw anything like it. You could just see the fella sort of fold up, in pieces, like a contraption. I says to Dick Gobbin: "Better take that side of him, Dick, he's gonna collapse," but Jim Haight, he just made a kind of shoving motion at Dick and I'll be doggone if he don't start to laugh—all folded up! An' he says, so you could hardly hear him through the laughin'—an' let me tell you fellas the stink of booze was enough to send you higher'n a kite—he says: "Don't tell my wife." And he comes along nice and quiet. Now wasn't that a

145

crazy thing for a fella to say who's just been arrested for murder? "Don't tell my wife." Facin' a murder rap an' thinkin' of sparin' his wife's feelin's! How could anybody keep it from her, anyway? Don't tell my wife! I tell you the fella's a nut.'

All Patrolman Gobbin said was: 'G-o-b-b-i-n. That's right, fellas. Hey, this'll give my kids a real kick!'

Part Four

19

War of the Worlds

Feb. 17, 1941

Mr Boris Connell
News & Features Syndicate
Press Ass'n Bldg.
Chicago, Ill.

Dear Boris:

Double Mickeys to you for that hot wire, but perhaps your celebrated news nose has been misled by the tons of garbage my fellow 'journalists' have been slinging back from Wrightsville.

I believe Jim Haight is innocent, and I'm going to say so in my column till I have no column. In my naïve way I still believe a man is innocent until he's proved guilty. Jim Haight has been condemned to death by all the smart lads and lassies sent here by their editors to dish out a Roman holiday for the great American mob. Somebody has to have principles. So I'm elected—plurality, one vote. And Wrightsville's in an ugly mood. People here talk about nothing else. Their talk is pure Fascism. It's going to be 'fun' watching them pick an 'unbiased' jury.

To appreciate what's happening, you've got to realize that only two months ago John F. and Hermione Wright were the lares and penates of this community. Today, they and their three swell daughters are untouchables—and everybody's scrambling to pick up the first stone. A slew of former Wright 'admirers' and 'friends' have been looking for a soft spot to jab the knife in; and are they jabbing! It's enough to make even me sick, and you know I've seen pretty nearly everything in the way of human meanness, malice, and downright cussedness.

It's a war of two worlds. The decent little world is hopelessly outclassed in armament, numbers, and about everything but guts and morale. The Wrights have a few real friends who are sticking by—Judge Eli Martin, Dr Milo Willoughby, a visiting writer named Ellery Smith (ever hear of him? *I* haven't!). Together they're putting up a propaganda battle. The Wrights are magnificent—in the face of everything, they're bunched solidly behind Jim Haight. Even this girl Lola Wright, who's been on the outs with her family for years, has moved back home; or at least she's there constantly. They're all fighting not only for Nora's husband but for her unborn child as well. Despite the tripe I dish out for my 'public' every day, I still believe in some fundamental decencies, and that little tyke can use a powerful voice!

Let me tell you something. I was in Jim's cell today in the County Courthouse, and I said to him: 'Jim, did you know your wife is going to have a baby?' He just sat down on his cell bunk and started to bawl, as if I'd hit him where a lady shouldn't.

I haven't been able to see Nora yet, though I may get Dr Willoughby's permission in a day or so. (I mean, since Jim's arrest.) Nora's collapsed, and she can't see anyone but her family. How would you like to be in her shoes? And if *she's* behind Jim—the man who's supposed to have plotted her death—then there's really something to fight for.

I know this is wasted time and paper, Boris, since your blood is composed of nine parts bourbon and one part club soda; so this is positively my last 'explanation.' From now on, if you want to know what's really happening in Wrightsville on the Haight murder case, read my column. And if you get nasty and break my contract before it runs out, I'll sue the N & F Syn and I'll keep suing it till I take away everything but that expensive bridgework behind your ruby lips.

As ever, ROBERTA ROBERTS

Roberta Roberts did not quite know the facts. Two days after Jim's arrest, Hermione Wright called a council of war. She closed the upstairs drawing-room doors with a grim bang. It was Sunday, and the family had just returned from church—Hermy had insisted that they attend services. They all looked weary from the ordeal. 'The question,' began Hermy, 'is what to do.'

'What can we do, Muth?' asked Pat tiredly.

'Milo.' Hermy took Doc Willoughby's big puffy hand. 'I want you to tell us the truth. How is Nora?'

'She's a sick girl, Hermy, a very sick girl.'

'That's not enough, Milo! How sick?'

Dr Willoughby's eyes shifted. 'Hard to say. She's dangerously nervous, excited, unstrung. Naturally her pregnancy isn't helping. Jim's arrest, thinking about the trial—she's got to be kept calmed down. Medicine alone won't do it. But if her nerves can be brought back to normal—'

Hermy patted his big hand absently. 'Then there's no question of what we've got to do.'

'When I see how worn-out Nora is—' said John F. in despair. 'She's begun to look the way she used to. How are we going—'

'There's one way, John,' said Hermy tightly. 'It's for all of us to get behind Jim and fight for him!'

'When he's ruined Nora's life?' cried John F. 'He's been bad luck from the day he came to Wrightsville!'

'John.' Hermy's voice was steel-lined. 'Nora wants it that way and, more important, for her health's sake she's got to *have* it that way. So it's going to be that way.'

'All *right*,' John F. almost shouted.

'John!' He subsided, muttering. 'And another thing. Nora mustn't know.'

'Mustn't know what?' demanded Pat.

'That we don't mean it.' Hermy's eyes began to redden up. 'Oh, that man! If Nora weren't his wife—'

Doc Willoughby said: 'So you think the boy's guilty, Hermione?'

'Think! If I'd known before about those three horrible letters, that medical book...Of course I think he's guilty!'

'The dirty dog,' muttered John F. 'He ought to be shot down, like a dirty dog.'

'I don't know,' moaned Pat. 'I just don't.'

Lola was smoking a cigarette. She flipped it into the fireplace viciously. 'Maybe I'm crazy,' she snapped. 'But I find myself feeling sorry for the twerp, and I don't usually spare any sympathy for murderers.'

'Eli, what's your opinion?' asked Hermy.

Judge Martin's sleepy face was grave. 'I don't know what young Bradford's got in the way of evidence. It's a highly circumstantial case. But on the other hand there's not a single fact I know of to cast doubt on the circumstances. I'd say Jim is in for a rough time.'

'Took generations to build up the Wright name,' mumbled John F., 'and one day to tear it down!'

'There's been enough damage done already,' sighed Pat. "When your own family runs out on you—'

'What's this?' demanded Lola.

'Aunt Tabitha, Lo. I thought you knew. She's closed up her house and gone to Los Angeles for a "visit" to Cousin Sophy's.'

'That Zombie still around?'

'Tabitha makes me sick!' said Hermione.

'You can't blame her so much, Hermy,' said John F. feebly. 'You know how she hates scandal—'

'I know I shan't run away, John! Nobody in this town's going to see me with *my* head hanging.'

'That's what I told Clarice,' chuckled Judge Martin. Then he rubbed his dry cheeks, like a cricket. 'Clarice would have come, Hermione, only—'

'I understand,' said Hermy quietly. 'Bless you for standing by us, Eli—you, and Milo, and you, Mr Smith. You more than anyone. After all, Judge Martin and Dr Willoughby are lifelong friends. But you're practically a stranger to us, and Patricia's told me how loyal you've been…'

'I've wanted to thank you, Smith,' said John F. awkwardly, 'but I think you know how hard it is—'

Ellery looked uncomfortable. 'Please. Don't think about me at all. I'll help all I can.'

Hermy said in a low voice: 'Bless you…Now that things have come out in the open, we'll completely understand, though, if you decide to leave Wrightsville—'

'I'm afraid I couldn't even if I wanted to,' smiled Ellery. 'The Judge will tell you I'm practically an accessory to the crime.'

'Suppressing evidence,' grinned Judge Eli. 'Dakin will have the hounds after you if you try to run away, Smith.'

'So you see? I'm stuck,' said Mr Queen. 'Let's say no more about it.' Pat's hand stole into Ellery's and squeezed hard.

'Then if we all understand one another,' declared Hermione in a firm tone, 'we're going to hire the best lawyer in the state to defend Jim. We're going to show Wrightsville a united front!'

'And if Jim's found guilty, Muth?' asked Pat quietly.

'We'll have done our best, dear. In the long run, such a verdict, hard as it seems, would be the best solution to our problem—'

'What a vile thing to say,' snapped Lola. 'Mother, that's not right or fair. You say that because you're convinced Jim's guilty. You're as bad as the rest of this town. Best solution—!'

'Lola, do you realize that if it were not for the intervention of providence,' Hermy cried, 'your sister would be a corpse this very minute?'

'Let's not quarrel,' said Pat wearily. Lola lit another cigarette, looking angry.

'And if Jim's acquitted,' said Hermy stiffishly, 'I'm going to insist that Nora divorce him.'

'Mother!' Now Pat was shocked. 'Even if a jury finds Jim *innocent*, you'll still believe he's guilty?'

'Now Hermy, that's not right,' said Judge Martin.

'I mean he's not the right man for my Nora,' said Hermy. 'He's brought her nothing but grief. Nora will divorce that man if *I've* got anything to say about it!'

'You won't,' said Doc Willoughby dryly.

Lola kissed her mother on the cheek. Ellery heard Pat gasp, and guessed that history had just been made. 'You old Trojan,' laughed Lola. 'When you get there you'll insist on running Heaven. Imagine—*you* urging a divorce!' And she added grimly: 'Why didn't you feel that way about *my* divorce from Claude?'

'This isn't...the same,' said Hermy, embarrassed. And suddenly Mr Queen saw a bright, bright light. There was an old antagonism between Hermione Wright and her daughter Lola that cut deep into their personalities. Pat was too young to have been a cause of irritation. But Nora—Nora had always been the preferred. Nora had always stood between Hermione and Lola emotionally, an innocent rope in a psychological tug-of-war. Hermy was saying to Judge Martin: 'We'll need an extra-fine lawyer for Jim, Eli. Whom can you suggest?'

'Will I do?' asked Judge Martin.

John F. was startled. 'Eli! You?'

'But Uncle Eli,' protested Pat, 'I thought—it's your court—I thought you'd have to sit—'

'In the first place,' said the old jurist dryly, 'that's not possible.

I'm involved. I was present at the scene of the crime. I am known to have strong ties with the Wright family. Legally and ethically, I can't sit on this case.' He shook his head. 'Jim will be tried before Judge Newbold. Newbold's a complete outsider.'

'But you haven't pleaded a case in fifteen years, Eli,' said John F. suspiciously.

'Of course, if you're afraid I won't do—' He smiled at their protestations. 'I forgot to mention that I'm retiring from the Bench, so...'

'You old fraud,' growled Dr Willoughby. 'John, Eli's quitting the Bench just to defend this case!'

'Now Eli, we can't let you do that,' said John F.

'Nonsense,' said the Judge gruffly. 'Don't go getting any sentimental ideas. Was going to retire anyway. Old Has-been Martin. Itching to get to work again, instead of dozing my life away in a robe. If you want a has-been in your corner, we won't say any more about it.'

Hermy burst into tears and ran from the room.

20

No Time for Pride

The next morning Pat rapped on Ellery's door and he opened it to find her dressed for the street. 'Nora wants to see you.' She looked around the room curiously. Ludie had already done the room, but it was briskly littered again, as if Ellery had been hard at work for some time.

'Right with you.' Ellery looked fatigued. He fussed with some pencil-scrawled papers on the desk; the typewriter carriage held a sheet. He slipped the cover over the portable and, putting the papers in a desk drawer, locked it. The key he dropped casually into his pocket, and put on his jacket.

'Working?' asked Pat.

'Well...yes. This way out, Miss Wright.' Mr Queen walked her out of his room and locked the door.

'Your novel?'

'In a way.' They went down to the second floor.

'What does "in a way" mean?'

'Yes and no. I've been...you might call it reconnoitering.' Ellery looked her over. 'Going out? You look cute.'

156

'I've a special reason for looking cute this morning,' murmured Pat. 'In fact, I'll have to look irresistible.'

'You do. But where are you going?'

'Can't a girl have any secrets from you, Mr Queen?' Pat stopped him outside Nora's room and looked him in the eye. 'Ellery, you've been going over your notes on the case, haven't you?'

'Yes.'

'Find anything?' she asked eagerly.

'No.'

'Damn!'

'It's a queer thing,' grumbled Ellery, putting his arm around her. 'Something's been annoying me for weeks. Flying around in my skull. Can't catch it…I thought it might be a fact—something trivial—that I'd overlooked. You know, I…well, I based my novel on you people—the facts, the events, the interrelationships. So everything's in my notes that's happened.' He shook his head. 'But I can't put my finger on it.'

'Maybe,' frowned Pat, 'it's a fact you don't *know*.'

Ellery held her off at arm's length. 'That,' he said slowly, 'is very likely. Do *you* know anything that—'

'You know if I did, I'd tell you, Ellery.'

'I wonder.' Then he shrugged and said: 'Well! Let's go in and see Nora.'

Nora was sitting up in bed, reading the *Wrightsville Record*. She was thinner, unhealthy-looking. Ellery was shocked to see how transparent the skin of her hands had grown. 'I always say,' grinned Mr Queen, 'that the test of a woman's attractiveness is—how does she look in bed of a winter's morning.'

Nora smiled wanly and patted the bed. 'Do I pass?'

'*Summa cum laude*,' said Ellery, sitting down beside her.

Nora looked pleased. 'Most of it's powder, lipstick—yes, and a dab of rouge on each cheek—and of course this ribbon in my hair is a help. Charming liar! Patty darling, sit down.'

'I really have to be going, Nora. You two can talk—'

'But Pats, I want you to hear this, too.' Pat glanced at Ellery;

he blinked, and she sat down in the chintz-covered chair on the other side of the bed. She seemed nervous, and Ellery kept watching her as Nora talked. 'First,' said Nora, 'I owe you an apology.'

'Who, me,' said Ellery, astonished. 'For what, Nora?'

'For having accused you of telling the police about those three letters and the toxicology book. Last week. When Chief Dakin said he was going to arrest Jim and I lost my head.'

'You see? I'd forgotten it. You do the same.'

Nora took his hand. 'It was a malicious thought. But for the moment I couldn't imagine who'd told them but you. You see, I thought they knew—'

'You weren't responsible, Nora,' said Pat. 'Ellery understands that.'

'But there's something else,' cried Nora. 'I can apologize for a nasty thought, but I can't wipe out what I did to Jim.' Her lower lip quivered. 'If not for me, they'd never have found out about those letters!'

'Nor dear,' said Pat, leaning over her, 'you know you mustn't. If you keep crying, I'll tell Uncle Milo and he won't let you have *any* company.'

Nora sniffled with her handkerchief to her nose. 'I don't know why I didn't burn them. Such a stupid thing—to keep them in that hatbox in my closet! But I had some idea I'd be able to find out who really wrote them—I was sure Jim hadn't—'

'Nora,' said Ellery gently. 'Forget it.'

'But I practically handed Jim over to the police!'

'That isn't true. Don't forget Dakin came here last week *prepared* to arrest Jim. Questioning you beforehand was just a formality.'

'Then you think those letters and the book don't make any essential difference?' asked Nora eagerly.

Ellery got up from the bed and looked out of the window at the winter sky. 'Well…not too much.'

'You're lying to me!'

'Mrs Haight,' said Pat firmly, 'you've had enough company for one morning. Ellery, scram.'

Ellery turned around. 'This sister of yours, Pat, will suffer more from doubt than from knowledge. Nora, I'll tell you exactly what the situation is.' Nora gripped her comforter with both hands. 'If Dakin was prepared to arrest Jim *before* he knew about the letters and the toxicology book, then obviously he and Carter Bradford thought they had a good case.' Nora made a tiny sound. '*With* the letters and the book, therefore, they just as obviously have a better case. Now that's the truth, you've got to face it, you've got to stop accusing yourself, you've got to be sensible and get well again, you've got to stand by Jim and give him courage.' He leaned over her and took her hand. 'Jim needs your strength, Nora. You have a strength he lacks. He can't face you, but if he knows you're behind him, never wavering, having faith—'

'Yes,' breathed Nora, her eyes shining. 'I have. Tell him I have.' Pat came around the bed and kissed Ellery on the cheek.

'Going my way?' asked Ellery as they left the house.

'Which way is that?'

'Courthouse. I want to see Jim.'

'Oh. I'll drive you down.'

'Don't go out of your way—'

'I'm going to the Courthouse, too.'

'To see Jim?'

'Don't ask me questions!' cried Pat a little hysterically.

They drove down the Hill in silence. There was ice on the road, and the chains sang cheerfully. Wrightsville looked nicely wintry, all whites and reds and blacks, no shading; it had the country look, the rich and simple cleanliness, of a Grant Wood painting. But in town there were people, and sloppy slush, and a meanness in the air; the shops looked pinched and stale; everybody was hurrying through the cold; no one smiled. In the Square they had to stop for traffic; a shopgirl recognized Pat and pointed her out with a lacquered fingernail to a pimpled youth in a leather storm-breaker. They whispered excitedly as Pat kicked the gas pedal. On the Courthouse steps Ellery said: 'Not *that* way, Miss Wright,' and steered Pat around to the side entrance.

'What's the idea?' demanded Pat.

'The press,' said Mr Queen. 'Infesting the lobby. I assume we'd rather not answer questions.'

They took the side elevator. 'You've been here before,' said Pat slowly.

'Yes.'

Pat said: 'I think I'll pay Jim a visit myself.'

The County Jail occupied the two topmost floors of the Courthouse. As they stepped out of the elevator into the waiting room, an odor of steam and Lysol rushed into their noses, and Pat swallowed hard. But she managed a smile for the benefit of Wally Planetsky, the officer on duty.

'If it ain't Miss Pat,' said the officer awkwardly.

'Hullo, Wally. How's the old badge?'

'Fine, fine, Miss Pat.'

'Wally used to let me breathe on his badge and shine it up when I was in grade school,' Pat exclaimed. 'Wally, don't stand there shifting from one foot to the other. You know what I'm here for.'

'I guess,' muttered Wally Planetsky.

'Where's his cell?'

'Judge Martin's with him, Miss Pat. Rules say only one visitor at a time—'

'Who cares about the rules? Take us to my brother-in-law's cell, Wally!'

'This gentleman a reporter? Mr Haight, he won't see any reporters excepting that Miss Roberts.'

'No, he's a friend of mine and Jim's.'

'I guess,' muttered Planetsky again; and they began a long march, interrupted by unlocking of iron doors, locking of iron doors, steps on concrete, unlocking and locking and steps through corridors lined with man-sized bird cages; and at each step the odor of steam and Lysol grew stronger, and Pat grew greener, and toward the last she clung tightly to Ellery's arm. But she kept her chin up.

'That's it,' murmured Ellery; and she swallowed several times in succession.

Jim sprang to his feet when he spied them, a quick flush coming to his sallow cheeks; but then he sat down again, the blood draining away, and said hoarsely: "Hello there, I didn't know you were coming.'

'Hello, Jim!' said Pat cheerily. 'How are you?'

Jim looked around his cell. 'All right,' he said with a vague smile.

'It's clean, anyway,' grunted Judge Martin, 'which is more than you could say about the *old* County Jail. Well, Jim, I'll be on my way. I'll drop in tomorrow for another talk.'

'Thanks, Judge.' Jim smiled the same vague smile up at the Judge.

'Nora's fine,' said Pat with an effort, as if Jim had asked.

'That's swell,' said Jim. 'Fine, uh?'

'Yes,' said Pat in a shrill voice.

'That's swell,' said Jim again.

Mercifully, Ellery said: 'Pat, didn't you say you had an errand somewhere? There's something I'd like to say to Jim in private.'

'Not that it will do you the least good,' said Judge Martin in an angry tone. It seemed to Ellery that the old jurist's anger was assumed for the occasion. 'This boy hasn't the sense he was born with! Come along, Patricia.'

Pat turned her pale face to Ellery, mumbled something, smiled weakly at Jim, and fled with the Judge. Keeper Planetsky relocked the cell door after them, shaking his head.

Ellery looked down at Jim; Jim was studying the bare floor of his cell. 'He wants me to talk,' mumbled Jim suddenly.

'Well, why not, Jim?'

'What could I say?'

Ellery offered him a cigarette. Jim took it, but when Ellery held a lighted match up he shook his head and slowly tore the cigarette to shreds. 'You could say,' murmured Ellery between puffs, 'you could say that you didn't write those three letters, or underline that paragraph on arsenic.'

For an instant Jim's fingers stopped tormenting the cigarette; then they resumed their work of destruction. His colorless lips flattened against his face in something that was almost a snarl.

'Jim.' Jim glanced at him, and then away. 'Did you really plan to poison Nora?' Jim did not even indicate that he had heard the question. 'You know, Jim, often when a man is guilty of a crime he's much better off telling the truth to his lawyer and friends than keeping quiet. And when he's not guilty, it's actually criminal to keep quiet. It's a crime against himself.' Jim said nothing. 'How do you expect your family and friends to help you when you won't help yourself?' Jim's lips moved. 'What did you say, Jim?'

'Nothing.'

'As a matter of fact, in this case,' said Ellery briskly, 'your crime of silence isn't directed half so much against yourself as it is against your wife and the child that's coming. How can you be so far gone in stupidity or listlessness that you'd drag them down with you, too?'

'Don't say that!' said Jim hoarsely. 'Get out of here! I didn't ask you to come! I didn't ask Judge Martin to defend me! I didn't ask for anything! I just want to be let alone!'

'Is that,' asked Ellery, 'what you want me to tell Nora?'

There was such misery in Jim's eyes as he sat, panting, on the edge of his cell bunk that Ellery went to the door and called Planetsky. All the signs. Cowardice. Shame. Self-pity...But that other thing, the stubbornness, *the refusal to talk about anything*, as if in the mere act of self-expression there were *danger* ...

As Ellery followed the guard down the eye-studded corridor a cell exploded in his brain with a great and disproportionate burst of light. He actually stopped walking, causing old Planet-sky to turn and look at him in surprise. But then he shook his head and strode on again. He'd almost had it that time—by sheer divination. Maybe the next time...

Pat drew a deep breath outside the frosted-glass door on the second floor of the County Courthouse, tried to see her reflection, poked nervously at her mink hat, tried out a smile or two, not too successfully, and then went in. Miss Billcox looked as if she were seeing a ghost. 'Is the Prosecutor in, Billy?' murmured Pat.

'I'll...see, Miss Wright,' said Miss Billcox, and fled.

Carter Bradford came out to her himself, in a hurry, 'Come in, Pat.' He looked tired, and astonished. He stood aside to let her pass, and as she passed she heard his uneven breathing. O Lord, she thought. Maybe. Maybe it isn't too late.

'Working?' His desk was covered with legal papers.

'Yes, Pat.' He went around his desk to stand behind it. One sheaf of bound papers lay open—he closed it surreptitiously and kept his hand on it as he nodded toward a leather chair. Pat sat down and crossed her knees.

'Well,' said Pat, looking around. 'The old office—I mean the new office—doesn't seem to have changed, Cart.'

'About the only thing that hasn't.'

'You needn't be so careful about that legal paper,' smiled Pat. 'I haven't got X-ray eyes.' He flushed and removed his hand. 'There isn't a shred of Mata Hari in my makeup.'

'I'm *not*—' Cart began angrily. Then he pushed his fingers through his hair in the old, old gesture. 'Here we are, scrapping again. Pat, you look simply delicious.'

'It's nice of you to say so,' sighed Pat, 'when I really am beginning to look my age.'

'Look your age! Why, you're—' Cart swallowed hard. Then he said, as angrily as before: 'I've missed you like hell.'

Pat said rigidly. 'I suppose I've missed you, too.' Oh, dear! That wasn't what she had meant to say at all. But it was hard, facing him this way, alone in a room together for the first time in so long—hard to keep from feeling...feelings.

'I dream about you,' said Cart with a self-conscious laugh. 'Isn't that silly?'

'Now, Cart, you know perfectly well you're just saying that to be polite. People don't dream about people. I mean in the way *you* mean. They dream about animals with long noses.'

'Maybe it's just before I drop off.' He shook his head. 'Dreaming or not dreaming, it's always the same. Your face. I don't know why. It's not such a wonderful face. The nose is wrong, and your mouth's wider than Carmel's, and you've got that ridiculous way of looking at people sidewise, like a parrot—'

And she was in his arms, and it was just like a spy drama, except that she hadn't planned the script exactly this way. *This* was to come after—as a reward to Cart for being a sweet, obliging, self-sacrificing boy. She hadn't thought of herself at all, assuming regal stardom. Certainly this pounding of her heart wasn't in the plot—not with Jim caged in a cell six stories above her head and Nora lying in bed across town trying to hold on to something. His lips were on hers and he was pressing, pressing.

'Cart. No. Not yet.' She pushed. 'Darling. Please—'

'You called me darling! Damn it, Pat, how could you play around with me all these months, shoving that Smith fellow in my face—'

'Cart,' moaned Pat. 'I want to talk to you...first.'

'I'm sick of talk! Pat, I want you so blamed much—' He kissed her mouth; he kissed the tip of her nose.

'I want to talk to you about Jim, Cart!' cried Pat desperately.

She felt him go cold in one spasm. He let her go and walked to the wall with the windows that overlooked the Courthouse plaza, to stare out without seeing anything, cars or people or trees or Wrightsville's gray-wash sky.

'What about Jim?' he asked in a flat voice.

'Cart. Look at me!' Pat begged.

He turned around. 'I can't do it.'

'Can't look at me? You are!'

'Can't withdraw from the case. That's why you came here today, isn't it—to ask me?'

Pat sat down again, fumbling for her lipstick. Her lips. Blobbed. Kiss. Her hands were shaking, so she snapped the bag shut. 'Yes,' she said, very low. 'More than that. I wanted you to resign the Prosecutor's office and come over to Jim's defense. Like Judge Eli Martin.'

Cart was silent for so long that Pat had to look up at him. He was staring at her with an intense bitterness. But when he spoke, it was with gentleness. 'You can't be serious. The Judge is an old man, your father's closest friend. And he wouldn't have been able to sit on this case, anyway. But I was elected to this office only a short time ago. I took an oath that means something to me. I hate to sound like some stuffed shirt of a politician looking for votes—'

'Oh, but you do!' flared Pat.

'If Jim's innocent, he'll go free. If he's guilty—you wouldn't want him to go free if he's guilty, would you?'

'He's *not* guilty!'

'That's something the jury will have to decide.'

'You've decided already! In your own mind, you've condemned him to death!'

'Dakin and I have had to collect the facts, Pat. We've *had* to. Don't you understand that? Our personal feelings can't interfere. We both feel awful about this thing...'

Pat was near tears now, and angry with herself for showing it. 'Doesn't it mean anything to you that Nora's whole life is tied up in this "thing," as you call it? That there's a baby coming? I know the trial can't be stopped, but I wanted *you* on our side, I wanted you to help, not hurt!' Cart ground his teeth together. 'You've said you love me,' cried Pat. 'How could you love me and still—' Horrified, she heard her own voice break and found herself sobbing. 'The whole town's against us. They stoned Jim. They're slinging mud at us. Wrightsville, Cart! A Wright founded this town. We were all born here—not only us kids, but Pop and Muth and Aunt Tabitha and the Bluefields and…I'm not the spoiled brat you used to neck in the back of your lizzie at the Grove in Wrightsville Junction on Saturday nights! The whole world's gone to pot, Cart—I've grown old watching it. Oh, Cart, I've no pride left—no defenses—say you'll help me! I'm afraid!' She hid her face, giving up the emotional battle. Nothing made any sense—what she'd just said, what she was thinking. Everything was drowning, gasping, struggling in tears.

'Pat,' said Cart miserably. 'I can't. I just can't.'

That did it. She was drowned now, dead, but there was a sort of vicious other-life that made her spring from the chair and scream at him. 'You're nothing but a selfish, scheming politician! You're willing to see Jim die and Pop, and Mother, and Nora, and me, and everyone suffer, just to further your own career! Oh, this is an *important* case. Dozens of New York and Chicago and Boston reporters to hang on your every word! Your name and photo—Young Public Prosecutor Bradford—brilliant—says this—my duty is—yes—no—off the record…You're a hateful, shallow *publicity hound!*'

'I've gone all through this in my mind, Pat,' Cart replied with a queer lack of resentment. 'I suppose I can't expect you to see it my way—'

Pat laughed. 'Insult to injury!'

'If I don't do this job—if I resign or step out—someone else will. Someone who might be a lot less fair to Jim. If I prosecute, Pat, you can be sure Jim will get a square deal—'

She ran out.

And there, on the side of the corridor opposite the Prosecutor's door, waiting patiently, was Mr Queen.

'Oh, *Ellery!*'

Ellery said gently: 'Come home.'

21

Vox Pops

'Ave, Caesar!' wrote Roberta Roberts at the head of her column under the date line of March fifteenth.

> He who is about to be tried for his life finds even the fates against him. Jim Haight's trial begins on the Ides of March before Judge Lysander Newbold in Wright County Courthouse, Part II, Wrightsville, U.S.A. This is chance, or subtlety…Kid Vox is popping furiously, and it is the impression of cooler heads that the young man going on trial here for the murder of Rosemary Haight and the attempted murder of Nora Wright Haight is being prepared to make a Roman Holiday.

And so it seemed. From the beginning there was a muttering undertone that was chilling. Chief of Police Dakin expressed himself privately to the persistent press as 'mighty relieved' that his prisoner didn't have to be carted through the streets of Wrightsville to reach the place of his inquisition, since the County Jail and the County Courthouse were in the same building. People were in such an ugly temper you would have imagined their hatred of the alleged poisoner to be inspired by the fiercest loyalty to the Wrights. But this was odd, because they were equally ugly towards the Wrights. Dakin had to assign two county detectives to escort the family to and from the Court-house. Even so, jeering boys threw stones, the tires of their cars were slashed mysteriously and the paint scratched with nasty words; seven unsigned letters of the 'threat' variety were delivered by a nervous Postman Bailey in one day alone. Silent, John F. Wright turned them over to Dakin's office; and Patrolman Brady himself caught the Old Soak, Anderson, standing precariously in the middle of the Wright lawn in bright daylight, declaiming not too aptly to the unresponding house Mark Antony's speech from Act III, Scene I of *Julius Caesar*. Charlie Brady hauled Mr Anderson to the town lockup hastily, while Mr Anderson kept yelling 'O parm me thou blee'n' piece of earth that I am meek an' zhentle with theshe—hup!—bushers!'

Hermy and John F. began to look beaten. In court, the family sat together, in a sort of phalanx, with stiff necks if pale faces; only occasionally Hermy smiled rather pointedly in the direction of Jim Haight, and then turned to sniff and glare at the jammed courtroom and toss her head, as if to say: 'Yes, we're all in this together—you miserable rubbernecks!'

There had been a great deal of mumbling about the impropriety of Carter Bradford's prosecuting the case. In an acid editorial Frank Lloyd put the *Record* on record as 'disapproving.' True, unlike Judge Eli Martin, Bradford had arrived at the fatal New Year's Eve party *after* the poisoning of Nora and Rosemary, so he was not involved either as participant or as witness. But Lloyd pointed out that 'our young, talented, but sometimes emotional Prosecutor has long been friendly with the Wright family, especially one member of it; and although we understand this friendship has ceased as of the night of the crime, we still question the ability of Mr Bradford to prosecute this case without bias. Something should be done about it.'

Interviewed on this point before the opening of the trial, Bradford snapped: 'This isn't Chicago or New York. We have a close-knit community here, where everybody knows everybody else. My conduct during the trial will answer the *Record*'s libelous insinuations. Jim Haight will get from Wright County a forthright, impartial prosecution based solely upon the evidence. That's all, gentlemen!'

Judge Lysander Newbold was an elderly man, a bachelor, greatly respected throughout the state as a jurist and trout fisherman. He was a square, squat, bony man who always sat on the Bench with his black-fringed skull sunk so deeply between his shoulders that it seemed an outgrowth of his chest. His voice was dry and careless; he had the habit, when on the Bench, of playing absently with his gavel, as if it were a fishing rod; and he never laughed.

Judge Newbold had no friends, no associates, and no commitments except to God, country, Bench, and the trout season. Everybody said with a sort of relieved piety that 'Judge Newbold is just about the best judge this case could have.' Some even thought he was *too* good. But they were the ones who were muttering. Roberta Roberts baptized these grumblers 'the Jimhaighters.'

It took several days to select a jury, and during these days Mr Ellery Queen kept watching only two persons in the courtroom—Judge Eli Martin, defense counsel, and Carter Bradford, Prosecutor. And it soon became evident that this would be a war between young courage and old experience. Bradford was working under a strain. He held himself in one piece, like a casting; there was a dogged something about him that met the eye with defiance and yet a sort of shame. Ellery saw early that he was competent. He knew his townspeople, too. But he was speaking too quietly, and occasionally his voice cracked.

Judge Martin was superb. He did not make the mistake of patronizing young Bradford, even subtly; that would have swung the people over to the prosecution. Instead, he was most respectful of Bradford's comments. Once, returning to their places from a low-voiced colloquy before Judge Newbold, the old man was seen to put his hand affectionately on Carter's shoulder for just an instant. The gesture said: You're a good boy;

169

we like each other; we are both interested in the same thing—
justice; and we are equally matched. This is all very sad, but necessary. The People are in good hands. The People rather liked it.
There were whispers of approval. And some were heard to say:
After all, old Eli Martin—he *did* quit his job on the Bench to
defend Haight. Can't get around that! Must be pretty convinced
Haight's innocent...And others replied: Go on. The Judge is John
F. Wright's best friend, that's why...Well, I don't know...The
whole thing was calculated to create an atmosphere of dignity
and thoughtfulness, in which the raw emotions of the mob could
only gasp for breath, and gradually expire.

Mr Ellery Queen approved. Mr Queen approved even more
when he finally examined the twelve good men and true. Judge
Martin had made the selections as deftly and surely as if there
were no Bradford to cope with at all. Solid, sober male citizens,
as far as Ellery could determine. None calculated to respond to
prejudicial appeals, with one possible exception, a fat man who
kept sweating; most seemed anxiously thoughtful men, with
higher than average intelligence. Men of the decent world, who
might be expected to understand that a man can be weak without being criminal.

For students of the particular, the complete court record of *People v. James Haight* is on file in Wright County—day after day after
day of question and answer and objection and Judge Newbold's
precise rulings. For that matter, the newspapers were almost as
exhaustive as the court stenographer's notes. The difficulty with
detailed records, however, is that you cannot see the tree for the
leaves. So let us stand off and make the leaves blur and blend into
larger shapes. Let us look at contours, not textures.

In his opening address to the jury, Carter Bradford said that
the jury must bear in mind continuously one all-important point:
that while Rosemary Haight, the defendant's sister, was murdered by poison, her death was not the true object of defendant's
crime. The true object of defendant's crime was to take the life of
defendant's young wife, Nora Wright Haight—an object so nearly accomplished that the wife was confined to her bed for six

weeks after the fateful New Year's Eve party, a victim of arsenic poisoning.

And yes, the State freely admits that its case against James Haight is circumstantial, but murder convictions on circumstantial evidence are the rule, not the exception. The only direct evidence possible in a murder case is an eyewitness's testimony as to having witnessed the murder at the moment of its commission. In a shooting case, this would have to be a witness who actually saw the accused pull the trigger and the victim fall dead as a result of the shot. In a poisoning case, it would have to be a witness who actually saw the accused deposit poison in the food or drink to be swallowed by the victim, and moreover who saw the accused hand the poisoned food or drink *to* the victim. Obviously, continued Bradford, such 'happy accidents' of persons witnessing the Actual Deed must be few and far between, since murderers understandably try to avoid committing their murders before an audience. Therefore nearly all prosecutions of murder are based on circumstantial rather than direct evidence; the law has wisely provided for the admission of such evidence, otherwise most murderers would go unpunished.

But the jury need not flounder in doubts about *this* case; here the circumstantial evidence is so clear, so strong, so indisputable, that the jury must find James Haight guilty of the crime as charged beyond any reasonable doubt whatsoever. 'The People will prove', said Bradford in a low, firm tone, 'that James Haight planned the murder of his wife a minimum of five weeks before he tried to accomplish it; that it was a cunning plan, depending upon a series of poisonings of increasing severity to establish the wife as subject to attacks of "illness," and supposed to culminate in a climactic poisoning as a result of which the wife was to die. The People will prove,' Bradford went on, 'that these preliminary poisonings did take place on the very dates indicated by the schedule James Haight had prepared with his own hand; that the attempted murder of Nora Haight and the accidental murder of Rosemary Haight did take place on the very date indicated by the same schedule.

'The People will prove that on the night under examination, James Haight and James Haight alone mixed the batch of cocktails among whose number was the poisoned cocktail; that James Haight and James Haight alone handed the tray of cocktails around to the various members of the party; that James Haight and James Haight alone handed his wife the poisoned cocktail from the tray, and even urged her to drink it; that she did drink of that cocktail, and fell violently ill of arsenic poisoning, her life being spared only because at Rosemary Haight's insistence she gave the rest of the poisoned cocktail to her sister-in-law after having merely sipped...a circumstance James Haight couldn't have foreseen.

'The People will prove,' Bradford went on quietly, 'that James Haight was in desperate need of money, that he demanded large sums of money of his wife while under the influence of liquor and, sensibly, she refused; that James Haight was losing large sums of money gambling; that he was taking other illicit means of procuring money; that upon Nora Haight's death her estate, a large one as the result of an inheritance, would legally fall to the defendant, who is her husband and heir-at-law.

'The People,' concluded Bradford, in a tone so low he could scarcely be heard, 'being convinced beyond reasonable doubt that James Haight did so plan and attempt the life of one person in attempting which he succeeded in taking the life of another and innocent victim—the People demand that James Haight pay with his own life for the life taken and the life so nearly taken.' And Carter Bradford sat down to spontaneous applause, which caused the first of Judge Newbold's numerous subsequent warnings to the spectators.

In that long dreary body of testimony calculated to prove Jim Haight's sole Opportunity, the only colorful spots were provided by Judge Eli Martin in cross-examination. From the first the old lawyer's plan was plain to Ellery: to cast doubt, doubt, doubt. Not heatedly. With cool humor. The voice of reason...Insinuate. Imply. Get away with whatever you can, and to hell with the rules of cross-examination. Ellery realized that Judge Martin was desperate.

'But you can't be *sure?*'

'N-no.'

'You didn't have the defendant under observation *every moment?*'

'Of course not!'

'The defendant *might* have laid the tray of cocktails down for a moment or so?'

'No.'

'Are you *positive?*'

Carter Bradford quietly objects: the question was answered. Sustained. Judge Newbold waves his hand patiently.

"Did you *see* the defendant prepare the cocktails?'

'No.'

'Were you in the living room *all* the time?'

'You know I was!' This was Frank Lloyd; and he was angry. To Frank Lloyd, Judge Martin paid special attention. The old gentleman wormed out of the newspaper publisher his relationship with the Wright family—his 'peculiar' relationship with the defendant's wife. He had been in love with her. He had been bitter when she turned him down for James Haight. He had threatened James Haight with bodily violence. Objection, objection, objection. But it managed to come out, enough of it to reawaken in the jury's minds the whole story of Frank Lloyd and Nora Wright—after all, that story was an old one to Wrightsville and everybody knew the details!

So Frank Lloyd became a poor witness for the People, and there was a doubt, a doubt. The vengeful jilted 'other' man. Who knows? Maybe—

With the Wright family, who were forced to take the stand to testify to the actual events of the night, Judge Martin was impersonal—and cast more doubts. On the 'facts.' Nobody actually *saw* Jim Haight drop arsenic into the cocktail. Nobody could be sure...of anything.

But the prosecution's case proceeded and, despite Judge Martin's wily obstructions, Bradford established: that Jim alone mixed the cocktails; that Jim was the only one who could have been certain the poisoned cocktail went to Nora, his intended victim, since he handed each drinker his or her cocktail; that Jim pressed Nora to drink when she was reluctant.

And the testimony of old Wentworth, who had been the attorney for John F.'s father. Wentworth had drawn the dead man's will. Wentworth testified that on Nora's marriage she received her grandfather's bequest of a hundred thousand dollars, held in trust for her until that 'happy' event.

And the testimony of the five handwriting experts, who agreed unanimously, despite the most vigorous cross-examination by Judge Martin, that the three unmailed letters addressed to Rosemary Haight, dated Thanksgiving, Christmas, and New Year's, and announcing far in advance of those dates the 'illness' of Nora Haight, the third actually announcing her 'death'— agreed unanimously that these damning letters were in the handwriting of the defendant, beyond any doubt whatever. For several days the trial limped and lagged while huge charts were set up in the courtroom and Judge Martin, who had obviously boned up, debated the finer points of handwriting analysis with the experts...unsuccessfully.

Then came Alberta Manaskas, who turned out a staunch defender of the public weal. Alberta evinced an unsuspected volubility. And, to judge from her testimony, her eyes, which had always seemed dull, were sharper than a cosmic ray; and her ears, which had merely seemed large and red, were more sensitive than a photoelectric cell. It was through Alberta that Carter Bradford brought out how, as the first letter had predicted, Nora took sick on Thanksgiving day; how Nora had another, and worse, attack of 'sickness' on Christmas Day. Alberta went into clinical detail about these 'sicknesses.'

Judge Martin rose to his opportunity. Sickness, Alberta? Now what kind of sickness would you say Miss Nora had on Thanksgiving and Christmas?

Sick! Like in her belly. (*Laughter.*)

Have *you* ever been sick like in your—uh—belly, Alberta? Sure! You, me, everyone. (*Judge Newbold raps for order.*)

Like Miss Nora?

Sure!

(Gently): You've never been poisoned by arsenic, though, have you, Alberta?

Bradford, on his feet. Judge Martin sat down smiling. Mr Queen noticed the sweat fringing his forehead.

Dr Milo Willoughby's testimony, confirmed by the testimony of Coroner Chic Salemson and the testimony of L.D. ('Whitey') Magill, State Chemist, established that the toxic agent which had made Nora Haight ill, and caused the death of Rosemary Haight, was arsenious acid, or arsenic trioxid, or arsenious oxid, or simply 'white arsenic'—all names for the same deadly substance. Henceforth prosecutor and defense counsel referred to it simply as 'arsenic.'

Dr Magill described the substance as 'colorless, tasteless, and odorless in solution, and of a high degree of toxicity.'

Q. (by Prosecutor Bradford)—It is a powder, Dr Magill? *A.*—Yes, sir.

Q.—Would it dissolve in a cocktail, or lose any of its effectiveness if taken that way? *A.*—Arsenic trioxid is very slightly soluble in alcohol, but since a cocktail is greatly aqueous it will dissolve quite readily. It is soluble in water, you see. No, it would lose none of its toxicity in alcohol.

Q.—Thank you, Dr Magill. Your Witness, Judge Martin.

Judge Martin waives cross-examination.

Prosecutor Bradford calls to the stand Myron Garback, proprietor of the High Village Pharmacy, Wrightsville. Mr Garback has a cold; his nose is red and swollen. He sneezes frequently and fidgets in the witness chair. From the audience Mrs Garback, a pale Irishwoman, watches her husband anxiously. Being duly sworn, Myron Garback testifies that 'sometime' during October of 1940—the previous October—James Haight had entered the High Village Pharmacy and asked for 'a small tin of Quicko.'

Q.—What exactly is Quicko, Mr Garback? *A.*—It is a preparation used for the extermination of rodents and insect pests.

175

Q.—What is the lethal ingredient of Quicko? *A.*—Arsenic tri-oxid. (*Sneeze. Laughter. Gavel.*)

Mrs Garback turns crimson and glares balefully about.

Q.—In highly concentrated form? *A.*—Yes, sir.

Q.—Did you sell the defendant a tin of this poisonous prepa-ration, Mr Garback? *A.*—Yes, sir. It is a commercial preparation, requiring no prescription.

Q.—Did the defendant ever return to purchase more Quicko? *A.*—Yes, sir, about two weeks later. He said he'd mislaid the can of stuff, so he'd have to buy a new can. I sold him a new can.

Q.—Did the defendant—I'll rephrase the question. What did the defendant say to you, and what did you say to the defen-dant, on the occasion of his first purchase? *A.*—Mr Haight said there were mice in his house, and he wanted to kill them off. I said I was surprised, because I'd never heard of house mice up on the Hill. He didn't say anything to that.

Cross-examination by Judge Eli Martin:—

Q.—Mr Garback, how many tins of Quicko would you esti-mate you sold during the month of October last? *A.*—That's hard to answer. A lot. It's my best-selling rat-killer, and Low Vil-lage is infested.

Q.—Twenty-five? Fifty? *A.*—Somewhere around there.

Q.—Then it's not unusual for customers to buy this poisonous preparation—purely to kill rats? *A.*—No, sir, not unusual at all.

Q.—Then how is it you remembered that Mr Haight pur-chased some—remembered it *for five months*? *A.*—It just stuck in my mind. Maybe because he bought two tins so close together, and it was the Hill.

Q.—You're positive it was two cans, two weeks apart? *A.*—Yes, sir. I wouldn't say it if I wasn't.

Q.—No comments, please; just answer the question. Mr Gar-back, do you keep records of your Quicko sales, listed by cus-tomer? *A.*—I don't have to, Judge. It's legal to sell—

Q.—Answer the question, Mr Garback. Have you a written record of James Haight's alleged purchases of Quicko? *A.*—No, sir, but—

Q.—Then we just have your word, relying on your memory of two incidents you allege to have occurred five months ago, that the defendant purchased Quicko from you?

Prosecutor Bradford: Your Honor, the witness is under oath. He has answered Counsel's question not once, but several times. Objection.

Judge Newbold: It seems to me witness has answered, Judge. Sustained.

Q.—That's all, thank you, Mr Garback.

Alberta Manaskas is recalled to the stand. Questioned by Mr Bradford, she testifies that she 'never seen no rats in Miss Nora's house.' She further testifies that she 'never seen no rat-killer, neither.'

On cross-examination, Judge Martin asks Alberta Manaskas if it is not true that in the tool chest in the cellar of the Haight house there is a large rat trap.

A.—Is there?

Q.—That's what I'm asking you, Alberta. *A.*—I guess there is, at that.

Q.—If there are no rats, Alberta, why do you suppose the Haights keep a rat trap?

Prosecutor Bradford: Objection. Calling for opinion.

Judge Newbold: Sustained. Counsel, I'll have to ask you to restrict your cross-examination to—

Judge Martin (humbly): Yes, Your Honor.

Emmeline DuPré, under oath, testifies that she is a Dramatic and Dancing Teacher residing at Number 468 Hill Drive, Wrightsville, 'right next door to Nora Wright's house.'

Witness testifies that during the previous November and December she 'happened to overhear' frequent quarrels between Nora and James Haight. The quarrels were about Mr Haight's heavy drinking and numerous demands for money. There was one markedly violent quarrel, in December, when Miss DuPré heard Nora Haight refuse to give her husband 'any more money.' Did Miss DuPré 'happen to overhear' anything to indicate why the defendant needed so much money?

177

A.—That's what shocked me so, Mr Bradford—

Q.—The Court is not interested in your emotional reactions, Miss DuPré. Answer the question, please. *A.*—Jim Haight admitted he'd been gambling, and losing plenty, and that's why he needed money, he said.

Q.—Was any name or place mentioned by either Mr or Mrs Haight in connection with the defendant's gambling? *A.*—Jim Haight said he'd been losing a lot at the *Hot Spot*, that scandalous place on Route 16—

Judge Martin: Your Honor, I move that this witness's entire testimony be stricken out. I have no objection to give-and-take in this trial—Mr Bradford has been extremely patient with me, and it is an admittedly difficult case, being so vaguely circumstantial—

Mr Bradford: May I ask Counsel to restrict his remarks to his objection, and stop trying to influence the jury by characterizing the case?

Judge Newbold: The Prosecutor is right, Counsel. Now what is your objection to this witness's testimony?

Judge Martin: No attempt has been made by the People to fix the times and circumstances under which witness allegedly overheard conversations between defendant and wife. Admittedly witness was not present in the same room, or even in the same house. How, then, did she 'overhear'? How can she be sure the two people *were* the defendant and his wife? Did she see them? Didn't she see them? I hold—

Miss DuPré: But I heard all this with my own ears!

Judge Newbold: Miss DuPré! Yes, Mr Bradford?

Mr Bradford: The People have put Miss DuPré on the stand in an effort to spare defendant's wife the pain of testifying to the quarrels—

Judge Martin: That's not my point.

Judge Newbold: No, it is not. Nevertheless, Counsel, I suggest you cover your point in cross-examination. Objection denied. Proceed, Mr Bradford.

Mr Bradford proceeds, eliciting further testimony as to quarrels between Jim and Nora. On cross-examination, Judge Martin reduces Miss DuPré to indignant tears. He brings out her physical position relative to the conversationalists—crouched by her bedroom window in darkness listening to the voices floating warmly across the driveway between her house and the Haight house—confuses her in the matter of dates and times involved, so that she clearly contradicts herself several times. The spectators enjoy themselves.

Under oath, J.P. Simpson, proprietor of Simpson's Pawnshop in the Square, Wrightsville, testifies that in November and December last James Haight pledged various items of jewelry at Simpson's Pawnshop.

Q.—What kind of jewelry, Mr Simpson? A.—First one was a man's gold watch—he took it off his chain to pawn it. Nice merchandise. Fair price—

Q.—Is this the watch? A.—Yes, sir. I remember givin' him a fair price—

Q.—Placed in evidence.

Clerk: People's exhibit thirty-one.

Q.—Will you read the inscription on the watch, Mr Simpson? A.—The what? Oh. 'To—Jim—from—Nora.'

Q.—What else did the defendant pawn, Mr Simpson? A.— Gold and platinum rings, a cameo brooch, and so on. All good merchandise. Very good loan merchandise.

Q.—Do you recognize these items of jewelry I now show you, Mr Simpson? A.—Yes, sir. They're the ones he pawned with me. Gave him mighty fair prices—

Q.—Never mind what you gave him. These last items are all women's jewelry, are they not? A.—That's right.

Q.—Read the various inscriptions. Aloud. A.—Wait till I fix my specs. 'N.W.'—'N.W.'—'N.W.H.'—'N.W.'

Nora's jewelry is placed in evidence.

Q.—One last question, Mr Simpson. Did the defendant ever redeem any of the objects he pawned with you? A.—No, sir. He just kept bringing me new stuff, one at a time, an' I kept givin' him fair prices for 'em.

Judge Martin waives cross-examination.

Donald Mackenzie, President of the Wrightsville Personal Finance Corporation, being duly sworn, testifies that James Haight had borrowed considerable sums from the PFC during the last two months of the preceding year.

Q.—On what collateral, Mr Mackenzie? A.—None.

Q.—Isn't this unusual for your firm, Mr Mackenzie? To lend money without collateral? A.—Well, the PFC has a *very* liberal loan policy, but of course we usually ask for collateral. Just business, you understand. Only, since Mr Haight was Vice-President of the Wrightsville National Bank and the son-in-law of John Fowler Wright, the company made an exception in his case and advanced the loans on signature only.

Q.—Has the defendant made any payments against his indebtedness, Mr Mackenzie? A.—Well, no.

Q.—Has your company made any effort to collect the moneys due, Mr Mackenzie? A.—Well, yes. Not that we were worried, but—well, it was five thousand dollars, and after asking Mr Haight several times to make his stipulated payments and getting no satisfaction, we—I finally went to the bank to see Mr Wright, Mr Haight's father-in-law, and explained the situation, and Mr Wright said he hadn't known about his son-in-law's loan but of course he'd make it good himself, and I wasn't to say anything about it—to keep it confidential. I would have, too, only this trial and all—

Judge Martin: Objection. Incompetent, irrelevant—

Q.—Never mind that, Mr Mackenzie. Did John F. Wright repay your company the loan in full? A.—Principal and interest. Yes, sir.

Q.—Has the defendant borrowed any money since January the first of this year? A.—No, sir.

Q.—Have you had any conversations with the defendant since January the first of this year? A.—Yes. Mr Haight came in to see me in the middle of January and started to explain why he hadn't paid anything on his loan—said he'd made some bad investments—asked for more time and said he'd surely pay back his debt. I said to him that his father-in-law'd already done that.

Q.—What did the defendant say to that? A.—He didn't say a word. He just walked out of my office.

Judge Martin cross-examines.

Q.—Mr Mackenzie, didn't it strike you as strange that the Vice-President of a banking institution like the Wrightsville National Bank, and the son-in-law of the President of that bank, should come to *you* for a loan? A.—Well, I guess it did. Only I figured it was a confidential matter, you see—

Q.—In a confidential matter, without explanations or collateral, on a mere signature, you still advanced the sum of five thousand dollars? A.—Well, I knew old John F. would make good if—

Mr Bradford: Your Honor—

Judge Martin: That's all, Mr Mackenzie.

Not all the evidence against Jim Haight came out in the courtroom. Some of it came out in Vic Carlatti's, some in the Hollis Hotel Tonsorial Parlor, some in Dr Emil Poffenberger's dental office in the Upham Block, some in Gus Olesen's *Roadside Tavern*, and at least one colorful fact was elicited from the bibulous Mr Anderson by a New York reporter, the scene of the interview being the pedestal of the Low Village World War Memorial, on which Mr Anderson happened to be stretched out at the time.

Emmeline DuPré heard the Luigi Marino story through Tessie Lupin. Miss DuPré was having her permanent done in the Lower Main Beauty Shop where Tessie worked, and Tessie had just had lunch with her husband Joe, who was one of Luigi Marino's barbers. Joe had told Tessie, and Tessie had told Emmy DuPré, and Emmy DuPré...

Then the town began to hear the other stories, and the old recollections were raked over for black and shining dirt. And when it was all put together, Wrightsville began to say: Now there's something funny going on. Do you suppose Frank Lloyd was right about Carter Bradford's being the Wrights' friend and all? Why doesn't he put Luigi and Dr Poffenberger on the stand?

181

And Gus Olesen? And the others? Why, this all makes it plain as day that Jim Haight wanted to kill Nora! He *threatened* her all over town!

Chief Dakin was tackled by Luigi Marino before court opened one morning when the Chief came in for a quick shave. Joe Lupin listened from the next chair with both hairy ears. 'Say, Chefe!' said Luigi in great excitement. 'I been lookin' all over for-a you! I just remember something hot!'

'Yeah, Luigi? Once over, and take it easy.'

'Las' Novemb'. Jim-a Haight, he come in here one day for I should cut-a his hair. I say to Mist' Haight, "Mist' Haight, I feel-a fine. You know what? I'm-a gonna get hitched!" Mist' Haight he say that's-a good, who's-a the lucky gal? I say: "Francesca Botigliano. I know Francesca from the ol' countree. She been workin' by Saint-a Louey, but I propose-a in a lett' an' now Francesca she's-a comin' to Wrights-a-ville to be Mrs Marino—I send-a her the ticket an' expense-a mon' myself. Ain't that something?" You remember I get-a married, Chefe...'

'Sure, Luigi. Hey, take it easy!'

'So what-a does Mist' Haight say? He say: "Luigi, nev' marry a poor gal! There ain't-a no per-cent-age in it!" You see? He marry that-a gal Nora Wright for her mon'! You get-a Mist' Bradford put me on-a stand. I'll tell-a dat story!'

Chief Dakin laughed. But Wrightsville did not. To Wrightsville it seemed logical that Luigi's story should be part of the trial testimony. It would show that he married Nora Wright for her money. If a man would marry a woman for her money, he'd poison her for it, too...Those ladies of Wrightsville who were so unfortunate as to have lawyers in the family heard a few pointed remarks about 'admissible' testimony.

Dr Poffenberger had actually gone to Prosecutor Bradford before the trial and offered to testify. 'Why, Haight came to me last December, Cart, suffering from an abscessed wisdom tooth. I gave him gas, and while he was under the influence of the gas he kept saying: "I'll get rid of her! I'll get rid of her!" And then he said: "I need that money for myself. I want that money for myself!" Doesn't that prove he was planning to kill her, and why?'

'No,' said Bradford wearily. 'Unconscious utterances. Inadmissible testimony. Go 'way, Emil, and let me work, will you?'

Dr Poffenberger was indignant. He repeated the story to as many of his patients as would listen, which was practically all of them.

Gus Olesen's story reached the Prosecutor's ears by way of Patrolman Chris Dorfman, Radio Division (one car). Patrolman Chris Dorfman had 'happened' to drop into Gus Olesen's place for a 'coke' (*he* said), and Gus, 'all het up,' had told him what Jim Haight had once said to him, Gus, on the occasion of a 'spree.' And now Patrolman Chris Dorfman was all het up, for he had been wondering for weeks how he could muscle into the trial and take the stand and get into the papers.

'Just what is it Haight is supposed to have said, Chris?' asked Prosecutor Bradford.

'Well, Gus says Jim Haight a couple of times drove up to the *Tavern* cockeyed and wanting a drink, and Gus says he'd always turn him down. Once he even called up Mrs Haight and asked her to come down and get her husband, he was raisin' Cain, plastered to the ears. But the thing Gus remembers that I think you ought to get into your trial, Mr Bradford, is when one night Haight was in there, drunk, and he kept ravin' about wives, and marriage, and how lousy it all was, and then said: "Nothin' to do but get rid of her, Gus. I gotta get rid of her quick or I'll go nuts. She's drivin' me nuts!"'

'Statements under the influence of liquor,' groaned Cart. 'Highly questionable. Do you want me to lose this case on reversible error? Go back to your radio car!'

Mr Anderson's story was simplicity itself. With dignity he told the New York reporter: 'Sir, Mr Haight an' I have quaffed the purple flagon on many an occasion together. Kindred spirits, you understand. We would meet in the Square an' embrace. Well do I recall that eventful evening in "dark December," when "in this our pinching cave," we discoursed "the freezing hours away"! *Cymbeline,* sir; a much-neglected master work...'

'We wander,' said the reporter. 'What happened?'

'Well, sir, Mr Haight put his arms about me and he said, Quote: "I'm going to kill her, Andy. See 'f I don't! I'm going to kill her dead!"'

'Wow,' said the reporter, and left Mr Anderson to go back to sleep on the pedestal of the Low Village World War Memorial.

But this luscious morsel, too, Prosecutor Bradford refused; and Wrightsville muttered that there was 'something phony,' and buzzed and buzzed and buzzed.

The rumors reached Judge Lysander Newbold's ears. From that day on, at the end of each court session, he sternly admonished the jury not to discuss the case with anyone, not even among themselves.

It was thought that Eli Martin had something to do with calling the rumors to Judge Newbold's attention. For Judge Martin was beginning to look harried, particularly in the mornings, after breakfast with his wife. Clarice, who served in her own peculiar way, was his barometer for readings of the temper of Wrightsville. So a fury began to creep into the courtroom, and it mounted and flew back and forth between the old lawyer and Carter Bradford until the press began to nudge one another with wise looks and say 'the old boy is cracking.'

Thomas Winship, head cashier of the Wrightsville National Bank, testified that James Haight had always used a thin red crayon in his work at the bank, and produced numerous documents from the files of the bank, signed by Haight in red crayon.

The last exhibit placed in evidence by Bradford—a shrewd piece of timing—was the volume Edgcomb's *Toxicology,* with its telltale section marked in red crayon...the section dealing with arsenic. This exhibit passed from hand to hand in the jury box, while Judge Martin looked 'confident' and James Haight, by the old lawyer's side at the defense table, grew very pale and was seen to glance about quickly, as if seeking escape. But the moment passed, and thenceforward he behaved as before— silent, limp in his chair, his gray face almost bored.

184

At the close of Friday's session, March the twenty-eighth, Prosecutor Bradford indicated that he 'might be close to finished,' but that he would know better when court convened the following Monday morning. He thought it likely the People would rest on Monday. There was an interminable conversation before the Bench, and then Judge Newbold called a recess until Monday morning, March the thirty-first.

The prisoner was taken back to his cell on the top floor of the Courthouse, the courtroom emptied, and the Wrights simply went home. There was nothing to do but wait for Monday...and try to cheer Nora up. Nora lay on the chaise longue in her pretty bedroom, plucking the roses of her chintz window drapes. Hermy had refused to let her attend the trial; and after two days of tears, Nora had stopped fighting, exhausted. She just plucked the roses from the drapes.

But another thing happened on Friday, March the twenty-eighth. Roberta Roberts lost her job. The newspaper woman had maintained her stubborn defense of Jim Haight in her column throughout the trial—the only reporter there who had not already condemned 'God's silent man,' as one of the journalistic wits had dubbed him, to death. On Friday Roberta received a wire from Boris Connell in Chicago, notifying her that he was 'yanking the column.' Roberta telegraphed a Chicago attorney to bring suit against News & Features Syndicate. But on Saturday morning there was no column.

'What are you going to do now?' asked Ellery Queen.

'Stay on in Wrightsville. I'm one of those pesky females who never give up. I can still do Jim Haight some good.'

She spent the whole of Saturday morning in Jim's cell, urging him to speak up, to fight back, to strike a blow in his own defense. Judge Martin was there, quite pursy-lipped, and Ellery; they heard Roberta's vigorous plea in silence. But Jim merely shook his head, or made no answering gesture at all—a figure bowed, three-quarters dead, pickled in some strange formaldehyde of his own manufacture.

185

22

Council of War

The whole week end stood between them and Monday. So on Saturday night Nora invited Roberta Roberts and Judge Eli Martin to dinner to 'talk things over' with the family. Hermione wanted Nora to stay in bed, because of her 'condition'; but Nora said: 'Oh, Mother, it will do me lots more good to be up on my feet and going through some motions!' So Hermy wisely did not press the point.

Nora was beginning to thicken noticeably about the waist; her cheeks were puffy and unhealthy-looking suddenly, and she walked about the house as if her legs were stuffed with lead. When Hermione questioned Dr Willoughby anxiously, he said that 'Nora's getting along about as well as we can expect, Hermy.' Hermy didn't dare ask him any more questions. But she rarely left Nora's side, and she would go white if she saw Nora try to lift so much as a long biography.

After dinner, which was tasteless and uneasy, they all went into the living room. Ludie had tightly flapped the blinds and lit a fire. They sat before it with the uncomfortable stiffness of people who know they should say something, but cannot think of what. There was no solace anywhere, not even in the friendly flames. It was impossible to relax—Nora was too much there. 'Mr Smith, you haven't said much tonight,' remarked Roberta Roberts at last.

Nora looked at Ellery beseechingly; but he avoided her eyes. 'There hasn't been too much to say, has there?'

'No,' the newspaper woman murmured. 'I suppose not.'

'As I see the problem before us, it's not intellectual, or emotional, but legal. Faith isn't going to acquit Jim, although it may bolster his spirits. Only facts can get him off.'

'And there aren't any!' cried Nora.

'Nora dearest,' moaned Hermy. 'Please. You heard what Dr Willoughby said about getting upset.'

'I know, Mother, I know.' Nora glanced eagerly at Judge Eli Martin, whose long fingers were bridged before his nose as he glowered at the fire. 'How does it look, Uncle Eli?'

'I wouldn't want to deceive you, Nora.' The old jurist shook his head. 'It looks just as bad as it possibly can.'

'You mean Jim hasn't got a chance?' she wailed.

'There's always a chance, Nora,' said Roberta Roberts.

'Yes,' sighed the Judge. 'You never can tell about a jury.'

'If there was only something we could *do*,' said Hermy helplessly.

John F. burrowed more deeply into his smoking jacket.

'Oh, you people!' cried Lola Wright. 'Moaning the blues! I'm sick of this sitting around, wringing our hands—' Lola flung her cigarette into the flames with disgust.

'So am I,' said Pat between her teeth. 'Sick as the devil.'

'Patricia darling,' said Hermy, 'I'm sure you'd better stay out of this discussion.'

'Of course, Momsy,' said Lola with a grimace. '*Your* baby. You'll never see Pat as anything but a long-legged brat who wouldn't drink her nice milk and kept climbing Emmy DuPré's cherry tree!'

Pat shrugged. Mr Ellery Queen regarded her with suspicion.

Miss Patricia Wright had been acting peculiarly since Thursday. Too quiet. Over-thoughtful for a healthy extrovert. As if she were brewing something in that fetching skullpan of hers. He started to say something to her, but lit a cigarette instead. The Gold Rush of '49, he thought, started with a battered pan in a muddy trickle of water. Who knows where the Fact may be found?

'Ellery, what *do* you think?' pleaded Nora.

'Ellery's been mulling over the case looking for a loophole,' Pat explained to Judge Martin.

'Not legally,' Ellery hastened to explain as the Judge's brows went up. 'But I've been handling crime facts so long in fiction that I've—uh—acquired a certain dexterity in handling them in real life.'

'If you juggle *these* with any success,' growled the old lawyer, 'you're a magician.'

'Isn't there *anything*?' Nora cried.

'Let's face it, Nora,' said Ellery grimly. 'Jim's in a hopeless position. You'd better prepare yourself...I've gone over the whole case. I've sifted every grain of evidence in the hopper, I've weighed every known fact. I've re-examined each incident a dozen times. And I haven't found a loophole. There's never been so one-sided a case against a defendant. Carter Bradford and Chief Dakin have built a giant, and it will take a miracle to topple it over.'

'And I,' said Judge Eli dryly, 'am no Goliath.'

'Oh, I'm prepared all right,' said Nora with a bitter laugh. She twisted about violently in her chair and dropped her face on her arms.

'Sudden movements!' said Hermy in an alarmed voice. 'Nora, you've *got* to be careful!' Nora nodded without raising her head. And silence entered, to fill the room to bursting.

'Look here,' said Ellery at last. He was a black man against the flames. 'Miss Roberts, I want to know something.'

The newspaper woman said slowly: 'Yes, Mr Smith?'

'You've lost your column because you chose to buck public opinion and fight for Jim Haight.'

'This is still a free country, thank God,' said Roberta lightly. But she was sitting very still.

'Why have you taken such a remarkable interest in this case— even to the point of sacrificing your job?'

'I happen to believe Jim Haight is innocent.'

'In the face of all the evidence against him?'

She smiled. 'I'm a woman. I'm psychic. That's two reasons.'

'No,' said Ellery.

Roberta got to her feet. 'I'm not sure I like that,' she said clearly. 'What are you trying to say?' The others were frowning. There was something in the room that crackled more loudly than the burning logs.

'It's too beautiful,' mocked Mr Queen. 'Too, too beautiful. Hard-boiled newspaper woman renounces livelihood to defend total stranger who—all the facts and all the world agree—is guilty as Cain. There's an excuse for Nora—she's in love with the man. There's an excuse for the Wrights—they want their son-in-law cleared for the sake of their daughter and grandchild. But what's yours?'

'I've told you!'

'I don't believe you.'

'You don't. What am I supposed to do—care?'

'Miss Roberts,' said Ellery in a hard voice, 'what are you concealing?'

'I refuse to submit to this third degree.'

'Sorry! But it's plain you do know something. You've known something from the time you came to Wrightsville. What you know has *forced* you to come to Jim's defense. *What is it?*'

The newspaper woman gathered her gloves and silver-fox coat and bag. 'There are times, Mr Smith,' she said, 'when I dislike you very much...No, please, Mrs Wright. Don't bother.' She went out with a quick step.

Mr Queen stared at the space she had just vacated. 'I thought,'

189

he said apologetically, 'I might be able to irritate it out of her.'

'I think,' said Judge Martin reflectively, 'I'll have a heart-to-heart talk with that female.'

Ellery shrugged. 'Lola.'

'Me?' said Lola surprised. 'What did I do, teacher?'

'You've concealed something, too.'

Lola stared. Then she laughed and lit a cigarette. 'You *are* in a Scotland Yard mood tonight, aren't you?'

'Don't you think the time has come,' smiled Mr Queen, 'to tell Judge Martin about your visit to the back door of Nora's house just before midnight New Year's Eve?'

'Lola!' gasped Hermy. 'You were *there?*'

'Oh, it's nothing at all, Mother,' said Lola impatiently. 'It hasn't a thing to do with the case. Of course, Judge, I'll tell you. But as long as we're being constructive, how about the eminent Mr Smith getting to work?'

'At what?' asked the eminent Mr Smith.

'My dear Smarty-Pants, you know a lot more than you've let on!'

'Lola,' said Nora, in despair. 'Oh, all this wrangling—'

'Don't you think,' cried Pat, 'that if there were something Ellery could do, he'd do it?'

'I dunno,' said Lola critically, squinting at the culprit through her cigarette smoke. 'He's a tough 'un to figure.'

'Just a minute,' said Judge Martin. 'Smith, if you know anything at all, I want to put you on the stand!'

'If I thought going on the stand for you would help, Judge,' protested Ellery, 'I'd do it. But it won't. On the contrary, it would hurt—a lot.'

'Hurt Jim's case?'

'It would just about cement his conviction.'

John F. spoke for the first time. 'You mean you *know* Jim is guilty, young man?'

'I didn't say that,' growled Ellery. 'But my testimony would make things look so black against him—it would establish so

clearly that no one but Jim could have poisoned that cocktail—
that you wouldn't be able to shake it with the Supreme Court to
help you. *I mustn't take the stand.'*

'Mr Smith.' Chief Dakin, alone... 'Sorry to bust in this way,
folks,' said the police chief gruffly, 'but this was one subpoena I
had to serve myself.'

'Subpoena? On me?' asked Ellery.

'Yes, sir. Mr Smith, you're summoned to appear in court Monday morning to testify for the People in the case of People
Against James Haight.'

Part Five

23

Lola and the Check

'I got one, too,' murmured Lola to Ellery Queen in the courtroom Monday morning.

'Got one what?'

'A summons to testify today for the beloved People.'

'Strange,' muttered Mr Queen.

'The pup's got something up his sleeve,' said Judge Martin. 'And what's J.C. doing in court?'

'Who?' Ellery looked about.

'J.C. Pettigrew, the real estate man. There's Bradford whispering to him. J.C. can't know anything about this case.'

Lola said in a strangled voice. 'Oh, nuts,' and they stared at her. She was very pale.

'What's the matter, Lola?' asked Pat.

'Nothing. I'm sure it can't possibly—'

'Here's Newbold,' said Judge Martin, hastily standing up. 'Remember, Lola, just answer Carter's questions. Don't volunteer information. Maybe,' he whispered grimly as the bailiff shouted to the courtroom to rise, 'maybe I've got a trick or two myself on cross-examination!'

*   *   *

J.C. Pettigrew sat down in the witness chair shaking and swabbing his face with a blue polka-dot handkerchief, such as the
farmers around Wrightsville use. Yes, his name is J.C. Pettigrew,
he is in the real estate business in Wrightsville, he's been a friend
of the Wrights for many years—his daughter Carmel is Patricia
Wright's best friend. (Patricia Wright compresses her lips. Her
'best friend' has not telephoned since January first.)

There was an aqueous triumph about Carter Bradford this
morning. His own brow was slick with perspiration, and he and
J.C. kept up a duet of handkerchiefs.

Q.—I hand you this cancelled check, Mr Pettigrew. Do you
recognize it? A.—Yep.

Q.—Read what it says. A.—The date—December thirty-first,
nineteen-forty. Then it says: pay to the order of cash, one hundred dollars. Signed J.C. Pettigrew.

Q.—Did you make out this check, Mr Pettigrew? A.—I did.

Q.—On the date specified—the last day of last year, the day of
New Year's Eve? A.—Yes, sir.

Q.—To whom did you give this check, Mr Pettigrew? A.—To
Lola Wright.

Q.—Tell us the circumstances of your giving Miss Lola Wright
this check for a hundred dollars, please. A.—I sort of feel funny
about…I mean, I can't help it…Well, last day of the year, I was
just cleaning up at my office in High Village when Lola came in.
Said she was in a bad spot, and she'd known me all her life, and
could I let her have a hundred dollars. I saw she was worried—

Q.—Just tell us what she said and you said. A.—Well, that's
all, I guess. I gave it to her. Oh, yes. She asked for cash. I said I
didn't have any cash to spare, and it was past banking hours, so
I'd give her a check. She said: 'Well, if it can't be helped, it can't
be helped.' So I made out a check, she said thanks, and that's all.
Can I go now?

Q.—Did Miss Wright tell you what she wanted the money
for? A.—No, sir, and I didn't ask her.

196

The check was placed in evidence, and when Judge Martin, who had been about to demand the deletion of all J.C.'s remarks, turned the check over and saw what was written on the other side, he blanched and bit his lip. Then he waved his hand magnanimously and declined to cross-examine. J.C. stumbled and almost fell, he was so anxious to get off the stand. He sent Hermy a sickly smile. His face was steaming, and he kept swabbing it.

Lola Wright was nervous as she took the oath, but her gaze was defiant, and it made Carter Bradford flush. He showed her the check in evidence. 'Miss Wright, what did you do with this check when you first received it from J.C. Pettigrew on December thirty-first last?'

'I put it in my purse,' said Lola. There were titters. But Judge Martin frowned, so Lola sat up straighter.

'Yes I know,' said Carter, 'but to whom did you give it?'

'I don't remember.'

Foolish girl, thought Ellery. He's got you. Don't make things worse by being difficult. Bradford held the check up before her. 'Miss Wright, perhaps this will refresh your memory. Read the endorsement on the back, please.'

Lola swallowed. Then she said in a low voice: '"James Haight."' At the defense table James Haight unaccountably seized that instant to smile. It was the weariest smile imaginable. Then he sank into apathy again.

'Can you explain how James Haight's endorsement appears on a check you borrowed from J.C. Pettigrew?'

'I gave it to Jim.'

'When?'

'That same night.'

'Where?'

'At the house of my sister Nora.'

'At the house of your sister Nora. Have you heard the testimony here to the effect that you were not present at the house of your sister Nora during the New Year's Eve party?'

'Yes.'

'Well, were you or weren't you?'

There was something in Bradford's voice that was a little cruel, and Pat writhed in her seat in front of the rail, her lips saying: 'I hate you!' almost aloud.

'I did stop at the house for a few minutes, but I wasn't at the party.'

'I see. Were you invited to the party?'

'Yes.'

'But you didn't go?'

'No.'

'Why not?'

Judge Martin objected, and Judge Newbold sustained him. Bradford smiled. 'Did anyone see you but your brother-in-law, the defendant?'

'No. I went around to the back door of the kitchen.'

'Then did you *know* Jim Haight was in the kitchen?' asked Carter Bradford quickly.

Lola grew pink. 'Yes. I hung around outside in the back yard till I saw, through the kitchen window, that Jim came in. He disappeared in the butler's pantry, and I thought there might be someone with him. But after a few minutes I decided he was alone, and knocked. Jim came out of the pantry to the kitchen door, and we talked.'

'About what, Miss Wright?'

Lola glanced at Judge Martin in a confused way. He made as if to rise, then sank back.

'I gave Jim the check.' Ellery was leaning far forward. So that had been Lola's mission! He had not been able to overhear, or see, what had passed between Jim and Lola at the back door of Nora's kitchen that night.

'You gave him the check,' said Bradford courteously. 'Miss Wright, did the defendant ask you to give him money?'

'No!'

Ellery smiled grimly. Liar—of the genus white.

'But didn't you borrow the hundred dollars from Mr Petti-grew for the purpose of giving it to the defendant?'

'Yes,' said Lola coolly. 'Only it was in repayment of a debt I owed Jim. I owe everybody, you see—chronic borrower. I'd bor-rowed from Jim some time before, so I paid him back, that's all.'

And Ellery recalled that night when he had trailed Jim to Lola's apartment in Low Village, and how Jim had drunkenly demanded money and Lola had said she didn't have any...Only it wasn't true that on New Year's Eve Lola had repaid a 'debt.' Lola had made a donation to Nora's happiness.

'You borrowed from Pettigrew to pay Haight?' asked Carter, raising his eyebrows. (*Laughter.*)

'The witness has answered,' said Judge Eli.

Bradford waved. 'Miss Wright, did Haight ask you for the money you say you owed him?'

Lola said, too quickly: 'No, he didn't.'

'You just decided suddenly, on the last day of the year, that you'd better pay him back—without any suggestion from him?' Objection. Argument. At it again.

'Miss Wright, you have only a small income, have you not?' Objection. Argument. Heat now. Judge Newbold excused the jury. Bradford said sternly to Judge Newbold: 'Your Honor, it is impor-tant to the People to show that this witness, herself in badly reduced circumstances, was nevertheless somehow induced by the defendant to get money for him, thus indicating his basic char-acter, how desperate he was for money—all part of the People's case to show his gain motive for the poisoning.' The jury was brought back. Bradford went at Lola once more, with savage per-sistence. Feathers flew again; but when it was over, the jury was convinced of Bradford's point, juries being notoriously unable to forget what judges instruct them to forget.

But Judge Martin was not beaten. On cross-examination he sailed in almost with joy. 'Miss Wright,' said the old lawyer, 'you have testified in direct examination that on the night of New Year's Eve last you called at the back door of your sister's house. What time was that visit, do you recall?'

'Yes. I looked at my wrist watch, because I had a—a party of my own to go to in town. It was just before midnight— fifteen minutes before the New Year was rung in.'

'You also testified that you saw your brother-in-law go into the butler's pantry, and after a moment or two you knocked and he came out to you, and you talked. Where exactly did that conversation take place?'

'At the back door of the kitchen.'

'What did you say to Jim?'

'I asked him what he was doing, and he said he was just finishing mixing a lot of Manhattan cocktails for the crowd—he'd about got to the maraschino cherries when I knocked, he said. Then I told him about the check—'

'Did you see the cocktails he referred to?'

The room rustled like an agitated aviary, and Carter Bradford leaned forward, frowning. This was important—this was the time the poisoning must have taken place. After that ripple of sound, the courtroom was very still. 'No,' said Lola. 'Jim had come from the direction of the pantry to answer the door, so I know that's where he'd been mixing the cocktails. From where I was standing, at the back door, I couldn't see into the pantry. So of course I couldn't see the cocktails, either.'

'Ah! Miss Wright, had someone sneaked into the kitchen from the main hall or the dining room while you and Mr Haight were talking at the back door, would you have been able to see the person?'

'No. The door from the dining room doesn't open into the kitchen; it leads directly into the pantry. And while the door from the hall does open into the kitchen and *is* visible from the back door, I couldn't see it because Jim was standing in front of me, blocking my view.'

'In other words, Miss Wright, while you and Mr Haight were

talking—Mr Haight with his back to the rest of the kitchen, you unable to see most of the kitchen because he was blocking your view—someone *could* have slipped into the kitchen through the hall door, crossed to the pantry, and retraced his steps without either of you being aware of what had happened or who it had been?'

'That's correct, Judge.'

'Or someone could have entered the pantry through the dining room during that period, and neither you nor Mr Haight could have seen him?'

'Of course we couldn't have seen him. I told you that the pantry is out of sight of—'

'How long did this conversation at the back door take?'

'Oh, five minutes, I should think.'

'That will be all, thank you,' said the Judge triumphantly.

Carter Bradford climbed to his feet for a redirect examination. The courtroom was whispering, the jury looked thoughtful, and Carter's hair looked excited. But he was very considerate in manner and tone. 'Miss Wright, I know this is painful for you, but we must get this story of yours straight. *Did* anyone enter the pantry either through the kitchen or the dining room while you were conversing at the back door with Jim Haight?'

'I don't know. I merely said someone could have, and we wouldn't have known the difference.'

'Then you can't really say that someone *did*?'

'I can't say someone did, but by the same token I can't say someone didn't. As a matter of fact, it might very easily have happened.'

'But you *didn't* see anyone enter the pantry, and you *did* see Jim Haight come out of the pantry?'

'Yes, but—'

'And you saw Jim Haight go back into the pantry?'

'No such thing,' said Lola with asperity. 'I turned around and went away, leaving Jim at the door!'

'That's all,' said Carter softly; he even tried to help her off the stand, but Lola drew herself up and went back to her chair haughtily.

'I should like,' said Carter to the Court, 'to recall one of my previous witnesses. Frank Lloyd.'

As the bailiff bellowed: 'Frank Lloyd to the stand!' Mr Ellery Queen said to himself: 'The build-up.'

Lloyd's cheeks were yellow, as if something were rotting his blood. He shuffled to the stand, unkempt, slovenly, tight-mouthed. He looked once at Jim Haight, not ten feet away from him. Then he looked away, but there was evil in his green eyes. He was on the stand only a few minutes. The substance of his testimony, surgically excised by Bradford, was that he now recalled an important fact which he had forgotten in his previous testimony. Jim Haight had not been the only one out of the living room during the time he was mixing the last batch of cocktails before midnight. There had been one other.

Q.—And who was that, Mr Lloyd? A.—A guest of the Wrights'. Ellery Smith.

You clever animal, thought Ellery admiringly. And now I'm the animal, and I'm trapped...What to do?

Q.—Mr Smith left the room directly after the defendant? A.— Yes. He didn't return until Haight came back with the tray of cocktails and started passing them around.

This is it, thought Mr Queen. Carter Bradford turned around and looked directly into Ellery's eyes. 'I call,' said Cart with a snap in his voice, 'Ellery Smith.'

24

Ellery Smith to the Stand

As Mr Ellery Queen left his seat, and crossed the courtroom foreground, and took the oath, and sat down in the witness chair, his mind was not occupied with Prosecutor Bradford's unuttered questions or his own unuttered answers. He was reasonably certain what questions Bradford intended to ask, and he was positive what answers he would give. Bradford knew, or guessed, from the scene opened up to him by Frank Lloyd's delayed recollection, what part the mysterious Mr 'Smith' had played that bitter night. So one question would lead to another, and suspicion would become certainty, and sooner or later the whole story would have to come out. It never occurred to Ellery that he might frankly lie. Not because he was a saint, or a moralist, or afraid of consequences; but because his whole training had been in the search for truth, and he knew that whereas murder will not necessarily out, the truth must. So it was more practical to tell the truth than to tell the lie. Moreover, people expected you to lie in court, and therein lay a great advantage, if only you were clever enough to seize it.

No, Mr Queen's thoughts were occupied with another question altogether. And that was: How to turn the truth, so damning to Jim Haight on its face, to Jim Haight's advantage? That would be a shrewd blow, if only it could be delivered; and it would have the additional strength of unexpectedness, for surely young Bradford would never anticipate what he himself, now, on the stand, could not even imagine.

So Mr Queen sat waiting, his brain not deigning to worry, but flexing itself, exploring, dipping into its deepest pockets, examining all the things he knew for a hint, a clue, a road to follow.

Another conviction crept into his consciousness as he answered the first routine questions about his name and occupation and connection with the Wright family, and so on; and it arose from Carter Bradford himself. Bradford was disciplining his tongue, speaking impersonally; but there was a bitterness about his speech that was not part of the words he was uttering. Cart was remembering that this lean and quiet-eyed man theoretically at his mercy was, in a sense, an author of more than books—he was the author of Mr Bradford's romantic troubles, too. Patty's personality shimmered between them, and Mr Queen remarked it with satisfaction; it was another advantage he held over his inquisitor. For Patty blinded young Mr Bradford's eyes and drugged his quite respectable intelligence. Mr Queen noted the advantage and tucked it away and returned to his work of concentration while the uppermost forces of his mind paid attention to the audible questions.

And suddenly he saw how he could make the truth work for Jim Haight! He almost chuckled as he leaned back and gave his whole mind to the man before him. The very first pertinent question reassured him—Bradford was on the trail, his tongue hanging out.

'Do you recollect, Mr Smith, that we found the three letters in the defendant's handwriting as a result of Mrs Haight's hysterical belief that you had told us about them?'

'Yes.'

'Do you also recall two unsuccessful attempts on my part that day to find out from you what you knew about the letters?'

'Quite well.'

Bradford said softly: 'Mr Smith, today you are on the witness stand, under oath to tell the whole truth. I now ask you: Did you know of the existence of those three letters before Chief Dakin found them in the defendant's house?'

And Ellery said: 'Yes, I did.'

Bradford was surprised, almost suspicious. 'When did you first learn about them?'

Ellery told him, and Bradford's surprise turned into satisfaction. 'Under what circumstances?' This was a rapped question, tinged with contempt. Ellery answered meekly.

'Then you knew Mrs Haight was in danger from her husband?'

'Not at all. I knew there were three letters saying so by implication.'

'Well, did you or did you not believe the defendant wrote those letters?'

Judge Martin made as if to object, but Mr Queen caught the Judge's eye and shook his head ever so slightly.

'I didn't know.'

'Didn't Miss Patricia Wright identify her brother-in-law's handwriting for you, as you just testified?'

Miss Patricia Wright, sitting fifteen feet away, looked murder at them both impartially.

'She did. But that did not make it so.'

'Did you check up yourself?'

'Yes. But I don't pretend to be a handwriting expert.'

'But you must have come to some conclusion, Mr Smith?'

'Objection!' shouted Judge Martin, unable to contain himself. 'His conclusion.'

'Strike out the question,' directed Judge Newbold.

Bradford smiled. 'You also examined the volume belonging to

the defendant, Edgcomb's *Toxicology*, particularly pages seventy-one and seventy-two, devoted to arsenic, with certain sentences underlined in red crayon?'

'I did.'

'You knew from the red-crayon underlining in the book that if a crime *were* going to be committed, death by arsenic poisoning was indicated?'

'We could quarrel about the distinction between certainty and probability,' replied Mr Queen sadly, 'but to save argument—let's say I knew; yes.'

'It seems to me, Your Honor,' said Eli Martin in a bored voice, 'that this is an entirely improper line of questioning.'

'How so, Counsel?' inquired Judge Newbold.

'Because Mr Smith's thoughts and conclusions, whether certainties, probabilities, doubts, or anything else, have no conceivable bearing upon the facts at issue.'

Bradford smiled again, and when Judge Newbold asked him to limit his questions to events and conversations, he nodded carelessly, as if it did not matter. 'Mr Smith, were you aware that the third letter of the series talked about the "death" of Mrs Haight as if it had occurred on New Year's Eve?'

'Yes.'

'During the New Year's Eve party under examination, did you keep following the defendant out of the living room?'

'I did.'

'You were keeping an eye on him all evening?'

'Yes.'

'You watched him mix cocktails in the pantry?'

'Yes.'

'Now do you recall the last time before midnight the defendant mixed cocktails?'

'Distinctly.'

'Where did he mix them?'

'In the butler's pantry off the kitchen.'

'Did you follow him there from the living room?'

'Yes, by way of the hall. The hall leads from the foyer to the rear of the house. He entered the kitchen and went into the pantry; I was just behind him but stopped in the hall, beside the door.'

'Did he see you?'

'I haven't the faintest idea.'

'But you were careful not to be seen?'

Mr Queen smiled. 'I was neither careful nor careless. I just stood there beside the half-open hall door to the kitchen.'

'Did the defendant turn around to look at you?' persisted Bradford.

'No.'

'But *you* could see *him?*'

'Clearly.'

'What did the defendant do?'

'He prepared some Manhattan cocktails in a mixing glass. He poured some into each of a number of clean glasses standing on a tray. He was reaching for the bottle of maraschino cherries, which had been standing on the pantry table, when there was a knock at the back door. He left the cocktails and went out into the kitchen to see who had knocked.'

'That was when Miss Lola Wright and the defendant had the conversation just testified to?'

'Yes.'

'The tray of cocktails left in the butler's pantry were visible to you all during the period in which the defendant conversed with Lola Wright at the kitchen back door?'

'Yes, indeed.'

Carter Bradford hesitated. Then he asked flatly: 'Did you see anyone go near those cocktails between the time the defendant left them in the pantry and the time he returned?'

Mr Queen replied: 'I saw no one, because there wasn't anyone.'

'The pantry remained absolutely empty during that period?'

'Of organic life—yes.'

Bradford could scarcely conceal his elation; he made a brave but unsuccessful effort. On the mourners' bench inside the railing the Wrights turned stone-faced. 'Now, Mr Smith, did you see the defendant return to the pantry after Lola Wright left?'

'I did.'

'What did he do?'

'He dropped a maraschino cherry from the bottle into each cocktail, using a small ivory pick. He picked up the tray in both hands and carefully walked through the kitchen toward the door at which I was standing. I acted casual, and we went into the living room together, where he immediately began distributing the glasses to the family and guests.'

'On his walk from the pantry to the living room with the tray, did anyone approach him except yourself?'

'No one.'

Ellery waited for the next question with equanimity. He saw the triumph gather in Bradford's eyes.

'Mr Smith, wasn't there something else you saw happen in that pantry?'

'No.'

'Nothing else happened?'

'Nothing else.'

'Have you told us *everything* you saw?'

'Everything.'

'*Didn't you see the defendant drop a white powder into one of those cocktails?*'

'No,' said Mr Queen. 'I saw nothing of the sort.'

'Then on the trip from the pantry to the living room?'

'Both Mr Haight's hands were busy holding the tray. He dropped no foreign substance of any kind into any of the cocktails at any time during their preparation or while he carried the tray into the living room.'

And then there was an undercurrent jabber in the room, and the Wrights glanced at one another with relief while Judge Martin wiped his face and Carter Bradford sneered almost with sound. 'Perhaps you turned your head for two seconds?'

'My eyes were on that tray of cocktails continuously.'

'You didn't look away for even a second, eh?'

'For even a second,' said Mr Queen regretfully, as if he wished he had, just to please Mr Bradford.

Mr Bradford grinned at the jury—man to man; and at least five jurors grinned back. Sure, what could you expect?—a friend of the Wrights'. And then everybody in town knew why Cart Bradford had stopped seeing Pat Wright. This Smith bird had a case on Patty Wright. So...

'And you didn't see Jim Haight drop arsenic into one of those cocktails?' insisted Mr Bradford, smiling broadly now.

'At the risk of seeming a bore,' replied Mr Queen with courtesy, 'no, I did not.' But he knew he had lost with the jury; they didn't believe him. He knew it, and while the Wrights didn't know it yet, Judge Martin did; the old gentleman was beginning to sweat again. Only Jim Haight sat unmoved, unchanged, wrapped in a shroud.

'Well, then, Mr Smith, answer this question: Did you see anyone else who had the *opportunity* to poison one of those cocktails?'

Mr Queen gathered himself, but before he could reply Bradford snapped: 'In fact, did you see anyone else who *did* poison one of those cocktails—anyone other than the defendant?'

'I saw no one else but—'

'In other words, Mr Smith,' cried Bradford, 'the defendant James Haight was not only in the *best* position, but he was in the *only* position, to poison that cocktail?'

'No,' said Mr Smith. And then *he* smiled. You asked for it, he thought, and I'm giving it to you. The only trouble is, I'm giving it to myself, too, and that's foolishness. He sighed and wondered what his father, Inspector Queen, no doubt reading about the case in the New York papers and conjecturing who Ellery Smith was, would have to say when he discovered Mr 'Smith's' identity and read about this act of puerile bravado.

Carter Bradford looked blank. Then he shouted: 'Are you aware that this is perjury, Smith? You just testified that no one else entered the pantry! No one approached the defendant while he was carrying the cocktails into the living room! Allow me to repeat a question or two. *Did* anyone approach the defendant during his walk to the living room with the tray?'

'No,' said Mr Queen patiently.

'*Did* someone else enter the pantry while the defendant was talking to Lola Wright at the back door?'

'No.'

Bradford was almost speechless. 'But you just said—! Smith, who but James Haight *could* have poisoned one of those cocktails, by your own testimony?'

Judge Martin was on his feet, but before he could get the word 'Objection' out of his mouth, Ellery said calmly: '*I could*.' There was a wholesale gasp before him and then a stricken silence. So he went on: 'You see, it would have been the work of ten seconds for me to slip from behind the door of the hall, cross the few feet of kitchen to the pantry unobserved by Jim or Lola at the back door, drop arsenic into one of the cocktails, return the same way…'

And there was Babel all over again, and Mr Queen looked down upon the noise makers from the highest point of his tower, smiling benignly. He was thinking: It's full of holes, but it's the best a man can do on short notice with the material at hand.

Over shouting, and Judge Newbold's gavel, and the rush of reporters, Carter Bradford bellowed in triumph: '*Well, DID you poison that cocktail, Smith?*'

There were several instants of quiet again, during which Judge Martin's voice was heard to say feebly: 'I object—' and Mr Queen's voice topped the Judge's by adding neatly: 'On constitutional grounds—'

Then hell broke loose, and Judge Newbold broke his gavel off at the head, and roared to the bailiff to clear the damn courtroom, and then he hog-called a recess until the next morning and practically ran into his chambers, where it is presumed he applied vinegar compresses to his forehead.

25

The Singular Request of Miss Patricia Wright

By the next morning several changes had taken place. Wrightsville's attention was temporarily transferred from one Jim Haight to one Ellery Smith. Frank Lloyd's newspaper came out with a blary edition reporting the sensational facts of Mr Smith's testimony; and an editorial which said, in part:—

The bombshell of Mr. Smith's testimony yesterday turns out to be a dud. There is no possible case against this man. Smith has no possible motive. He had not known Nora or James Haight or any of the Wrights before he came to Wrightsville last August. He has had practically no contact with Mrs. Haight, and less than that with Rosemary Haight. Whatever his reason for the quixotic nature of his farcical testimony yesterday—and Prosecutor Bradford is to be censured for his handling of the witness, who obviously led him on—it means nothing. Even if Smith were the only other person aside from Jim Haight who could have poisoned the fatal cocktail on New Year's Eve, he could not possibly have been sure that the one poisoned cocktail would reach Nora Haight, whereas Jim Haight could have and, in effect, did. Nor could

Smith have written the three letters, which are indisputably in the handwriting of James Haight. Wrightsville and the jury can only conclude that what happened yesterday was either a desperate gesture of friendliness on Smith's part or a cynical bid for newspaper space by a writer who is using Wrightsville as a guinea-pig.

The first thing Bradford said to Ellery on the stand the next morning was:—'I show you the official transcript of your testimony yesterday. Will you please begin to read?'

Ellery raised his brows, but he took the transcript and read:

'"Question: What is your name? Answer: Ellery Smith—"'

'Stop right there! That *is* what you testified, isn't it—that your name is Ellery Smith?'

'Yes,' said Ellery, beginning to feel cold.

'Is Smith your real name?'

Ho hum, thought Ellery. The man's a menace. 'No.'

'An assumed name, then?'

'Order in the court!' shouted the baliff.

'Yes.'

'What is your real name?'

Judge Martin said quickly: 'I don't see the point of this line of questioning, Your Honor. Mr Smith is not on trial—'

'Mr Bradford?' said Judge Newbold, who was looking curious.

'Mr Smith's testimony yesterday,' said Bradford with a faint smile, 'raised a certain logical question about what the People allege to have been the defendant's unique opportunity to poison the cocktail. Mr Smith testified that he himself was in a position to have poisoned the cocktail. My examination this morning, then, must necessarily include an examination of Mr Smith's character—'

'And you can establish Mr Smith's character by bringing out his true name?' asked Judge Newbold, frowning.

'Yes, Your Honor.'

'I think I'll allow this, Counsel, pending testimony.'

212

'Will you please answer my last question,' said Bradford to Ellery. 'What is your real name?'

Ellery saw the Wrights looking bewildered—all but Pat, who was biting her lip with vexation as well as perplexity. But it was quite clear to him that Bradford had been busy through the intervening night. The name 'Queen' carried no theoretical immunity against a charge of murder, of course; but as a practical measure its revelation would banish from the minds of the jury any notion that its well-known bearer could have had anything to do with the crime. The jig was up. Ellery Queen sighed and said: 'My name is Ellery Queen.'

Judge Martin did his best, under the circumstances. The punctuality of Bradford's timing became evident. By putting Ellery on the stand Bradford had given the defense a handhold to an important objective. But the objective was lost in the revelation of Ellery's true identity. Judge Martin hammered away at the anvil of one point. 'Mr Queen, as a trained observer of criminal phenomena, you were interested in the possibilities of this case?'

'Immensely.'

'That is why you kept James Haight under unrelaxing observation New Year's Eve?'

"That, and a personal concern for the Wright family.'

'You were watching for a possible poisoning attempt on Haight's part?'

'Yes,' said Ellery simply.

'Did you see any such attempt on Haight's part?'

'I did not!'

'You saw James Haight make no slightest gesture or motion which might have concealed a dropping of arsenic into one of the cocktail glasses?'

'I saw no such gesture or motion.'

'And you were watching for that, Mr Queen?'

'Exactly.'

'That's all,' said Judge Martin in triumph.

The newspapers all agreed that Mr Ellery Queen, who was in Wrightsville seeking material for a new detective story, had seized upon this hell-sent opportunity to illuminate the cause of dark letters with some national publicity. And Bradford, with a grim look, rested for the People.

The week end intervened, and everybody involved in the case went home or to his hotel room or, as in the case of the out-of-town newspaper people, to their cots in the lobby of the Hollis; and all over town people were agreeing that it looked black for Jim Haight, and why shouldn't it—he did it, didn't he? The roadhouses and taverns were jammed over the week end, and there was considerable revelry. On Friday night, however, the unofficial committee for the defense of James Haight met again in the Wright living room, and the atmosphere was blue with despair. Nora said to Ellery, to Judge Martin, to Roberta Roberts: 'What do you think?'—painfully and without hope; and all they could do was shake their heads.

'Queen's testimony would have helped a great deal more,' growled old Judge Eli, 'if that jury weren't so dad-blamed set on Jim's guilt. No, Nora, it looks bad, and I'm not going to tell you anything different.' Nora stared blindly into the fire.

'To think that you've been Ellery Queen all along,' sighed Hermy. 'I suppose there was a time when I'd have been thrilled, Mr Queen. But I'm so washed-out these days—'

'Momsy,' murmured Lola, 'where's your fighting spirit?'

Hermy smiled, but she excused herself to go upstairs to bed, her feet dragging. And after a while John F. said: 'Thanks, Queen,' and went off after Hermy, as if Hermy's going had made him a little uneasy.

And they sat there without speaking for a long time, until Nora said: 'At least, Ellery, what you saw confirms Jim's innocence. That's something. It ought to mean *something*. Heavens,' she cried, 'they've got to believe you!'

'Let's hope they do.'

'Judge Martin,' said Roberta suddenly. 'Monday's your day to begin howling. What are you going to howl about?'

'Suppose you tell me,' said Judge Martin.

Her glance fell first. 'I have nothing to tell that could help,' she said in a faint voice.

'Then I *was* right,' murmured Ellery. 'Don't you think others might make better judges—' Something crashed. Pat was on her feet, and the sherry glass from which she had been sipping lay in little glittery fragments in the fireplace, surrounded by blue flames.

'What's the matter with *you*?' demanded Lola. 'If this isn't the screwiest family!'

'I'll tell you what's the matter with me,' panted Pat. 'I'm through sitting on my—sitting around and imitating Uriah Heep. I'm going to *do* something!'

'Patty,' gasped Nora, looking at her younger sister as if Pat had suddenly turned into a female Mr Hyde.

Lola murmured: 'What in hell are you babbling about, Patticums?'

'I've got an idea!'

'The little one's got an idea,' grinned Lola. 'I had an idea once. Next thing I knew I was divorcing a heel and everybody began to call me an amptray. Siddown, Snuffy.'

'Wait a moment,' said Ellery. 'It's possible. What idea, Pat?'

'Go ahead and be funny,' said Pat hotly. 'All of you. But I've worked out a plan, and I'm going through with it.'

'What kind of plan?' demanded Judge Martin. 'I'll listen to anyone, Patricia.'

'Will you?' jeered Pat. 'Well, I'm not talking. You'll know when the time comes, Uncle Eli! You've got to do just one thing—'

'And that is?'

'To call me as *the last witness for the defense!*'

The Judge began in bewilderment: 'But what—?'

'Yes, what's stewing?' asked Ellery quickly. 'You'd better talk it over with your elders first.'

'There's been too much talk already, Grandpa.'

'But what do you think you're going to accomplish?'

'I want three things.' Pat looked grim. 'Time, last crack at the witness stand, and some of your new Odalisque Parfum, Nora ... Accomplish, Mr Queen? *I'm going to save Jim!*' Nora ran out of the room, using her knitting as a handkerchief. 'Well, I will!' said Pat, exasperated. And she added, in a gun-moll undertone: 'I'll show that Carter Bradford!'

26

Juror Number 7

'We will take,' said old Eli Martin to Mr Queen in the courtroom Monday morning, as they waited for Judge Newbold to enter from chambers, 'what the Lord provides.'

'Meaning what?' asked Ellery.

'Meaning,' sighed the lawyer, 'that unless providence intercedes, my old friend's son-in-law is a fried squab. If what I've got is a defense, may God help all petitioners for justice!'

'Legally speaking, I'm a blunderbuss. Surely you've got some sort of defense?'

'Some sort, yes.' The old gentleman squinted sourly at Jim Haight, sitting near by with his head on his breast. 'I've never had such a case!' he exploded. 'Nobody tells me anything—the defendant, the Roberts woman, the family...why, even that snippet Patricia won't talk to me!'

'Patty...' said Ellery thoughtfully.

'Pat wants me to put her on the stand, and I don't even know what for! This isn't law, it's lunacy.'

'She went out mysteriously Saturday night,' murmured Ellery, 'and again last night, and she came home very late both times.'

'While Rome burns!'

'She'd been drinking Martinis, too.'

'I forgot you're something of a sleuth. How did you find that out, Queen?'

'I kissed her.'

Judge Martin was startled. 'Kissed her? You?'

'I have my methods,' said Mr Queen, a whit stiffly. Then he grinned. 'But this time they didn't work. She wouldn't tell me what she'd been doing.'

'Odalisque Parfum,' sniffed the old gentleman. 'If Patricia Wright thinks a sweet *odeur* is going to divert young Bradford... He looks undiverted to me this morning. Doesn't he to you?'

'An immovable young man,' agreed Mr Queen uneasily.

Judge Martin sighed and glanced over at the row of chairs inside the railing, where Nora sat with her little chin raised high and a pallid face between her mother and father, her gaze fixed beggingly upon her husband's motionless profile. But if Jim was conscious of her presence, he made no sign. Behind them the courtroom was jammed and whispery.

Mr Queen was furtively scanning Miss Patricia Wright. Miss Patricia Wright had an Oppenheim air this morning—slitted eyes, and a certain enigmatic expression about the mouth Mr Queen had kissed in the interests of science the night before...in vain. Perhaps not quite in vain...

He became aware that Judge Eli was poking his ribs. 'Get up, get up. You ought to know something about courtroom etiquette! Here comes Newbold.'

'Good luck,' said Ellery absently.

The first witness Judge Martin called to testify in defense of Jim Haight was Hermione Wright. Hermy crossed the space before the Bench and mounted the step to the witness chair if not quite like royalty ascending the throne, then at least like royalty ascending the guillotine. On being sworn, she said 'I do' in a firm, if tragic, voice. Clever, thought Ellery. Putting Hermy on the stand. Hermy, mother of Nora. Hermy, who of all persons in the world

218

except Nora should be Jim Haight's harshest enemy—Hermy to testify for the man who had tried to kill her daughter! The courtroom and jury were impressed by the dignity with which Hermy met all their stares. Oh, she was a fighter! And Ellery could detect the pride on the faces of her three daughters, a queer shame on Jim's, and the faint admiration of Carter Bradford.

The old lawyer led Hermione skillfully through the night of the crime, dwelling chiefly on the 'gaiety' of the occasion, how happy everyone had been, how Nora and Jim had danced together like children, and incidentally how much Frank Lloyd, who had been Bradford's chief witness to the events of the evening, had had to drink; and the Judge contrived, through Hermy's helpless, 'confused' answers, to leave the impression with the jury that no one there could possibly have said for certain what had happened so far as the cocktails were concerned, let alone Frank Lloyd—unless it was Mr Ellery Queen, who'd had only one drink before the fatal toast to 1941.

And then Judge Martin led Hermione around to a conversation she had had with Jim shortly after Jim and Nora returned from their honeymoon—how Jim had confided in his mother-in-law that Nora and he suspected Nora was going to have a baby, and that Nora wanted it to be kept a secret until they were 'sure,' except that Jim said he was so happy he couldn't keep it in any longer, he had to tell someone, and Hermy wasn't to let on to Nora that he'd blabbed. And how ecstatic Jim had been at the prospect of being father to Nora's child—how it would change his whole life, he said, give him a fresh push towards making a success of himself for Nora and the baby—how much he loved Nora...more every day.

Carter Bradford waived cross-examination with almost a visible kindliness. But there was a little whiff of applause as Hermy stepped off the witness stand.

Judge Martin called up a roll of character witnesses as long as Judge Newbold's face. Lorrie Preston and Mr Gonzales of the bank, Brick Miller the bus driver, Ma Upham, young Manager Louie Cahan of the Bijou, who had been one of Jim's bachelor cronies, Miss Aikin of the Carnegie Library—that *was* a surprise, as Miss Aikin had never been known to say a kind word about anybody, but she managed to say several about Jim Haight despite the technical limitations of 'character' testimony— chiefly, Ellery suspected, because Jim had patronized the Library in the old days and broken not a single one of Miss Aikin's numerous rules...The character witnesses were so many, and so socially diversified, that people were surprised. They hadn't known Jim Haight had so many friends in town. But that was exactly the impression Judge Martin was trying to make. And when John F. clambered to the stand and said simply and directly that Jim was a good boy and the Wrights were behind him heart and soul, people remarked how old John F. looked—'aged a lot these past couple of months, John F. has'—and a tide of sympathy for the Wrights began to creep up in the courtroom until it was actually lapping Jim Haight's shoes.

During the days of this character testimony, Carter Bradford maintained a decent respect for the Wrights—just the proper note of deference and consideration, but a little aloof, as if to say: 'I'm not going to badger your people, but don't expect my relationship with your family to influence my conduct in this courtroom one iota!'

Then Judge Martin called Lorenzo Grenville. Lorenzo Grenville was a drippy-eyed little man with hourglass cheeks and a tall Hoover collar, size sixteen, out of which his neck protruded like a withered root. He identified himself as a handwriting expert.

Mr Grenville agreed that he had sat in the courtroom from the beginning of the trial; that he had heard the testimony of the People's experts regarding the authenticity of the handwriting in the three letters alleged to have been written by the defendant; that he had had ample opportunity to examine said letters, also undisputed samples of the defendant's true handwriting; and

220

that in his 'expert' opinion there was grave reason to doubt James Haight's authorship of the three letters in evidence.

'As a recognized authority in the field of handwriting analysis, you do not believe Mr Haight wrote the three letters?'

'I do not.' (The Prosecutor leers at the jury, and the jury leers back.)

'Why don't you believe so, Mr Grenville?' asked the Judge.

Mr Grenville went into punctilious detail. Since he drew almost exactly opposite conclusions from the identical data which the jury had heard the People's experts say proved Jim Haight *had* written those letters, several jurymen were not unnaturally confused; which contented Judge Martin.

'Any other reasons for believing these letters were not written by the defendant, Mr Grenville?'

Mr Grenville had many which, edited, became a question of composition. 'The phrasing is stilted, unnatural, and is not like the defendant's ordinary letter style at all.' Mr Grenville cited chapter and verse from Haight letters in evidence.

'Then what is your opinion, Mr Grenville, as to the authorship of the three letters?'

'I am inclined to consider them forgeries.'

Mr Queen would have felt reassured, but he happened to know that a certain defendant in another case *had* written a check which Mr Lorenzo Grenville just as solemnly testified to be a forgery. There was no slightest doubt in Ellery's mind about the Haight letters. They *had* been written by Jim Haight, and that's all there was to it. He wondered what Judge Martin was up to with the unreliable Mr Grenville.

He found out at once. 'Is it your considered opinion, Mr Grenville,' purred Judge Eli, 'that it would be easy, or difficult, to forge Mr Haight's handwriting?'

'Oh, very easy,' said Mr Grenville.

'Could *you* forge Mr Haight's handwriting?'

'Certainly.'

'Could you forge Mr Haight's handwriting *here and now?*'

221

'Well,' said Mr Grenville apologetically, 'I'd have to study the handwriting a while—say two minutes!'

Bradford was on his feet with a bellow, and there was a long, inaudible argument before Judge Newbold. Finally, the Court allowed the demonstration, the witness was provided with pen, paper, ink, and a photostatic copy of one of Jim Haight's acknowledged samples of handwriting—it happened to be a personal note written to Nora by Jim on the Wrightsville National Bank stationery, and dated four years before—and the courtroom sat on the edge of its collective seat. Lorenzo Grenville squinted at the photostat for exactly two minutes. Then, seizing the pen, he dipped it into the ink, and with a casual air wrote swiftly on the blank paper. 'I'd do better,' he said to Judge Martin, 'if I had my own pens to work with.'

Judge Martin glanced earnestly at what his witness had written, and then, with a smile, passed the sheet around the jury box, together with the photostat of Jim's undisputed handwriting. From the amazement on the jurors' faces as they compared the photostat with Grenville's forgery, Ellery knew the blow had told.

On cross-examination, Carter had only one question to ask the witness. 'Mr Grenville, how many years has it taken you to learn the art of forging handwriting?'

It seemed Mr Grenville had spent his whole life at it.

Victor Carlatti to the stand. Yes, he is the owner of a roadhouse on Route 16 called the *Hot Spot*. What sort of establishment is it? A night club.

Q.—Mr Carlatti, do you know the defendant, James Haight? A.—I've seen him around.

Q.—Has he ever visited your night club? A.—Yeah.

Q.—Drinking? A.—Well, a drink or two. Once in a while. It's legal.

Q.—Now, Mr Carlatti, there has been testimony here that James Haight allegedly admitted to Mrs Haight that he had 'lost money gambling' in your establishment. What do you know about this? *A.*—It's a dirty lie.

Q.—You mean James Haight has never gambled in your night club? *A.*—Sure he never. *Nobody* ever—

Q.—Has the defendant borrowed any money from you? *A.*— He nor nobody else.

Q.—Does the defendant owe you a single dollar? *A.*—Not a chip.

Q.—As far as you know, has the defendant ever 'lost' any money in your establishment? Gambling or any other way? *A.*— Maybe some broad may have took him to the cleaners while he was feeling happy, but he never shelled out one cent in my place except for drinks.

Q.—You may cross-examine, Mr Bradford.

Mr Bradford murmurs, 'With pleasure,' but only Judge Eli hears him, and Judge Eli shrugs ever so slightly and sits down.

Cross-examination by Mr Bradford:—

Q.—Carlatti, is it against the law to operate a gambling parlor? *A.*—Who says I operate a gambling parlor? Who says?

Q.—Nobody 'says,' Carlatti. Just answer my question. *A.*—It's a dirty frame. Prove it. Go ahead. I ain't gonna sit here and take no double-cross—

Judge Newbold: The witness will refrain from gratuitous remarks, or he will lay himself open to contempt. Answer the question.

A.—What question, Judge?

Q.—Never mind. Do you or do you not run roulette, faro, craps, and other gambling games in the back of your so-called 'night club'? *A.*—Am I supposed to answer dirty questions like that? It's an insult, Judge. This kid ain't dry behind the ears yet, and I ain't gonna sit here and take—

Judge Newbold: One more remark like that —

Judge Martin: It seems to me, Your Honor, that this is improper cross. The question of whether the witness runs a gambling

223

establishment or not was not part of the direct examination.

Judge Newbold: Overruled!

Judge Martin: Exception!

Mr Bradford: If Jim Haight did owe you money lost at your gambling tables, Carlatti, you'd have to deny it, wouldn't you, or face prosecution on a charge of running a gambling establishment?

Judge Martin: I move that question be stricken—

A.—What is this? All of a sudden all you guys are getting angels. How do you think I been operating—on my sex appeal? And don't think no hick judge can scare Vic Carlatti. I got plenty of friends, and they'll see to it that Vic Carlatti ain't going to be no fall guy for some old goat of a judge and some stinker of a D.A.—

Judge Newbold: Mr. Bradford, do you have any further questions of this witness?

Mr Bradford: I think that will be quite sufficient, Your Honor.

Judge Newbold: Clerk, strike the last question and answer. The jury will disregard it. The spectators will preserve the proper decorum or the room will be cleared. Witness is held in contempt of court. Bailiff, take charge of the prisoner.

Mr Carlatti puts up his dukes as the bailiff approaches, roaring: 'Where's my mouthpiece? This ain't Nazzee Goimany!'

When Nora took the oath and sat down and began to testify in a choked voice, the court was like a church. She was the priestess, and the people listened to her with the silent unease of a sinning congregation confronted by their sins...Surely the woman Jim Haight had tried to do in would be against him? But Nora was not against Jim. She was for him, every cell in her. Her loyalty filled the courtroom like warm air. She made a superb witness, defending her husband from every charge. She reiterated her love for him and her unquestioning faith in his innocence. Over and over. While her eyes kept coming back to the object of her testimony, those scant few feet away, who sat with his face lowered, wearing a dull red mask of shame, blinking at the tips of his unpolished shoes.

'The idiot might be more cooperative!' thought Mr Queen angrily.

Nora could give no factual evidence to controvert the People's case. Judge Martin, who had put her on the stand for her psychological value, did not touch upon the two poisoning attempts preceding New Year's Eve; and in a genuine act of kindness, Carter Bradford waived cross-examination and the opportunity to quiz her on those attempts. Perhaps Bradford felt he would lose more in good will by grilling Nora than by letting her go.

Mr Queen, a notorious sceptic, could not be sure.

Nora was to have been Judge Martin's last witness; and indeed he was fumbling with some papers at the defense table, as if undecided whether to proceed or not, when Pat signalled him furiously from inside the railing, and the old gentleman nodded with a guilty, unhappy look and said: 'I call Patricia Wright to the stand.' Mr Queen sat forward in the grip of a giant tension he could not understand.

Obviously at a loss where to begin, Judge Martin began a cautious reconnaissance, as if seeking a clue. But Pat took the reins out of his hands almost at once. She was irrepressible—deliberately, Ellery knew; but why? What was she driving at?

As a defense witness, Pat played squarely into the hands of the People. The more she said, the more damage she did to Jim's cause. She painted her brother-in-law as a scoundrel, a liar—told how he had humiliated Nora, stolen her jewelry, squandered her property, neglected her, subjected her to mental torment, quarrelled with her incessantly...Before she was half through, the courtroom was sibilating. Judge Martin was perspiring like a coolie and trying frantically to head her off, Nora was gaping at her sister as if she were seeing her for the first time, and Hermy and John F. slumped lower and lower in their seats, like two melting waxworks.

Judge Newbold interrupted Pat during a denunciation of Jim and an avowal of her hatred for him. 'Miss Wright, are you aware that you were called as a witness for the defense?'

Pat snapped: 'I'm sorry, Your Honor. But I can't sit here and see all this hush-hush going on when we all know Jim Haight is guilty—'

'I move—' began Judge Martin in an outraged bellow.

'Young woman—' began Judge Newbold angrily.

But Pat rushed on. 'And that's what I told Bill Ketcham only last night—'

'*What!*'

The explosion came from Judge Newbold, Eli Martin, and Carter Bradford simultaneously. And for a moment the room was plunged in an abyss of surprise; and then the walls cracked, and Bedlam piled upon Babel, so that Judge Newbold pounded with his third gavel of the trial, and the bailiff ran up and down shushing people, and in the press row someone started to laugh as realization came, infecting the whole row, and the row behind that. 'Your Honor,' said Judge Martin above the din, 'I want it to go on record here and now that the statement made by my witness a moment ago comes to me as an absolute shock. I had no faintest idea that—'

'Just a moment, just a moment, Counsel,' said Judge Newbold in a strangled voice. 'Miss Wright!'

'Yes, Your Honor?' asked Patty in a bewildered way, as if she couldn't imagine what all the fuss was about.

'Did I hear you correctly? Did you say you told *Bill Ketcham* something last night?'

'Why, yes, Your Honor,' said Pat respectfully. 'And Bill agreed with me—'

'I object!' shouted Carter Bradford. 'She's got it in for me! This is a put-up job—!'

Miss Wright turned innocent eyes on Mr Bradford.

'One moment, Mr Bradford!' Judge Newbold leaned far forward on the Bench. 'Bill Ketcham agreed with you, did he? What did he agree with you about? What else happened last night?'

'Well, Bill said Jim was guilty, all right, and if I'd promise to—' Pat blushed—'well, if I'd promise him a certain something, he'd see to it that Jim got what was coming to him. Said he'd talk to the others on the jury, too—being an insurance man, Bill said, he could sell anything. He said I was his dream girl, and for me he'd climb the highest mountain—'

'Silence in the court!' bellowed Judge Newbold.

And there was silence. 'Now, Miss Wright,' said Judge Newbold grimly, 'are we to understand that you had this conversation last night with the William Ketcham who is Juror Number 7 in this trial?'

'Yes, Your Honor,' said Pat, her eyes wide. 'Is anything wrong with that? I'm sure if I had known—' The rest was lost in uproar.

'Bailiff, clear the room!' screamed Judge Newbold.

'Now, then,' said Judge Newbold. 'Let's have the rest of it, if you please!'—so frigidly that Pat turned *café au lait* and tears appeared in the corners of her eyes.

'W-we went out together, Bill and I, last Saturday night. Bill said we oughtn't to be seen, maybe it wasn't legal or something, so we drove over to Slocum to a hot spot Bill knows, and —and we've been there every night since. I said Jim was guilty, and Bill said sure, he thought so too—'

'Your Honor,' said Judge Martin in a terrible voice, 'I move—'

'Oh, you do!' said Judge Newbold. 'Eli Martin, if your reputation weren't... You there!' he roared at the jurist. 'Ketcham! Number 7! Get up!'

Fat Billy Ketcham, the insurance broker, tried to obey, half hoisted himself, fell back again, and finally made it. He stood there in the rear row of the jury box, swaying a little, as if the box were a canoe.

'William Ketcham,' snarled Judge Newbold, 'have you spent

'Yes,' pointed out Mr Queen dryly. 'But look at Judge Martin's.'

Old Eli Martin came over to Pat and he said: 'Patricia, you've placed me in the most embarrassing position of my life. I don't care about that, or the ethics of your conduct, so much as I do about the fact that you probably haven't helped Jim's chances, you've hurt them. No matter what Newbold says or does—and he really hasn't any choice—everybody will know you did this deliberately, and it's bound to bounce back on Jim Haight.' And Judge Martin stalked away.

'I suppose,' said Lola, 'you can't scratch an ex-judge without stuffiness leaking out. Don't you worry, Snuffles! You gave Jim a zero-hour reprieve—it's better than he deserves, the dumb ox!'

'I wish to state in preamble,' said Judge Newbold coldly, 'that in all my years on the Bench I have encountered no more flagrant, disgraceful example of civic irresponsibility. William Ketcham!' He transfixed Juror Number 7, who looked as if he were about to faint, with a stern and glittering eye 'Unfortunately, there is no statutory offense with which you can be charged, unless it can be shown that you have received property or value of some kind. For the time being, however, I order the Commissioner of Jurors to strike your name from the panel of jurors, and never so long as you are a resident of this State will you be permitted to exercise your privilege of serving on a jury.'

William Ketcham's expression said that he would gladly relinquish many more appreciated rights for the privilege of leaving the courtroom that very instant.

'Mr Bradford—' Carter looked up, thin-lipped and black-angry—'you are requested to investigate the conduct of Patricia Wright with a view toward determining whether she willfully and deliberately sought to influence Juror Number 7. If such intention can be established, I ask you to draw an indictment charging Patricia Wright with the appropriate charge—'

'Your Honor,' said Bradford in a low voice, 'the only conceiv-

'Yes,' pointed out Mr Queen dryly. 'But look at Judge Martin's.'

Old Eli Martin came over to Pat and he said: 'Patricia, you've placed me in the most embarrassing position of my life. I don't care about that, or the ethics of your conduct, so much as I do about the fact that you probably haven't helped Jim's chances, you've hurt them. No matter what Newbold says or does—and he really hasn't any choice—everybody will know you did this deliberately, and it's bound to bounce back on Jim Haight.' And Judge Martin stalked away.

'I suppose,' said Lola, 'you can't scratch an ex-judge without stuffiness leaking out. Don't you worry, Snuffles! You gave Jim a zero-hour reprieve—it's better than he deserves, the dumb ox!'

'I wish to state in preamble,' said Judge Newbold coldly, 'that in all my years on the Bench I have encountered no more flagrant, disgraceful example of civic irresponsibility. William Ketcham!' He transfixed Juror Number 7, who looked as if he were about to faint, with a stern and glittering eye. 'Unfortunately, there is no statutory offense with which you can be charged, unless it can be shown that you have received property or value of some kind. For the time being, however, I order the Commissioner of Jurors to strike your name from the panel of jurors, and never so long as you are a resident of this State will you be permitted to exercise your privilege of serving on a jury.'

William Ketcham's expression said that he would gladly relinquish many more appreciated rights for the privilege of leaving the courtroom that very instant.

'Mr Bradford—' Carter looked up, thin-lipped and black-angry—'you are requested to investigate the conduct of Patricia Wright with a view toward determining whether she willfully and deliberately sought to influence Juror Number 7. If such intention can be established, I ask you to draw an indictment charging Patricia Wright with the appropriate charge—'

'Your Honor,' said Bradford in a low voice, 'the only conceiv-

able charge I can see would be corrupting a juror, and to establish corruption it seems to me necessary to show consideration. And in this case it doesn't seem as if there was any consideration—'

'She offered her body!' snapped Judge Newbold.

'I did not!' gasped Pat. 'He asked for it, but I didn't—'

'Yes, Your Honor,' said Bradford, blushing, 'but it is a moot point whether that sort of thing constitutes legal consideration—'

'Let's not get entangled, Mr Bradford,' said Judge Newbold coldly. 'The woman is clearly guilty of embracery if she attempted to influence a juror improperly, whether she gave any consideration or not!'

'Embracery? What's that?' muttered Pat. But no one heard her except Mr Queen, who was chuckling inside.

'Also,' continued Judge Newbold slamming a book down on a heap of papers, 'I shall recommend that in future trials coming under the jurisdiction of this court, juries shall be locked in, to prevent a recurrence of this shameful incident.

'Now.' He glared at Billy Ketcham and Pat, and then at the jury. 'The facts are clear. A juror has been influenced in a manner prejudicial to the rights of the defendant to a fair trial. This is by the admission of both parties involved. If I permitted this trial to continue, it could only bring an appeal to a superior court which must, on the record, order a new trial. Consequently, to save further and needless expense, I have no choice. I regret the inconvenience and waste of time caused the remaining members of the jury; I deplore the great expense of this trial already incurred by Wright County. Much as I regret and deplore, however, the facts leave me no recourse but to declare People Against James Haight a mistrial. I do so declare, the jury is discharged with the apology and thanks of the Court, and the defendant is remanded to the custody of the Sheriff until the date of a new trial can be set. Court is adjourned!'

27

Easter Sunday: Nora's Gift

The invading press retreated, promising to return for the new trial; but Wrightsville remained, and Wrightsville chortled and raged and buzzed and gossiped until the very ears of the little Buddha clock on Pat's dresser were ringing.

William Ketcham, by a curious inversion, became the town hero. The 'boys' stopped him on the street corners to slap his back, he sold five insurance policies he had long since given up, and, as confidence returned, he related some 'details' of his relationship with Miss Patricia Wright on the critical nights in question which, when they reached Pat's ears by way of Carmel Pettigrew (who was phoning her 'best friend' again), caused Miss Wright to go downtown to Mr Ketcham's insurance office in the Bluefield Block, grasp Mr Ketcham firmly by the collar with the left hand, and with the right slap Mr Ketcham's right cheek five ringing times, leaving assorted marks in the damp white flesh.

'Why five?' asked Mr Queen, who had accompanied Miss Wright on the excursion and had stood by, admiring, while she cleansed her reputation.

Miss Wright flushed. 'Never mind,' she said tartly. 'It was—exact—retribution. That lying, bragging—!'

'If you don't watch out,' murmured Mr Queen, 'Carter Bradford will have another indictment to draw against you—this one for assault and battery.'

'I'm just waiting,' said Pat darkly. 'But he won't. He knows better!' And apparently Cart did know better, for nothing more was heard from him about Pat's part in the debacle.

Wrightsville prepared for the Easter holidays. The Bon Ton did a New York business in dresses and spring coats and shoes and underwear and bags, Sol Gowdy put on two 'extras' to help in his Men's Shop, and the Low Village emporia were actually crowded with mill and factory customers.

Mr Ellery Queen shut himself up in his quarters on the top floor of the Wright house and, except for meals, remained incommunicado. Anyone looking in on him would have been puzzled. He was doing exactly nothing visible to the uninitiated eye. Unless it was to consume innumerable cigarettes. He just sat still in the chair by the window and gazed out at the spring sky, or patrolled the room with long strides, head bent, puffing like a locomotive. Oh, yes. If you looked hard, you could see a mass of notes on his desk—a mess of a mass, for the papers were scattered like dead leaves in autumn. And indeed the wind of Ellery's fury had scattered them so. They lay there discarded, and a mockery.

So there was nothing exciting in *that* direction. Nor anywhere else, except possibly in Nora's. It was strange about Nora. She had stood up so gallantly under the stresses of the arrest and trial that everyone had begun taking her for granted. Even Hermione thought of nothing but Nora's 'condition' and the proper care of the mother; and there old Ludie was of infinitely more practical use. Old Ludie said a woman was a woman, and she was made to have babies, and the less fuss you made over Nora's 'condition' the better off they'd both be—Nora *and* the little one. Eat good plain food, with plenty of vegetables and milk and fruit, don't go gallivantin', go easy on the candy and do plenty of walking and mild exercise, and the good Lord would do the rest. Ludie had incessant quarrels about it with Hermione, and at least one memorable tiff with Dr Willoughby.

But the pathology of the nervous system was so much Sanskrit to Ludie; and while the others were better informed, only two persons close to Nora suspected what was going to happen, and at least one of them was helpless to avert the catastrophe. That was Mr Queen; and he could only wait and watch. The other was Doc Willoughby, and the doctor did all he could— which meant tonic and daily examinations and advice, all of which Nora ignored.

Nora went to pieces of a sudden. On Easter Sunday, just after the family had returned from church, Nora was heard laughing in her bedroom. Pat, who was fixing her hair in her own room down the hall and was the nearest, got there first, alarmed by a queer quality in Nora's laughter. She found her sister in a swollen heap on the floor, rocking, laughing her head off while her cheeks changed from red to purple to yellow-ivory. Her eyes were spumy and wild, like a sea storm.

They all ran in then, and among them managed to drag Nora onto the bed, and loosen her clothes, while she laughed and laughed as if the tragedy of her life were the greatest joke in the world. Ellery telephoned Dr Willoughby, and set about with the assistance of Pat and Lola to arrest Nora's hysteria. By the time the doctor arrived, they had managed to stop the laughter, but Nora was shaking and white and looked about her with frightened eyes.

'I can't understand—it,' she gasped. 'I was—all right. Then—everything...Ooh, I *hurt*.'

Dr Willoughby chased them all away. He was in Nora's room for fifteen minutes. When he came out he said harshly: 'She's got to be taken to the hospital. I'll arrange it myself.'

And Hermy clutched at John F., and the girls clung to each other, and nobody said anything while a big hand took hold of them and squeezed.

The Wrightsville General Hospital was understaffed for the day, since it was Easter Sunday and a holiday. The ambulance did not arrive for three quarters of an hour, and for the first time within the memory of John F. Wright, Dr Milo Willoughby was heard to swear—a long, loud, imagistic curse, after which he clamped his jaws together and went back to Nora. 'She'll be all right, Hermy,' said John F.; but his face was gray. If Milo swore, it was bad!

When the ambulance finally came, the doctor wasted no time in further anathema. He had Nora whisked out of the house and away, leaving his car at the Wright curb to accompany her in the ambulance. They glimpsed Nora's face for an instant as the interns carried her downstairs on a stretcher. The skin lay in coils that jerked this way and that, as if they had a life of their own. The mouth was twisted into a knot, and the eyes were opalescent with agony.

Mercifully, Hermione did not see that face; but Pat did, and she said to Ellery in flat horror: 'She's in horrible pain, and she's scared to death, Ellery! Oh, Ellery, do you think—?'

'Let's be getting over to the hospital,' said Ellery.

He drove them. There was no private pavilion at the Wrightsville General; but Doc Willoughby had a corner of the Women's Surgical Ward screened off and Nora put to bed there. The family was not admitted to the ward; they had to sit in the main waiting room off the lobby. The waiting room was gay with Easter posies and sad with the odor of disinfectant. It sickened Hermy, so they made her comfortable on a mission-wood settee, where she lay with tightly closed eyes. John F. just pottered about, touching a flower now and then, and saying once how nice it felt to have the spring here again. The girls sat near their mother. Mr Queen sat near the girls. And there was nothing but the sound of John F.'s shoes whispering on the worn flowered rug.

*   *   *

And then Dr Willoughby came hurrying into the waiting room, and everything changed—Hermy opened her eyes, John F. stopped exploring, the girls and Ellery jumped up.

'Haven't much time,' panted the doctor. 'Listen to me. Nora has a delicate constitution. She's always been a nervy girl. Strain, aggravation, worry, what she's gone through—the poisoning attempts, New Year's Eve, the trial—she's very weak, very badly run-down...'

'What are you trying to say, Milo?' demanded John F., clutching his friend's arm.

'John, Nora's condition is serious. No point in keeping it from you and Hermy. She's a sick girl.' Dr Willoughby turned as if to hurry away.

'Milo—wait!' cried Hermy. 'How about the...baby?'

'She's going to have it, Hermy. We've got to operate.'

'But—it's only six months!'

'Yes,' said Dr Willoughby stiffly. 'You'd better all wait here. I've got to get ready.'

'Milo,' said John F. 'If there's anything—money—I mean, get anybody—the best—'

'We're in luck, John. Henry Gropper is in Slocum visiting his parents over Easter; classmate of mine; best gynaecologist in the East. He's on his way over now.'

'Milo—' wailed Hermy. But Dr Willoughby was gone.

And now the waiting began all over again, in the silent room with the sun beating in and the Easter posies approaching their deaths fragrantly. John F. sat down beside his wife and took her hand. They sat that way, their eyes fixed on the clock over the waiting-room door. Seconds came and went and became minutes. Lola turned the pages of a *Cosmopolitan* with a torn cover. She put it down, took it up again.

'Pat,' said Ellery. 'Over here.'

John F. looked at him, Hermy looked at him, Lola looked at him. Then Hermy and John F. turned back to the clock, and Lola to the magazine.

'Where?' Pat's voice was shimmering with tears.

'By the window. Away from the family.' Pat trudged over to the farthest bank of windows with him. She sat down on the window seat and looked out. He took her hand. 'Talk.'

Her eyes filled. 'Oh, Ellery—'

'I know,' he said gently. 'But you just talk to me. Anything. It's better than choking on the words inside, isn't it? And you can't talk to *them*, because they're choking, too.' He gave her a cigarette, and held a match up, but she just fingered the cigarette, not seeing it or him. He snuffed the flame between two fingers and then stared at the fingers.

'Talk...' said Pat bitterly. 'Well, why not? I'm so confused. Nora lying there—her baby coming prematurely—Jim in jail a few squares away—Pop and Mother sitting here like two old people...*old*, Ellery. They are old.'

'Yes, Patty,' murmured Ellery.

'And we were so happy before,' Pat choked. 'It's all like a foul dream. It can't be us. We were—*everything* in this town! Now look at us. Dirtied up. Old. They spit on us.'

'Yes, Patty,' said Ellery again.

'When I think of how it happened...How *did* it happen? Oh, I'll never face another holiday with any gladness!'

'Holiday?'

'Don't you realize? Every last awful thing that's happened—happened on a holiday! Here's Easter Sunday—and Nora's on the operating table. When was Jim arrested? On St Valentine's Day! When did Rosemary die, and Nora get so badly poisoned? On New Year's Eve! And Nora was sick—poisoned—on Christmas Day, and before that on Thanksgiving Day...'

Mr Queen was looking at Pat as if she had pointed out that two plus two adds up to five. 'No. On that point I'm convinced. It's been bothering me for weeks. But it's coincidence. Can't be anything else. No, Patty...'

'Even the way it started,' cried Patty. 'It started on Hallowe'en! Remember?' She stared at the cigarette in her fingers; it was pulpy ruin now. 'If we'd never found those three let-

236

ters in that toxicology book, everything might have been different, Ellery. *Don't* shake your head. It might!'

'Maybe you're right,' muttered Ellery. 'I'm shaking my head at my own stupidity—' A formless something took possession of his mind in a little leap, like a struck spark. He had experienced that sensation once before—how long ago it seemed!—but now the same thing happened. The spark died and he was left with a cold, exasperating ash which told nothing.

'You talk about coincidence,' said Pat shrilly. 'All right, call it that. I don't care what you call it. Coincidence, or fate, or just rotten luck. But if Nora hadn't accidentally dropped those books we were moving that Hallowe'en, the three letters wouldn't have tumbled out and they'd probably be in the book still.'

Mr Queen was about to point out that the peril to Nora had lain not in the letters but in their author; but again a spark leaped, and died, and so he held his tongue.

'For that matter,' Pat sighed, 'if the most trivial thing had happened differently that day, maybe none of this would have come about. If Nora and I hadn't decided to fix up Jim's new study—if we hadn't opened that box of books!'

'*Box* of books?' said Ellery blankly.

'I brought the crate up myself from the cellar, where Ed Hotchkiss had put it when he cabbed Jim's stuff over from the railroad station after Jim and Nora got back from their honeymoon. Suppose I hadn't opened that box with a hammer and screwdriver? Suppose I hadn't been able to *find* a screwdriver? Or suppose I'd waited a week, a day, even another hour...Ellery, what's the matter?'

For Mr Queen was standing over her like the judgment of the Lord, a terrible wrath on his face, and Patty was so alarmed she shrank back against the window. 'Do you mean to sit there and tell me,' said Mr Queen in an awful quietude, 'that those books—the armful of books Nora dropped—those books were *not* the books usually standing on the living-room shelves?' He shook her, and she winced at the pressure of his fingers on her

shoulder. 'Pat, answer me! You and Nora weren't merely transferring books from the living-room bookshelves to the new
shelves in Jim's study upstairs? You're *sure* the books came from
that box in the cellar?'

'Of course I'm sure,' said Pat shakily. 'What's the matter with
you? A nailed box. I opened it myself. Why, just a few minutes
before you came in that evening I'd lugged the empty wooden
box back to the cellar, with the tools and wrapping paper and
mess of bent nails—'

'It's...fantastic,' said Ellery. One hand groped for the rocker
near Pat. He sat down, heavily.

Pat was bewildered. 'But I don't get it, Ellery. Why all the dra-
matics? What difference can it make?'

Mr Queen did not answer at once. He just sat there, pale, and
growing perceptibly paler, nibbling his nails. And the fine lines
about his mouth deepened and became hard, and there
appeared in his silvery eyes a baffled something that he concealed very quickly—almost as quickly as it showed itself. 'What
difference?' He licked his lips.

'Ellery!' Pat was shaking *him* now. 'Don't act so mysterious!
What's wrong? Tell me!'

'Wait a minute.' She stared at him, and waited. He just sat.
Then he muttered: 'If I'd only *known*. But I couldn't have...Fate.
The fate that brought me into that room five minutes late. The
fate that kept you from telling me all these months. The fate that
concealed the essential fact!'

'But Ellery—'

'Dr Willoughby!'

They ran across the waiting room. Dr Willoughby had just
blundered in. He was in his surgical gown and cap, his face
mask around his throat like a scarf. There was blood on his
gown, and none in his cheeks.

'Milo?' quavered Hermione. 'Well, well?' croaked John F. 'For
God's sake, Doc!' cried Lola. Pat rushed up to grab the old man's
thick arm.

238

'Well,' said Dr Willoughby in a hoarse voice, and he stopped. Then he smiled the saddest smile and put his arm around Hermy's shoulder, quite dwarfing her. 'Nora's given you a real Easter present...Grandma.'

'Grandma,' whispered Hermy.

'The baby!' cried Pat. 'It's all *right?*'

'Fine, fine, Patricia. A perfect little baby girl. Oh, she's very tiny—she'll need the incubator—but with proper care she'll be all right in a few weeks.'

'But Nora,' panted Hermy. 'My Nora.'

'How is Nora, Milo?' demanded John F.

'Is she out of it?' Lola asked.

'Does she know?' cried Pat. 'Oh. Nor must be so happy!'

Dr Willoughby glanced down at his gown, began to fumble at the spot where Nora's blood had splattered. 'Damn it all,' he said. His lips were quivering. Hermione screamed.

'Gropper and I—we did all we could. We couldn't help it. We worked over her like beavers. But she was carrying too big a load. John, don't look at me that way...' The doctor waved his arms wildly.

'Milo—' began John F. in a faint voice.

'She's dead, that's all!'

He ran out of the waiting room.

Part Six

Chapter 28

The Tragedy on Twin Hill

He was looking at the old elms before the new Courthouse. The old was being reborn in multitudes of little green teeth on brown gums of branches; and the new already showed weather streaks in its granite, like varicose veins. There is sadness, too, in spring, thought Mr Ellery Queen. He stepped into the cool shadows of the Courthouse lobby and was borne aloft.

'No time for visitors to be visitin',' said Wally Planetsky sternly. Then he said: 'Oh. You're that friend of Patty Wright's. It's a hell of a way to be spendin' the Easter Sunday, Mr Queen.'

'How true,' said Mr Queen. The keeper unlocked an iron door, and they trudged together into the jail. 'How is he?'

'Never saw such a man for keepin' his trap shut. You'd think he'd taken a vow.'

'Perhaps,' sighed Mr Queen, 'he has...Anyone been in today to see him?'

'Just that newspaper woman, Miss Roberts.' Planetsky unlocked another door, locked it carefully behind them.

'Is there a doctor about?' asked Ellery unexpectedly.

Planetsky scratched his ear and opined that if Mr Queen was feelin' sick...

'Is there?'

'Well, sure. We got an infirmary here. Young Ed Crosby—that's Ivor Crosby the farmer's son—he's on duty right now.'

'Tell Dr Crosby I may need him in a very little while.'

The keeper looked Ellery over suspiciously, shrugged, unlocked the cell door, locked it again, and shuffled away. Jim was lying on his bunk, hands crossed behind his head, examining the graph of sky blue beyond the bars. He had shaved, Ellery noted; his clean shirt was open at the throat; he seemed at peace.

'Jim?'

Jim turned his head. 'Oh, hello, there,' he said. 'Happy Easter.'

'Jim—' began Ellery again, frowning.

Jim swung his feet to the concrete floor and sat up to grip the edge of his bunk with both hands. No peace now. Fear. And that was strange...No, logical! When you came to think of it. When you *knew*. 'Something's wrong,' said Jim. He jumped to his feet. 'Something's wrong!'

Ellery grimaced. This was the punishment for trespassing. This was the pain reserved for meddlers. 'I'm all for you, Jim—'

'What is it?' Jim made a fist.

'You've got a great deal of courage, Jim—'

Jim stared. 'She's...It's Nora.'

'Jim, Nora's dead.' Jim stared, his mouth open. 'I've just come from the hospital. The baby is all right. A girl. Premature delivery. Instruments. Nora was too weak. She didn't come out of it. No pain. She just died, Jim.'

Jim's lips came together. He turned around and went back to his bunk and turned around again and sat down, his hands reaching the bunk before he reached it.

'Naturally, the family...John F. asked me to tell you, Jim. They're all home now, taking care of Hermione. John F. said to tell you he's terribly sorry, Jim.'

Stupid, thought Ellery. A stupid speech. But then he was usually the observer, not a participant. How did one go about drawing the agony out of a stab to the heart? Killing without hurting—for as much as a second? It was a branch of the art of violence with which Mr Queen was unacquainted. He sat helplessly on the contraption which concealed Wright County's arrangement for the physical welfare of its prisoners, and thought of symbolism. 'If there's anything I can do—'

That wasn't merely stupid, thought Ellery angrily; that was vicious. Anything he could do! Knowing what was going on in Jim's mind! Ellery got up and said: 'Now Jim. Now wait a minute, Jim—'

But Jim was at the bars like a great monkey, gripping two of them, his thin face pressed as hard between two adjacent ones as if he meant to force his head through and drag his body after it. 'Let me out of here!' he kept shouting. 'Let me out of here! Damn all of you! I've got to get to Nora! Let me out of here!' He panted and strained, his teeth digging into his lower lip and his eyes hot and his temples bulging with vessels. 'Let me out of here!' he screamed. A white froth sprang up at the corners of his mouth.

When Dr Crosby arrived with a black bag and a shaking Keeper Planetsky to open the door for him, Jim Haight was flat on his back on the floor and Mr Queen knelt on Jim's chest holding Jim's arms down, hard, and yet gently, too. Jim was still screaming, but the words made no sense. Dr Crosby took one look and grabbed a hypodermic.

Twin Hill is a pleasant place in the spring. There's Bald Mountain off to the north, almost always wearing a white cap on its green shoulders, like some remote Friar Tuck; there's the woods part in the gulley of the Twins, where boys go hunting woodchuck and jack rabbit and occasionally scare up a wild deer; and there are the Twins themselves, two identical humps of hill all densely populated with the dead.

The east Twin has the newer cemeteries—the Poor Farm burial ground pretty far down, in the scrub, the old Jewish cemetery, and the Catholic cemetery; these are 'new' because not a head-stone in the lot bears a date earlier than 1805.

But the west Twin has the really old cemeteries of the Protestant denominations, and there you can see, at the very bald spot of the west Twin, the family plot of the Wrights, the first Wright tomb—Jezreel Wright's—in its mathematical center. Of course, the Founder's grave is not exposed to the elements—the wind off Bald Mountain does things to grass and topsoil. John F.'s grandfather had built a large mausoleum over the grave—handsome it is, too, finest Vermont granite, white as Patty Wright's teeth. But inside there's the original grave with its little stick of headstone, and if you look sharp you can still make out the scratches on the stone—the Founder's name, a hopeful quotation from the Book of Revelation, and the date 1723.

The Wright family plot hogs pretty nearly the whole top of the west Twin. The Founder, who seems to have had a nice judgment in all business matters, staked out enough dead land for his seed and his seed's seed to last for eternity. As if he had faith that the Wrights would live and die in Wrightsville unto Judgment Day. The rest of the cemetery, and the other burial grounds, simply took what was left. And that was all right with everyone, for after all didn't the Founder found? Besides, it made a sort of show place. Wrightsvillians were forever hauling outlanders up to Twin Hill, halfway to Slocum Township, to exhibit the Founder's grave and the Wright plot. It was one of the 'sights.'

The automobile road ended at the gate of the cemetery, not far from the boundary of the Wright family plot. From the gate you walked—a peaceful walk under trees so old you wondered they didn't lie down and ask to be buried themselves out of plain weariness. But they just kept growing old and droopier. Except in spring. Then the green hair began sprouting from their hard black skins with a sly fertility, as if death were a great joke. Maybe the graves so lush and thick all over the hillside had something to do with it.

Services for Nora—on Tuesday, April the fifteenth—were private. Dr Doolittle uttered a few words in the chapel of Willis Stone's Eternal Rest Mortuary, on Upper Whistling Avenue in High Village. Only the family and a few friends were present— Mr Queen, Judge and Clarice Martin, Dr Willoughby, and some of John F.'s people from the bank. Frank Lloyd was seen skulking about the edge of the group, straining for a glimpse of the pure still profile in the copper casket. He looked as if he had not taken his clothes off for a week, or slept during that time. When Hermy's eye rested on him, he shrank and disappeared...Perhaps twenty mourners in all.

Hermy was fine. She sat up straight in her new black, eyes steady, listening to Dr Doolittle; and when they all filed past the bier for a last look at Nora, she merely grew a little paler, and blinked. She didn't cry. Pat said it was because she was all cried out. John F. was a crumpled, red-nosed little derelict. Lola had to take him by the hand and lead him away from the casket to let Mr Stone put the head section in place. Nora had looked very calm and young. She was dressed in her wedding gown. Just before they went out to the funeral cars, Pat slipped into Mr Stone's office. When she came back she said: 'I just called the hospital. Baby's fine. She's growing in that incubator like a little vegetable.' Pat's lips danced, and Mr Queen put his arm about her.

Looking back on it, Ellery saw the finer points of Jim's psychology. But that was after the event. Beforehand it was impossible to tell, because Jim acted his part perfectly. He fooled them all, including Ellery.

Jim came to the cemetery between two detectives, like an animated sandwich. He was 'all right.' Very little different from the Jim who had sat in the courtroom—altogether different from the Jim Ellery had sat upon in the cell. There was a whole despair about him so enveloping that he had poise, and self-control, even dignity. He marched along steadily between his two guards, ignoring them, looking neither to right nor to left, on the path under the aged trees up to the top of the hill where the

247

newly turned earth gaped, like a wound, to receive Nora. The cars had been left near the gate.

Most of Wrightsville watched from a decent distance—let us give them that. But they were there, silent and curious; only occasionally someone whispered, or a forefinger told a story.

The Wrights stood about the grave in a woebegone group, Lola and Pat pressing close to Hermione and their father. John F.'s sister Tabitha had been notified, but she had wired that she was ill and could not fly to the funeral from California, and the Lord in His wisdom taketh away, and perhaps it was all for the best may she rest in peace your loving sister Tabitha. John F. made a wad out of the wire and hurled it blindly; it landed in the early morning fire Ludie had lit against the chill in the big old house. So it was just the immediate family group, and Ellery Queen, and Judge Eli Martin and Clarice and Doc Willoughby and some others; and, of course, Dr Doolittle. When Jim was brought up, a mutter arose from the watchers; eyes became very sharp for this meeting; this was very nearly 'the best part of it.' But nothing remarkable happened. Or perhaps it did. For Hermy's lips were seen to move, and Jim went over to her and kissed her. He paid no attention to anyone else; after that he just stood there at the grave, a thin figure of loneliness.

During the interment service a breeze ran through the leaves, like fingers; and indeed Dr Doolittle's voice took on a lilt and became quite musical. The evergreens and lilies bordering the grave stirred a little, too. Then, unbelievably, it was over, and they were shuffling down the walk, Hermy straining backward to catch a last glimpse of the casket which could no longer be seen, having been lowered into the earth. But the earth had not yet been rained upon it, for that would have been bestial; that could be done later, under no witnessing eyes but the eyes of the gravediggers, who were a peculiar race of people. So Hermy strained, and she thought how beautiful the evergreens and the lilies looked, and how passionately Nora had detested funerals.

The crowd at the gate parted silently. Then Jim did it.

One moment he was trudging along between the detectives, a dead man staring at the ground; the next he came alive. He tripped one of his guards. The man fell backward with a thud, his mouth an astonished O even as he fell. Jim struck the second guard on the jaw, so that the man fell on his brother officer and they threshed about, like wrestlers, trying to regain their feet. In those few seconds Jim was gone, running through the crowd like a bull, bowling people over, spinning people around, dodging and twisting...

Ellery shouted at him, but Jim ran on. The detectives were on their feet now, running too, revolvers out uselessly. To fire would mean hitting innocent people. They pushed through, cursing and ashamed.

And then Ellery saw that Jim's madness was not madness at all. For a quarter way down the hill, past all the parked cars, stood a single great car, its nose pointed away from the cemetery. No one was in it; but the motor had been kept running, Ellery knew, for Jim leaped in and the car shot forward at once. By the time the two detectives reached a clear space, and fired down the hill, the big limousine was a toy in the distance. It was careering crazily and going at a great speed. And after another few moments, the detectives reached their own car and took up the chase, one driving, the other still firing wildly. But Jim was well out of range by this time and everyone knew he had a splendid chance of escaping. The two cars disappeared.

For some moments there was no sound on the hillside but the sound of the wind in the trees. Then the crowd shouted, and swept over the Wrights and their friends, and automobiles began flying down the hill in merry clouds of dust, as if this were a paid entertainment and their drivers were determined not to miss the exciting climax.

Hermy lay on the living-room settee, and Pat and Lola were applying cold vinegar compresses to her head while John F. turned the pages of one of his stamp albums with great deliberation, as if it were one of the most important things in the world.

He was in a corner by the window to catch the late afternoon light. Clarice Martin was holding Hermy's hand tightly in an ecstasy of remorse, crying over her defection during the trial and over Nora and over this last shocking blow. And Hermy—Hermy the Great!—was comforting her friend!

Lola slapped a new compress so hard on her mother's forehead that Hermy smiled at her reproachfully. Pat took it away from her angry sister and set it right.

At the fireplace Dr Willoughby and Mr Queen conversed in low tones. Then Judge Martin came in from outdoors. And with him was Carter Bradford.

Everything stopped, as if an enemy had walked into camp. But Carter ignored it. He was quite pale, but held himself erect; and he kept from looking at Pat, who had turned paler than he. Clarice Martin was frankly frightened. She glanced quickly at her husband, but Judge Eli shook his head and went over to the window to seat himself by John F. and watch the fluttering pages of the stamp album, so gay with color.

'I don't want to intrude, Mrs Wright,' said Carter stiffishly. 'But I had to tell you how badly I feel about—all this.'

'Thank you, Carter,' said Hermy. 'Lola, stop babying me! Carter, what about—' Hermy swallowed—'Jim?'

'Jim got away, Mrs Wright.'

'I'm *glad*,' cried Pat. 'Oh, I'm so very glad!'

Carter glanced her way. 'Don't say that, Patty. That sort of thing never winds up right. Nobody "gets away." Jim would have been better…advised to have stuck it out.'

'So that you could hound him to his death, I suppose! All over again!'

'Pat.' John F. left his stamp album where it was. He put his thin hand on Carter's arm. 'It was nice of you to come here today, Cart. I'm sorry if I was ever harsh with you. How does it look?'

'Bad, Mr Wright.' Carter's lips tightened. 'Naturally, the alarm is out. All highways are being watched. It's true he got away, but it's only a question of time before he's captured—'

'Bradford,' inquired Mr Queen from the fireplace, 'have you traced the getaway car?'

'Yes.'

'Looked like a put-up job to me,' muttered Dr Willoughby. 'That car was in a mighty convenient place, and the motor was running!'

'Whose car is it?' demanded Lola.

'It was rented from Homer Findlay's garage in Low Village this morning.'

'Rented!' exclaimed Clarice Martin. 'By whom?'

'Roberta Roberts.'

Ellery said: 'Ah,' in a tone of dark satisfaction, and nodded as if that were all he had wanted to know. But the others were surprised.

Lola tossed her head. 'Good for her!'

'Carter let me talk to the woman myself just now,' said Judge Eli Martin wearily. 'She's a smart female. Insists she hired the car just to drive to the cemetery this morning.'

'And that she left the motor running by mistake,' added Carter Bradford dryly.

'And was it a coincidence that she also turned the car about so that it pointed down the hill?' murmured Mr Queen.

'That's what I asked her,' said Carter. 'Oh, there's no question about her complicity, and Dakin's holding her. But that doesn't get Jim Haight back, nor does it give us a case against this Roberts woman. We'll probably have to let her go.' He said angrily: 'I never did trust that woman!'

'She visited Jim on Sunday,' remarked Ellery reflectively.

'Also yesterday! I'm convinced she arranged the escape with Jim then.'

'What difference does it make?' Hermy sighed. 'Escape—no escape—Jim won't ever escape.' Then Hermy said a queer thing, considering how she had always claimed she felt about her son-in-law and his guilt. Hermy said: 'Poor Jim,' and closed her eyes.

The news arrived at ten o'clock that same night. Carter Bradford came over again and this time he went directly to Pat Wright and took her hand. She was so astonished she forgot to snatch it away. Carter said gently: 'It's up to you and Lola now, Pat.'

'What...on earth are you talking about?' asked Pat in a shrill tight voice.

'Dakin's men have found the car Jim escaped in.'

'*Found* it?'

Ellery Queen rose from a dark corner and came over into the light. 'If it's bad news, keep your voices down. Mrs Wright's just gone to bed, and John F. doesn't look as if he could take any more today. Where was the car found?'

'At the bottom of a ravine off Route 478A, up in the hills. About fifty miles from here.'

'Lord,' breathed Pat, staring.

'It had crashed through the highway rail,' growled Carter, 'just past a hairpin turn. The road is tricky up there. Dropped about two hundred feet—'

'And Jim?' asked Ellery.

Pat sat down in the love seat by the fireplace, looking up at Cart as if he were a judge about to pronounce doom. 'Found in the car.' Cart turned aside. 'Dead.' He turned back and looked humbly at Pat. 'So that's the end of the case. It's the end, Pat...'

'Poor Jim,' whispered Pat.

'I want to talk to you two,' said Mr Queen. It was very late. But there was no time. Time had been lost in the nightmare. Hermione had heard and Hermione had gone to pieces. Strange that the funeral of her daughter should have found her strong, and the news of her son-in-law's death weak. Perhaps it was the crushing tap after the heavy body blows. But Hermy collapsed, and Dr Willoughby spent hours with her trying to get her to sleep. John F. was in hardly better case: he had taken to trembling, and the doctor noticed it, and packed him off to bed in a guest room while Lola assisted with Hermy and Pat helped her

252

father up the stairs...Now it was over, and they were both asleep, and Lola had locked herself in, and Dr Willoughby had gone home, sagging. 'I want to talk to you two,' said Mr Queen.

Carter was still there. He had been a bed of rock for Hermy this night. She had actually clung to him while she wept, and Mr Queen thought this, too, was strange. And then he thought: No, this is the rock, the last rock, and Hermy clings. If she lets go, she drowns, they all drown. That is how she must feel. And he repeated: 'I want to talk to you two.'

Pat was suspended between worlds. She had been sitting beside Ellery on the porch, waiting for Carter Bradford to go home. Limply and far away. And now Carter had come out of the house, fumbling with his disreputable hat and fishing for some graceful way to negotiate the few steps of the porch and reach the haven of night shadows beyond, on the lawn.

'I don't think there's anything you can have to say that I'd want to hear,' said Carter huskily; but he made no further move to leave the porch.

'Ellery—don't,' said Pat, taking his hand in the gloom.

Ellery squeezed the cold young flesh. 'I've got to. This man thinks he's a martyr. *You* think you're being a heroine in some Byronic tragedy. You're both fools, and that's the truth.'

'Good night!' said Carter Bradford.

'Wait, Bradford. It's been a difficult time and an especially difficult day. And I shan't be in Wrightsville much longer.'

'Ellery!' Pat wailed.

'I've been here much too long already, Pat. Now there's nothing to keep me—nothing at all.'

'Nothing...at all?'

'Spare me your tender farewells,' snapped Cart. Then he laughed sheepishly and sat down on the step near them. 'Don't pay any attention to me, Queen. I'm in a fog these days. Sometimes I think I must be pretty much of a drip.'

Pat gaped at him. 'Cart—*you*? Being humble?'

'I've grown up a bit these past few months,' mumbled Cart.

'There's been a heap of growing up around here these past few months,' said Mr Queen mildly. 'How about you two being sensible and proving it?'

Pat took her hand away. 'Please, Ellery—'

'I know I'm meddling, and the lot of the meddler is hard,' sighed Mr Queen. 'But just the same, how about it?'

'I thought you were in love with her,' said Cart gruffly.

'I am.'

'Ellery!' cried Pat. 'You never *once*—'

'I'll be in love with that funny face of yours as long as I live,' said Mr Queen wistfully. 'It's a lovely funny face. But the trouble is, Pat, that you're not in love with *me*.' Pat stumbled over a word, then decided to say nothing. 'You're in love with Cart.'

Pat sprang from the porch chair. 'What if I was! Or am! People don't forget hurts and burns!'

'Oh, but they do,' said Mr Queen. 'People are more forgetful than you'd think. Also, they have better sense than we sometimes give them credit for. Emulate them.'

'It's impossible,' said Pat tightly. 'This is no time for silliness, anyway. You don't seem to realize what's happened to us in this town. We're pariahs. We've got a whole new battle on our hands to rehabilitate ourselves. And it's just Lola and me now to help Pop and Muth hold their heads up again. I'm not going to run out on them now, when they need me most.'

'I'd help you, Pat,' said Cart inaudibly.

'Thanks! We'll do it on our own. Is that all, Mr Queen?'

'There's no hurry,' murmured Mr Queen.

Pat stood there for a moment, then she said goodnight in an angry voice and went into the house. The door huffed. Ellery and Carter sat in silence for some time.

'Queen,' said Cart at last.

'Yes, Bradford?'

'This isn't over, is it?'

'What do you mean?'

'I have the most peculiar feeling you know something I don't.'

'Oh,' said Mr Queen. Then he said: 'Really?'

Carter slapped his hat against his thighs. 'I won't deny I've been pigheaded. Jim's death has done something to me, though. I don't know why it should, because it hasn't changed the facts one iota. He's still the only one who could have poisoned Nora's cocktail, and he's still the only one who had any conceivable motive to want her to die. And yet...I'm not so sure any more.'

'Since when?' asked Ellery in a peculiar tone.

'Since the report came in that he was found dead.'

'Why should that make a difference?'

Carter put his head between his hands. 'Because there's every reason to believe the car he was driving didn't go through that rail into the ravine by accident.'

'I see,' said Ellery.

'I didn't want to tell that to the Wrights. But Dakin and I both think Jim drove that car off the road deliberately.'

Mr Queen said nothing.

'And somehow that made me think—don't know why it should have—well, I began to wonder. Queen!' Carter jumped up. 'For God's sake, tell me if you know! I won't sleep until I'm sure. *Did Jim Haight commit that murder?*'

'No.'

Carter stared at him. 'Then who did?' he asked hoarsely.

Mr Queen rose, too. 'I shan't tell you.'

'Then you do know!'

'Yes,' sighed Ellery.

'But Queen, you can't—'

'Oh, but I can. Don't think it's easy for me. My whole training rebels against this sort of—well, connivance. But I like these people. They're nice people, and they've been through too much. I shouldn't want to hurt them any more. Let it go. The hell with it.'

'But you can tell me, Queen!' implored Cart.

'No. You're not sure of yourself, not yet, Bradford. You're rather a nice chap. But the growing-up process—it's been retarded.' Ellery shook his head. 'The best thing you can do is forget it,

255

and get Patty to marry you. She's crazy in love with you.'

Carter grasped Ellery's arm so powerfully that Ellery winced. 'But you've *got* to tell me!' he cried. 'How could I...knowing that anyone...any *one* of them...might be ...?'

Mr Queen frowned in the darkness. 'Tell you what I'll do with you, Cart,' he said at last. 'You help these people get back to normal in Wrightsville. You chase Patty Wright off her feet. Wear her down. But if you're not successful, if you feel you're not making any headway, wire me. I'm going back home. Send me a wire in New York and I'll come back. And maybe what I'll have to say to you and Patty will solve your problem.'

'Thanks,' said Carter Bradford hoarsely.

'I don't know that it will,' sighed Mr Queen. 'But who can tell? This has been the oddest case of mixed-up people, emotions, and events I've ever run across. Goodbye, Bradford.'

29

The Return of Ellery Queen

This, thought Mr Ellery Queen as he stood on the station platform, makes me an admiral all over again. The second voyage of
Columbus...He glanced moodily at the station sign. The tail of
the train that had brought him from New York was just disap-
pearing around the curve at Wrightsville Junction three miles
down the line. He could have sworn that the two small boys
swinging their dirty legs on the hand truck under the eaves of
the station were the same boys he had seen—in another century!—on his first arrival in Wrightsville. Gabby Warrum, the station agent, strolled out to stare at him. Ellery waved and made
hastily for Ed Hotchkiss's cab, drawn up on the gravel. As Ed
drove him 'uptown,' Ellery's hand tightened in his pocket about
the telegram he had received the night before. It was from Carter
Bradford, and it said simply: 'COME. PLEASE.'

He had not been away long—a matter of three weeks or so—
but just the same it seemed to him that Wrightsville had
changed. Or perhaps it would be truer to say that Wrightsville
had changed *back*. It was the old Wrightsville again, the town he
had come into so hopefully the previous August, nine months

ago. It had the same air of unhurried peace this lovely Sunday afternoon. Even the people seemed the old people, not the maddened horde of January and February and March and April. Mr Queen made a telephone call from the Hollis Hotel, then had Ed Hotchkiss drive him up the Hill. It was late afternoon and the birds were whizzing and chirping at a great rate around the old Wright house. He paid Ed off, watched the cab chug down the Hill, and then strolled up the walk. The little house next door— the house of Nora and Jim—was shuttered up; it looked opaque and ugly in its blindness. Mr Queen felt a tremor in his spine. That *was* a house to avoid. He hesitated at the front steps of the big house, and listened. There were voices from the rear gardens. So he went around, walking on the grass. He paused in the shadow of the oleander bush, where he could see them without being seen.

The sun was bright on Hermy, joggling a brand-new baby carriage in an extremely critical way. John F. was grinning, and Lola and Pat were making serious remarks about professional grandmothers, and how about giving a couple of aunts a chance to practise, for goodness' sake? The baby would be home from the hospital in just a couple of weeks! Mr Queen watched, unobserved, for a long time. His face was very grave. Once he half turned away, as if he meant to flee once and for all. But then he saw Patricia Wright's face again, and how it had grown older and thinner since last he had seen it; and so he sighed and set about making an end of things. After five minutes of delicate reconnaissance he managed to catch Pat's eye while the others were occupied—caught her eye and put his finger to his lips, shaking his head in warning.

Pat said something casual to her family and strolled towards him. He backed off, and then she came around the corner of the house and flew into his arms. 'Ellery! Darling! Oh, I'm so *glad* to see you! When did you come? What's the mystery for? Oh, you bug—I *am* glad!' She kissed him and held him close, and for a moment her face was the gay young face he had remembered.

He let her sprinkle his shoulder, and then he took her by the hand and drew her towards the front of the house. 'That's your convertible at the curb, isn't it? Let's go for a ride.'

'But Ellery, Pop and Muth and Lola—they'll be heartbroken if you don't—'

'I don't want to disturb them now, Patty. They look really happy, getting ready for the baby. How is she, by the way?' Ellery drove Pat's car down the Hill.

'Oh, wonderful. Such a clever little thing! And do you know? She looks just like—' Pat stopped. Then she said quietly: 'Just like Nora.'

'Does she? Then she must be a beautiful young lady indeed.'

'Oh, she is! And I'll swear she knows Muth! Really, I mean it. We can't *wait* for her to come home from the hospital. Of course, Mother won't let *any* of us touch little Nora—that's her name, you know—when we visit her—we're there practically *all* the time! except that I sneak over there alone once in a while when I'm not supposed to...Little Nora is going to have Nora's old bedroom—ought to see how we've fixed it up, with ivory furniture and gewgaws and big teddy bears and special nursery wallpaper and all—anyway, the little atom and I have secrets...well, we do!...of course, she's out of the incubator...and she gurgles at me and hangs on to my hand for dear life and *squeezes*. She's so fat, Ellery, you'd laugh!'

Ellery laughed. 'You're talking like the old Patty I knew—'

'You think so?' asked Pat in a queer voice.

'But you don't *look*—'

'No,' said Pat. 'No, I don't. I'm getting to be an old hag. Where are we going?'

'Nowhere in particular,' said Ellery vaguely, turning the car south and beginning to drive towards Wrightsville Junction.

'But tell me! What brings you back to Wrightsville? It must be us—couldn't be anyone else! How's the novel?'

'Finished.'

'Oh, grand! Ellery, you never let me read a word of it. How does it end?'

'That,' said Mr Queen, 'is one of my reasons for coming back to Wrightsville.'

'What do you mean?'

'The end,' he grinned. 'I've ended it, but it's always easy to change the last chapter—at least, certain elements not directly concerned with mystery plot. You might be a help there.'

'Me? But I'd love to! And—oh, Ellery. What am I thinking of? I haven't thanked you for that magnificent gift you sent me from New York. And those wonderful things you sent Muth, and Pop, and Lola. Oh, Ellery, you shouldn't have. We didn't do anything that—'

'Oh, bosh. Seeing much of Cart Bradford lately?'

Pat examined her fingernails. 'Oh, Cart's been around.'

'And Jim's funeral?'

'We buried him next to Nora.'

'Well!' said Ellery. 'You know, I feel a thirst coming on. How about stopping in somewhere for a long one, Patty?'

'All right,' said Pat moodily.

'Isn't that Gus Olesen's *Roadside Tavern* up ahead? By gosh, it is!' Pat glanced at him, but Ellery grinned and stopped the car before the tavern, and helped her out, at which she grimaced and said men in Wrightsville didn't do things like that, and Ellery grinned again, which made Pat laugh; and they walked into Gus Olesen's cool place arm in arm, laughing together; and Ellery walked her right up to the table where Carter Bradford sat waiting in a coil of knots, and said: 'Here she is, Bradford. C.O.D.'

'Pat,' said Cart, his palms flat on the table.

'Cart!' cried Pat.

'Good morrow, good morrow,' chanted a cracked voice; and Mr Queen saw old Anderson the Soak, seated at a nearby table

260

with a fistful of dollar bills in one hand and a row of empty whisky glasses before him.

'Good morrow to you, Mr Anderson,' said Mr Queen; and while he nodded and smiled at Mr Anderson, things were happening at the table; so that when he turned back there was Pat, seated, and Carter seated, and they were glaring at each other across the table. So Mr Queen sat down, too, and said to Gus Olesen: 'Use your imagination, Gus.' Gus scratched his head and got busy behind the bar.

'Ellery.' Pat's eyes were troubled. 'You tricked me into coming here with you.'

'I wasn't sure you'd come, untricked,' murmured Mr Queen.

'*I* asked Queen to come back to Wrightsville, Pat,' said Cart hoarsely. 'He said he'd—Pat, I've tried to see you, I've tried to make you understand that we can wipe the past out, and I'm in love with you and always was and always will be, and that I want to marry you more than anything in the world—'

'Let's not discuss *that* any more,' said Pat. She began making pleats in the skirt of the tablecloth. Carter seized a tall glass Gus set down before him; and Pat did, too, with a sort of gratitude for the diversion; and they sat in silence for a while, drinking and not looking at each other.

At his table old Anderson had risen, one hand on the cloth to steady himself, and he was chanting:—

'I believe a leaf of grass is no less than the journey-work of the stars,
And the pismire is equally perfect, and a grain of sand, and the egg of the
  wren,
And the tree-toad is a chef-d'oeuvre of the highest,
And the running blackberry would adorn the parlors of heaven—'

'Siddown, Mr Anderson,' said Gus Olesen gently. 'You're rockin' the boat.'

'Whitman,' said Mr Queen, looking around. 'And very apt.'

Old Anderson leered, and went on:—

'And the narrowest hinge in my hand puts to scorn all machinery,
And the cow, crunching with depressed head, surpasses any statue,
And a mouse is miracle enough to stagger sextillions of infidels!'

And with a courtly bow the Old Soak sat down again and began to pound out rhythms on the table. 'I was a poet!' he shouted. His lips waggled. 'And l-look at me now...'

'Yes,' said Mr Queen thoughtfully. 'That's very true indeed.'

'Here's your poison!' said Gus at the next table, slopping a glass of whisky before Mr Anderson. Then Gus looked very guilty and, avoiding the startled eyes of Pat, went quickly behind his bar and hid himself in a copy of Frank Lloyd's *Record*. Mr Anderson drank, murmuring to himself in his gullet.

'Pat,' said Mr Queen, 'I came back here today to tell you and Carter who was really responsible for the crimes Jim Haight was charged with.'

'Oh,' said Patty, and she sucked in her breath.

'There are miracles in the human mind, too. You told me something in the hospital waiting room the day Nora died—one little acorn fact—and it grew into a tall tree in my mind.'

'"And a mouse,"' shouted Mr Anderson exultantly, '"is miracle enough to stagger sextillions of infidels!"'

Pat whispered: 'Then it wasn't Jim after all...Ellery, no! Don't! Please! No!'

'Yes,' said Ellery gently. 'That thing is standing between you and Cart. It's a question mark that would outlive you both. I want to erase it and put a period in its place. Then the chapter will be closed and you and Cart can look each other in the eye again with some sort of abiding faith.' He sipped his drink, frowning. 'I hope!'

'You hope?' muttered Cart.

'The truth,' said Ellery soberly, 'is unpleasant.'

'Ellery!' cried Pat.

262

'But you're not children, either of you. Don't delude your-selves. It would stand between you even if you married...the uncertainty of it, the not-knowing, the doubt and the night-and-day question. It's what's keeping you apart, and what has kept you apart. Yes, the truth is unpleasant. But at least it *is* the truth, and if you know the truth, you have knowledge; and if you have knowledge, you can make a decision with durability...Pat, this is surgery. It's cut the tumor out, or die. Shall I operate?'

Mr Anderson was singing 'Under the Greenwood Tree' in a soft croak, beating time with his empty whisky glass. Patty sat up perfectly straight, her hands clasped about her glass. 'Go ahead...Doctor.' And Cart took a long swallow, and nodded.

Mr Queen sighed. 'Do you recall, Pat, telling me in the hospi-tal about the time I came into Nora's house—last Hallowe'en—and found you and Nora transferring books from the living room to Jim's new study upstairs?' Pat nodded wordlessly. 'And what did you tell me? That the books you and Nora were lug-ging upstairs you had just removed from a *nailed box*. That you'd gone down into the cellar just a few minutes before I dropped in, seen the box of books down there all nailed up, exactly as Ed Hotchkiss had left it when he cabbed it from the station weeks and weeks before...*seen the box intact and opened it yourself.*'

'A box of books?' muttered Carter.

'That box of books, Cart, had been part of Jim's luggage which he'd shipped from New York to Wrightsville when he came back to Wrightsville to make up with Nora. He'd checked it at the Wrightsville station, Cart. It was at the station all the time Jim and Nora were away on their honeymoon; it was brought to the new house only on their return, stored down in the cellar, and on Hallowe'en Pat found that box still intact, still nailed up, still unopened. That was the fact I hadn't known—the kernel fact, the acorn fact, that told me the truth.'

'But how, Ellery?' asked Pat, feeling her head.

'You'll see in a moment, honey. All the time, I'd assumed that the books I saw you and Nora handling were merely being transferred from the living-room bookshelves to Jim's new study upstairs. I thought they were *house books,* books of Jim's and Nora's that had been in the house for some time. It was a natural assumption—I saw no box on the living-room floor, no nails—'

'I'd emptied the box and taken the box, nails, and tools down to the cellar just before you came in,' said Pat. 'I told you that in the hospital that day.'

'Too late,' growled Ellery. 'When I came in, I saw no evidence of such a thing. And I'm no clairvoyant.'

'But what's the point?' frowned Carter Bradford.

'One of the books in the wooden box Patty opened that Hallowe'en,' said Ellery, 'was Jim's copy of Edgcomb's *Toxicology.*'

Cart's jaw dropped. 'The marked passage about arsenic!'

'Not only that, but it was from between two pages of that volume that the three letters fell out.'

This time Cart said nothing. And Pat was looking at Ellery with deep quotation marks between her eyebrows.

'Now, since the box had been nailed up in New York and sent to General Delivery, Wrightsville, where it was held, and the toxicology book with the letters in it was found by us directly after the box was unpacked—the letters fell out as Nora dropped an armful of books quite by accident—then the conclusion is absolutely inescapable: *Jim could not possibly have written those three letters in Wrightsville.* And when I saw that I saw the whole thing. The letters *must* have been written by Jim in New York—*before* he returned to Wrightsville to ask Nora for the second time to marry him, *before* he knew that Nora would accept him after his desertion of her and his three-year absence!'

'Yes,' mumbled Carter Bradford.

'But don't you see?' cried Ellery. 'How can we now state with such fatuous certainty that the sickness and death Jim predicted for his 'wife' in those three letters *referred to Nora?* True, Nora was Jim's wife when the letters were found, *but she was NOT his wife, nor could Jim have known she would BE his wife, when he originally wrote them!*'

264

He stopped and, even though it was cool in Gus Olesen's tap-room, he dried his face with a handkerchief and took a long pull at his glass. At the next table, Mr Anderson snored.

Pat gasped: 'But Ellery, if those three letters didn't refer to Nora, then the whole thing—the whole thing—'

'Let me tell it my way,' said Mr Queen in a harsh voice. 'Once doubt is raised that the "wife" mentioned in the three letters was Nora, then two facts that before seemed irrelevant simply shout to be noticed. One is that the letters bore *incomplete dates*. That is, they marked the month, and the day of the month, *but not the year*. So the three holidays—Thanksgiving, Christmas, and New Year's—which Jim had written down on the successive letters as marking the dates of his "wife's" illness, more serious illness, and finally death, might have been the similar dates of one, two, or even three years before! Not 1940 at all but 1939, or 1938, or 1937...

'And the second fact, of course, was that not once did any of the letters refer to *the name Nora;* the references were consistently to *"my wife."*

'If Jim wrote those letters in New York—before his marriage to Nora, before he even knew Nora would marry him—then Jim could not have been writing about *Nora's* illness or *Nora's* death. And if we can't believe this —an assumption we all took for granted from the beginning of the case—then the whole struc-ture which postulated *Nora* as Jim's intended poison victim col-lapses.'

'This is incredible,' muttered Carter. 'Incredible.'

'I'm confused,' moaned Patty. 'You mean—'

'I mean,' said Mr Queen, 'that Nora was never threatened, Nora was never in danger...*Nora was never meant to be murdered.*'

Pat shook her head violently, and groped for her glass. 'But that opens up a whole new field of speculation!' exclaimed Carter. 'If Nora wasn't meant to be murdered—ever, at all—'

'What are the facts?' argued Ellery. 'A woman did die on New Year's Eve: Rosemary Haight. When we thought Nora was the intended victim, we said Rosemary died by accident. But now that we know Nora *wasn't* the intended victim, surely it follows that Rosemary did NOT die by accident—*that Rosemary was meant to be murdered from the beginning?'*

'Rosemary was meant to be murdered from the beginning,' repeated Pat slowly, as if the words were in a language she didn't understand.

'But Queen—' protested Bradford.

'I know, I know,' sighed Ellery. 'It raises tremendous difficulties and objections. But with Nora eliminated as the intended victim, it's the only logical explanation for the crime. So we've got to accept it as our new premise. Rosemary was *meant* to be murdered. Immediately I asked myself, Did the three letters have anything to do with Rosemary's death? Superficially, no. The letters referred to the death of Jim's wife—'

'And Rosemary was Jim's sister,' said Pat with a frown.

'Yes, and besides Rosemary had shown no signs of the illnesses predicted for Thanksgiving Day and Christmas Day. Moreover, since the three letters can now be interpreted as two or three years old or more, they no longer appear necessarily criminal. They can merely refer to the natural death of a previous wife of Jim's—not Nora, but *a first wife whom Jim married in New York* and who died there some New Year's Day between the time Jim ran out on Nora and the time he came back to marry Nora.'

'But Jim never said anything about a first wife,' objected Pat.

'That wouldn't prove he hadn't had one,' said Cart.

'No,' nodded Ellery. 'So it all might have been perfectly innocent. Except for two highly significant and suspicious factors: first, that the letters were written but never mailed, as if no death *had* occurred in New York; and second, that a woman did actually die in Wrightsville on New Year's Day of 1941, as written by Jim in his third and last letter a long time before it happened. Coincidence? My gorge rises at the very notion. No, I saw that there must be *some* connection between Rosemary's death and the three letters Jim wrote—he did write them, of course; poor

Judge Eli Martin's attempt to cast doubt on their authenticity during the trial was a brave but transparent act of desperation.'

Mr Anderson woke up, looking annoyed. But Gus Olesen shook his head. Mr Anderson tottered over to the bar. '"Landlord,"' he leered, '"fill the flowing bowl until it does run over!"'

'We don't serve in bowls, and besides, Andy, you've had enough,' said Gus reprovingly. Mr Anderson began to weep, his head on the bar; and after a few sobs, he fell asleep again.

'What connection,' continued Mr Queen thoughtfully, 'is possible between Rosemary Haight's death and the three letters Jim Haight wrote long, long before? And with this question,' he said, 'we come to the heart of the problem. For with Rosemary the intended victim all along, the use of the three letters can be interpreted as a stupendous blind, a clever deception, *a psychological smoke-screen to conceal the truth from the authorities!* Isn't that what happened? Didn't you and Dakin, Bradford, instantly dismiss Rosemary's death as a factor and concentrate on Nora as the intended victim? But that was just what Rosemary's murderer would want you to do! You ignored the actual victim to look for murder motives against the ostensible victim. And so you built your case around Jim, who was the only person who could possibly have poisoned *Nora*, and never for an instant sought the real criminal—*the person with the motive and opportunity to poison Rosemary.*'

Pat was by now so bewildered that she gave herself up wholly to listening. But Carter Bradford was following with a savage intentness, hunched over the table and never taking his eyes from Ellery's face. 'Go on!' he said. 'Go on, Queen!'

'Let's go back,' said Mr Queen, lighting a cigarette. 'We now know Jim's three letters referred to a hidden, a never-mentioned, a first wife. If this woman died on New Year's Day two or three years ago, why didn't Jim mail the letters to his sister? More important than that, why didn't he disclose the fact to you or Dakin when he was arrested? Why didn't Jim tell Judge Martin, his attorney, that the letters didn't mean Nora, for use as a possible defense in his trial? For if the first wife were in all truth dead, it would have been a simple matter to corroborate—the attending physician's affidavit, the death certificate, a dozen things. *But Jim kept his mouth shut.* He didn't by so much as a sober word indicate that he'd married another woman between the time he and Nora broke up almost four years ago and the time he returned to Wrightsville to marry her. Why? Why Jim's mysterious silence on this point?'

'Maybe,' said Pat with a shiver, 'because he'd actually planned and carried out the murder of his first wife.'

'Then why didn't he mail the letters to his sister?' argued Cart. 'Since he'd presumably written them for that eventuality?'

'Ah,' said Mr Queen. 'The very counterpoint. So I said to myself: Is it possible that the murder Jim had planned of his first wife *did not take place at the time it was supposed to?*'

'You mean she was alive when Jim came back to Wrightsville?' gasped Pat.

'Not merely alive,' said Mr Queen; he slowly ground out the butt of his cigarette in an ash tray. 'She followed Jim here.'

'The first *wife?*' Carter gaped.

'She came to *Wrightsville?*' cried Pat.

'Yes, but not as Jim's first wife. Not as Jim's any-wife.'

'Then who—?'

'*She came to Wrightsville,*' said Ellery, '*as Jim's sister.*'

Mr Anderson came to life at the bar, and began: 'Landlord—!'

'Go home,' said Gus, shaking his head.

'Mead! Nepenthe!' implored Mr Anderson.

'We don't carry that stuff,' said Gus.

'As Jim's sister,' whispered Pat. 'The woman Jim introduced to us as his sister Rosemary *wasn't his sister at all?* She was his *wife?*'

'Yes.' Ellery motioned to Gus Olesen. But Gus had the second round ready. Mr Anderson followed the tray with gleaming eyes. And no one spoke until Gus returned to the bar.

'But Queen,' said Carter, dazed, 'how in hell can you know *that?*'

'Well, whose word have we that the woman who called herself Rosemary Haight was Jim Haight's sister?' demanded Ellery. 'Only the word of Jim and Rosemary, and they're both dead...However, that's not how I know she was his first wife. I know that because I know who really killed her. And knowing who really killed her, it just isn't possible for Rosemary to have been Jim Haight's sister. The only person she could have been, the only person against whom the murderer had motive, was Jim's first wife; as you'll see.'

'But Ellery,' said Pat, 'didn't you tell me yourself that day, by comparing the woman's handwriting on Steve Polaris's trucking receipt with the handwriting on the flap of the letter Jim received from "Rosemary Haight," that that proved the woman *was* Jim's sister?'

'I was wrong,' said Mr Queen, frowning. 'I was stupidly wrong. All that the two signatures proved, really, was that *the same woman had written them both.* That meant only that the woman who showed up here was the same woman who wrote Jim that letter which disturbed him so. I was misled by the fact that on the envelope she had signed the name "Rosemary Haight." Well, she was just using that name. I was wrong, I was stupid, and you should have caught me up, Patty. Let's drink!'

'But if the woman who was poisoned New Year's Eve was Jim's first wife,' protested Carter, 'why didn't Jim's real sister come forward after the murder? Lord knows the case had enough publicity!'

'If he had a sister,' mumbled Patty. 'If he had one!'

'Oh, he had a sister,' said Ellery wearily. 'Otherwise, why should he have written those letters to one? When he originally penned them, in planning the murder of his then-wife—the murder he didn't pull off—he expected those letters to give him an appearance of innocence. He expected to send them to his real sister, Rosemary Haight. It would have to be a genuine sister to stand the searchlight of a murder investigation, or he'd really be in a mess. So Jim had a sister, all right.'

'But the papers!' said Pat. 'Cart's right, Ellery. The papers were full of news about "Rosemary Haight, sister of James Haight," and how she *died* here in Wrightsville. If Jim had a real sister Rosemary, surely she'd have come lickety-split to Wrightsville to expose the mistake?'

'Not necessarily. But the fact is—Jim's sister *did* come to Wrightsville, Patty. Whether she came to expose the mistake I can't say; but certainly, after she'd had a talk with her brother Jim, she decided to say nothing about her true identity. I suppose Jim made her promise to keep quiet. And she'd kept that promise.'

'I don't follow, I don't follow,' said Cart irritably. 'You're like one of those fellows who keep pulling rabbits out of a hat. You mean the real Rosemary Haight's been in Wrightsville all these months, calling herself by some other name?'

Mr Queen shrugged. 'Who helped Jim in his trouble? The Wright family, a small group of old friends whose identities, of course, are unquestionable, myself, and...one other person. And that person a woman.'

'Roberta!' gasped Pat. '*Roberta Roberts, the newspaper woman!*'

'The only outsider of the sex that fits,' nodded Ellery. 'Yes, Roberta Roberts. Who else? She "believed" in Jim's innocence from the start, she fought for him, she sacrificed her job for him, and at the end—in desperation—she provided the car by which Jim escaped his guards at the cemetery. Yes, Roberta's the only one who *could* be Jim's sister, from the facts; it explains all the peculiarities of her conduct. I suppose "Roberta Roberts" has been her professional name for years. But her real name is Rosemary Haight!'

'So that's why she cried so at Jim's funeral,' said Pat softly. And there was no sound but the swish of Gus Olesen's cloth on the bar and Mr Anderson's troubled muttering.

'It gets clearer,' growled Cart at last. 'But what I don't understand is why Jim's first wife came to Wrightsville *calling* herself Jim's sister.'

'And why,' added Pat, 'Jim permitted the deception. It's mad, the whole thing!'

'No,' said Ellery, 'it's frighteningly sane, if you'll only stop to think. You ask why. I asked why, too. And when I thought about it, I saw what must have happened.' He drank deeply of the contents of the frosty glass. 'Look. Jim left almost four years ago on the eve of his wedding to Nora, as a result of their quarrel about the house. He went to New York, I should suppose desperately unhappy. But remember Jim's character. An iron streak of independence—that's usually from the same lode as stubbornness and pride. They kept him from writing to Nora, from coming back to Wrightsville, from being a sensible human being; although of course Nora was as much to blame for not understanding how much standing on his own feet meant to a man like Jim. At any rate, back in New York, Jim's life—as he must have thought—blasted, Jim ran into this woman. We all saw something of her—a sultry, sulky wench, quite seductive...especially attractive to a man licking the wounds of an unhappy love affair. On the rebound, this woman hooked Jim. They must have been miserable together. Jim was a good solid boy, and the woman was a fly-by-night, selfish and capable of driving a man quite mad with exasperation. She must have made his life intolerable, because Jim wasn't the killing type and still he did finally plan to kill her. The fact that he planned each detail of her murder so carefully, even to writing those letters to his sister *in advance*—a silly thing to do!—shows how obsessed he became with the necessity of being rid of her.'

'I should think,' said Pat in a sick voice, 'that he could have divorced her!'

Ellery shrugged again. 'I'm sure that if he could have, he would. Which leads me to believe that, at first, she wouldn't give him a divorce. The leech, genus homo, sex female. Of course, we

271

can't be sure of anything. But Cart, I'm willing to lay you odds that if you followed the trail back you'd discover (a) that she refused to give him a divorce, (b) that he then planned to murder her, (c) that she somehow got wind of his plans, was frightened, ran away from him, causing him to abandon his plans, and (d) that she later informed him that she had got a divorce!

'Because what follows makes all that inevitable. We know that Jim was married to one woman—we know that subsequently he came rushing back to Wrightsville and asked *Nora* to marry him. He would only have done that if *he thought he was free of the first.* But to think so, she must have given him reason. So I say she told him she'd got a divorce.

'What happened? Jim married Nora; in his excited emotional state he completely forgot about those letters which had been lying in the toxicology book for heaven knows how long. Then the honeymoon. Jim and Nora returned to Wrightsville to take up their married life in the little house...and the trouble began. Jim received a letter from his "sister." Remember that morning, Patty? The postman brought a letter, and Jim read it and was tremendously agitated, and then later he said it was from his "sister" and wouldn't it be proper to ask her to Wrightsville for a visit...' Pat nodded.

'The woman who turned up claiming to be Jim's sister—and whom we accepted as his sister and introduced as his sister—was, we now know, not his sister at all but his first wife.

'But there's a more factual proof that the letter was from the first wife...the business of the identical signatures on the charred flap of the letter Jim received and on Steve Polaris's receipt for the visitor's luggage. So it *was* the first wife who wrote to Jim, and since Jim could scarcely have relished the idea of her coming to Wrightsville, it must have been *her* idea, not his, and that's what her letter to him was about.

'But why did she write to Jim and appear in Wrightsville as Jim's sister at all? In fact, why did Jim permit her to come? Or, if he couldn't keep her from coming, why did he connive at the deception after her arrival and keep it a secret until her death and *still* afterward? There can be one reason: *she had a powerful hold over him.*

'Confirmation of that? Yes. Jim was "squandering" lots of money—and mark that his squandering habits coincided in point of time with the arrival of his first wife in Wrightsville! Why was he pawning Nora's jewelry? Why did he borrow five thousand dollars from the Wrightsville Personal Finance Corporation? Why did he keep bleeding Nora for cash? Why? Where did all that money go? Gambling, you said, Cart. And tried to prove it in court—'

'But Jim himself admitted to Nora that he gambled the money away, according to the testimony,' protested Carter.

'Naturally if his secret wife was blackmailing him, he'd have to invent an excuse to Nora to explain his sudden appetite for huge sums of cash! The fact is, Cart, you never did *prove* Jim was losing all that money gambling in Vic Carlatti's *Hot Spot.* You couldn't find a single eyewitness to his gambling there, or you'd have produced one. The best you could get was an eavesdropper who overheard *Jim* say to Nora that he'd been gambling! Yes, Jim drank a lot at the *Hot Spot*—he was desperate; but he wasn't gambling there.

'Still, that money was going somewhere. Well, haven't we postulated a woman with a powerful hold on him? Conclusion: *He was giving Rosemary that money*—I mean, the woman who called herself Rosemary, the woman who subsequently died on New Year's Eve. He was giving it on demand to the cold-blooded creature he had to continue calling his sister—the woman he'd actually been married to!'

'But what could the hold on him have been, Ellery?' asked Pat. 'It must have been something terrific!'

'Which is why I can see only one answer,' said Ellery grimly. 'It fits into everything we know like plaster of Paris into a mold. Suppose the woman we're calling Rosemary—the first wife—never *did get a divorce*? Suppose she'd only fooled Jim into believing he was free? Perhaps by showing him forged divorce papers? Anything can be procured for money! Then the whole thing makes sense. Then Jim, when he'd married Nora, had committed bigamy. Then he was in this woman's clutches for good...She warned Jim in advance by letter and then came to Wrightsville posing as his sister so that she could blackmail him on the spot without exposing her true identity to Nora and the family! So now we know why she posed as his sister, too. If she exposed her real status, her power over Jim was gone. She wanted money, not revenge. It was only by holding a *threat* of exposure over Jim's head that she would be able to suck him dry. To do that she had to pretend to be someone else...And Jim, caught in her trap, had to acknowledge her as his sister, had to pay her until he went nearly insane with despair. Rosemary knew her victim. For Jim couldn't let Nora learn the truth—'

'No,' moaned Pat.

'Why not?' asked Carter Bradford.

'Once before, when Jim ran out on her, he'd humiliated Nora frightfully in the eyes of her family and the town—the town especially. There are no secrets or delicacies, and there is much cruelty, in the Wrightsvilles of this world; and if you're a sensitive, inhibited, self-conscious Nora, public scandal can be a major tragedy and a curse to damn your life past regeneration. Jim saw what his first defection had done to Nora, how it had driven her into a shell, made her over into a frightened little person half crazy with shame, hiding from Wrightsville, from her friends, even from her family. If a mere jilting at the altar did that to Nora, what wouldn't the shocking revelation that she'd married a bigamist do to her? It would drive her mad; it might even kill her.

'Jim realized all that...The trap Rosemary laid and sprung was Satanic. Jim simply couldn't admit to Nora or let her find out that she was not a legally married woman, that their marriage was not a true marriage, and that their coming child...

Remember Mrs Wright testified that Jim knew almost as soon as it happened that Nora was going to have a baby.'

'This,' said Carter hoarsely, 'is damnable.'

Ellery sipped his drink and then lit a fresh cigarette, frowning at the incandescent end for some time. 'It gets more difficult to tell, too,' he murmured at last. 'Jim paid and paid, and borrowed money everywhere to keep the evil tongue of that woman from telling the awful truth which would have unbalanced Nora, or killed her.'

Pat was close to tears. 'It's a wonder poor Jim didn't embezzle funds at Pop's bank!'

'And in drunken rages Jim swore he'd "get rid of her"—that he'd "kill her"—and made it plain that he was speaking of his "wife." Of course he was. He was speaking of the only legal wife he had—the woman calling herself Rosemary Haight and posing as his sister. When Jim foolishly made those alcoholic threats *he never meant Nora at all.*'

'But it seems to me,' muttered Cart, 'that when he was arrested, facing a conviction, to keep quiet *then*—'

'I'm afraid,' replied Mr Queen with a sad smile, 'that Jim in his way was a great man. He was willing to die to make up to Nora for what he had done to her. And the only way he could make up to her was to pass out in silence. He unquestionably swore his real sister, Roberta Roberts, to secrecy. For to have told you and Chief Dakin the truth, Cart, Jim would have had to reveal Rosemary's true identity, and that meant revealing the whole story of his previous marriage to her, the divorce-that-wasn't-a-divorce, and consequently Nora's status as a pregnant, yet unmarried, woman. Besides, revealing the truth wouldn't have done *him* any good, anyway. For Jim had infinitely more motive to murder Rosemary than to murder Nora. No, he decided the best course was to carry the whole sickening story with him to the grave.'

Pat was crying openly now.

'And,' muttered Mr Queen. 'Jim had still another reason for keeping quiet. The biggest reason of all. A heroic, an epic, reason. I wonder if you two have any idea what it is.' They stared at him, at each other. 'No,' sighed Mr Queen. 'I suppose you wouldn't. The truth is so staggeringly simple that we see right through it, as if it were a pane of glass. It's two-plus-two, or rather two-minus-one; and those are the most difficult calculations of all.'

A bulbous organ the color of fresh blood appeared over his shoulder; and they saw that it was only Mr Anderson's wonderful nose. '*O vita, misero longa! felici brevis!*' croaked Mr Anderson. 'Friends, heed the wisdom of the ancients...I suppose you are wondering how I, poor wretch, am well-provided with lucre this heaven-sent day. Well, I am a remittance man, as they say, and my ship has touched port today. *Felici brevis!*' And he started to fumble for Patty's glass.

'Why don't you go over there in the corner and shut up, Andy?' shouted Cart.

'Sir,' said Mr Anderson, going away with Pat's glass, '"the sands are number'd that make up my life; Here must I stay and here my life must end."' He sat down at his table and drank quickly.

'Ellery, you can't stop now!' said Pat.

'Are you two prepared to hear the truth?'

Pat looked at Carter, and Carter looked at Pat. He reached across the table and took her hand. 'Shoot,' said Carter.

Mr Queen nodded. 'There's only one question left to be answered—the most important question of all: who really poisoned Rosemary? The case against Jim had shown that he alone had opportunity, that he alone had motive, that he alone had control of the distribution of the cocktails and therefore was the only one who could have been positive the poisoned cocktail reached its intended victim. Further, Cart, you proved that Jim had bought rat poison and so could have had arsenic to drop into the fatal cocktail. All this is reasonable and, indeed, unassailable—*if* Jim meant to kill Nora, to whom he handed the cocktail. But now we know Jim never intended to kill Nora at all!—that the real victim from the beginning was meant to be Rosemary, and only Rosemary!

'So I had to refocus my mental binoculars. Now that I knew *Rosemary* was the intended victim, was the case just as conclusive against Jim as when Nora was believed to be the victim? Well, Jim still had opportunity to poison the cocktail; with Rosemary the victim he had infinitely greater motive; he still had a supply of arsenic available. BUT—with Rosemary the victim, did Jim control the *distribution* of the fatal cocktail? Remember, he handed the cocktail subsequently found to contain arsenic to Nora...Could he have been sure the poisoned cocktail would go to *Rosemary?*

'*No!*' cried Ellery, and his voice was suddenly like a knife. 'True, he handed Rosemary a cocktail previous to that last round. But that previous cocktail had not been poisoned. In that last round *only Nora's cocktail*—the one that poisoned both Nora and Rosemary—had arsenic in it! If *Jim* had dropped the arsenic into the cocktail he handed Nora, how could he know that *Rosemary* would drink it?

'He couldn't know. It was such an unlikely event that he couldn't even dream it would happen...imagine it, or plan it, or count on it. Actually, *Jim was out of the living room*—if you'll recall the facts—*at the time Rosemary drank Nora's cocktail*. So this peripatetic mind had to query: Since *Jim* couldn't be sure Rosemary would drink that poisoned cocktail, who *could* be sure?'

Carter Bradford and Patricia Wright were pressing against the edge of the table, still, rigid, not breathing.

Mr Queen shrugged. 'And instantly—two minus one. Instantly. It was unbelievable, and it was sickening, and it was the only possible truth. Two minus one—one. Just one...Just one other person had opportunity to poison that cocktail, for just one other person handled it before it reached Rosemary! Just one other person had motive to kill Rosemary and could have

277

utilized the rat poison for murder which Jim had bought for innocent, mice-exterminating purposes...perhaps at someone else's suggestion. Remember he went back to Myron Garback's pharmacy a second time for another tin, shortly after his first purchase of Quicko, telling Garback he had "mislaid" the first tin? How do you suppose that first tin came to be "mislaid"? With what we now know, isn't it evident that it wasn't mislaid at all, but stolen and stored away by the only other person in Jim's house with motive to kill Rosemary?'

Mr Queen glanced at Patricia Wright and at once closed his eyes, as if they pained him. And he stuck the cigarette into the corner of his mouth and said through his teeth: *'That person could only have been the one who actually handed Rosemary the cocktail on New Year's Eve.'*

Carter Bradford licked his lips over and over. Pat was frozen. 'I'm sorry, Pat,' said Ellery, opening his eyes. 'I'm frightfully, terribly sorry. But it's as logical as death itself. And to give you two a chance, I had to tell you both.'

Pat said faintly: 'Not Nora. Oh, *not Nora!'*

30

The Second Sunday in May

'A drop too much to drink,' said Mr Queen quickly to Gus Olesen. 'May we use your back room, Gus?'

'Sure, sure,' said Gus. 'Say, I'm sorry about this, Mr Bradford. That's good rum I used in those drinks. And she only had one—Andy took her second one. Lemmy give you a hand—'

'We can manage her all right, thank you,' said Mr Queen, 'although I do think a couple of fingers of bourbon might help.'

'But if she's sick—' began Gus, puzzled. 'Okay!'

The Old Soak stared blindly as Carter and Ellery helped Pat, whose eyes were glassy chips of agony, into Gus Olesen's back room. They set her down on Gus's old horsehair black leather couch, and when Gus hurried in with a glass of whisky Carter Bradford forced her to drink. Pat choked, her eyes streaming; then she pushed the glass aside and threw herself back on the tufted leather, her face to the wall. 'She feels fine already,' said Mr Queen reassuringly. 'Thanks, Gus. We'll take care of Miss Wright.' Gus went away, shaking his head and muttering that that was good rum—he didn't serve rat poison like that chiseling greaseball Vic Carlatti over at the *Hot Spot*.

Pat lay still. Carter stood over her awkwardly. Then he sat down and took her hand. Ellery saw her tanned fingers go white with pressure. He turned away and strolled over to the other side of the room to examine the traditional Bock Beer poster. There was no sound at all, anywhere.

Until he heard Pat murmur: 'Ellery.' He turned around. She was sitting up on the couch again, both her hands in Carter Bradford's; he was holding on to them for dear life, almost as if it were he who needed comforting, not she. Ellery guessed that in those few seconds of silence a great battle had been fought, and won. He drew a chair over to the couch and sat down facing them. 'Tell me the rest,' said Pat steadily, her eyes in his. 'Go on, Ellery. Tell me the rest.'

'It doesn't make any difference, Patty darling,' mumbled Cart. 'Oh, you know that. You know it.'

'I know it, Cart.'

'Whatever it was, darling—she was sick. I guess she was always a neurotic, always pretty close to the borderline.'

'Yes, Cart. Tell me the rest, Ellery.'

'Pat, do you remember telling me about dropping in to Nora's a few days after Rosemary arrived, in early November, and finding Nora "trapped" in the serving pantry?'

'You mean when Nora overheard Jim and Rosemary having an argument?'

'Yes. You said you came in at the tail end and didn't hear anything of consequence. And that Nora wouldn't tell you what she'd overheard. You said Nora had the same kind of look on her face as that day when those three letters tumbled out of the toxicology book.'

'Yes...' said Pat.

'That must have been the turning point, Pat. That must have been the time when Nora learned the whole truth—by pure accident, she learned from the lips of Jim and Rosemary themselves that Rosemary wasn't his sister but his wife, that she herself was not legally married...the whole sordid story.' Ellery examined his hands. 'It...unbalanced Nora. In a twinkling her whole world came tumbling down, and her moral sense and mental health with it. She faced a humiliation too sickening to be faced. And Nora was emotionally weakened by the unnatural life she'd been leading for the years between Jim's sudden desertion and her marriage to him...Nora slipped over the line.'

'Over the line,' whispered Pat. Her lips were white.

'She planned to take revenge on the two people who, as her disturbed mind now saw it, had shamed her and ruined her life. She planned to kill Jim's first wife, the hated woman who called herself Rosemary. She planned to have Jim pay for the crime by using the very tools he'd manufactured for a similar purpose years before and which were now, as if by an act of providence, thrust into her hand. She must have worked it out slowly. But work it out she did. She had those three puzzling letters that were puzzling no longer. She had Jim's own conduct to help her create the illusion of his guilt. And she found in herself a great strength and a great cunning; a talent, almost a genius, for deceiving the world as to her true emotions.'

Pat closed her eyes, and Carter kissed her hand.

'Knowing that we knew about the letters—you and I, Pat—Nora deliberately carried out the pattern of the three letters. She deliberately swallowed a small dose of arsenic on Thanksgiving Day so that it would seem to us Jim was following his schedule. And recall what she did immediately after showing symptoms of arsenic poisoning at the dinner table? She ran upstairs and gulped great quantities of milk of magnesia, which, as I told you later that night in my room, Pat, is an emergency antidote for arsenic poisoning. Not a well-known fact, Patty. *Nora had looked it up.* That doesn't prove she poisoned herself but it's significant when you tack it onto the other things she did.

'Patty, must I go on? Let Carter take you home—'

'I want the whole thing,' said Pat. 'This moment, Ellery. Finish.'

'That's my baby,' said Carter Bradford huskily.

'I said "the other things she did,"' said Ellery in a low tone.

'Recall them! If Nora was as concerned over Jim's safety as she pretended, would she have left those three incriminating letters to be found in her hatbox? Wouldn't any wife who felt as she claimed to feel about Jim have burned those letters instantly? But no—*Nora saved them*...Of course. She knew they would turn out to be the most damning evidence against Jim when he was arrested, and she made sure they survived to be used against him. As a matter of cold fact, how *did* Dakin eventually find them?'

'Nora...Nora called our attention to them,' said Cart feebly. 'When she had hysterics and mentioned the letters, which we didn't even know about—'

'Mentioned?' cried Ellery. 'Hysterics? My dear Bradford, that was the most superb kind of acting! She pretended to be hysterical, she pretended that *I* had already told you about the letters! In saying so, she established the existence of the letters for your benefit. A terrible point, that one. But until I knew Nora was the culprit, it had no meaning for me.' He stopped and fumbled for a cigarette.

'What else, Ellery?' demanded Pat in a shaky voice.

'Just one thing. Pat, you're sure—You look ill.'

'What else?'

'Jim. *He was the only one who knew the truth*, although Roberta Roberts may have guessed it. Jim knew *he* hadn't poisoned the cocktail, so he *must* have known only Nora could have. *Yet Jim kept quiet*. Do you see why I said before that Jim had a more sublime reason for martyrizing himself? *It was his penance, his self-imposed punishment*. For Jim felt himself to have been completely responsible for the tragedy in Nora's life—indeed, for driving Nora into murder. So he was willing to take his licking silently and without complaint, as if that would right the wrong! But agonized minds think badly. Only...Jim couldn't *look* at her. Remember in the courtroom? Not once. He wouldn't, he couldn't look at her. He wouldn't see her, or talk to her, before, during, or after. That would have been too much. For after all she *had*—' Ellery rose. 'I believe that's all I'm going to say.'

Pat sank back on the couch to rest her head against the wall. Cart winced at the expression on her face. So he said, as if somehow it softened the blow and alleviated the pain: 'But Queen, isn't it possible that Nora and Jim together, *as accomplices*—?'

Ellery said rapidly: 'If they'd been accomplices, working together to rid themselves of Rosemary, would they have deliberately planned the crime in such a way that Jim, one of the accomplices, would turn out to be the only possible criminal? No. Had they combined to destroy a common enemy, they would have planned it so that *neither* of them would be involved.'

And then there was another period of quiet, behind which tumbled the water of Mr Anderson's voice in the taproom. His words all ran together, like rivulets joining a stream. It was pleasant against the malty odor of beer.

And Pat turned to look at Cart; and oddly, she was smiling. But it was the wispiest, lightest ghost of a smile.

'No,' said Cart. 'Don't say it. I won't hear it.'

'But Cart, you don't know what I was going to say—'

'I do! And it's a damned insult!'

'Here—' began Mr Queen.

'If you think,' snarled Cart, 'that I'm the kind of heel who would drag a story like this out for the edification of the Emmy DuPrés of Wrightsville, merely to satisfy my sense of "duty," then you're not the kind of woman I want to marry, Pat!'

'I couldn't marry you, Cart,' said Pat in a stifled voice. 'Not with Nora—not my own sister—a…a…'

'She wasn't responsible! She was sick! Look here, Queen, drive some sense into—Pat, if you're going to take that stupid attitude, I'm through—I'll be damned if I'm not!' Cart pulled her off the sofa and held her to him tightly. 'Oh, darling, it isn't Nora, it isn't Jim, it isn't your father or mother or Lola or even you I'm really thinking of…Don't think I haven't visited the hospital. I—I have. I saw her just after they took her out of the incubator. She glubbed at me, and then she started to bawl, and— damn it, Pat, we're going to be married as soon as it's decent, and we're going to carry this damn secret to the grave with us, and we're going to adopt little Nora and make the whole damn thing sound like some impossible business out of a damn book—that's what we're going to do! Understand?'

'Yes, Cart,' whispered Pat. And she closed her eyes and laid her cheek against his shoulder.

When Mr Ellery Queen strolled out of the back room he was smiling, although a little sadly.

He slapped a ten-dollar bill down on the bar before Gus Olesen and said: 'See what the folks in the back room will have, and don't neglect Mr Anderson. Also, keep the change. Goodbye, Gus. I've got to catch the train for New York.'

Gus stared at the bill. 'I ain't dreaming, am I? You ain't Santa Claus?'

'Not exactly, although I just presented two people with the gift of several pounds of baby, complete down to the last pearly toenail.'

'What is this?' demanded Gus. 'Some kind of celebration?'

Mr Queen winked at Mr Anderson, who gawped back. 'Of course! Hadn't you heard, Gus? Today is Mother's Day!'